Nilanjan P. Choudhury's most recent novel is *Shillong Times*, a coming-of-age story set against the ethnic conflict in Shillong in the 1980s. It has been widely praised as a significant contribution to North-east literature. His debut novel, a mythological thriller entitled *Bali and the Ocean of Milk*, was a best-seller. His subsequent writings include *The Case of the Secretive Sister*, a contemporary detective caper set in Bangalore and two plays on science history—*The Square Root of a Sonnet* and *The Trial of Abdus Salam*, which received wide critical acclaim and have been staged across multiple cities in India and the US. Nilanjan studied at IIM, Ahmedabad, and IIT, Kanpur. He grew up in Shillong and now lives in Bangalore with his family. He can be reached at www.nilanjan.net

Praise for *Shillong Times*

'A punch to the gut...a ripping good yarn written with a deft touch...'
– *Hindustan Times*

'Leavened with humour, the fault-lines between the two communities, Khasi and Bengali, are delineated in superb set pieces.' – *The Hindu Literary Review*

'Filled with laughter, sharp observations, perfect scripting and historical details, the book is a must-read.' – *Mathrubhumi*

'Superb, with its delightful fusion of style and content.' – *Kitaab.org*

'This delightful novel about growing up in Shillong in the 1980s has the power to create an unforgettable map of that place in one's mind. A moving story of friendship that transcends the barriers of communities.'

– Hansda Sowvendra Shekhar,
Sahitya Akademi Award-winning novelist

Praise for *The Case of the Secretive Sister*

'Packed with wild cat-and-mouse chases...hidden identities...hilarious policemen...pepper spray cans...wicked auto drivers—all delivered with good doses of laughs.' – *The Telegraph*

'A delightful read. May the Chatterjee Institute of Detection keep on sleuthing in sequels.' – Jug Suraiya, author and columnist

Praise for *Bali and the Ocean of Milk*

'A ripping good yarn, the fast-paced action given resonance by echoes of current moral, political and social issues.' – *The Times of India*

'A spicy concoction of myth, human drama, social satire and humour. Revisit our ancient myths, discovering their contemporary resonance with plenty of chuckles along the way.' – *Deccan Herald*

'A grand and frothy manthan of myth, magic, palace intrigue, Wodehouse-ian humour and more! A modern-day Aristophanes!' – Mahesh Dattani, Sahitya Akademi Award-winning playwright and film-maker

Song of the Golden Sparrow

A NOVEL HISTORY OF FREE INDIA

Nilanjan P. Choudhury

SPEAKING
TIGER

SPEAKING TIGER BOOKS LLP
125A, Ground Floor, Shahpur Jat, near Asiad Village,
New Delhi 110049

First published by Speaking Tiger Books 2023

ISBN: 978-93-5447-120-9
eISBN: 978-93-5447-130-8

10 9 8 7 6 5 4 3 2 1

Typeset in Garamond Premier Pro by SÜRYA, New Delhi

Printed at Chaman Enterprises, New Delhi

For Pampa and Sumedha
My constant (if cranky) companions through many winters and springs
Know that you have always been the wind below my wings.

'History is natural selection. Mutant versions of the past struggle for dominance; new species of fact arise, and old, saurian truths go to the wall, blindfolded and smoking last cigarettes.'

—Salman Rushdie

CONTENTS

Prologue

It is a truth universally acknowledged but rarely remembered that the smallest incident, the humblest nobody, can set into motion an avalanche of events, great and small, that even the wisest cannot foresee.

A butterfly flaps its wings in Brazil and a tendril of air quivers above the coffee-black Amazon, nudging a breeze off course. The breeze bumps into a trade wind passing the tip of Tierra Del Fuego, startling it into furious speed. The wind sweeps over the vast blue expanse of the Pacific and swells into a hundred-mile-wide air current which whips across the globe—whistling through the kimonos of geriatric geishas in Kyoto, shrieking past the star-kissed temple spires of Angkor Vat, slowing down for an instant at the go-go parlours of Patpong—and finally thunders into the Bay of Bengal, where it explodes into Hurricane Haloom, sending cars, cows and kathi-roll carts whooshing over the Victoria Memorial in Calcutta, until at last it finds release over the parched plains of Eastern Bihar, flooding the kharif crop and causing the price of onions to shoot up by 93 per cent, and the serving prime minister being booted out in the general elections three weeks later.

So, what should be the resolution of the microscope through which we examine history? What should be the first brush stroke of the hapless historian in his doomed quest to paint the staggering tapestry of the life of a nation? Pouting prime ministers, over-priced onions or fluttering butterflies? Where, oh where, to begin? Aye, therein lies the rub.

For lack of a better alternative, then, let us start at the very beginning. Yes, yes, I know there is no such thing; that in the great chakra of Time that is forever turning, turning, the end is the beginning and vice versa for all eternity. But we must begin *somewhere*. So let us begin with me, the aforesaid hapless historian.

Let us begin with hubris; with stupidity.

***

High upon the snow-covered cliffs of Mount Kailash, hidden from mortal eyes, lies the kingdom of Alaka. It is the abode of Lord Kubera, the god of wealth, guardian of the North, overlord of the yakshas. Battered by blizzards and assaulted by avalanches, it is about as warm and inviting as an unheated swimming pool in Siberia. But of all the places in Alaka, the coldest, the most forbidding is the Court of Justice—a cavernous hall carved out of a craggy wall of frozen rock. Icy winds tear through its hollow chambers, screaming like angry banshees, striking terror into the souls of the trembling convicts who are summoned there to answer for their crimes. Convicts such as I.

On the dark day that my tale begins, I found myself in the very heart of the dreaded Chamber of Justice—the Altar of the Accused. It stood at the centre of a semi-circle around which sat nine pisachas—nine undead demons of the afterworld, who were to be the judges for my case. Their blood-red eyes glowered at me as I stood quaking in the heavy iron chains that bound me from head to heel.

'The court is now in session,' the nine judges announced in one sepulchral voice, their bones rattling ominously with every word that they uttered. 'Let the trial begin.' A tenth pisacha, more bloodless and bonier than the rest, glided out of the shadows and planted his skeletal self in front of me. An expectant hush descended upon the courtroom. An old, sinking feeling swelled inside my stomach. My crime was a serious one and my tail twitched nervously in dread of the punishment that surely awaited me. What would it be—a thousand lashes of the whip, solitary imprisonment, tomatoes in my hilsa curry? (You think there are no Bengalis in the otherworld? No maach, no Rabindra Sangeet? How little you know!)

With an effort of will, I tried to stop the morbid thoughts that were sweeping through my imagination like locusts over a field of grain. But it wasn't easy. For I am one of God's chosen pessimists—the sort that makes hand sanitizer out of a bottle of Old Monk rum. Just in case....

'Your name?' croaked the inquisitor.

'Prem Chandra, milord,' I replied.

'Full name!' he growled.

'Prem Chandra Guha, milord,' I replied.

'Your trade?'

'Custodian of History.'

'Father's name and trade?' he asked.

'Bipan Chandra,' I replied. 'Custodian of History.'

'So both of you are Custodians of History? Like father, like son, eh?' the inquisitor asked with a crooked smile.

'Yes, milord. It runs in the family, so to speak. Papa's area is Ancient History and mine is Modern. I expect my children's will be Post-Modern,' I replied with a crooked smile that matched his.

I know that I should have been taking the inquisition more seriously. But I was beginning to tire of these meaningless formalities. I mean, they surely knew what my job was. It was what had led to my arrest in the first place. So why waste time? Quite frankly, I preferred to hear the sentence right away instead of being stretched out on this rack of long-winded legal niceties. In any case, I had less hopes of being acquitted than I had of getting a Diwali bonus from Ravana, or, which is more to the point, from his elder brother and my magnificent but not-so-munificent master, Kubera.

The anticipation of a punishment can sometimes be worse than its execution. Be over and done with it already, I muttered under my breath.

'I shall now state the charges against the accused, Prem Chandra Guha,' the inquisitor's voice reverberated through the courtroom like a headbanging skeleton inside a coffin. He grasped a scroll of parchment and began to read: 'Seven moons ago, on the seventh night of Shravan, the accused yaksha Prem Chandra Guha was assigned to guard duty at the treasury, in the Chamber of Modern History.'

A quick digression may be in order here. I don't know if you know this, but we yakshas are nature spirits, semi-divine beings, blessed with many rare magical powers such as shape-shifting, levitation and flirtation. We are called by all sorts of fancy names—sentinels, Guardians of the Galaxy, Bahadur, chowkidar and what not.

But basically, we yakshas are security guards. From the moment we are born, to the moment of our death, there is but one purpose to our lives—to protect the treasures of our master, Lord Kubera. It was the job of a lifetime, for the man has a lot of treasures, And I mean a *lot*. Kubera's stock may have fallen a little in these modern times but back in the day, he was da man—the Burger King of the Satya Yug, a whopping triple decker of Bezos, Buffet and Bill Gates rolled into one, with a side of Adani fries thrown in for free.

The riches he had amassed over the ages had been stashed in the state treasury. And that's where I had spent most of my adult life—guarding Kubera's ill-gotten gains. And it wasn't just me. Thousands of us yakshas slaved night and day, in the most abysmal working conditions, to guard the obscene wealth of a single man. And we barely made minimum wage. Seriously, even the poorest migrant workers from Bengal and Bihar have it better than us. Yaksha lives didn't matter and they never would.

I hated my job. I really did. But I had little choice. Thanks to an immutable caste system, the only profession that a yaksha can take up, is that of security guard. I've lost count of how many times I've heard my father tell me—'Prem *khoka* (beta), you are a yaksha and we yakshas are born to be guards.'

But I didn't want to become a security guard. It was my dream to become an engineer or a doctor. I like creating, building things, helping people. Given a choice, I wanted to save lives, not take them. My stomach churns at the very thought of the killing, slashing and garroting that is the lot of every yaksha. Why, I even fell ill the first time I had to dissect a dakini in my third year at university.

It's the same with my gandharva friends. They are supposed to become musicians when they grow up. Or dancers. Two career choices—take your pick. Now Chitrasena, my good friend, wanted to study accountancy and become a money lender. But no! The moment his father came to know of it, he threw away all the cost accounting books that Chitrasena had been hiding under his pillow and said: 'Musicians should have nothing to do with money!' He shoved a tanpura into Chitrasena's hand, and forced the poor boy to do riyaaz for twelve hours a day. And that was the end of one fine financier.

My father was no different. 'Any more of this girlish talk of becoming an engineer or doctor, and I'll throw you out of the house,' he warned me. 'Guard you are and guard you must be.'

And so it was that I became sentry Number 17307 in the Kubera Corps. Soon after I completed my guard training I was assigned to the treasury. I went into depression almost immediately. For no job in the world is as soul-sucking as that of a security guard's (with the possible exception of TV news anchors). My thwarted dreams shattered my peace of mind and my misery kept me awake, night after night.

I tried everything possible to get some sleep—glugged down wine, puffed endless chillums of ganja, read every mind-numbing book that I could borrow from the university library, from the novels of James Joyce to the poems of Bjørnstjerne Bjørnson and even The Foundations of Multi-variate Calculus. But not a wink of sleep could I get.

Except on that one fateful night in Shravan, when I slept for eight hours straight. It was the sweetest sleep that I had had in months. But when the dawn came, it was to demand from me a terrible price for those eight exquisite hours.

***

The inquisitor had at last come to the crux of the matter: 'Prem Chandra Guha, on the seventh night of Shravan, you fell asleep at your post. You failed in your sacred duty to guard the Chamber of Modern History. You admit this?'

'Yes,' I replied. There was no point denying it. When my supervisor had discovered me the following morning, my snores were louder than the trumpeting of wild elephants in heat.

'And just how did you fall asleep?' demanded the inquisitor.

'Well, what can I say?' I shrugged. 'I was getting bored stiff. So, I decided to take a look at what it was that I was guarding. I went inside the Chamber of History and opened one of the golden chests that were lying around. It was full of dusty, old parchments. Moth-eaten, most of—' I had to stop. The collective jaws of the nine demon judges had dropped to their collar bones and the inquisitor looked as if he would have had a heart attack, had there been a heart beating beneath those bleached, white ribs.

'Moth-eaten! You, you...!' he stuttered. 'You miserable, lowly yokel of a yaksha! You dared to lay your hands on the chronicles of our history? The most precious of all our treasures?'

I shrugged. 'I was bored, milord. If I didn't do *something,* I'd go mad. The soul of a security guard wearies—'

'Spare us your sob stories,' the inquisitor thundered. 'What did you do after taking them out?'

'I read them. Or rather I tried to,' I said. 'For timepass, you know.'

'Timepass!' the inquisitor hissed like an angry rattlesnake.

'Umm...yes.'

'And then?'

'Then...I dozed off. Reading them, I mean,' I replied with a nervous giggle. 'Never thought it would happen. I'm a certified insomniac you see. But—'

'But?'

'But it wasn't exactly riveting stuff, you know. In fact, it was a little...umm...boring.'

'Boring?' the inquisitor's bloodless lips tightened into a knife edge.

Excruciatingly boring! Even worse than Arundhati Roy's essays! Dull enough to make even *you* drop dead a second time, milord, I wanted to say, but I kept my mouth shut. Mostly to stop my foot from going in any further. A few inches more and it would emerge from my other end...

But how I wished I had never set my eyes on those accursed chronicles! Then I wouldn't have read them. And I wouldn't have fallen asleep. And I wouldn't have been discovered in the morning, with those damned parchments scattered around my supine self. A few of them at any rate. While I had been blissfully snoring, an uncaring wind had blown the rest to god knows where. When I awoke, I found that the parchments were gone and I was trussed up in chains.

'Do you realise that because of *you,* these so called 'boring' chronicles are now lost forever?' the inquisitor's teeth rattled in barely controlled indignation.

'Yes,' I said, trying to look as sorry as I could.

'The chronicles of our history! Gone! Our most priceless possession, our greatest treasure! Gone! Precious beyond gold and diamonds! More precious than the broken bow of Rama, or the Pushpaka Vimana, or the Syamantaka gem, or the—'

'Yes, yes I know,' I interrupted. Ufff! How the old bag of bones could go on and on! I cleared my throat and said: 'But aren't you overreacting just a little bit, your highness? Surely, they can be written again? A blessing in disguise, if you ask me. Honestly, I think even I would be able to do a better job than what was in there.'

A pin-drop silence fell in the courtroom.

'Really?' the inquisitor said at last, stroking his chin with his bony fingers. 'Now that's a very interesting thought,' he said with a toothy smirk. He creaked across to the judges and whispered something to them. It seemed to amuse them for they all started cackling in ghoulish glee.

A familiar voice sounded in my head: 'Oh, my poor son! How many times have I warned you that your pride would be your ruin? Only a fool or a politician would attempt the rewriting of history. Even the gods cannot change the past. But you were always too clever by half and now your cockiness will cost you dear.'

'Baba?' I looked around but my father was nowhere to be seen. I was truly alone. And royally rogered. I panicked.

'Your most magnificent honours,' I whimpered. 'I am very sorry for—'

The inquisitor held up his hand and cut me short: 'Enough! We have heard quite enough from you. Now we will speak and you will listen,' he turned to the judges. 'Milords and miladies, are you ready to pronounce your judgment?'

'Yes, we are,' intoned the nine pisachas.

With the bushy end of my tail, I dabbed the sweat dripping from my horns, as the nine judges continued: 'We find the accused Shri Prem Chandra Guha guilty of destroying the most precious possession of our world—the chronicles of our past! Worse still, his description of our history as 'boring', shows his absolute and wilful disrespect for our glorious and ancient civilization. As a punishment for these heinous crimes, Shri Guha is banished from these lands for a period of one hundred years. Furthermore—'

'No!' I let out a wail of agony. 'Not exile! Not one hundred years! Please, your honours! No!'

'Furthermore,' the judges went on, 'Shri Guha is to spend this time in writing a historical account of the land to which he is exiled.'

'What!' I croaked.

'Furthermore, since Shri Guha fancies himself to be better than our greatest historians, his own account must be sufficiently interesting to hold the undivided attention of this court. It must not, to use his own words, be *boring*. Or else—'

'But your exalted highnesses, I was only joking,' I pleaded tearfully. 'I can't write to save my life.'

'Ah, but that is exactly what you must now do,' the judges smirked. 'For unless you are able to produce a suitably riveting history of the land of your exile, you will be banished for another one hundred years.'

Another hundred years! My knees gave way and I crumpled to the floor as I heard them say: 'And now by the powers vested in us, we command the accused, Prem Chandra Guha to proceed to his exile in the land of—' they paused dramatically before resuming: 'in the land of Bharatavarsha. Or India, as she is now called.'

I gasped in horror. India! The shock sent my eyeballs rolling skywards, until only the whites were visible. I fell into a swoon and the darkness overcame me. The last thing I remember, was a single word echoing inside my head like the ominous background score of an Ekta Kapoor serial—*India, India, India!*

Book One

The Problem with History

When I came to my senses, I found myself lying at the foot of Mount Kailash. I was still in shock and it took a while for the reality of the situation to sink in. So, they had thrown me out after all! The heartless devils! My home, my parents, all the gorgeous yakshinis that I had lusted after (but who had never given me so much as a second glance!)—they had taken everything away from me. *Everything.* My head sank to my knees as I let out a wail of despair. One hundred years of exile! And in India of all places! And that too modern India!

Of all the places on earth, why, oh, why did it have to be India! Why not Brazil or the Bahamas...or Tahiti...Timbuctoo even. I would have somehow survived in any of those places—one hand clasping a can of beer, the other a beach goddess. But one hundred years in India! It really was the pits.

Now if I had been put into a time machine and sent to ancient India, things would have been just hunky-dory. I could have spent my days racing on nuclear-powered chariots, gotten a long overdue nose job done by the best plastic surgeons, and sipped soma-ras every evening. But modern India? Urrgghh! Even in distant Kailash, everyone had heard of India's steep descent from its glorious past to its ignominious present—it was a crowded, chaotic, poverty-stricken land, sucked dry of all its fabled goodness and gold by two centuries of colonial rule. The very thought of spending the next one hundred years there, rubbing shoulders with millions upon millions of the desperate unwashed made my skin crawl. Who knew what lay in store for me there?

You would think that as a divine thing—well, at least a supernatural one—I would be able to look into the past, present, future, infinity—that all the little blink-and-they're-gone centuries of human history would be visible to me in an instant. That I would know exactly what awaited me and spare myself the worst. Alas, no. Baba was right, I was unripe, too raw a banana even for a decent kachkolar tarkari. For one desperate moment, I even wondered if I should try and sneak back home. But it was impossible. Kubera's defences were impregnable. I knew that the moment I set foot on Mount Kailash again, I would be blown to bits. I spent the rest of the day wallowing in self-pity. It was only around dusk that I was finally able get a grip on myself.

I began to analyze my situation a little more calmly. I couldn't do anything about my exile—except make sure that it wasn't extended by another hundred years. But for that I would have to write a history of India—a history so mind-blowing, that even that bloodless devil of an inquisitor, would be compelled to keep turning its pages until he developed an exquisitely painful tennis elbow. That would be my revenge and my redemption.

All of a sudden, I began to feel a little better. From the depths of my despair, there arose a small bubble of hope. Even as one hundred years of servitude loomed ahead of me, there was a small voice inside my head which said—*Listen, Prem khoka, there may be something here. This may be the opportunity you have been waiting for all this while—to write the deathless prose that will win you the hearts of countless, breathless readers. From lowly custodian to famous chronicler! In writing the history of India, you will also write your own.*

My lack of experience was a slight problem, of course. But it wasn't fatal. I mean, how difficult was it to become a historian, really? After all, every Ram, Shyam, Shashi and Romila was writing his or her own version of history these days. The past was to them what clay is to a potter—a protean, malleable thing. I made up my mind. Yes, I Prem Chandra Guha, would also grasp the sands of time and pour them into a mould of my own making. Like Hitler, Nehru and Mandela and so many others, my pen would turn the poison of imprisonment into the amrit of art.

Life may have given me a bottle of hand sanitizer. But I would make a single malt out of it.

***

The distillation of hand sanitizer into whisky is a simple, chemical process. But the distillation of time into recorded history, is of an alchemy most complex. For the sirens of history can lure the novice historian into a bottomless sea of stories and songs, in which he is doomed to drown.

Therefore, like the sailors aboard Odysseus' ship, I must block my ears against the million-tongued sirens of time who tempt me with their tales of infinite variety (which age cannot wither, nor badly written NCERT textbooks stale). And like Odysseus himself, I must bind myself to a single mast, a single story, in the hope that within it are contained the stories of millions, like the million melodies contained inside a single raga. Bound thus, to the mast of the single story, I must navigate my ship across the vast ocean of India's history, with a prayer to Mnemosyne and to Saraswati to guide my leaky boat to the harbour at the end of time, with my sanity and pencil lead intact.

In short, I must not be an enthu-cutlet and overdo things.

I must willy-nilly cherry-pick a few random threads in the giant fabric that is Bharatavarsha, and hope to catch a glimpse of the entire tapestry. It is a liberating thought! For all of a sudden, the dead weight of history is off my back. It is as if someone sauntered across to the titan Atlas, carrying the earth on his shoulders, and said to him: 'Hello there...why don't you go suck on an olive or something, while I hold that thing up for you?'

Suddenly, I am no longer burdened by the need to be comprehensive, correct, or dare I say it, even truthful. For what is truth but fact filtered through the sieve of perception and prejudice? Therefore, I shall merrily go where my whims and fancies take me. Upwards and onwards then!

***

If history is the study of humankind, the question that naturally arises is: which human or humans? Traditionally, most scholars have been obsessed with kings and queens and princes and presidents i.e. assorted big-shots and boneheads whose decisions have apparently turned the tides of time. But what about the little people behind the big people? What about the backstabbing courtiers and the back-rubbing courtesans whose subtle influences may have shaped the moods and decisions of the aforesaid decision-makers?

Aye, who speaks for the butterflies flapping up the storms?

The question is not one of mere academic interest. For example, it is well known that the political differences between Jinnah and Gandhi had become irreconcilable in the summer of 1930, when the Poona Pact was about to be signed. But what is not so well known is the reason behind the rift, which is as follows.

One fateful morning in April, Jinnah was waiting to meet Gandhi-ji for a crucial discussion on the future of the country. But he found himself waiting for an inordinately long time as Gandhi-ji was preoccupied with one of his favourite morning rituals—an enema. Probably feeling like shit, an insulted Jinnah stormed out, and they say, from that moment onwards, he never quite got along with Gandhi-ji.

It was a turning point in India's history—one that was to reaffirm Jinnah's faith in the Two Nation Theory and ultimately lead to the Partition of 1947. This we all know.

But what many may not know is that Gandhi-ji's touching faith in enemas originated from the advice given to him by an unknown Ayurveda doctor from Rajkot. So was this obscure doctor as much a maker of history as he was a maker of emetics? And when the story of Partition is told, where should it begin—with Jinnah, Gandhi or the Ayurveda doctor?

As I was grappling with questions such as these, there suddenly popped into my head, an old Tamizh proverb—*'One only has to squeeze a grain of rice to know if the pot has boiled.'* In modern-day statistics this is called random sampling. The more I thought about it, the more sense it made to me—if I had to write the history of an entire nation, then random sampling was my only hope. Blind chance would have to lead me to a suitable randomly chosen sample. And s/he would be the single grain of rice that would give voice to the teeming millions bubbling inside the gigantic degchi that was India.

The theory was sound. But I was wondering how exactly I would carry out my cunning plan, when like a bolt of lightning, I was struck by an enema-inspired idea.

What if I were to assume the form of a bird, I said to myself, and take off into the skies? I would keep flying across the length and breadth of India until one of my droppings fell on someone's head. And that someone would become my grain of rice, the grain which I would squeeze, until the truth dripped out of him (or her) and flowed onto the pages of my chronicles.

A distastefully scatological scheme, I admit. Crude, vulgar, without a trace of dignity. But the more I thought about it, the more the idea appealed to me. It was an excellent strategy to shift the vexing problem of random selection from my mind to my hind.

In a flash, I made my decision. I would become a bird and scour the skies of India in search of my subject. But what bird? The peacock? National bird of my impending karmabhoomi? Nah—too flashy. An eagle? Too regal. A hawk? But the prospect of a hundred-year diet of field rats, made my non-violent soul go bilious-green. That sort of ruled out vultures, owls and most other non-veg birds. No, I decided: it would have to be a small bird, a common, inconspicuous bird that could come and go as it wanted, without attracting attention. Something like a crow, or even better—a sparrow...a chidiya, as they called it in India. Come to think of it, hadn't India herself been called a chidiya...*sone ki chidiya...*

For centuries, wasn't that the epithet by which India had been known? *Sone ki chidiya...India,* the golden sparrow...

Yes, I rubbed my horns in glee. A sparrow would be perfect, the ideal guise for an unobtrusive observer. Sparrows were found everywhere—in the great cities and small towns, in the vast forests and the high mountains. No one would notice me, no one would hide their true nature from a mere sparrow. My bird-on-the-wall view of the times, would give me enough juice to slake the thirst of the thirstiest, most pyaasa pisacha. My decision was made. It was time to act.

Closing my eyes, I began to recite the Bahurupee mantra that would transform me into any form that I wished to assume. As soon as I had finished, my arms turned into wings, my nose into a beak, my toes into little claws and my hard, hairy chest softened into the yellowy down of a bird's breast.

I hopped around a bit to check if all my newly formed parts were in working order. They seemed to be all right. Well—there was no reason to hang around here any longer. I had my work cut out. My golden wings gleamed in the sun as I took off into the skies. I soared past the foothills of Mount Kailash and as I was flying over the majestic Himalayas, a flash of light caught my eye.

It was a sunbeam bouncing off a thin trickle of clear, blue water, spurting out of a mountain face. I was at Tapovan, birthplace of the mighty Ganga. My tryst with India had begun. Now it was up to blind chance to lead me to the masthead to which I would bind myself, and steer my ship through the turbulent tides of India's history.

Tryst with Destiny

The sun was hovering above the lip of the western horizon, when I arrived in the forests of Betla in the Chhota Nagpur plateau in the eastern part of the country. I glided onto the low branch of a tamarind tree and perched myself upon it. I had been flying all through the day and I badly needed a break. A bio-break to be precise. My long flight had taken me over desolate lands devoid of any humans and I had been loath to let my statistically significant offering fall upon barren ground. But now, my precious payload was pressing down upon my nether regions with a furious urgency, and I could no longer ignore its call.

'Oh, the hell with it,' I said and let go.

A moment later, I heard an angry cry. 'Stupid bird! Couldn't find any other place to shit?'

I peered down from my perch. A boy of about nine or ten was standing below the tree, cursing the blessing that I had just bestowed upon his head. As far as heads went, it wasn't particularly impressive. The best that could be said about it, was that it had plenty of hair. But it was dusty and unkempt and looked like the disorderly nest of a feminist crow who preferred Gloria Steinem to *Good Housekeeping*. The bits below the head were nothing to write home about either—he was a skinny little runt, the sort you see in every nook and corner of India. His chest had caved in, his ribs poked out, and his large eyes were dark with hunger. He wore a banian and a pair of dirty shorts and his face was blackened with grease.

In short, he looked sorrier than an armadillo's arse.

Ignoring the boy's curses, I examined my surroundings. Beside the tamarind tree, stood a ramshackle wooden shed in which a blue Morris Minor car had been parked. A small signboard sat askew upon the roof. It said:

Vishwakarma Motor Works

Your car is our karma

I looked around. I seemed to be on some sort of highway that ran through a forest. On either side of the road were dense jungles and the only sign of human civilization was this car shed. The boy scurried into it and emerged with a jug of water. He was splashing the water on his hair to clean it out, when I hopped onto the bonnet of the car.

'Hooshh! Hooshh!' the boy yelled. 'If you dirty that car, I'll feed you to the wolves!' He grabbed a stone and hurled it at me.

I made a rude sound at him and fled to the roof of the shed. This did not look like the beginning of a beautiful friendship. But then what was to be done? *Alea jacta est* and all that—the die, or rather, the dropping had been cast. If this was where blind chance had led me, then so be it.

'Here's looking at you, kid,' I muttered under my breath as I embarked upon the study of my ill-chosen grain of rice.

***

Half an hour had passed. The boy had spent most of it underneath the chassis of the Morris Minor. Clearly, he was a car mechanic. And a fairly good one at that, it would seem. Every now and then, his hand would pop out from beneath the car, expertly pick up a wrench or a screwdriver and return to work.

But after a while it was getting boring to watch him and so I decided to look around a bit. I flew into the shed. It was bare apart from a rickety plywood table that stood in the far corner. A few grimy tools and a newspaper were lying on it. I flicked open the newspaper with my claws. It was dated 15 August 1947. I was about to start reading it when an angry voice interrupted me.

'You're back again!' The boy was glaring at me, a nasty-looking spanner clutched in his raised hand.

'Don't you dare throw that thing at me!' I squawked.

'Get out of here then!' the boy spat. He was about to take a swipe at me with the spanner, when he stopped himself and stared curiously at me. 'Who are you? Haven't seen you here before.'

My breast puffed up in self-importance. 'My name is Prem Chandra Guha, Custodian of History, Third Class. I come from the snows of Mount Kailash,' I declaimed.

'Good for you,' replied the boy. 'You can go back there now.'

I nearly toppled over in shock. It suddenly struck me that I was speaking Avianese, the language of the birds, but the boy could understand me without any problem. Not that such things were unknown. In the past, birds and humans did have the occasional chat—for instance, the famous one between Jatayu and Ravana (which unfortunately, ended quite badly for the poor bird). But that was aeons ago. This was 1947, for god's sake! Birds and men didn't talk to each other anymore.

'You...understand what I am saying, boy?' I asked him very slowly.

'Of course,' he yawned. 'You have a horrible accent, though.'

I barely registered the insult as I scratched my head and asked: 'But how?'

'Oh, birds are really easy to understand,' the boy shrugged. 'They have no brains and hardly any vocabulary. Four-legged animals are tougher. But I can manage. Goats, horses, deer, wolves—I can talk to them all. Fish are the most difficult. Can't do that yet.'

'And just how did you learn to speak to animals?' I asked.

'She taught me,' he replied, pointing at the tamarind tree. I now noticed the young girl who was seated at the foot of the tree. She had a woven reed basket filled with small, reddish berries. She was probably about the same age as the boy, ten or so, but a good three inches taller. A faded, cotton half-sari was draped around her slender frame, and she looked older than her years.

'So...that girl and you...both of you can speak to animals?' I asked.

'Yes. But she's much better than me. She's a Santhal, you see,' the boy replied.

'And what is a Santhal?' I asked.

'Rajinder Seth says they are Adivasis, illiterate junglees,' the boy said. 'They live in that forest there,' he pointed a greasy finger at the dense jungles across the road. 'City people say that the Santhals can even talk to the trees and the winds and the river.'

'Yes, we can. We Santhals are the greatest tribe in all of Bharat-disom,' said a thin, sharp voice. 'We are the first, the cleverest, and the bravest!' I turned to see the girl standing behind me. Without so much as a hi-hello to me, the impudent little brat promptly launched into a song.

The Santhals were there,
When the earth was born.
Our bodies were warmed
By the world's first dawn.

From rocks and stones,
Were forged our bones.
Rainwater and red mud,
Flowed in our veins as blood.

We swam with the fishes
And sang with the birds
Our god is earth mother,
And we know of no other.

But then came the dikus,
With spear and gun.
Some with a million gods,
And some with one.

The dikus tried to devour,
The earth that we till.
But the greedy dikus
Our brave warriors did kill.

The arrows of the Santhals,
Made earth mother free
The blood of the Santhals,
Made Bharat-disom free.

'Doesn't she sing well?' said the boy, gazing admiringly at her.

'Yes, not bad,' I was forced to admit. 'What's a *diku* by the way?'

'Outsiders,' the girl said. 'Enemies of the Santhals. They want to take all that we have. They want us to become like them. But we don't fear them. They fear us because they know that our arrows are more powerful than their guns.'

'I see. But don't you think this business of the Santhals making all of Bharat-disom free, might just be a wee bit exaggerated? Have you seen this?' I pointed my claw at the big, bold headlines sprawled across the front page of the newspaper.

BIRTH OF INDIA'S FREEDOM

Mr Nehru Calls for Big Effort from People
Incessant Striving Task of Future

'He can't read,' the girl said, smirking at the boy. 'He's never gone to school.'

'Oh yes?' the boy snapped. 'And you have, is it?'

'I don't want to!' said the girl. 'My father says all this reading-writing is useless.'

'It's not,' the boy replied. 'I want to go to school and learn to read and write!'

'What for?' returned the girl. 'Will reading teach you which plant will cure a snake bite and which a fever? Will counting 1-2-3 tell you how to smell the wind and say when the rains will come?'

'And what is the use of knowing such things? No one will pay even one paisa for them. But if I could read and write, I would get a job in an office or a factory. And I could stay in Netarhat town instead of this stupid garage in the middle of this stupid jungle!'

'It's you that's stupid! My father says that the jungle is our teacher, the best teacher there is.'

'Because your father doesn't know of anything outside the jungle. But there is a big world out there and I want to see it,' a dreamy look entered the boy's eyes. 'I want to see the whole wide world. And I will do it. One day I will do it! I am not going to rot in this garage, repairing cars for that bastard Rajinder Seth! I will live in the big city, inside a big house with electric lights and a soft bed. I will buy a red Morris car, and have a driver who will take me wherever I want to go, and two fat servants who will do whatever I tell them.'

'And a fat wife who will beat you every night,' sniggered the girl, as she ducked a pebble that the boy flung at her.

'Now, now, children, no fighting,' I said, with a professorial wag of my wing. I turned to the boy. 'Shall we get properly introduced? I've told you my name. Why don't you tell me yours?'

The boy looked at me suspiciously. 'Manhoos,' he muttered after a while.

'Manhoos!' I squawked. 'What sort of name is that?'

'It's my name, okay! Why is *your* bottom tickling?' the boy hissed like an angry snake.

'It means unlucky,' the girl explained.

'Better than your name at least!' the boy snapped. 'Mary! Hah—what a stupid name!'

I let out a low whistle. 'Holy mother of god! The last person I expected to meet in this jungle was a Mary.'

'She's a Kristchan,' the boy said. 'The white dikus made her Kristchan. And her father and her mother and her whole tribe. At least I'm not a stupid Kristchan like them.'

Mary's face darkened. 'They told baba that if he became Kristchan, then they would give him a gardening job in Netarhat church. Baba told them that two years ago, some other people had also promised him a job if he became something called a Hindu. So, Baba became a Hindu. But they never gave him a job. Then the Kristchan fellows told Baba that they did not lie like the Hindu fellows because their holy book had some rule against telling lies. Baba told them okay, fine. I can become Hindu or Kristchan or whatever you want as long as I get a job. And so we became Kristchan. But the Kristchans also didn't give him or anyone else any jobs. Only lectures about some man called Jisu and how much he loved sheep. And they built a funny temple in the village which they call chaarch. There's no god inside it, only two pieces of wood like this,' she placed one forefinger above another to make a cross sign.

'I told you, your father is stupid! You are all stupid, all you junglees—' Manhoos broke off and let out a yelp as Mary snapped off a twig of the tamarind tree and gave him a sharp whack on his bottom.

'Now, Manhoos, my boy,' I intervened hastily, 'tell me about your father and mother. Where are they?'

The boy threw me a furious glare. 'Who are you to ask me so many questions? Just get lost! Go!' he spat and walked off in a huff.

'You talk too much, you know?' Mary said to me. 'Why did

you have to bring up his mother? She's dead...and he blames himself for it.'

'But why?'

'She died while giving birth to him. That's why his father named him Manhoos. Don't speak of her again. Or he'll bite off your little head.' She looked up at the setting sun. 'Anyway, I have to go now. It's late,' she grabbed the basket of berries and bounded across the road, into the jungle.

'What a pity,' I sighed, as I watched her disappear behind the trees. 'Just when we were getting to know each other better.'

'She'll be back here tomorrow to sell her berries,' Manhoos growled behind me. 'Now, please just shut up and let me work. Rajinder Seth will skin me alive, if I don't get this car ready today.' He grabbed a rag cloth and began to polish the bonnet of the Morris with a fierce energy.

In spite of his disdain towards his superiors, I was beginning to warm up to my grain of rice. He had a certain *je ne sais quoi* that piqued my curiosity. There was more to him than met the eye...and the girl as well. Meanwhile, as a budding historian, it was probably a good idea to start improving my general knowledge. The newspaper seemed a good place to begin.

As I skimmed through its pages, it became clear that I had arrived on a day of tremendous historical significance—15 August 1947. The pages of the newspaper were crammed with advertisements, celebrating the birth of free India.

'Construct Your House of Independence with Dalmia Cement'
'Buy Kopran: India's National Toothpaste—as Popular as the Flag of Free India'
'Write with P.M. Bagchi Inks: The Ink that History Uses; Letters that Burn with Undying Flames'

Squeezed in between these patriotic urgings to loosen one's purse strings, was the text of a speech made by Pandit Nehru, on the previous night in Delhi.

'Long years ago,' Nehru-ji had declared, *'we made a tryst with destiny, and now the time comes when we shall redeem our pledge, not wholly or in full measure, but very substantially. At the stroke of the midnight hour, when the world sleeps, India will awake to life and freedom...'*

It went on and on—rousing stuff about souls, sufferings and tears, until it finally ended on an alarmingly earnest note that sent shivers down my spine: *'And so we have to labour and to work, and work hard, to give reality to our dreams. Those dreams are for India, but they are also for the world.'*

I set aside the newspaper and gazed curiously at Manhoos. His hands were moving back and forth over the bonnet of the car like a pair of well-oiled pistons, polishing it until it gleamed. Nehru-ji would have been pleased to see his advice being taken so seriously, I said to myself. But would mere hard work be enough to make Manhoos' dreams come true? I doubted it. I could not see how this illiterate, orphaned urchin would ever be able to overcome his obvious disadvantages and graduate from polishing cars to driving them.

The faint strains of a lilting melody now intruded into my musings. It was clear as a bell, yet soft as a sigh—a million-voiced song, that seemed to be coming from a vast distance...

'Jana gana mana, adhinayaka jaya he
Bharata bhagya vidhaata'

I immediately snapped to attention. Instinctively, I knew what the song was. Raising my wing to my forehead, I gave a sharp salute. It would not do to be charged with sedition for disrespecting the national anthem, on my very first day in India. But as I listened, I was struck by the sheer beauty of the song. It was majestic and tranquil as the ocean, yet quick and playful as a mountain spring. Soon I was lost in the poetry of its words and the magic of its melody.

And so, on the first dusk of freedom, deep in the forests of Betla, a golden sparrow stood ramrod straight, singing the song of Bharat. And even as I sang, I could not help but wonder what lay in store for her and her three hundred and fifty million children, especially the two whom I had just met.

But as a fellow bard had once said, who can look into the seeds of time and say which one would grow and which would not? Perhaps in the magical soil of a hard-won freedom, a million seeds like Manhoos and Mary would awaken to life and make their own trysts with destiny.

Manhoos and Mary

Two years had passed since India had become independent. But it had as little effect on Manhoos' life as a mosquito bite on a rhino's rump. In fact, he was probably worse off now than before. Taking a leaf out of Kubera's book, the vile Rajinder Seth, was making poor Manhoos work twice as hard, without increasing his wages by a single paisa. It was as if the crown of India had passed from the white King of England to the Red Queen of Wonderland, and Manhoos was running faster and faster, to stay in the same place.

By this time, I had come to know a fair bit about him. As Mary had told me, his mother had died while giving birth to him. Grief-stricken, his father had named his newborn son, Manhoos—the unlucky one. Apparently, he had an elder sister as well, who had mothered him for a while. But when he was four, she had died of diarrhoea and there remained only his father to take care of little Manhoos.

Manhoos did not know much about his father, except that he was illiterate and desperately poor and had come from his ancestral village somewhere near the Bihar-Nepal border to Netarhat town in search of work. After doing all sorts of odd jobs, he was finally able to find steady employment in the stone-cutting quarry on the outskirts of town. And ever since Manhoos could remember, his father had been breaking big rocks into little rocks and little rocks into littler ones.

When Manhoos turned six, his father found him a job at Rajinder Seth's garage. The hours were long and the wages paltry. But Seth-ji gave him two rotis for lunch and a biscuit and tea in the evening, which was quite enough for a boy of six. Young Manhoos worked hard and to everyone's surprise, he turned out to have a knack for machines. Although his milk teeth would have fallen out if he had tried to say accelerator or carburettor, he had an intuitive understanding of how such things worked. By the time he was eight, he was carrying out several minor repairs by himself and Rajinder Seth rewarded him by increasing his daily rations to three rotis and two biscuits.

But man does not live by bread alone and Manhoos experienced little of the usual joys of childhood. Life was hard and brutish and it took a turn for the worse when his father died of lung disease—the result of constantly inhaling the fine dust of the rocks that he had crushed for years. With his father gone, Rajinder Seth's garage became Manhoos' home. There he lived and worked—repairing cars by day and resting his tired head on a tyre by night, too exhausted even to dream of school and city lights and soft pillows.

It was grim stuff, straight out of a Ritwik Ghatak film. But like a ray of light that can sometimes brighten the gloomiest Ghatak film, there was a sunbeam to dispel the darkness of Manhoos' life—Mary.

***

Mary lived in the Santhal village, inside the Betla jungles, about eight miles away from the highway. When she turned six, she was made to squat on the side of the highway and sell the wild berries that her mother would gather from the forest. But she was hardly able to sell anything. For although the highway linked two important towns, Netarhat and Ranchi, there wasn't exactly bumper to bumper traffic on it. After all it was 1949, and the total number of vehicles in India at the time, was probably less than the number of cars stuck at Silk Board signal in Bangalore, in 2022. (Ah! Progress!) And the few cars that did come along, would simply zoom past Mary, leaving in their wake a cloud of dust and a basketful of unsold berries.

After several weeks of wandering up and down the highway in search of business, Mary stumbled upon Rajinder Seth's garage. She soon realised that it was the ideal location to set up shop. It was the only garage for miles around and a popular pitstop for passing vehicles. Every time a car halted there, Mary would scamper to its side, thrusting her basket of berries at the passengers.

Mary's efforts bore fruit—sales were certainly better than before.

But in the intervals between one car and the next, time lay heavy on her hands and she spent much of it with the only other person of her size in the vicinity—Manhoos. Unfortunately, he wasn't quite the lady of leisure that she was. Rajinder Seth kept his nose pressed firmly against the grindstone and from morning to night, Manhoos was busy cleaning out carburettors, replacing clutch pads or changing tyres. He barely had a moment to call his own, let alone share it with Mary. But this did not deter her.

Every afternoon, after Rajinder Seth had sunk into his after-lunch siesta, Mary would hop across from the tamarind tree to the garage, to have a chat with Manhoos. It was usually a one-sided conversation for she was a talker, while he was more of a grunter. Manhoos would silently tend to the underbelly of some malfunctioning vehicle, while Mary would regale him with stories of the forest and her Santhal village.

One afternoon, with Rajinder Seth's snores rumbling in the background, she said: 'You know, yesterday we went to the Koyal river to catch fish. Do you know how we catch fish?' Without waiting for a reply, she went on: 'I just have to call them and they come to me. We wait until they are swimming around my knees, and then my friends quickly spear them with a sharp stick.'

'That's cruel,' Manhoos muttered.

'Yes, I don't like doing it either,' Mary sighed. 'But what to do? We have to eat right? But we first say sorry to them and their children, and we pray for their souls and only then do we catch them.'

'What language do fish speak?' asked Manhoos.

'Meendarin, of course,' Mary replied. 'If you want, I can teach you. Anyway, my mother roasted the poor fish on a wood fire, with wild pepper and mushrooms. It tasted so good that I can't even tell you.'

Manhoos heaved a deep sigh. I could almost feel the loneliness that was gnawing inside him. I could see how badly he missed having a family and a home of his own. I felt just like him...

'If only you could stay in our village,' Mary continued. 'I even asked my father once if you could live with us in our house.'

Manhoos' ears pricked up. 'What did he say?' he asked hopefully.

'He said that he can't afford to feed one more mouth,' replied

Mary, with the appalling honesty of children. 'So, you can't stay with us.'

Manhoos' face fell. After a moment's pause to absorb the disappointment, he snapped: 'That's fine by me. Who wants to stay in your stupid village anyway! I'm going to live in a big city.'

'If only you could see our village once, you wouldn't say that. It's the most beautiful village in Bharat-disom.'

Every time Mary spoke of her village, Manhoos' insides would whine with desire to go there. But he merely shrugged his shoulders and said: 'Maybe I'll see it someday. When I have the time.'

'You'll never have time,' said Mary. 'That Rajinder Seth never gives you even a day off.'

Manhoos grunted as Mary went on: 'Why are you so scared of him? Why do you put up with all his beatings and gaalis?'

Mary was right. Rajinder Seth treated poor Manhoos worse than a mongrel, as generous with his slaps as he was tightfisted with holidays and money. But Manhoos bore it all without a murmur of protest.

'At least he gives me two meals a day and seven rupees every month,' he said. 'If it wasn't for him, I would starve to death.'

'You call this living? What a coward you are! If you can't ask, I'll ask Seth-ji to give you an off-day. And then I'll take you to see our—' Mary broke off with a sudden yelp.

Rajinder Seth was standing behind Mary, a clump of her curly hair grasped in his fist. He was a short, pot-bellied man in his mid-forties, with a thick black moustache that bristled above his bulbous paan-stained lips. He tightened his grip on Mary's hair and said: 'Haven't I told you before, don't disturb this boy when he is at work. Does your father pay his salary?'

Manhoos was lying below the chassis of a car. He slithered out as quickly as he could and said: 'Let her go, Seth-ji. We were only talking. I was doing my work.'

'You talk back to me and I'll beat you so badly that you won't know your face from your arse!' Rajinder Seth yelled.

'Seth-ji, just let her go! Otherwise, I'll—' Manhoos hissed through gritted teeth. His eyes were dark slits of hate. He held a wrench in his hand, his fingers tightening around it until the knuckles turned pale.

Rajinder stared at Manhoos in astonishment. A moment later, he swung back his arm and his fist slammed into the boy's face. With a howl of pain, Manhoos toppled over, clutching his nose. A stream of blood gushed out of his nostrils, and trickled down his chin.

'*Bhenchod bhikhari ka bachcha!* (You sister-fucking beggar's son),' Rajinder Seth roared. 'You talk to me like that again and I'll cut your tongue out.' He turned to Mary and said: 'If I ever see you here again, I'll break your bones. And his too. You understand? Now go! And don't come back here again, you junglee bitch!'

With a violent shove he sent her crashing to the ground. She landed smack on her face. The basket flew out of her hands and the berries scattered all over the garage. Manhoos went pale, his breath shallow and quick. But my eyes were on Mary. That scrawny little girl was standing up to Seth-ji's assault with such a devil-may-care attitude that she reminded me of...well...me.

Without a word, she brushed away the blood dripping from her cut lip, with the casual air of someone powdering her nose. Then she got back on her feet and began to silently gather the fallen berries into her basket. And as she did so, she threw a quick look at Manhoos and said: 'Don't worry about me, I'm fine. You just stay quiet and do your work today. I will be back here tomorrow morning and fix this bastard.'

Her voice was soft and low. Besides she was speaking in Avianese, so that Rajinder Seth would have no clue what she was saying. But I could understand her well enough and her words had me all a-flutter in anticipation. Seth-ji was headed for trouble. Big trouble. I could not wait to see what it was.

***

The following morning, Mary arrived at the garage and planted herself in front of Rajinder Seth. His lips twisted into an angry scowl, but before he could move a muscle, Mary opened her basket and held it below his nose. Inside it sat a king cobra, its speckled coils gleaming like a polished spring. Like a kite in the breeze, the hood rose and swayed above Seth-ji's forehead, its diamond shaped shadow flitting across his brow.

Seth-ji's cheeks turned the colour of discarded engine oil, as Mary said: 'This is my friend, Lukabarsi.'

The cobra's forked tongue flickered out, sniffing curiously at the droplets of terror oozing out of Rajinder Seth's ashen skin. 'He doesn't like people who hit his friends. That means me and my friend here,' she nodded her head at Manhoos, who as usual, was mucking about under the chassis of a car.

Manhoos crawled out as quickly as he could and said: 'Mary, please! What are you doing? Seth-ji, I am really sorry that—'

'Shut up, Manhoos,' Mary cut him off. 'I'll take care of this.' She turned to Seth-ji and said: 'Listen Seth-ji, I brought Lukabarsi here because he wants to make you an offer.' The cobra hissed loudly. 'He says it's an offer you can't refuse,' she stroked the snake's hood. 'Don't be shy, Luka. Tell him.'

A series of hisses emerged from the snake. After he finished, Mary said: 'This is what Luka says. One—you must never again, so much as even raise your voice against Manhoos or me, let alone lifting a finger. Two—you must increase Manhoos' pay by twelve annas. Three—alternate Sundays are to be given as off days. Manhoos will not work on these days. Do you understand?'

Seth-ji managed to nod his head. 'Good,' said Mary. 'If you agree, then Luka will leave you and your family alone. If you don't, he will bite all of you and you will die slow, horrible and painful deaths. Now, do you accept Luka's offer?'

'Yes,' Seth-ji gasped.

'Good. Like he said, it is an offer you can't refuse,' said Mary. 'And remember, if you ever break your word, that very night, Lukabarsi will make sure that you sleep with the fishes. You understand?'

'Yes,' Seth-ji somehow croaked and collapsed on the floor with a soft thud, his body limp as a punctured tyre. Manhoos' jaw dropped; his eyes bulged in disbelief. His gaze shifted rapidly from Seth-ji to Mary and back. His awe for Mary knew no bounds, but at the same time, he was terrified of what Seth-ji would do to him once she had gone. But he needn't have worried. It took seven days for Rajinder Seth to recover from his encounter with Lukabarsi. They say he was never quite the same again.

***

With the defanging of Seth-ji, things were beginning to look up for Manhoos. He didn't have to work quite so hard as before and he had more time to spend with Mary. Naturally, his admiration and fondness for her had skyrocketed and he loved being with her.

One afternoon, they were sitting together and chatting, when Manhoos took Mary's hand in his and said shyly: 'Thank you. I don't know where I would be without you. The way you and Luka made baingan-bharta out of Seth-ji!' he giggled. 'I swear I won't forget it for the rest of my life.'

'*Arre jah*!' said Mary, pretending to be annoyed. 'I know you. The first chance you get, you will go to the city and forget all about me.'

'I won't. I promise. We will always be together.'

'We'll see. Anyway, even if you go to the city, don't become like the dikus.'

'What do you mean?'

'I mean don't become like Seth-ji. Always taking and taking. And eating and eating and becoming fat.'

'I'll never become like that.'

'We'll see. All dikus are the same—fat and greedy. My father told me that once upon a time, the whole world used to be a forest. And then the dikus came. And they cut down the jungles, killed the animals and birds, planted their fields of rice and wheat, made their roads and factories. They burnt our homes to build their houses and churches and temples. They destroyed everything.'

'But you still live in the forest, in your own homes.'

'Yes, but there are so few of us left. We may even be the last. My father told me that before the dikus came, there were one hundred thousand of us. All of Bharat-disom used to belong to our people. Now there are just a handful of us. And even our days may be numbered.'

'What do you mean?'

'The other day, one engine-babu came to our village from Ranchi. He came in a jeepo along with two police-babus who had guns with them.'

'Guns! What does a gun look like? Did you touch it?'

'Are you stupid? All the children stayed inside the house until they had gone. Father says police-babus and engine-babus are always up to mischief. Anyway, they ordered him to take them to the bamboo forest.'

'What for?'

'I thought they wanted to hunt deer. But no! It was for something quite weird. These dikus are mad, I'm telling you!'

'Why? What did they do?'

'Father says engine-babu dug a hole in the ground and took out a few handfuls of soil. He put it into a box and said he was going to take it to Ranchi to take a closer look. When father asked him what he was looking for, engine-babu smiled and said—*white gold*.'

'White gold? What nonsense! There is no such thing.'

'Exactly. I told you no, these dikus are mad! Anyway, father also told them the same thing. But engine-babu only laughed at him and said—*You are an unpadh junglee, an illiterate savage. You know nothing. There is a great treasure buried inside this forest. I can smell it—a giant pot of white gold that is more precious than real gold*.'

'A pot of white gold? More precious than real gold?'

'Yes, engine-babu even called it by a strange name—backside or something like that. He said if they could find it, then they would make a temple for it'

'A temple for a backside?' Manhoos frowned at this new word. I, on the other hand, almost fell off my perch laughing.

'Don't laugh about things you don't understand,' snapped Mary. 'My father said we must be very careful. Dikus can do anything for gold and temples. Even kill.' The lines on her young, weather-beaten face deepened. 'Anyway, maybe we are thinking too much. Let's talk of better things. You are coming with me to the village next Sunday, no? It's your first holiday!'

'Yes! Just six more days and I'll finally be able to see your home.'

'It will be great fun. We will get there by dawn when the koel is singing. We'll catch fish in the morning and bathe at noon, when the river is flowing like liquid gold. We'll dance in the full moon, with the Tumdak drums beating like our own hearts, when the scent of mahua and raat ki rani, the night jasmine is rising into the star-filled sky. Wait till you see it—it's magic, pure magic.'

'Yes, magic,' agreed Manhoos. He looked shyly at Mary and clasped his fingers over her. She gazed back and dropped her head on his shoulder.

All these years later, I can still see that droplet of time, suspended between the maws of the past and the future, that one ephemeral moment made eternal by the magic of first love, that one fleeting moment, in the ceaseless, swirling currents of time.

Temple of Gold

By virtue of our birth and training, we yakshas have an acute sixth sense that alerts us to imminent dangers long before ordinary mortals can see them coming. For example, the moment the Willys jeep screeched to a halt in front of Rajinder Seth's garage, I smelt trouble. It had a red beacon light flashing on its bonnet and spotless white towels draped over its seats, marking it out as the official vehicle of some government bigshot. Besides the driver, the jeep had two other occupants—two grey-haired, middle-aged men in solar topis and grey safari suits that stretched over their gently protruding paunches.

The sight sent Rajinder Seth's knickers into a right royal twist. '*Hey bhagwan,*' he mumbled in a trembling voice. 'Collector saab is here. And engineer saab too. What if they ask me to show my papers? I haven't renewed my license in years.'

But he needn't have worried. Thick black smoke was billowing out of the jeep's bonnet and all the men wanted was to get the vehicle fixed and be on their way. For a change, Seth-ji rolled up his own sleeves to get down to work, while Manhoos laid out chairs for the visitors. The two men sat themselves down and were soon in the middle of an animated conversation. Naturally, I had to eavesdrop.

'You are sure about this, Sharma?' the first man asked.

'One hundred and ten per cent, Varma-ji,' replied the second man. 'The soil test results from the Ranchi laboratory prove it beyond doubt. It is definitely bauxite.'

'Bauxite! I thought as much!' Varma exclaimed. 'Umm...Sharma?' he eyed the other shiftily.

'Yes, Varma-ji?'

'Remind me again, my dear boy, what exactly *is* bauxite? As you know, my degree is in English Literature, not Chemistry.'

'Aluminium ore, sir,' replied Sharma. 'From which we can make aluminium. It is the wonder metal of our age, sir. White gold! Can be used to make anything—from aeroplanes to hairpins.'

'White gold, eh? And exactly how much of this ore is there? How much aluminium can be made from it?'

'Oh, several lakh tonnes, sir. The ore deposits seem to be exceptionally rich.'

'Excellent! Excellent!' Varma beamed. 'I will finally have some good news to give to the Cabinet Secretary. So far, all I have been sending him are reports on riots and refugee camps. What an unending nightmare the Partition has been! The whole country has gone mad—killing, looting, raping!'

'What can you expect, Varma-ji? Seven million Muslims going from Hindustan to Pakistan and another seven million Hindus going the other way. There will be blood, no?'

'Yes, indeed, there will be blood,' a distant look entered the senior man's eyes as he said: '*...two peoples fanatically at odds / With their different diets and incompatible gods.../...in seven weeks it was done, the frontiers decided /A continent for better or worse divided.*'

'Nice,' said Sharma. 'You wrote this poem, sir?'

'No, no, it's one of these modern poets. Some fellow called Mr Auden. '*A continent for better or worse divided*'—well, thanks to Mr Radcliffe, that's the reality now, for better or for worse. At least things are not so bad in these parts. But in Lahore and Delhi and Calcutta, it is madness, I believe. My brother-in-law wrote to me from Delhi, saying that the whole city has become one big refugee colony. Over three lakh refugees in Kingsway Camp alone! I hear Calcutta is equally bad.'

'*Yeh daagh daagh ujaalaa, yeh shab-gazidaa seher / Woh intezaar tha jiska, yeh woh seher toh nahin,*' Sharma sighed. Varma, who was more familiar with English sonnets than Urdu couplets stared blankly at Sharma.

'Faiz Ahmed Faiz, sir,' said Sharma and provided a quick translation. 'This mottled light, this morning wounded by the night, this dawn which was awaited, it cannot be this.'

'How true. But what use is poetry in these times, Sharma, when people are busy cutting each other's throats?'

'Maybe they are cutting each other's throats, *because* they have forgotten poetry, Varma-ji.'

'Five years into this job, and all the poetry has gone out of my life, Sharma. Byron, Shelley, Keats—in college, I knew them like the back of my hand. Now, they are all but dead to me,' he spread out his hands in an expansive gesture and began to recite:

'I wandered lonely as a cloud
That floats on high o'er vales and hills,
When all at once I saw a crowd,
A host, of golden—'

'Daffodils,' Sharma completed the line with a smug smile. 'Wordsworth. I also know it, sir. It was in our Rapid Reader in sixth standard.'

'Not bad, my boy, not bad at all! But the daffodils are long gone and along with them, has gone the age of the poets. This is the age of engineers, Sharma—your age. Once the horrors of Partition are behind us, a new India will have to be built. And you are the people who will build it—with your roads and dams and factories. *Oh, brave new world, that hath such people in it,* etcetera, etcetera.'

A dreamy look entered Sharma's eyes. 'I like to think of them as temples, sir. The temples of modern India. They will drag our people out of the Dark Ages and throw them straight into the twentieth century.'

Varma sat upright. 'Temples of modern India, eh? Well said, my boy, well said. You are quite the poet yourself. I think I will mention that in my report to New Delhi. It's just the sort of thing that Nehru-ji seems to like. In fact, I should draft a letter right away, before I forget,' he pulled out a pen and a notepad from his pocket and began to write:

To,
The Cabinet Secretary
Government of India
New Delhi
My Dear Sir,
It is my delightful duty to inform you that we have discovered

extensive deposits of the aluminium ore, bauxite, in the forests of Betla in Netarhat district, which lies in my jurisdiction.

We are seized of the urgent need for the industrial development of the nation. Pursuant to this noble goal, we would like to embark upon the mining of the aforesaid ore and the rapid production of the concomitant aluminium metal, which will doubtless, bring great benefit to our great nation.

I seek your permission to begin the development of such mines, roads and factories necessary for this purpose. It will be my privilege to lead such a mission to build what I believe are the true temples of modern India.

I remain,
Your most faithful servant,
Shri A.K. Varma (ICS)
Collector, Netarhat District
Bihar.
Copy to: Shri Jawaharlal Nehru, Prime Minister, India.

'There, that should do the trick,' Varma said with a satisfied smile. 'I will send the letter today itself. Pandit Nehru is a man in a hurry. I expect that we will receive all the approvals soon. But you don't need to wait for the formal orders. You should start making your preparations.'

'Certainly, sir,' said Sharma. 'Don't worry about the technical side. I will manage that. But we may need help from the police. Perhaps even the army.'

Varma frowned. 'The army? What for?'

'There are some tribals who are living in that part of the forest, sir. A few hundred or so. They will have to be cleared out first, before we can start clearing the area for civil works.'

'So, what is the problem? Tell them to pack up and go somewhere else.'

'But what if they don't want to leave?'

'Seven million Muslims and seven million Hindus have just left their homes, Sharma. If they can leave, then so can a handful of tribals!'

'Yes, but—'

'How can a bunch of half-naked tribals hold an entire nation to ransom?' Varma slapped his thigh in agitation. 'India needs aluminium and she shall have it! These tribals must vacate their lands for the greater good. Of course, we will offer them a good rehabilitation package—houses, jobs, roads, etcetera etcetera. I'm sure they will understand if we tell them nicely. But if they don't, we will have to evict them.'

'But I don't think they will go easily, sir. They have been living there for centuries.'

'Then they have long overstayed their welcome. In any case, they are illegal occupants. I hope you know that according to the Forest Act of 1927, all forest lands belong to the Government of India. Which means, these people are encroaching on government property. They must leave. That is the law.'

'Pardon me, Varma-ji. But isn't the Forest Act a British law? Does it still hold good?' Sharma noticed the scowl on Varma-ji's face and hastened to explain. 'I mean, our own Constitution has come into effect since January this year. So, will the old British laws still hold? I'm only an engineer, you see, I don't really understand these things.'

'That's exactly why the Indian Civil Service is there, Sharma,' Varma-ji smiled. 'We are the iron frame holding the country together so it doesn't fall apart. And of course, the Forest Act of 1927 is still in force. It is a good law, so we have retained it. We have removed only the bad British laws, not the good ones. Can't throw the baby out with the bathwater, can we? Now, you don't worry yourself about such matters. Just sort out this tribal business and get down to work.'

'All right, sir. I only hope there won't be too much trouble. These Santhal fellows are good hunters, experts with bows and arrows.'

'Don't tell me you are scared, Sharma!' Varma-ji sniggered. 'If they have bows and arrows, then we have rifles. Not that I am saying we will use them. Of course not. After all, it's a free country now. The Santhals are also Indians like us. We are all equal. But that also means that we must all obey the same laws. Our very own laws, sanctified by our very own Constitution. And as per law, these people are illegal occupants.'

'True, sir. All Indians are legal, but some Indians are less legal than others,' Sharma said.

'You have hit the nail on the head, Sharma. If force has to be used to evict such illegal people, then so be it,' Varma-ji shrugged, 'what to do?'

'Very true sir. After all, you can't make an omelette without breaking eggs.'

'Or bring progress to the many, without breaking the legs of a few, if necessary. This is the time for strong and decisive leadership. It is our duty to do this for the people.'

'Exactly, sir. Democracy—for the people, of the peop—'

'Right, right,' Varma cut him off. 'But enough philosophy for one day. There is plenty of work to do. The first step will be to cordon off the forest and—' he stopped as Rajinder Seth shuffled up to his side.

'Your car is ready, Collector saab,' Rajinder Seth said with an oily smile.

'Good! About time too!' Varma-ji exclaimed. 'Sharma, the moment I reach office, I will inform the Superintendent of Police to be ready to remove these tribals—by force if necessary. Meanwhile, begin your preparations for the bauxite project...or rather, this temple of modern India, as I like to think of it.'

Well, at least the mystery of the backside temple had been solved. But it sent shivers down my spine to think that it would be built on the bones of Mary and her tribe. My first instinct was to warn her of the terrible danger that was dancing above their heads like the shadowy hood of Lukabarsi. But with a great effort of will, I held myself back.

For it was the burden of my song to only observe the sands of time, not leave my footprints on them. Besides, like the flapping of butterfly wings, the wagging of my tongue could trigger off a storm, even worse than the one that it was intended to prevent.

In any case, it wasn't the first time that innocent lives would be destroyed because of a temple. Nor would it be the last.

A feeling of deja poo swept over me at the gloomy realisation, that shit, like history, repeats itself. And there was little that anyone could do about it.

The Prince and the Pauper

On Sunday afternoon, Manhoos and Mary were sitting by the edge of the Koyal river, her gentle waves lapping their feet. They had spent the morning in Mary's village and after lunch she had suggested that they walk down to the river. The day seemed unreal to Manhoos, as if he were in a dream. He hadn't known that such times were possible, when all you did was listen to birdsong, watch butterflies and deer dance as you roamed the jungle without a care in the world.

'So, this is what being free really feels like,' Manhoos muttered, almost to himself.

'Didn't I tell you? The jungle is a special place,' Mary smiled.

'You people spend your days like this?' Manhoos asked. 'Just lazing around?'

'Sometimes. But we also work hard—sowing and harvesting, gathering fruits, hunting, making mahua.'

Manhoos took a moment to absorb this. 'But if there's so much to do here, why do you come all the way to the highway to sell a few berries?'

'Because we need the money, stupid.'

'Why? You keep saying the forest gives you everything.'

'Yes, but not knives or medicines or matchboxes. There are still some things which only money can buy. For everything else, there is the forest.'

Manhoos watched a dazzling blue kingfisher plunge into the river, and return to the surface with a silvery fish wriggling in its beak. 'It's so beautiful...this place,' he said.

'Yes...and I only hope it stays that way.' A dark shadow flitted across Mary's face.

'What's happened? Why are you looking so worried?'

Mary sighed. 'That engine-babu came here again, yesterday. With a police-babu. A different one this time. I think this one is a big babu.'

'How do you know?'

'He had three gold coins stitched to his shirt. Can you believe it? These dikus are so stupid. Always after gold. What is the use of something you can't eat, you can't make arrows from? But they keep wanting more and more of it. Now they are telling us that we may have to leave our village. So that they can dig out their stupid white gold!'

'They told you to go?' An icy knife stabbed at Manhoos' heart. 'Go where?'

'We asked. But they didn't give a clear answer. They only said they would find us another piece of land somewhere else. And give us money to build pucca cement houses, maybe even electricity. And engine-babu said that he'll try and get jobs for some of the men.'

'That's something at least. But what if they send you to some place far away?' said Manhoos. 'Suppose they send you to Dilli? Then what? How will we meet? How—' he grunted as Mary gave him a sharp poke in the ribs.

'Shut up! You are a real manhoos, you know!' she said. 'Stop saying such things. We are not going away anywhere. We said that to engine-babu and police-babu and I'm saying it to you. We will *not* go from here, no matter what!'

'Thank god!'

'You think it's the first time the dikus have tried to take away our lands? You think we don't know how to fight them? Just wait till they see our bows and arrows. They'll run with their tails between their legs.'

'You're not scared of fighting the police?'

Mary went quiet. 'Yes, I am,' she said after a while. 'We are all scared. But when we see the trees, the river, the birds...we know that we are fighting for them too. And that gives us strength. I'm telling you, Manhoos, the police won't find it easy to throw us out. We will fight them till our last breath.'

'Mary?'

'Yes?'

'I just wanted to say...if there is a fight, I will be with you, fighting by your side.'

'*Arre jah*!' sniggered Mary. 'You're such a darpoke, a real coward. When there's a fight, I know where you'll be. Hiding under a car! Owww!' she squealed as Manhoos yanked her pigtail. 'Sorry! I'm sorry! You're not a darpoke. You're brave as Birsa Munda. Happy?' she extended her hand, but Manhoos pushed it away roughly.

'Come on now. I was just joking,' she pleaded. 'All right, we'll fight the police together, okay? We will be together. Always. Okay?'

Manhoos did not reply. He was still angry at her. But after a while, her fingers reached out again and brushed against his and he could not help smiling. He found it as difficult to be angry at Mary, as at the afternoon breeze ruffling his hair.

'Yes, together. Always,' he said softly and clasped her hand.

For a while, all was quiet except for the rustle of leaves and the river breaking gently on the shore. But presently, the peace was broken by a sound so faint, that only my supernaturally sensitive ears could have detected it.

From the depths of some cavernous building in Lutyens' Delhi, emerged the sound of crinkling paper, as a nameless government clerk in the Cabinet Secretary's office placed Varma-ji's letter inside a file marked: *'Urgent: For Immediate Action.'*

***

One good thing about the Indian government is that files marked *'Urgent'* are usually treated as anything but. And so it was with Varma-ji's file. All through the spring of 1950, it went up, down and sideways, from one desk to another, with the directionless energy of Brownian motion. Spring turned to autumn, but the dog-eared file was still meandering through the labyrinthine corridors of power in Delhi.

Meanwhile an uneasy peace prevailed in the forests of Betla and by the winter of 1950, the Santhals began to feel that the danger may have passed them by. But I wasn't so sure. My ever alert sixth sense told me that the file was still hovering over their heads, like the sword of Damocles. It was only a matter of time before it fell on them.

One morning as Manhoos was taking apart a gear box, I hopped across to him and said: 'So, what do you think?'

'Think of what?' asked Manhoos.

'This white gold that the dikus are after? You think they've forgotten about it?'

'That's what Mary says. She says that the thought of Santhal arrows make the dikus piss in their pants.'

'Mary this and Mary that! You think your Mary knows everything!' I exclaimed. Although it was none of my business, I was getting a little worried at how close the boy had grown to Mary. They were as thick as thieves these days. 'Have you ever thought of what will happen to *you* when she goes away?'

'She's not going anywhere.'

'We'll see. It's a big world. She won't be here forever. Neither will you.'

'We will. We've sworn to be together,' he snapped. 'Always.'

'I thought you wanted to see the world?'

'I will. But with Mary. So, you can keep your stupid little mouth shut! Anyway, I have to get back to work. If I don't fix that man's car now, he's sure to complain to Seth-ji. Can you see how he's looking at me?'

I turned to see a man standing in front of the shed. He seemed to be around thirty but I couldn't be sure. It wasn't surprising that I hadn't noticed him until now, for he was the most average looking man I had ever seen. Everything about him was smack in the middle of the Bell curve—his height, weight, waist, his bland clothes, and his blander face. A cellophane man, if there ever was one, the sort of man that women look through and shopkeepers look past.

The stranger's gaze was fixed on Manhoos. A moment later he trotted up to us and cleared his throat awkwardly: 'Umm...excuse me, but if you don't mind, can I ask you something?'

'Yes, saab?' Manhoos replied.

'I couldn't help noticing that—' the man stopped and shook his head. 'No, I'm being stupid. It can't be...obviously not,' he mumbled to himself.

'What can't be, saab?' Manhoos asked.

The man squared his shoulders. 'All right, fine! I'll ask. Tell me something, boy—by any chance, were you talking to that sparrow?' the man pointed at me.

'Yes, I was,' Manhoos nodded.

'Really!' the stranger exclaimed. 'To think that I would ever see such a thing again...here of all—' he stopped, as if struck by a sudden thought. 'Tell me something, are you from Registan?'

'Registan? No, never heard it. But why do you ask, saab?'

'Because some years ago I had heard of a boy like you. He lived in a village in the hills of Registan. People said that he could speak with the birds and beasts. I thought it was just an old wives' tale. But apparently, he could talk to all sorts of animals, like they were his friends—pigeons, falcons, camels. Even horses.'

'What's so great about that? I can speak to horses as well. And wolves and deer and birds. Never spoken to a camel though. Never seen one. What is a camel?'

'A camel? It's like...well...never mind. But did you just say that you could speak to...horses?'

'Yes, horses are nice. Very soft-spoken.'

The stranger's eyebrows disappeared into his hairline. 'Really? Amazing! Astonishing!'

'It's easy,' shrugged Manhoos. He went on to tell the stranger how Mary had taught him to talk to animals.

'Oh, I see,' the stranger muttered, after Manhoos had finished. 'That may be so...yes, maybe. The jungle tribes have powers that city people don't understand.' A strange glitter flashed in his eyes. 'Tell me something, boy. Is there a horse somewhere nearby?'

'There were a few wild horses which used to graze in the forest. I used to chat with them sometimes. But I haven't seen them lately.'

The stranger's face fell. 'A pity. No other horses here?'

'None I've seen.'

'Tchah!' said the stranger. He paced up and down, as if in deep thought, when he smacked his forehead and halted. 'Of course! I have it!' he grabbed Manhoos' hand and said: 'Can you come with me to Netarhat town?'

'Netarhat? For what?'

'Tongas! There are tongas in Netarhat. Which means there are horses. I want to see you talking to them.'

Manhoos pulled his hand away. 'Why should I? And who are you?'

'I'll tell you everything. But first you tell me, will you come with me to Netarhat?' the stranger asked. Manhoos made no reply. 'Look—if you do as I say, I will give you three rupees. Yes?'

Manhoos bit his lip and frowned. I could see that he was sorely tempted by the stranger's offer. After nearly three years of being with him, I could read him like a book. I could almost see the cogs turning inside his head as he weighed the pros and cons—three rupees was a hell of a lot of money. Nearly half a month's wages. But who was this stranger and what was he up to? Suspicion and temptation battled inside Manhoos for a while, until he said: 'I don't think I can go. Seth-ji won't allow me.'

The stranger clucked his tongue. 'Tchh, I'll convince your Seth-ji. You leave that to me. But are *you* willing to come with me to Netarhat? If so, we will leave the moment the car is ready.'

'I can come...but Seth-ji—'

'Excellent!' the stranger cut him off. 'Now listen carefully. Don't worry about Seth-ji. I will drive you to Netarhat and back. If you do as I say, I will give you three rupees. And if I am pleased with you, I may even give you something extra. Something very special.'

'What, saab?'

'A grand dinner at the best hotel in Netarhat—the Buckingham Place Hotel. What do you say to that?'

Manhoos' eyes widened into twin moons. He tried to think what a grand dinner at the best hotel in town might be like, but his imagination was unequal to the task.

'You can eat anything you want—pulao, paneer, chicken, ice cream,' the stranger said.

'Ice cream?' Manhoos whispered. He had seen Seth-ji's fat, spoilt daughter, who was just about his age, eating ice cream. She sometimes came with her father to the garage and would sit there licking the delicious-looking stuff. It made his mouth water and his insides whine with hopeless desire. The last vestiges of his resistance crumbled to dust as he swallowed his saliva and said: 'Yes, babu, I'll come. I'll do whatever you tell me to.'

'Fantastic!' the stranger rubbed his hands in glee. 'Good. Now that we are friends, why don't you tell me your name?'

'Manhoos.'

The stranger grimaced. 'Well, Manhoos, I hope you won't live up to your name,' he said. Then in a low voice, he muttered to himself: 'Because that would definitely ruin my little plan, if it all works out that is...'

Manhoos couldn't hear him. But I could. Half a dozen questions immediately sprouted inside my head. What was this man's 'little plan'? Why did he seem so excited? Who *was* he anyway?

As if he had read my mind, the stranger said: 'I should introduce myself. Manhoos, I am Prince Surya Pratap Singh.'

Manhoos' eyebrows shot up. 'Prince? Like a Maharaja?' It was difficult to believe that this nondescript, shabbily attired stranger with his beat-up Morris car, was a king.

'Indeed. I was once the Maharaja of Registan,' the stranger replied. 'But now...now the British have gone. And with them have gone all the kings and queens of India. Gone to dust,' he suddenly looked ten years older. 'But as they say, once a king, always a king,' he gazed curiously at Manhoos. 'Who knows, with your help, I may even be able to get back my lost kingdom.'

'*My* help?' Manhoos said. Maharaja or not, the man was surely mad. What if he kidnapped him, slit his throat or something? He suddenly felt scared.

'Yes, with your help, Manhoos,' the prince replied. 'You see, I believe in destiny. Or else why should you suddenly appear out of nowhere, at the moment of my greatest need? It is a sign, Manhoos, a sign that our fates are joined. Destiny is showing us a path. A path that may lead to a gold mine.'

Manhoos' misgivings grew stronger. Was this man another gold-crazed diku, the sort that Mary had warned him about? How could he be trusted? And yet, the lure of three rupees and a grand dinner was almost impossible to resist...he wished he could have asked Mary what to do. She would have known. But she wasn't around. It was Sunday, her day off.

'What's the matter?' the prince said. 'If it's about your Seth-ji, then don't worry. A little extra payment for his services, and I'm sure he'll cooperate. But will you come or not?'

But Manhoos was still in two minds. Should he trust this diku with his strange talk of gold mines and lost kingdoms? It was risky no doubt. But then, nothing risked, nothing gained...the first ice cream of his life was inches away from his grasp, so close that he could see it, smell it. He could almost feel its cool sweetness melting in his mouth. A taste of the real thing would be worth a risk. Almost any risk.

'Yes, saab. I'll come with you,' said Manhoos.

The Horse Whisperer

One hour later, we were at the outskirts of Netarhat. All through the twenty-mile journey from the garage to the town, the prince had been chattering away. He clearly liked the sound of his own voice, but I didn't mind listening. For the story that he told us, was entwined with an important chapter in the history of this land.

Until three years ago, Prince Surya Pratap Singh had been the king of Registan, a small princely state to the west of Ajmer. He had ascended the throne in 1926, the last in a long line of Singhs to become king. For over twenty years, he had ruled his little kingdom well and his subjects had adored him (I took this with a pinch of salt, for which king would say otherwise...). Things were going all hunky-dory, until the summer of 1947, when disaster struck.

On the fourth of June 1947, Lord Mountbatten, the last Viceroy of India, declared that from the fifteenth of August that year, India would no longer be ruled by the King of England. Furthermore, the five hundred and sixty-three princely states of India would cease to be ruled by any king or queen, and would have to merge with either of the two independent republics of India or Pakistan. Having done his duty to King and country, Lord Mountbatten muttered a hurried 'God Save India' and boarded the first available boat to old Blighty, just in time to catch the racing season at Ascot.

The fate of the princely states now lay in the hands of that shrewd Congressman from Gujarat—Sardar Vallabhbhai Patel. A formidable character he was, blunt and powerful as a battering ram. He had an equally dangerous secretary—the smooth-talking V.P. Menon, his tongue like a switch blade cloaked in a silken sheath. And over the next few months, the five hundred and sixty-three royals of Hindustan got royally buggered by the Sardar and his secretary.

'*Baap re baap*! By god! What a pair they made!' the prince exclaimed. 'The Gujarati Iron Man and his Madrasi henchman ! One fine day, I received a telegram from Menon saying that he wanted to meet me. The next morning, he and Patel just walked into my palace, as if...as if they owned the place! The nerve! These Congressi fellows, who were in jail only months ago, were strutting about my palace in khadi chaddhis, like Roman emperors!

'Anyway, over breakfast, they told me how much the people of Registan would bless me if I joined the Indian Union. I said I needed time to think about it. But by lunch, they were casually talking of sending in three battalions of the Rajputana Rifles, just to keep an eye on my affairs. By tea-time, the two had arm-twisted me into signing the instrument of ascension. And with one stroke of the pen, I was forced to give away the throne that had belonged to our family for fourteen generations! Yes, when India won her independence, I lost mine. I lost everything—my kingdom, my palace, my estates, jewels, eunuchs...'

'At least you still have this car. It's a good one,' Manhoos lied. The prince's battered Morris was on its last legs but he was looking so downcast, that Manhoos felt sorry for him.

'Hah,' the prince grunted. 'I once had five cars, including a Rolls Royce Silver Ghost. But I had to sell them all. Not just my cars—my estates, my jewels, I sold everything. Even my palace! Sold it to a Marwari bania who wants to turn it into a hotel. My ancestral home's gone...sold for peanuts.'

'But why?' asked Manhoos.

'Who will pay good money for a three-hundred-year-old palace? It was falling apart, especially the plumbing. I think I was lucky to get what I did.'

'No, I meant why did you have to sell everything?'

'Why? To pay off my debts, what else. You see, my father and I, we both had a liking for the good life—French wines, Italian opera singers, tawaifs from Lucknow...that sort of thing. But when the bloody Congress government stripped me of my royal privileges, all those damned vendors and shopkeepers started hounding me for their payments. Some of them are still after me...,' the prince looked around furtively. 'You are just a child and you don't understand these things. But let me tell you this, boy. One day, I will become a rich man again. I will return to Registan with a chest full of money, and I will throw it at the faces of my debtors. You just watch.' A wealth of emotions flitted across the prince's face.

'Yes sir,' Manhoos nodded. Seeing that the prince had regained his composure, he asked: 'What about your family, Raja-saab?'

The prince's face darkened. 'Never had any children,' he replied. 'And my poor wife died soon after Registan was taken away from me. The Rani-sahiba was a proud woman. She couldn't bear the insults and threats of debtors knocking on the palace doors. She hid herself and just wasted away...she had lost the will to live, the doctors told me later. Ah, I miss her, Manhoos, I miss her.'

'So, you have no family? Just like me?' asked Manhoos.

'No family, no home, just like you,' said the prince. 'Maybe that's why destiny has brought us together.' Without a warning, the prince suddenly slammed on the brakes and the car screeched to a standstill.

'What the flying fu—' I started to squawk in alarm, when I saw the reason for the abrupt halt. By the side of the road, was a pair of tongas. And standing beside them were two horses, flicking away flies with their swishing tails.

***

A quick negotiation with the tongawallas, the exchange of two crisp one-rupee notes and it was all settled. The tongawallas were all too happy for the prince to use their horses as he pleased, as long as it didn't involve any bodily fluids.

The two horses, one chestnut and one black, were now munching on a pile of hay. The prince pointed at them and said: 'The moment of reckoning has come, Manhoos. Let's see if you can tell your friends to do what I want.'

'What do you want, saab?' asked Manhoos.

'Let's start with something easy,' the prince replied. 'Tell that chestnut horse to raise its right leg.'

'Okay, saab,' Manhoos pressed his fingers against his nostrils, opened his mouth and let out a shrill neighing sound. The horse looked up curiously at the boy and gave an answering neigh. Then it slowly lifted its right foot and waved its hoof at Manhoos.

'Amazing!' the prince whispered, his eyes bulging. 'Now, can you ask the black horse to raise its left hind leg?'

Manhoos made another neighing sound. The black horse neighed in reply and lifted its left hind leg.

The prince rubbed his hands in glee. His voice was hoarse as he said: 'And now...Manhoos beta, now can you ask both of them to run down the road? Tell them to go to that tree over there and return the same way.'

Manhoos cocked an eyebrow at the prince. He definitely had a few loose screws. But as long as he paid up, Manhoos thought, what went of his father? He issued a sharp command and the horses promptly clip-clopped down the road. They made a U-turn at the tree that the prince had indicated, and trotted back. In quick succession, the prince proceeded to ask for a canter, a gallop, a sudden turn, a stop and a start and several other manoeuvres of increasing complexity. But under Manhoos' directions, the horses executed them all to perfection. Even I was impressed, not to mention the tongawallas, whose jaws had dropped to their chests, or the prince who was positively dribbling with excitement.

After a full hour of horseplay, the prince seemed to be finally satisfied. He thumped Manhoos on the back and said: 'Well done, Manhoos beta! Well done!' he fished out his wallet and pressed three coins into the boy's palm.

Manhoos stared disbelievingly at the coins in his hand. Three whole rupees! All for himself? At that moment, even Kubera could not have felt richer than him. It took a while before he could speak. 'Thank you, saab,' he began to mumble at last, when he remembered something, the most important thing, in fact. 'Errr, Raja-saab...what about the dinner? And...ice cream?'

'Of course! Of course!' the prince beamed. 'You richly deserve it and you shall have it. The best dinner of your life. Now that our work here is done, we can go straight to Buckingham Place Hotel. There will be plenty to eat and plenty to talk about.'

As they were returning to the car, Manhoos sneaked a quick look at the coins clutched in his fist. He was relieved to see that all three coins were still there. But to his surprise, they felt much lighter now, than they had been only moments ago. He wondered whether he should have asked for more.

***

'You want some more?' smiled the prince.

Manhoos nodded. He was unable to speak for his mouth was filled with the most delicious ice cream that there was. Nothing, he decided, nothing in the world was better than a meal of pulao and chicken curry, followed by chocolate ice cream. As he scooped another divine spoonful into his mouth, it struck him how beautiful life could be. How sweet, and fragrant, and clean...everything was so clean—the gleaming cutlery, the table cloth, the spotless uniforms of the waiters. He sneaked a glance at his tattered, grease-stained shirt and shame washed over him. If only his clothes were like the waiter's...

'Enjoying yourself?' the prince asked.

'Yes,' mumbled Manhoos.

'Well, I am afraid you will have to eat up quickly. It's already quite late and I have to drop you back to the garage,' said the prince.

The spoon slipped from Manhoos' fingers and clattered to the floor. All thoughts of Seth-ji's rat-hole of a garage had been wiped out by the pleasures of Buckingham Place and the very idea of returning there made his stomach churn.

As if he had read Manhoos' mind, the prince said: 'Of course, you can also stay here tonight, if you want. I can book a room for you.'

'I can...stay here?' Manhoos stuttered.

'Yes, why not? We can leave tomorrow after breakfast. It's not a bad spread—juice, toast, eggs, butter.'

'Butter?' Manhoos whispered. He had only heard of this mysterious thing that was called 'butter' on Rajinder Seth's radio. 'Polson's Butter', an English lady would say in a beautiful memsahib voice—and some other things, of which he only understood the word 'bread'. Butter! In the memsahib's melting voice, it suggested something so rich and delicious that it made his mouth water.

'Polson Butter?' he asked in wonder now.

'Yes, yes, Polson's butter! As much as you want. After you have breakfast, we can go back to the garage. But...' the prince paused and examined his fingertips, 'but if you don't want to, then—'

'Then what Raja-saab?' Manhoos stared blankly at him.

'Then you can quit your job at the garage and come with me.'

Manhoos couldn't make head or tail of what the man saying: 'Leave my job...but why?' he asked haltingly.

'Because I have a better job for you and with better pay. Not just that, I can also take care of your other needs, roti, kapda and makaan. And makhkhan. All the food you can eat, good clothes to wear, a home. And butter, bread and jam as well.'

'Are you saying you can give me a job and money and—'

'And all those things I said. Yes, I can give you all that and more. But on one condition.'

'What?'

'That in return, you must do whatever I tell you to do. And you must keep it a secret. No one must ever know what you do for me. Do you agree?'

The sweet smell of vanilla and chocolate suddenly turned into the rancid odour of danger. Manhoos' palms turned clammy and he sneaked a quick look at the door, just in case he needed to make a run for it.

'Why do you look so scared, Manhoos?' the prince leaned forward. 'I am not a kidnapper, if that's what you think. Nor am I going to sell you off to some beggars' gang. It's very simple. I believe you can be useful to me. So, I am asking you to come and work for me.'

Manhoos' heart was hammering so hard that he was scared it might pop out of his ribs any moment. For years, he had dreamt of escaping from Seth-ji's garage. And now suddenly, it seemed that the dream was coming true. But at what price? Fear and hope chased through him, like a cat after her tail.

'What do you want me to do, Raja-saab?' Manhoos managed to say.

'I can see that you are good with both cars and horses. Very good. A person with those skills would come in very handy in my line of business.'

'You have a garage? Or are you a tongawalla?'

'Neither. I cannot tell you what the work is now. But I will, when the time is right,' the prince said. 'Don't worry, Manhoos beta. I'm not a bad person and I won't ask you to do anything wrong. All I can say now, is that you have nothing to lose and everything to gain. So will you trust me? Will you come with me?'

'Where to, Raja-saab?' asked Manhoos.

'Calcutta,' the prince replied.

A bolt of excitement shot through Manhoos. His father had once told him about Calcutta. It was the greatest city in India, his father had said, a city of millions to which millions more flocked each day, like moths to a flame. Manhoos had imagined its bright lights, its huge mansions, its streets paved with gold. But it was as unreachable as the moon and even in his wildest dreams, Manhoos couldn't have thought that he would ever see the place. The very idea took his breath away.

'Calcutta?' Manhoos managed to say at last.

'Yes. I have a house there, our ancestral haveli. It serves as a winter residence and I'm very fond of it. It's the only property that I haven't yet sold. And I won't either if I can help it. You can stay there with me.'

'I can stay with you...in your haveli in Calcutta?'

'Not forever, of course. Listen Manhoos, this is what I have in mind—you come and work for me in Calcutta. I will try you out for the next two weeks and see how it goes.'

'Only two weeks? What'll I do after that?'

'If things work out, then you can continue to work for me. But if they don't, then I will bring you back to Netarhat and you can return to your old job. What do you say?'

As Manhoos chewed on his fingernails, trying to collect his thoughts, I couldn't help wondering what the prince was up to. Was he laying a trap for the boy? If so, why? What was the secret work that he wanted Manhoos to do? I had no answers, except this—that if indeed, the prince was leading Manhoos up the garden path, then he had lined it with all the right goodies—ice cream, buttered toast and city lights. I doubted if the boy would be able resist such powerful seducements, no matter what the risk.

There was only one thing that might stop him—Mary. But would he value an old friendship over the possibility of a brand-new life? I did not have to wait long to know the answer to my question.

'I have decided,' Manhoos said. 'I will go with you to Calcutta.'

'And me too!' I said. 'I've always wanted to see Calcutta, the greatest city of the East.'

'He asked me. Not you,' Manhoos replied.

'What is your pet saying?' the prince asked, looking curiously at me.

'My pet?' Manhoos asked in a puzzled voice. 'Oh, you mean this silly sparrow.'

'I am not silly!' I bristled. 'And I am certainly not a pet! I am the pride of the yakshas, guardian of the great treasures of Kubera, beloved of—'

'You can bring him along, if you want,' the prince said over my indignant chirping. He hadn't of course, understood a word of what I'd said. 'He can keep you company, stop you from getting too homesick. After all, you will be going far away from home.'

'Yes, that I will,' said Manhoos softly. 'Maybe you are right. Maybe I do need someone to remind me of home.'

'He seems to be very happy that he's coming with us,' the prince beamed at me. 'So, all settled then. We will leave tomorrow morning—all three of us. Done?'

'Done!' I said with a wiggle of my wings as Manhoos nodded his head in agreement.

***

We were in Room 234 of Buckingham Place Hotel. The prince had insisted that we stay there so that we could leave directly for Calcutta, the next morning. For the first time in his life, Manhoos was discovering the pleasures of a proper bed, with a mattress and a soft, white pillow. But it paled in comparison to the excitement of going to the greatest city of the East, and he was wide awake into the wee hours of the night.

'Calcutta!' he said, hugging his knees. 'Isn't it amazing that I'm going there? What do you think it will be like?'

'No idea,' I replied. 'Fun, I hope.'

'I just can't believe it. I'm going to have a proper job, a proper home, a proper bed. I'm never going to see that dirty garage again.'

'Never say never again. He's only taking you on a two-week trial. If you can't make him happy, you will be right back to square one.'

'I won't. I'm going to work so hard, that Raja-saab will be forced to give me a permanent job in Calcutta. And I'll never come back here again.' All of a sudden his face turned pale, 'But Mary?' he smacked his forehead. 'What about Mary? I'd almost forgotten about her.'

'I can see that.'

'But what will Mary say when I tell her I am going?'

I shrugged.

'She will understand, won't she?' he asked biting his lip. 'I'm sure she will understand that this is the chance of a lifetime. That I can't miss it.'

'I guess so.'

'Anyway, it's not like we will never meet. As soon as Raja-saab gives me my first payment, I'll come back here and meet her.'

'Hmm.'

'And I'll write letters to her every day.'

'You can't write.'

'But once I go to Calcutta, I will learn how to. I will go to school like I always wanted to.'

'Mary can't read.'

Manhoos glared at me. 'I can't think of so many things. This is the chance of a lifetime! I can't miss it.'

'I agree,' I said. 'If I may suggest something, the best thing is to meet her tomorrow morning before you leave. Say a proper goodbye and then go. Who knows when you will be able to come back here?'

'You know, that's exactly what I was thinking. I'll meet her tomorrow...and say goodbye,' he paused and frowned. 'But what if—'

'But what?'

'It's just that I'm a little scared.'

'Scared of what?'

'I'm scared that if I meet her, I won't be able to leave. She'll tell me not to go with Raja-saab. Because he's a diku. And I won't be able to say no to her. And then I'll never be able to get out of Seth-ji's garage.'

'I see. But don't you think—'

'If I think of so many things, I won't be able to do anything,' Manhoos cut me off. 'I really wish I could meet her once. But this is a chance that I just can't miss.' His eyes moistened as he said to himself: 'But I will come back. I will come back soon and see you, Mary.'

'I'm sure you will. Now try and get some sleep. We have a long day ahead.'

Manhoos lay down on the bed, exhausted. But he was in a state of nervous tension, and tossed and turned all through the night. It was only when dawn was breaking that he finally fell into an uneasy sleep. About time too, I muttered and closed my eyes for a quick nap, when I heard a noise that made me feel uneasy. I turned my gaze in the direction from which it was coming.

A convoy of police jeeps and vans was rumbling down the highway in the direction of the Santhal village. I knew instinctively that terrible things were afoot. I swooped down and flew alongside the convoy. Each vehicle was packed with policemen in full battle gear—helmets, lathis, shields and .303 Enfield Rifles. At the head of the convoy was a Willys jeep, beacon light flashing, white towels draped over its seats. Inside it sat Sharma and a police officer who had three gold medals pinned to his sharp khaki uniform. There was a dog-eared file in Sharma's hands which read: *Approved. Top Priority.*

A chill ran through me as I heard the blare of a police siren.

So this was it. The conch had been blown, the axe had been sharpened. All that remained was for the ritual sacrifices to be made and the construction of Varma's temple would begin. Luckily, Calcutta-bound Manhoos' head would be nowhere near the chopping block.

But I wasn't so sure about Mary's.

Calcutta

We left the hotel after a quick breakfast of toast and eggs and soon we were on the highway. I, of course, made no mention of the police convoy I had seen earlier that morning. It would only make Manhoos feel even worse and that was the last thing I wanted. The pain of leaving his childhood behind was like a knife twisting inside him. And the guilt of leaving like a thief at night, without so much as a goodbye to Mary, gnawed at his heart like a caged rat. The poor boy looked so miserable, that I couldn't help feeling sorry for him.

But the human mind is a malleable thing, especially if it is that of a twelve-year-old. And as we drove down the winding roads of the Chhota Nagpur Plateau, Manhoos began to feel better. I could see that the past was quickly ebbing out of his head and the future was seeping in. A part of him may still have been lingering in the forest, but another part was already looking ahead.

But I was looking back. Even as we sped away from the past, I could not forget the little girl who had been such an important part of it. And suddenly, without warning, a vision rose before me. Only a few yakshas have ever had the gift of an omniscient gaze, and I certainly did not. I still don't. Sometimes, only sometimes, we yakshas are shown a little scrap of the future, or an event unfolding light years away from us. Why this happens, we have never understood, and it always surprises us, unsettles us. What I saw that day—I wish I had never seen it. It would scar me for all time.

A throng of terrified villagers were huddled together in a clearing in the centre of a village I recognised as Mary's. Surrounding them was a company of policemen, their Enfield rifles aimed at the villagers' heads. I desperately searched for Mary but I couldn't see her. Moments later, I heard the crack of gunfire. The smell of cordite filled the air as a little red flower bloomed on the forehead of some nameless Santhal. He crashed to the ground, a bow and arrow clutched in his hands. Screams followed. Another crack and another red flower bloomed—this time on someone's chest. More screams. A child leapt wailing at a policeman and was thrown back against a tree with a bullet in his neck. Small mercy, I suppose, that he was dead before his skull cracked.

Soon, there was more cordite than I could bear to smell and more red-flowered corpses than I could bear to see. I forced myself and took one last look at the row of fallen Santhal warriors, just in case Mary was one of them. But so many dead bodies had piled up by now that I couldn't be sure.

***

In more ways than one, the past was over and the future was fast approaching.

We were on the Grand Trunk Road that would take us all the way to Calcutta. The ancient Oxford Morris was rattling down the highway that for two millennia had straddled the breadth of Hindustan, from the mountains of Kabul in the west to the mouth of the Ganga in the east. All day long we travelled, halting only at night to rest in wayside serais until three days later, we had crossed the dusty plains of Bihar to arrive at the lush paddy fields of Purnea in Bengal. A few hours later, we had reached the gateway to our final destination.

In front of us, stood the Howrah Bridge, its cantilevered trusses vaulting across the Hooghly, like the arms of a sleeping steel giant. Drifting below in its placid-green waters, was a small wooden boat. The boatman was singing as he rowed his boat, and the strains of his full-throated bhatiyali song reached our ears—*'Amay bhashaili re, amay dubaili re, okul doriyar bujihi paar nai re'*—(In your waters, I float; in your waters, I sink; in your shoreless waters that have no end).

'How far are we from Calcutta?' asked Manhoos.

'Almost there. Just across the bridge,' the prince replied.

Manhoos' gaze shifted to the far bank of the river. Even from the distance, he could see buildings that were so high that they seemed to touch the sky. In their shadows lay a patchwork of streets filled with cars, bullock carts, rickshaws, bicycles and people—countless numbers of people, great masses of people jostling against each other like a swarm of angry bees. The forest of people that lay ahead suddenly seemed darker and more dangerous than the forest that he had left behind. Here he was—a stranger in a strange land, his fate in the hands of another stranger. If only Mary was with him, he thought, he wouldn't have felt so alone then, so scared...

'What work do you want me to do for you?' asked Manhoos. 'You said you'll tell me once we reach Calcutta.'

'I will, very soon,' the prince's teeth flashed through his parted lips. 'Don't worry. The work will be interesting, if nothing else. And there's good money in it.'

He pressed down on the accelerator and the Oxford Morris sped across the Howrah Bridge. Moments later, we were on the other side of the river. The Rubicon had been crossed. Manhoos was in the city of his dreams, the city of dreadful night.

***

The prince's mansion stood on a leafy by-lane in Jodhpur Park. It was a large, single-storied building designed in what could only be called the Greco-Roman-Registani architectural style. Fluted Corinthian pillars held up a dome-shaped canopy above the front porch. Marble statues of fat, pouting Cupids stood on either side of the front door, their arrows pointed at walls adorned with miniature paintings of dancing nautch girls, preening peacocks and other such touristy tat. A square stone slab at the entrance read: 'Registan Manor.'

'So, what do you think of your new home?' the prince asked Manhoos.

The grandeur of his new surroundings had stunned Manhoos into silence. This wasn't a home. It was a palace, straight out of the fairy-tales that his father used to tell him once upon a time. His eyes turned into rasogollas as we followed the prince into the mansion. A vast living room greeted us. A dusty chandelier was swinging from its high roof and the stuffed heads of a variety of wild beasts looked down upon us from the walls—antlered deer, snarling leopards and even a gaping black bear. Luckily there were no birds...

'This is the baithak-khana, the drawing room,' said the prince. 'Or rather, it used to be,' he grimaced as he scanned the room. A thick shroud of dust had settled over the heavy teak furniture, the white marble floor had turned grey and the curtains looked as if they hadn't been washed in years.

'Prahlad! Where are you Prahlad?' the prince roared.

A bent old man emerged out of nowhere. He wore a tattered white uniform and an equally tattered white moustache. He threw himself at the prince's feet and said: 'Malik! Sir, you are here!'

'Yes, Prahlad! I am here,' the prince replied. 'But I am not at all pleased to be here!'

'Why, malik?' the old man asked.

'Why?' the prince thundered. 'What have you done to the house? Just look at it! It's worse than a beggar's hut.'

'What to do, Raja-saab?' the old man croaked. 'You haven't sent any money in the last six months. All the other servants have left. Only I stayed behind. But how much can I do by myself? I am old and—'

'All right, all right!' the prince cut him off. 'Don't talk too much. Now that I am here, you don't have to worry about money anymore. I will take care of it. Or rather, this boy will,' the prince bared his teeth at Manhoos. 'Won't you, beta?'

'Money? I...I'll try my best saab but I—,' Manhoos stammered.

'Not try. You will do it,' the prince patted Manhoos on his back. 'Prahlad, this is Manhoos. He will be staying here for some time. Show him to the small bedroom. And after that go to Rahman Mian's shop and tell him to come here at once.'

'*Ji huzoor*,' the old servant nodded.

The prince turned to Manhoos. 'Go have a bath and get ready. Rahman Mian will be here soon to take your measurements.'

'What measurements, saab?' asked Manhoos.

'Measurements for your new clothes,' the prince replied.

'New clothes?' Manhoos eyes lit up like a Venetian chandelier. 'For me?'

'Yes,' the prince said as he scanned Manhoos from head to toe. 'You can't wear these clothes in the places we will be going to.'

'Where are we going?' asked Manhoos.

'You'll find out soon,' the prince said shortly. 'Also, one more thing. You will have to change your name.'

Manhoos frowned. 'What's wrong with my name?' he said. 'My father gave it to me.'

'And I am giving you a new name. A better name.'

'But why, saab?'

'I can't go around calling you Manhoos in a place like Calcutta. People will laugh at me. And at you. No, no, I have decided—you must change your name. I will call you Manu. What do you say to that?'

Manhoos did not know what to say. Everything was changing so quickly, everything was so different, so new...it felt as if the ground was slipping under his feet. There was no anchor to steady him, nothing familiar to which he could cling—except his name. And now even that was being taken away. A tiny spark of rebellion flared up inside him. What right did anyone have to take away the name that his own father had given him? But a moment later, it struck him, that apart from his name, there was nothing that he had received from his father. Raja-saab had given him chicken curry and ice cream, a new home, new clothes, new hope. If all he wanted in return was to give him a new name, then so be it. Like Seth-ji would discard old tools and replace them with new ones, the old Manhoos would have to step aside for the new Manu.

'All right, Raja-saab,' Manhoos nodded. 'You can call me Manu.'

And so it was that Manhoos the unlucky one, became Manu the first one, poised to take his first steps into an uncertain new world in his newly tailored clothes.

Book Two

Show Business

'Who is that?' asked Manu. His attention had been drawn to a tall, middle-aged man attired in a pale grey suit and a black fedora hat. He seemed to be an important person. A knot of people was milling around him, their arms extended in handshakes, heads bobbing respectfully in greeting, as he tried to make his way past them.

'That is Shri Ghanshyam Das Birla, the biggest industrialist of India,' the prince whispered conspiratorially. 'Used to live in a small town in Rajasthan not far from my kingdom. Came to Calcutta thirty years ago and look where he is today—Chairman of Hindustan Motors, founder of UCO Bank etcetera, etcetera. Capitalist, socialist and philanthropist all rolled into one. Great friend of Gandhi-ji's. Poor Bapu even breathed his last at Birla-ji's haveli in Delhi.'

'He's Gandhi-ji's friend?' Manu was impressed. He had heard about how the great Gandhi-ji had freed India, by telling three hundred million Indians to spit on the British, so that they would drown in a sea of saliva.

'Not just Gandhi-ji's. Nehru's, Patel's, Ambedkar's—the lot. Has the whole government in his pocket and from what I hear, is taking full advantage of it. When he started out in life, he was just an ordinary shopkeeper, a mamooli dukandaar. And look at what he has become today. But one day, I will become as rich as—' he broke off abruptly and bowed low.

Another tall gentleman in a suit and fedora hat had entered the enclosure. 'Good morning, Sir Biren!' the prince exclaimed. 'How wonderful to see you here! And you too, Lady Ranu! Such an unexpected pleasure,' he said, extending his hand to the woman who was at Sir Biren's side.

She was the second most beautiful woman that Manu had seen in his brief life. Mary of course, was the first, and nothing would ever change that. But this slim, fair woman with her huge, kohl-lined eyes, took his breath away.

'May I say how absolutely spiffing you are looking, Lady Ranu!' the prince gushed.

From his imposing height, Sir Biren looked down at the prince and said: 'And you are?'

'I am Prince Surya Pratap Singh. We had met five years ago at the Viceroy's reception in Fort William. Don't you remember?'

'Can't say we do, old chap. Well...it was nice meeting you... prince...err...what did you say your name was, old fruit?'

'Prince Surya Pratap Singh,' the prince said. 'Ruler of the princely state of Regi—'

'Ah, yes, yes, of course,' Sir Biren hurriedly cut in, 'Well then Suraj, old boy, chuffed to meet you,' he threw a quick glance at Manu. 'And your...son too. But we must run along now. Don't want to miss our little flutter now, do we?'

Sir Biren and Lady Ranu hurried away, but their whispered mutterings reached Surya Pratap's ears: *'These nouveau riche people! So crass! Typical Hindi-wallahs! They are ruining Calcutta, I tell you. Spiffing, indeed! Such a poseur that man is. Who on earth is he? I haven't the faintest, dear.'*

The prince watched their receding figures, his face red as a brick. 'Nouveau riche they call me! Me? Did you hear that?'

'Yes, but I couldn't understand much,' Manu replied. 'Birds and animals, I can understand, but not these babus buk-bukking in English. I don't know what they were saying, but I don't like them.'

'They called me a *kal ka nawab,* a king without a crown. Me, who until yesterday could have bought and sold ten of them, just like that!' he snapped his fingers. 'Who are they?' asked Manu.

'That man is Sir Biren Mookerjee,' spat the prince. 'Chairman of IISCO, the Indian Iron & Steel Company. The woman is Lady Ranu Mookerjee, his wife. Used to be one of Tagore's handpicked disciples. The cream of society. All these Mookerjees, Birlas, Tatas—I tell you Manu, these are the kings of modern India, the new royalty.'

'You are also a king,' Manu said loyally.

'I'm only yesterday's news,' the prince's shoulders slumped. 'Stale, good for nothing, and nothing in my pocket.'

'You are a kind and good-hearted person,' said Manu. 'And that's king enough for me.'

'You think so?' the prince gave a wry smile and straightened his shoulders. 'Nice of you to say so, Manu. But you know what? I am in the mood to become a real king once again. And you're going to help me, won't you?'

'I'll try my best,' said Manu.

'That's my boy,' the prince slapped Manu on his back. 'You know what you have to do, right? The plan is absolutely clear?'

'Yes, all clear,' Manu replied.

'Excellent,' said the prince. 'Let's get down to business then. And like they say, there's no business like show business!'

***

There were few in the Royal Calcutta Turf Club who could remember the last time that Show Business had won a race. There were fewer still who knew that the regal mare traced her ancestry to the thoroughbred warhorses from Arabia which had once graced the stables of Emperor Shahjahan. With her gleaming black hide and white socked hooves, Show Business had once been the pride and joy of every jockey who had ridden her to victory in every major derby of the country.

But her glory days were long gone. Like the prince, Show Business was yesterday's news. It was perhaps for this reason that he had decided to place his bet on her—one has-been rooting for another. The stakes were high—a full five thousand rupees, almost a tenth of all his savings.

The bookie had looked up in astonishment at the prince's wager. 'Odds on Show Business are fifty to one,' said the bookie. 'Sure you want to put all that money on her?'

'Yes,' replied the prince and muttering the Hanuman Chalisa under his breath, he placed his bet.

He then made his way to the members' stand and took a seat in the front row. Five thousand rupees gone...the die had been cast. What if it rolled the wrong way? What if his grand plan failed and his dreams came crashing down like a house of cards?

It was all up to the boy now. They had gone through every detail of the plan with a fine-toothcomb and Manu had been confident that it would work. As a precaution, they had even paid a visit to the tonga-pulling horses in the Maidan to find out if Manu had the same facility with Bengali horses as he had with Bihari ones. The tests had gone off just as smoothly as they had in Netarhat.

Any moment now, and the race would begin. With a pair of binoculars, the prince made a quick scan of the surroundings. The horses were at the starting line, impatiently pawing the ground. The jockeys were hunched over their backs, taut as bowstrings. The referee's pistol was raised in the air, ready to be fired.

The perspiring prince swung his binoculars to the public stands at the far end of the race course. In spite of the dense mass of people squished together like sardines in a can, it did not take him long to locate Manu. With his tuxedo and bow-tie, he stood out in the rabble like a nun in a nudist camp. The boy was in the perfect position for the job—just behind the guard rails at the very edge of the racing track, about ten metres away from the finishing line...

The crack of a pistol shot. A cloud of dust. And the horses were off. All except one.

Show Business was still glued to her position on the starting line. The jockey kicked, yelled, and swore at her but she refused to budge an inch, casually swishing her tail at imaginary flies.

From high above in the members' stand, the prince yelled: 'Show Business! Move your bloody butt!' He shot out of his seat, hopping up and down in anguish when he noticed Lady Ranu staring at him with a horror that she usually reserved for people who played Rabindra Sangeet tunes on the Hawaiian guitar.

Casting all niceties to the wind, the prince bellowed again: 'Show Business! Get off your goddamned arse, you stupid horse!' Why wasn't Manu following the plan! He was supposed to be telling Show Business to run as if his life depended on it.

But the Olympic spirit seemed to have suddenly come over Show Business. She now decided that participation was more important than winning. With a shake of her mane, she shuffled forward with the enthusiasm of a schoolboy being summoned to the headmaster's office. The rest of the horses were leagues ahead by now. They had curved past the last bend of the oval track and were thundering down the final straight stretch. Tipu Sultan, the bookies' favourite was in the lead. It was only a matter of seconds before he would breast the finishing tape.

All was lost now. There was no hope. The prince sank heavily into his seat, clutching his head in despair when the sound of an uproar jerked him out of his misery. He looked up and his jaw dropped at the sight of the bizarre tableau that had unfolded on the racetrack.

All the horses had come to a standstill, frozen in their positions like flies stuck in a honey pot. Barely a yard away from the finishing line, stood Tipu Sultan. At his tail, was Moonlight Romance, nonchalantly nibbling on a blade of grass. Just behind her stood Princess Charming, rubbing noses with Pyare Miyan and so it went, till the last horse standing motionless at the end of the line. The jockeys were yelling furiously at the horses, tugging their reins, digging in their stirrups. But their efforts were in vain—not a single horse stirred a muscle, not a single horse moved one step forward.

Apart from Show Business that is.

She was still ambling down the track, her leisurely gait clearly indicating that she didn't believe in the rat race even if it was between horses. The onlookers watched in pin-drop silence as she continued her unhurried stroll round the track and at last entered the final stretch. She trotted past her immobile colleagues, greeting each one with a friendly neigh and soon she was at the head of the line, next to Tipu Sultan. Acknowledging his presence with a regal nod of her head, Show Business clip-clopped forward and touched her nose to the finishing tape. Manu may have changed the script but he had won the day.

In its one hundred and five years of existence, the Royal Calcutta Turf Club had never witnessed a silence, such as the one that followed the victorious return of Show Business. And then the hush was broken by three sounds that followed each other in quick succession. The first came from a tuxedo-clad boy in the public stands—a high-pitched neigh that sounded suspiciously like *shabaash*! The second was a jubilant cry of 'Hip, hip, hooray!' that came from the front row of the members' stand.

And the third was a low moan that emerged from Lady Ranu Mookerjee, fainting, as a wild-eyed prince enfolded her in a bear hug and smacked a loud kiss on her rouged cheek.

Yeh Azaadi Jhootha Hai

Six months had passed since that morning at the Royal Calcutta Turf Club when the prince's gamble had paid off in spectacular fashion. It was the first of many such successes. The prince kept placing his bets and Manu kept winning them for him. The boy was getting better at it by the day. He had even invented a new set of techniques to avoid any suspicion. He no longer brought a horse to a dramatic halt in the middle of a race. Instead, they were made to slow down, or make a late start, and at other times, rear up on their forelegs to unseat their jockeys.

Meanwhile, the prince was also taking great care to cover his tracks. He shrewdly mixed his bets between favourites and long-shots, camouflaging the occasional big win with several modest losses. So far no one had smelt a rat. The money was rolling in and with it, the good times.

The dilapidated Oxford Morris was replaced by a spanking new red Studebaker imported from Germany. The mansion was renovated, its greyed walls painted the brightest pink that the Imperial Chemicals Company had to offer. The Venetian glass chandeliers were polished until they sparkled like diamonds and the brand-new electric bulbs inside them burned like little yellow stars in the night.

The prince was immensely grateful to Manu. If it wasn't for the strange boy from Betla, he would still have been trying to make his frayed ends meet on a paltry government pension. But now, the old, near-forgotten pleasures were finally back in his life—fine wines and women, servants and soirees. There was so much that Manu had given him. And in return, he had given the boy much as well—a room of his own, a bathroom with running hot and cold water, soft pillows, buttered rolls and ice creams. And when Manu had expressed his desire to go to school, the prince even appointed a private tutor for him.

'It is good that you want to study,' the prince told Manu. 'In free India, every child should be able to read and write. But unfortunately, I don't think any school in Calcutta will admit you.'

'Why not?' Manu asked.

'You are almost thirteen now, but you don't even know A, B, C. You are too far behind other boys of your age,' the prince said. 'No school will take you.'

'But you said you would send me to school,' Manu said, the disappointment spilling over into his voice. 'You promised!'

'You don't have to go to school to get an education. In fact, it may have the opposite effect,' the prince said. 'I think it will be best if a private tutor comes and teaches you.'

Now Calcutta may not have many things going for it, but it has never had a shortage of private tutors. This was as true in 1951 as it is today. Soon, an over-educated, under-employed young man was appointed as Manu's tutor. He came in three days a week and taught the boy English, Hindi and Arithmetic. It cost the prince ten rupees a month. But he didn't mind, because it made Manu happy. Manu was the goose that was laying the golden eggs and happy geese laid more eggs.

But unlike geese, it is the destiny of human beings never to be happy. Manu had everything that he had ever dreamt of, and more. But he wasn't happy. Once the initial excitement of city lights, soft beds and private tutors had subsided, his old discontents bubbled to the surface.

One morning, he was sitting at the breakfast table nibbling gloomily on a piece of toast, when he let out a sigh: 'I wish Mary was here. I miss her so much. Sometimes I wish I had never left Betla.'

'You're mad!' I exclaimed, perching myself on his shoulder. 'Don't you see how lucky you are? You should kiss the prince's feet for giving you a life that most people can only dream of.'

'Don't you think I know that? He's given me everything, more than any father would,' Manu replied. 'But what have I done to deserve so much,' he pointed at the lavish breakfast spread, 'when Mary is still selling berries.'

Clearly the poor boy was suffering from survivor's guilt. 'Don't think so much,' I said. 'Mary's bad luck is very good and yours is the opposite. Now just eat your toast and be happy.'

'But I can't be happy until I see her. I must see her. Otherwise, I won't be at peace. But whenever I ask Raja-saab if I can go to Betla, he says, later. He says there are more races coming up and he can't let me go now.'

'Don't you think he has a right to say that, after all he's done for you?'

'And haven't I done anything for him? Haven't I made pots of money for him? I'm telling you, I will go to Betla, whether he allows me or not.'

The sound of gunshots and the screams of dying Santhals rang in my head. 'That's not a good idea at all. You should stay right here in Calcutta.'

He ignored me and said: 'What is the point of having so much if I'm not free to do what I want? I feel trapped. And what am I doing anyway? Tricking racehorses to make money! I feel like a fraud, like I'm living a lie.'

***

Manu wasn't the only person who was feeling like he was living a lie. There were others who had started to say that the golden egg of India's freedom was a sham, a fraud perpetrated on the people by the Congress party. And to express their discontent, they had coined a slogan that was spreading like wildfire across the country:

'Yeh azaadi jhootha hai.'
This freedom is a lie.

One morning, we had gone out for a stroll in Dhakuria Lake, when we noticed a man pasting a poster on the wall of a roadside tea stall. He was tall and thin, with a scraggly beard that looked as if it hadn't been trimmed in months. He had a pot of glue in one hand and a beedi dangling from the corner of his mouth.

The poster caught Manu's eye. He squinted at the picture of the hammer and sickle that had been hand-painted upon it. '*Yeh azaadi jhootha hai,*' Manu haltingly read out the words that appeared below the picture. He turned to the bearded man and asked: 'Is this an advertisement for shoes?'

The man looked down at Manu and smiled. 'No, my young friend. *Joota* means shoes. *Jhootha* means untrue. This is the slogan of our party. It means—this freedom is a lie.'

'Oh,' Manu said. 'It should be *azaadi jhoothi hai*, then. Why confuse people?'

The man laughed. 'Grammar is the privilege of the rich, my friend.'

'I don't understand what that means, dada. Anyway, why does your party think our azaadi is a lie? Isn't freedom a good thing?'

'True freedom is,' the stranger smiled. 'But the freedom we have got is nothing but a sham!'

'How can you say that?' said Manu. 'The British have gone.'

'But has the suffering gone? Don't you see it all around you? People are starving, grown men are dropping dead like flies from disease, children are begging on the streets instead of going to school, while our netas are living in bungalows and driving around in their fancy cars.'

Manu thought of the prince's mansion and the new Studebaker gleaming in the garage. 'I'm sorry,' he mumbled in an embarrassed voice. 'I don't know much about such things. I don't come out very often. I'm not allowed to.'

'Ah, but you should step out of your house sometimes and see what's happening. You don't seem all that young to me either. How old are you? Fourteen?'

'I think so,' Manu said. 'Who are you?'

'Me? I'm just a humble party worker,' the stranger replied. 'You can call me Dipu-da.'

'What does a party worker do?'

'We are Communists. We want to expose the lie of freedom that the Congress thugs have been trying to brainwash the people into believing.'

'Raja-saab also says that the Congressis are thugs.'

'Then your Raja-da is absolutely right. The Communist Party needs more people like him, who can see the truth. Would he be interested in meeting us?'

'I'll ask him. He may be. He hates the Congress,' Manu said. 'Where do you stay? Is your home nearby?'

A dark shadow crossed Dipu-da's face. 'Home? I've forgotten what that means. But once upon a time, I did have a home.'

'Where is it?'

'Gone. Gone forever,' he took a drag on his beedi and let out a cloud of grey smoke. 'They call us *bastuhara* now, those who have lost everything.'

'But where are you from?' Manu persisted.

'Where? The other Bengal, the Bengal that has gone forever. They call it East Pakistan these days. I come from Khulna District,' he took another drag of the beedi. 'We lived in a small village by the Rupsha river. We had our own house, thirty bighas of land, three ponds filled with the sweetest of fishes. We had everything a man could need. But then Partition came, and with it ruin and destruction. We lost everything. We had to flee to India with nothing more than the clothes on our back.'

'Where are you staying now?'

'Bijoygarh Refugee Camp. It's just down the road.' He looked curiously at Manu. 'Maybe you would you like to see it, my friend?'

'No, no. I should be getting back home now,' Manu replied. 'Raja-saab doesn't like it if I am out for too long.'

'It's only a ten-minute walk from here. Come, my friend. Come and see how we live. Come and see what the Congress has done to us. Then go back home and tell your Raja-da about it.'

Manu chewed on his lower lip for a moment. 'All right,' he said. 'I'll come.'

***

I don't know why Manu chose to trust a total stranger and risk following him to some unknown destination. Perhaps he saw it as a tiny act of rebellion against the prince. Perhaps he was tired of living in a bubble and wanted a glimpse of the real world. But mostly, I think it was because he saw something of himself in Dipu-da—a stranger in a strange land, caught between an unreturnable past and an uncertain future.

Whatever be the reason, Manu and I followed Dipu-da and

fifteen minutes later we had arrived before the gates of a walled enclosure. Within it stood row upon row of tunnel-shaped shelters, with semi-circular roofs made of corrugated steel.

'This is Bijoygarh Refugee Colony,' Dipu-da said. 'This is my home and home to thirty thousand others like me. There are other camps like this all over Bengal—Azadgarh, Sealdah, Cossipore. Two lakh refugees are living like this today.'

Manu peered through the iron rails of the gate. Several people were lounging outside the shelters. Some were stretched out on the ground while others leaned listlessly against the walls. Great blue-green flies were buzzing over their bloated bellies. He was wondering why they weren't swatting away the flies, when he realised with a shock, that they were all dead.

It took a while before Manu could find his voice. 'Those people are all...dead?' he gasped.

'Yes,' replied Dipu-da.

'But why...why are they just lying around like that...in the open?' Manu stammered.

'There's no room for the living here, what to say of the dead,' Dipu-da replied. 'Dysentery, cholera, tuberculosis—people are dying like flies. Dying faster than we can get rid of their corpses. The trucks come only once a week to dump the dead bodies in the jungles behind the camp for hyenas and rats to finish the job. But they aren't fast enough.'

The door of the nearest shelter swung open, providing a glimpse within. It seemed as if an entire village had been crammed into a single room—thirty, perhaps forty families, people squeezed so tightly against each other that it seemed that they would have to crawl over each other's heads if they had to move anywhere.

A group of toothless crones was huddled in the centre of the room, cracking jokes and guffawing. Next to them sat a bunch of young men playing cards and puffing on beedis. Every three yards or so stood a makeshift clay oven, over which the evening meal was being cooked. The smoke of the burning firewood curled into the air and joined a cacophony of voices—children crying, women chattering, young couples whispering sweet nothings.

Suddenly a stench hit him with the force of a punch to his gut.

A gasp escaped him, as his gaze shifted to the far corner of the room, from where it appeared to be coming. A bloated, stinking corpse lay there. 'Come, you've seen enough for one day,' Dipu-da placed a hand on Manu's shoulder and tried to pull him away.

But Manu could not drag his eyes away from the dead body. He watched in dread fascination as a pair of giant furry rats scampered across the half-naked corpse, pausing to nibble at its flesh. A moment later, his horror was replaced by astonishment, when his gaze fell on a young couple, lying on the floor inches away from the corpse. The boy was stretched out on top of the girl. His head was buried in her breasts and they were both moaning loudly.

It took Manu a while to realise that they were making love, rutting each other with a fierce hunger. Their emaciated young bodies rocked against each other, oblivious to the others in the room and the stench of death all around them.

The bile erupted inside Manu's mouth. He bent over double and retched. A pool of yellow slime spread at his feet.

'Easy, easy,' Dipu-da rubbed him on the back. 'Didn't I tell you to look away?'

Manu shoved Dipu-da away roughly. Still retching, he somehow managed to stagger to his feet, and make a run for it.

'You can't run away from reality, my friend,' Dipu-da called out from behind. 'The government is the real enemy. We must fight it together. Come and join our fight, comrade.'

But Manu could barely register what Dipu-da was saying. There was only one thought in his head—to get as far away from the horror as possible...get back home...a home that smelt of freshly washed sheets and lavender soap, not raw sewage and fresh death.

The Prince's Dream

Some things once seen, are impossible to unsee. I could almost read Manu's mind, so fond had I (to my surprise) become of him by now. The horrors of Bijoygarh refused to leave Manu, clinging to him like an evil spirit. He had nightmares of rats gnawing at dead bodies and corpses squirming together in the throes of lovemaking. He would wake up in the middle of the night, shuddering and sweating, as if he was in the grip of a harsh fever. After Bijoygarh, a terrible fear had possessed Manu—the fear of loss.

When he slept, he would clutch at his pillow, scared that someone would snatch it from him; when he ate, he would gobble down his food as if it were his last meal; and every day he would count the clothes in his cupboard to check if any were missing. But his greatest fear was of losing his home, of becoming a bastuhara.

So great had his dread of homelessness become that he had excised from his mind all thoughts of returning to Betla to meet Mary. What if it angered Raja-saab? What if he threw him out as soon as he broached the topic? What if he refused to let him back in once he left?

The more he thought about it, the more he became convinced that his past was a threat to his future. He would have to forget Mary, the forest, the river. He would have to bury his past to build his future—a future in which he was safe, protected from the dangers that could burst upon him any moment.

But when he took stock of his present, his future seemed fragile and full of uncertainties. Here he was—a fourteen-year-old orphan, illiterate, lost in a city that he knew nothing of. He had no one to call his own except a stranger who was using him for his own purposes. Yes, he was lucky to have a roof over his head and food on his plate. But for how long? The prince once had his own palace, his own kingdom, seven cars...but he had lost them all. The Santhals had an entire forest to themselves, but the government had threatened to take it away. Dipu-da once had thirty bighas of land and three fishponds. But they were gone. The thousands who lived inside Bijoygarh camp had been stripped of everything. The dead had been denied even the dignity of a funeral pyre.

Nothing was permanent...no one was safe...especially from the government. Raja-saab, Dipu-da and the refugees, the Santhals—they had been mere sport for the government, cruelly betrayed by the very men in whom they had placed their trust. As for Manu himself, what had the government ever done for him? Nothing. Orphaned equally by his dead parents and an uncaring state, he had had to fend for himself since the age of six.

His mind went back to the poster in the tea-stall: '*Yeh azaadi jhootha hai.*' It was true, thought Manu. The only *azaadi* he had seen so far was the freedom of the government to do as it pleased. The people were as enslaved as ever.

'*The government is the real enemy, and we must fight it together. Come and join our fight, comrade.*' Dipu-da's parting words came back to him. Was he right, Manu wondered? Was fighting the government the only way to protect oneself against it?

***

One Sunday evening, when the prince was having a quiet drink, Manu sat next to him and asked: 'Why aren't you a Communist?'

The prince was so startled by Manu's question that he nearly choked on his whisky. 'Are you mad? Why should I be a Communist?'

'Because you hate the Congress, and the Communists are fighting against them.'

'An enemy's enemy isn't always a friend, Manu. I don't like the Congressis. They are corrupt as hell. But I can't stand the Commies either. They are anarchists. A dangerous lot!'

'Are they worse than the Congress?'

'Difficult to say which is worse. The Congressis believe in the unequal distribution of wealth, mostly by pocketing it all for themselves. The Communists believe in the equal distribution of poverty. But why are you asking me all these questions?'

'Nothing. A Communist was talking to me the other day. He called me comrade. He wants me to join their party. He wants to meet you as well.'

'What! What are you up to these days, Manu? You stay a mile away from these fellows, do you hear?' the prince almost shouted. 'They are nothing but trouble! You keep away from all this nonsense politics if you want to stay with me. You understand?'

'Yes, Raja-saab,' Manu stammered, taken aback by the intensity of the prince's reaction.

'I'm sorry I got angry. But there is something important that I wanted to tell you.'

'Yes, Raja-saab?'

'The thing is, I'm done with racing. I won't need your help with the horses anymore.'

Manu's heart sank. The sceptre of homelessness loomed in front of him. 'Then what will I do, Raja-saab?'

'I have other plans,' said the prince. 'Big plans.'

***

The prince had always known that his horse-racing days would not last forever. It was merely the means to an end, not the end in itself. The last couple of years had been excellent, but of late, his winning ways had begun to raise eyebrows. There were whispers of foul play and they were growing louder by the day. The writing on the wall was clear—he would have to exit the racing business before it got too hot to handle.

Luckily, Manu's golden eggs had brought in a nice bit of money. He had collected enough capital to think of running his own business—something that he had always wanted to do. Ever since he had lost Registan, the prince had been toying with the idea of becoming an industrialist. He dreamt of the day when the name of Surya Pratap Singh would be taken in the same breath as that of Tata-Birla. For they were the movers and shakers of free India, the new royalty.

About three weeks ago, he had got a lucky break. The son of an old Bengali industrialist, Mr Haldar, had decided not to become a dirty capitalist like his father, preferring instead to publish a little magazine. Enraged by his son's attitude, Mr Haldar had thrown him out of the house and had put up his factory for sale. It was a small manufacturing unit located in Uttarpara but enjoyed a good reputation in the market for the quality of its products. Even Hindustan Motors used its bushings and bearings in their Ambassador cars.

The prince read the sale notice in the newspapers and had put in a bid to buy out the factory. If the deal worked out, then he would be one step closer to his dream. A dream that had been made possible by Manu. The prince looked fondly at the boy and said: 'Yes, Manu, I hope I will be getting into a new business very soon.'

'What sort of business?'

'I'm buying a factory that manufactures bushings and bearings. I've already thought of its name—Regal Bearings. What do think?'

'Very nice, Raja-saab.'

'Regal Bearings will go places, I tell you. Because we will take it places—you and I.'

'Me? I don't know anything about how bushings and bearings are made.'

'Ah, but you are a good mechanic. You will pick up. Listen, Manu—I couldn't have started my business without your help, and I feel I owe you something. So, this is my proposal—I will continue to pay for your studies. The private tutor will come and teach you, like he is doing today. But once you are able to do some basic reading, writing and calculations, you will start working for me in the factory. After all, who needs an MA-BA in the bushings line? So, what do you think of that?'

Manu did not know what to say. All he knew was that he still had a home and that was all that he wanted. He merely gave a grateful nod. 'Yes, Raja-saab. Whatever you say.'

'Good. I am hoping we should be able to start soon. But before you begin work with me, I have a condition.'

'Yes?'

'I won't stand it if you mix with any Communists,' the prince said. 'This city is full of them and as you grow older, you will meet more of them. You are to stay well clear of them. Because all they want to do is shout slogans and shut down factories. And I simply cannot afford that when I am just starting my business. Am I perfectly clear?'

'Yes, Raja-saab,' Manu nodded.

'When I came to Calcutta, I told myself that I would make it big.' The prince took a sip of his whisky. 'And I will. Regal Bearings is only the beginning. Once I start making some serious money, I may even get into politics.'

'Politics? But you said you hate the Congress and Communists both.'

'There is a third party these days—a new one. The Jana Sangh. I'm thinking of meeting them one of these days. Industrialist to MLA to minister, maybe even Chief...' he broke off. 'Stick with me, Manu, and who knows where we may reach. The sky is the limit.'

A Ray of Hope

By the winter of 1954, Prince Surya Pratap Singh had achieved the dubious distinction of becoming moderately famous. He was the Managing Director of Regal Bearings Ltd, one of Calcutta's fastest growing business houses. The media had taken note of it and on one occasion *The Statesman* had even published a tiny single column article on the prince. It wasn't undeserved, for the little factory that he had bought from the disgruntled Mr Haldar, had grown quickly to become one of the largest manufacturers of bushings and bearings in Eastern India. These days, Regal Bearings was supplying parts to every company worth its name in the region.

Not that the journey had been easy. Politicians and bureaucrats had to be bribed regularly and aggressive trade unions had to be humoured in order to keep the wheels of the factory running smoothly. But the prince was fairly satisfied with what he had accomplished in three short years. Of course, there was still a long way to go before he became as famous as Tata-Birla, but he had no doubt that one day, he would get there.

Manu hadn't done too badly for himself either. He would be eighteen soon—tall, handsome, well-dressed and at ease with the ways of the city. He had studied hard and was proficient in Hindi and English, and had a good head for numbers. Since the last two years, he had also been working as a mechanic at Regal Bearings. His job was to maintain and repair the many complicated pieces of machinery on the shop floor and his natural aptitude for such things served him well. Driven by his old fears of losing the only home that he had, Manu put his heart and soul into his work. He would arrive at the factory at eight in the morning and put in at least twelve hours of work, even on weekends and holidays.

Impressed by his hard work, the prince had rewarded him with a salary of ten rupees per month. It did not take long for Manu to realise that if there was money in one's pocket, then the world could be a rather nice place. Soon eighteen-year-old Manu was discovering the pleasures of Calcutta. One of his favourites was Firpo's Hotel on Park Street where he promptly fell in love with its two primary attractions—the jelly-bellied Miss Shefali, the first cabaret dancer of India and the belly-expanding Gateau Millefeuilles, the last word in unpronounceable desserts from France.

In short, by 1954, Manu had put his past behind him and his eyes were firmly on the future. The memories of Seth-ji's garage, the forest and Mary had become hazy and blurred as an old photograph, bleached sepia by the bright neon lights of the city.

It was the year in which the greasy urchin from the Betla forests had turned into a tall, elegantly attired young man about town, who could tell the difference between a butter knife and a steak knife. 1954 was also the year in which another tall, elegant man would change the course of Manu's life, as dramatically as he had changed the course of world cinema.

***

On the evening of 21 December 1954, at six p.m. sharp, a visitor arrived at the prince's mansion. He was well over six feet tall, with a rugged face that looked as if it had been carved out of granite.

'My name is Ray, Satyajit Ray,' he said in a rich baritone that reverberated like an old church bell. His diction was clipped and clear as any Englishman's, but his spotless white dhoti and kurta marked him out as the archetype of the Bengali gentleman, a bhadralok. He held out his hand to the prince and said: 'Prince Surya Pratap Singh, I presume?'

'Just Mr Singh. I am only an ordinary citizen these days, just like everyone else,' the prince replied. 'Welcome to my humble abode, Mr Ray. Do take a seat,' he said, waving the visitor to the sofa.

With a regal nod, Mr Ray lowered himself into the sofa and said: 'Thank you. I am grateful to you for agreeing to meet me. My colleague Ravi Shankar suggested that you might be able to help me.'

'Yes, yes, I happened to bump into Ravi at the club last week and he requested me to meet you. How could I refuse? I know Ravi since he was this much,' the prince lowered his palm to his knee. 'His father, Shyam Shankar Choudhury, and I were good friends. Ah, those were the good old days, Mr Ray. I was ruler of Registan and Shyam Shankar was the dewan of Jhalawar, our neighbouring state. A fine gentleman he was, very competent in business affairs. Although, his son Ravi has turned out to be quite the opposite. He's become some sort of *musician*, I believe,' he said wrinkling his nose as if he had smelt something foul.

'That is correct,' boomed Mr Ray. 'Ravi Shankar is a very fine sitar player. In fact, he is composing the music for my film.'

'Young people these days, I tell you!' the prince sighed. 'Doing films, music and what-not. I don't know how they make a living. But tell me, what can I do for you?'

'Let me come straight to the point, Mr Singh. I am in urgent need of funds to complete my film. I have been running from pillar to post to raise money, when Ravi Shankar mentioned that you might be able to help. I am told you are a successful industrialist and that your family has always been a patron of the arts.'

'You may be right there. You see this?' The prince indicated the high-roofed living room. 'In my father's time, this room used to be the jalsaghar, the music room. There would be all-night singing and dancing, the finest liquor from France. Famous baijis would come here from Benares. Rasoolan Bai, Gauhar Jaan—they have all sung in this room. But those days are gone now, Mr Ray, all gone.'

A gleam appeared in Mr Ray's eyes. He fished out a small notebook from his pocket and scribbled the following words on it—*jalsaghar, Benares baiji, all gone!*

'Coming to the films business, I know nothing of it,' the prince went on. 'But I am willing to give you a fair hearing. How much money do you need? As a businessman, I am open to any investment which can provide a good return.'

'The film is almost complete Mr Singh. I just need a little more money for shooting the final scenes. About ten thousand rupees or so should do it.'

'Ten thousand, eh? That's not a small amount. What is the name of this film? What's it about?'

'It's called *Pather Panchali*—the song of the road. It is set in the village of Nischindipur where Harihar Roy, a priest, makes a meagre living and dreams of a better career as a playwright. He lives with his wife, two young children, Durga and Apu, and an old cousin, Indir Thakrun. But life is hard and poverty forces—'

'Can you please be brief?' the prince interrupted, glancing at his watch. 'I have to leave soon to attend Lady Ranu's party at the Bengal Club.'

Mr Ray's eyebrows knotted in a frown. He took a deep breath and rattled away: 'Harihar leaves village for work, Indir dies, Durga dies, Harihar returns, surviving characters leave village for Benares. The end. In short, it is the story of a poor family's struggle for survival in rural Bengal.'

'Struggle?' The prince gave a crooked smile. 'Why are you Bengalis so fond of this word—struggle? What is so special about it? Who is not struggling, Mr Ray? Rich or poor—everyone has their own struggles. Look at me. I am a self-made man. I used to have a palace ten times the size of this house. I had my own army, two garrisons of soldiers stationed in a fortress that rivalled those of Chittoor and Jaisalmer. The fortress of gold, people used to call it. It was made of the finest yellow limestone that glittered in the sun. But I lost everything. However, with my hard work and—'

'Extraordinary, most extraordinary,' Mr Ray interrupted. 'Mr Singh, what you are saying is most interesting. May I take some notes? Just in case I forget.' He quickly scribbled down the words *yellow limestone, golden fortress, sonar kella(?)* in his notepad and said: 'Please go on, you were saying—'

'What I was saying, Mr Ray,' said the prince testily, 'is that there are so many interesting and inspiring tales to tell. My own life story, for example. Why can't you make a film on that instead of this poor village family and their miserable lives? Who will want to watch such a film? As it is Ravi is playing his *tyaaan tyaaan* sitar for your film, isn't it? So, no chance of any singing and dancing, correct?'

'Correct,' said Mr Ray, a thundercloud darkening his face.

'Any fights? Any romance?'

Mr Ray stood up straight, his towering figure casting a shadow on the prince. He looked down his patrician nose and said: 'No song. No dance. No fights. No romance.'

'Then no money either, Mr Ray,' the prince threw up his hands. 'I am sorry to say that if this is the type of film you want to make, then no person in his right mind will spend his money to watch it.'

'And I am also sorry to say that I have wasted your valuable time, Mr Singh,' said Mr Ray. 'However, you have not wasted mine. This has been an extraordinarily useful meeting for me. You have given me much to think about,' he tapped a finely wrought finger on his notepad. 'Thank you,' he said and strode out of the room.

'Hah!' snorted the prince after Mr Ray had left. 'What these young fellows are up to these days I don't understand! Wasting their time on nonsense—films, music, novels! There is not one paisa to be made from such things. And all they can talk about is poor people. These Communists just love poverty! That fellow Ray, for example. Can't even tell a good story from a bad one. You saw how I offered him my life story to make his film. I may even have produced it for him. But he refused. Why? Only because I am not poor. Nothing will come of this glorification of poverty, I tell you, Manu. Just mark my words.'

***

But the prince couldn't have been more wrong. In the summer of 1955, Mr Ray finally managed to finish his film. *Pather Panchali* went on to make history. Its crowning glory came in the summer of 1956, when it won a prize at the Cannes film festival. It even became an unexpected box office success, thanks to the great unwashed masses of Calcutta who, having suddenly discovered the Bengali French Cannes-ection, turned up in large numbers to watch the film. And before young Satyajit could say *haw-jaw-baw-raw-law*, he found himself hoisted upon the pedestal that had lain vacant since the death of Tagore and the mysterious disappearance of Bose.

The meteoric rise of Ray did not escape the prince's attention. 'Looks like I missed a good opportunity, Manu,' rued the prince, one evening. 'You remember that Ray fellow who had come here? Yes? Well, it seems his film is a super-duper hit. If I had invested in it, I would have made a good return.'

'Does it really matter, Raja-saab? The business is doing quite well,' said Manu.

'Yes, yes, I know, baba. Bushings and bearings are all very well, but the film line is different. Glamour, publicity, hobnobbing with important people—these are the perks of the film industry,' said the prince, as he tapped on a newspaper. 'Have you seen this?'

Manu glanced at the headlines—'*Satyajit Ray to be Felicitated by Chief Minister.*'

'I have been wondering about something, Manu,' the prince said. 'You know I used to do theatre quite regularly in Registan before I became king. Lead roles, standing ovations every time,' he closed his eyes and declaimed in loud, quivering tones: '*Oh, how much sharper than a serpent's tooth, it is to have a thankless child*. Old-timers still remember my King Lear. I was just wondering...'

'If you should become a film actor?' asked Manu.

'Why not, eh? Why not?' the prince slapped his thigh. 'I could produce my own films, no? That way the lead role would also be guaranteed. Less cost, more publicity. What do you think?'

'Surely you can't be serious?'

'Why not? As you say, the business is doing well. I can invest some of the money.'

'But will you have the time for such things?'

'Ah, I am glad you mentioned that. You know, Manu, I have been thinking of handing over some of my responsibilities to you.'

'To me?'

'Yes, why not? You've been working for almost five years now and you are very good at it. You understand all the machinery, the workers know you. And the most important thing is that I can trust you. You are still a little young, but nineteen is not a spring chicken. I think it's time for you to take some load off me—supervising the shop floor, for example. Then I would have a lot more time to explore other things.' A distant look entered his eyes as he stroked his moustache thoughtfully. 'Surya Singh, industrialist, film star, politician...why not eh, why not?'

Manu tried to picture the tepid-faced prince as a film star but failed. Not wanting to hurt his feelings, he remained silent, as the prince went on: 'Manu, I have made up my mind. I want you to meet this Ray fellow and find out if we can do something together.'

'Make a film together you mean?'

'Basically. A film in which I have a meaty role. This chap is the talk of the town and it's always a good idea to hitch one's wagon to a rising star. We must strike when the iron is hot. Only last evening at the club, someone was saying that he is making his second film these days...whatsisname now...*Apaar...Apu* or something like that. They even published a photo of him with one of the actors—a fellow called Kan...something...'

'Kanu Banerjee,' Manu corrected him. He had read about *Aparajito* in the newspapers.

'That's the one. Zero charisma the fellow had,' said the prince. 'I would have made a much better choice. Manu, go and meet Ray. Find out if he is looking for a producer for his films. Or a good actor. I can be both, you know. You should also drop a diplomatic hint along those lines to him, you understand?'

'Yes, but why don't you meet him yourself and speak directly?'

'Tchah!' the prince waved his hand. 'That would only make me look desperate. The only way to get something in this world is to pretend that you don't want it. No, Manu, it is you who must go.'

'All right, if that's what you want,' Manu shrugged. 'But I have no idea where to find him.'

'I believe he is shooting in Indrapuri Studios these days. You know the place? It's in Tollygunge. Take an off-day tomorrow and meet Mr Ray. If he shows any interest then set up a meeting between us. You understand?'

Manu nodded obediently. He wondered what it was about films, that could make paupers dream of becoming princes, and a prince dream of becoming a pauper—as long as it was the lead role.

Indrapuri

Kinnaris, yallis, yakshas...the sculpted figures of a menagerie of mythical beings adorned the colonnade of pillars that led into a luxuriantly decorated hall. At the far end of the hall stood a golden throne upon which sat a plump, sour-faced man, stroking his luxuriant black moustache. Rubies and sapphires adorned his stubby fingers and strings of pearls sparkled over his silken robes. For a moment, I thought I was back in Kubera's court. The décor was as offensively gaudy and the man squatting on the throne was just as ugly. But then I saw the beedi in his hands and came back to reality.

We were on the sets of *Jai Ma Manasa*. Mr Ray was shooting in the studio next door and he had peremptorily turned down Manu's request to meet him. It would take two hours at least before he was free, Mr Ray told Manu, and returned to his camera. There was nothing to be done but wait for the great man to finish. We wandered around aimlessly inside Indrapuri studios, until we stumbled upon the sets of *Jai Ma Manasa*.

In contrast to the funereal gloom of *Aparajito*, things were a great deal more lively here. Manu decided it would be good to watch the film shoot to kill time. We quickly slipped into a throng of technicians and general hangers-on and tried to blend in. Luckily, the sets were as chaotic as a Bengali wedding and everyone was too busy ordering everyone else, to notice us.

But after a while, the chaos subsided. The lights came on, and an expectant hush descended upon the sets. A hennaed make-up man applied a final layer of greasepaint on the face of the mustachioed actor and said: 'All ready, dada. You are ready. And ladies also ready.'

As if on cue, a gaggle of apsaras traipsed in and arrayed themselves around the golden throne. Silver anklets twinkled on their feet and their black kohl-ed eyes flashed dangerously, sending Manu's heart into a cartwheel. They weren't exactly Urvashi and Rambha but a couple of them could certainly give Miss Shefali a run for her money...

'All ready?' barked the director.

'Ready, sir,' replied the mustachioed actor, stubbing out his beedi. 'What do I have to do in this scene?'

'Just behave like Indra, you fool,' the director replied. 'Apsaras will dance, you will drink wine and look lustfully at them. No need to act. Just be yourself. That's why you got this role in the first place. Understood?'

'Understood, sir,' the actor said. Then with a frown he said: '*Accha* sir, you want full lusty or medium lusty? For example, should I sniff the jasmine garland on my wrist, when I am checking out the ladies? Maybe with little bit of winking?'

'I will pull off your moustache if you try to be over-smart,' the director snapped. 'Please understand your role. You are Indra, king of the gods. Not some loose character drunkard in a *bai-ji's kotha*! You should balance your lustiness with some dignity also, no? Please remember this is a family film.'

'Got it, sir. Then I'll do medium lusty, sir.'

'Yes, that's right. Okay? All ready? Let's start then. Silence. Lights, camera and...action!'

A scrawny young boy in shorts and vest darted before the throne, a clapper board clutched in his hands. '*Jai Ma Manasa*. Scene 23. Shot 1. Take 1,' he yelled in a nasal voice, and clacked shut the flaps of the clapper board. The cameras whirred into life and a song blared out on the loudspeaker:

'In the golden palace of your love,
My heart flutters like a long-lost dove.'

The apsaras swayed and swirled to the music, as Indra gawked at them with expressions that alternated between the dignified and the lecherous.

'In the garden of your adoring glances,
My mind like an innocent peacock dances.'

I was rather enjoying myself when an angry bellow spoilt all the fun.

'What the hell is happening? Why has that girl stopped dancing?' the director yelled. His finger was pointed at a slim, dark-skinned apsara, who was frozen in her position. She was still as a block of stone, her gaze fixed on Manu.

'You?' she whispered, her kohl-lined eyes widening with disbelief.

Manu stared back at the apsara. Several moments passed before he found his voice. 'Mary?' he managed to say at last.

***

It had been three hours since Manu had been pacing up and down the street outside Indrapuri Studios. He had barely been able to exchange a word with Mary, when the director had booted him out of the studio. But before leaving, he had been able to tell her that he would be waiting for her outside. She had looked so shocked that he wasn't sure she had even heard him. He glanced at his watch for the umpteenth time, trying to control his impatience. What was taking her so long? Was it even Mary in the first place? Or had he imagined the whole thing?

It was nearly five in the evening before Mary finally stepped out of the main gate of the studio. She stared at him blankly for a while before mumbling: 'It's really you then...you're real.'

Manu nodded. 'Yes, it's me.'

'I'm sorry you had to wait,' Mary said. 'I am not allowed to leave until I finish my shift.'

'That's okay,' Manu mumbled. All this while, he hadn't been able to think of anything except Mary but now that she was finally in front of him, he didn't know what to say. Nor did she. They could only stare at each other as if they were ghosts. Mary had the worn-out, emaciated appearance of someone who hadn't had a decent meal in a while. Now that her face was shorn of make-up, the fine web of lines cutting across her pallid cheeks was visible. She bore little resemblance to the bejewelled apsara of Indra's court nor to the vivacious young girl whom he had deserted six years ago.

'You look just the same,' Manu mumbled. 'I'd have recognised you anywhere.'

'*Bakwas*,' Mary gave a wan smile. 'I'm old now. We're both old,' her gaze swept over him. 'But you look like you've done well for yourself, I must say. Proper suited-booted gentleman you've become, almost like engineer-babu,' she gave his hand a gentle squeeze. 'You know, when I saw you on the sets this morning, I thought you were a ghost.'

'So did I.'

'But how on earth did you land up there? Where have you been all these years? What are you doing here in Calcutta?'

'I have the same questions,' Manu replied. 'What are *you* doing here? And why are you dancing in a film?'

'What can I say? It's been such a strange journey. The police, the dolphins, the—'

'Dolphins! What on earth—'

'I'll tell you everything. But you tell me first. You owe me an explanation,' said Mary. 'Lots of explanations. You disappear one fine day and then...you suddenly appear out of the blue. Who do you think you are? Why did you leave—'

'Wait, wait,' Manu held up his hand. 'There's lots to talk about and we can't do it here on the street. Can we go somewhere else?'

'Where?' asked Mary.

'A restaurant? I know a nice place on Park Street,' Manu replied. 'You look like you could do with some food.'

'Yes, that I could,' Mary replied. 'I haven't been eating much of late.'

'Why?'

'It's just that...well...life hasn't been very easy.'

'Why? What's happened?'

She cut him off. 'Can we go to that restaurant of yours, first? I'll tell you everything.'

'Including the dolphins?'

'That too. But after I have a bite. I'm starving.'

The Dolphins

A tuxedoed waiter padded up to their table and placed a plate of chicken tikkas and two glasses of red wine before them. 'Madam, sir, enjoy your meal,' he said and departed discreetly.

Manu nodded his thanks as Mary scanned the surroundings. They were seated at a corner table of Mocambo Restaurant, next to a large bay window, overlooking Park Street. It was early evening, but the restaurant was already thrumming with revellers—bow-tied men in dinner jackets creased sharp as knives, women in silk sarees, sipping cocktails as they toyed with their pearl necklaces. In the far corner of the room, a svelte woman in a sequined golden gown was crooning a breathy jazz number.

'Very fancy place, this. I wish we had gone somewhere else,' mumbled Mary, as she furtively patted down the pleats of her faded cotton sari. 'I'm not even properly dressed.'

'You look just fine,' Manu lied. 'I thought you would like this place. Their Chicken a la Kiev is really good. We can order a plate, if you want.'

Mary frowned at the glass of wine. 'This is sharaab? Looks like Coca Cola.'

Manu smiled. 'It's called red wine. It's not bad. Try it.'

Mary took a sip of her wine and let out a satisfied sigh. 'Not as good as mahua but it will do.' Then she cocked an eyebrow at him. 'Air-conditioned restaurants, firangi sharaab. Didn't know Calcutta was like this. Looks like that prince of yours is taking good care of you.'

During the drive from Indrapuri to Park Street, Manu had given her a quick account of his six-year long journey from Betla to Calcutta—starting from his chance encounter with the prince, the horse races, his home, and his work at Regal Bearings. She had listened in silence and he didn't know what to make of it. He had expected her to be disappointed and angry by his sudden disappearance from Betla and his transformation into a diku. But she did not seem to be. Her calmness was unnerving. It occurred to him that she was no longer the Mary he had known six years ago, but a different person altogether, a stranger almost.

'You've changed, Manhoos,' Mary said. 'Or should I say Manu?'

'Manu is probably better. I've gotten used to it.'

'I can see that. So, what else have you got used to?'

'Come on, Mary. You know me. At heart, I'm just the same old Manhoos,' he said. 'But enough about me. I have been going on and on. It's time you told me about yourself. I am dying to know.'

'All right,' she replied and took another sip of wine. And as Pam Crain's angelic voice belted out *Stella by Starlight*, Mary told him her tale.

***

On the morning that Manhoos had left Netarhat, Mary had woken up earlier than usual. No one else was up and she had gone down to the river alone to take her bath. She had barely stepped into the water when she saw a strange creature leap out of it. She had never seen anything like it before. It had a long, thin beak, a rounded belly, and a pair of wing-like flippers that protruded from its sides. It looked like a cross between a bird and a fish. Every now and then, a plume of water spurted out of the top of its head in a graceful arc. Mary was staring in fascination at the bird-fish when it began to speak to her, with a clarity and a vocabulary that was almost human.

He was neither fish nor bird, the creature informed her, but a *soos*.

'A soos? What is that?' asked Mary.

'That's what the locals call us. I think in English we are called river dolphins. Not many of us here, so I'm not surprised you haven't seen any of us yet. Here, take a closer look at me,' the dolphin said and swam right up to Mary's feet. He stood upright, half his body out of the water.

He had travelled all the way from the Mahanadi river, which had once been his home, said the dolphin. It had been a long and hard journey. For hundreds of miles, he and the other dolphins of his pod had swum down the Mahanadi into the salty seas of the Bay of Bengal, then upstream along the Baitarani river until at last, they had found refuge in the quiet currents of the Koyal, deep inside the forest.

'I can't tell you how peaceful it is here, madam Mary,' said the dolphin, blowing out a jet of water. 'After what happened to us in the Mahanadi, this place is like heaven.'

'What happened?' Mary asked.

'The dam, madam! The damned Hirakud dam,' the dolphin hissed, his snout quivering in fury. 'That bloody dam nearly killed us. And not just us—fishes, crocodiles, otters, snails, everyone. Overnight, we were all made homeless! The day the government started building that massive barrage across the Mahanadi, we knew that our days were numbered. We were terrified of what would happen to us. But luckily, Shushuki kept her head.'

'Shushuki?' asked Mary.

'The leader of our pod—as brave as she is wise. She rallied us around and led us out of danger. We swam down endless rivers and seas, until we finally arrived here. But not all. More than half of us died on the way.'

Tears streamed from the dolphin's eyes as he told her of his childhood days in the Mahanadi, and his friends, and their adventures together. Mary was transfixed by his account, when Shushuki and the other dolphins of the pod joined him. They wanted to know everything about Mary, and soon she was chatting and playing with them like they were old friends. They were such pleasant company, that she lost track of time. It was only when the shadows had lengthened, that she realised how late it was. She bade goodbye to the dolphins and hurried back to the village.'

'But there was no village,' Mary said, her face turning grey and old.

'Meaning?' Manu asked.

'It had been burnt down.'

'Burnt down?' Manu gasped.

'Everything. The houses, the fields, even that stupid Kristchan church. Everything had turned into ashes,' Mary said.

'But...who did it?'

'Who else but the police? It must have been them. There were tyre marks in the soil. I found bullets lodged in the trees. And arrows. My guess is that the police must have come that morning to throw us out, so that they could build their backside temple. My people must have fought back...and lost...'

'But where are they now? Your family, your father, mother...'

'Don't know. Must be dead,' Mary muttered. 'Please...give me a... minute. It's not easy for me to speak of these things.'

'I understand,' said Manu and placed his hand on hers.

She drained the rest of the wine, and after a few moments, she said: 'The police must have either killed them or taken them to some other place. I don't know. What does it matter? Either way they are as good as dead. When I saw that burnt down village, I was too numb even to cry. I have never felt so helpless in my life. I ran into the jungle, screaming out everyone's names, in the hope that I would find someone. I searched every inch of the forest, all the way till the highway. There was nothing. But I didn't give up. For the next three days, I kept looking for them,' she gazed at him. 'And I looked for you too, you know. But you had vanished. Just like everyone else. Rajinder Seth had no idea where you had gone.'

Manu's head sank to his chest. 'I'm terribly sorry. I told you why I had to leave so suddenly.'

'It's okay. I understand,' Mary gave a small smile. 'If I had been in your place, I would probably have done the same. After all, we all have to survive. But all the same, I wish you had been there. I was so alone. Everyone I ever knew had gone. All of them...' she stopped.

'At least you are still here,' Manu squeezed her hand. 'You're still alive.'

'I wished I wasn't. I didn't feel like living anymore. I just wanted to lay down and die. But those damned dolphins didn't let me do even that!'

'The dolphins?'

'Yes, after three days of useless searching, I couldn't take it anymore. I tied a rock around myself and stepped into the river. I was sinking into the water...the pain was going away...I could even see their faces—my mother's, my father's, all my friends'...it was bliss.

But those bloody dolphins! Wouldn't even let me drown in peace!'

She was almost about to lose consciousness, Mary continued, when she felt something pushing hard against her. A dolphin was pressing its snout against her back, stopping her from sinking. It was soon joined by three more dolphins and together they lifted her out of the water. She struggled to free herself from them, but they were strong and nimble and despite her best efforts, she could not manage to drown herself. They dragged her to the shore, and pushed her away with their snouts every time she tried to dive back in. She cursed, threatened and begged them to let her have her way but they refused to hear a word of it.

'All life is sacred,' they said to her. 'You cannot destroy life—neither yours nor anyone else's.'

'I have lost everything,' replied Mary. 'I don't want to live anymore.'

'We too have lost much,' said the dolphins. 'Half our pod died on our way here—our families and friends, our children. But we haven't given up, have we? You cannot give up either. We won't let you.'

For three days, they were her constant companions, never letting her out of their sight. Whenever she tried to escape them, they would call out to her with cries that were so heartrending that she could not bear to ignore them.

'They forced me to keep living, those stupid dolphins,' said Mary. 'And the problem is that the more you live, the tougher it becomes to die. After a few days, the pain started getting duller. It was still terrible, but I found that I was able to bear it. Seeing that I was a little better, the dolphins sat me down for a talk. They said it was time for me to go and live in some place where there were other people.'

'All animals need to live with their own kind. Even humans,' the dolphins said to me. 'You can't stay with us forever. We will be very sad to see you go but the jungle isn't the right place for you anymore. You won't be able to live here all by yourself.'

'To tell you the truth, by now, I was desperate to get away from the forest myself,' said Mary. 'Every tree and every animal, every bird and every butterfly reminded me of the old days. I was desperate to go. Go to a place so far away that my memories would not be able to follow me.'

'I can understand,' Manu said.

'I don't think you can. Anyway, that's when Shushuki suggested that I go to Calcutta,' said Mary.

'That's where everyone is going these days,' Shushuki said to me. 'Of course, it's a terrible place for fishes. Those horrible Calcuttans just love eating them. But they say, it's a good place for people—especially the poor and homeless.'

'Who says?' I asked her. 'What do you know about Calcutta?'

'Oh, we know,' Shushuki replied. 'We have swum up the Hooghly. We have seen things, heard things from the local fishes.'

'What sort of things?'

'For example, that no one starves in Calcutta. There are refugee camps all over the city, where even the poorest can find food and shelter.'

'But how will I get there?' I asked. 'Calcutta must be thousands of miles from here.'

'If there's a will there's a way. Calcutta is far from here. But you are clever and strong. We know you can do it if you want.'

'I thought about it for a day or two. I wasn't scared of the journey. I knew that if I waited long enough on the highway, I could probably get some kind person to give me a ride up to Calcutta. But was I ready to go to a strange, new place full of strange people? How would I live there? What would I do? But in the end, I decided to follow Shushuki's advice. My old life had been destroyed. If I had to make a fresh start, I wanted to do it as far away from Betla as possible. The next day, I walked to the highway and hitched a ride with a truck driver who was headed here. Four days later, he dropped me off at Sealdah station. Since then, six years have passed. And here I am.'

'Yes, here you are. And just how did you start dancing as an apsara in films?'

'Oh that happened because of the party. They helped me find a job in Indrapuri Studios.'

'What party?'

'The Communist party of course,' said Mary. 'Is there any other worth the name?'

The Communist

Mary had been lost when she first arrived in Calcutta, a solitary grain of sand among the millions that had been washed up to the shores of that great city. For the first few weeks she had lived on the streets, ragpicking, scavenging for food, scrounging for odd jobs, begging...

'And worse,' the lines on Mary's face deepened. 'I don't want to talk of it.'

'That's all right,' said Manu. He didn't want to hear of it either. He could guess.

'By now I was cursing myself for having believed the dolphins. It wasn't their fault of course. I had chosen to come to Calcutta. But I had no idea that things would be so bad here. I almost decided to go back to Betla. If it hadn't been for Dipu-da, I probably would have.'

'Dipu-da?'

'He was a volunteer with the Council at the time.'

'What Council?'

'The United Central Refugee Council. Or the UCRC as they call themselves. Most of the people in it are from the party.'

'The Communist party?'

'Yes. Dipu-da found me looking for food in a garbage dump. He took pity on me and took me to Bijoygarh Colony. That's where I stayed for the next three years.'

'You stayed there!' Manu exclaimed. In a flash, the aroma of Chicken a la Kiev gave way to the stench of rotting human flesh and he was back in Bijoygarh.

'Yes, Manu, I wasn't as lucky as you,' Mary said. 'I had no Prince Charming to take care of me. For three years I lived with death, dysentery and cholera, with rats and fleas and half humans,' she shuddered.

'I know,' Manu muttered under his breath.

'But Bijoygarh Colony changed my life,' said Mary. 'A terrible but beautiful place. A place where people shared whatever little they had with each other—food, clothes, medicines. There was even a school inside the colony. Ranjan-jethu, a retired school teacher from Faridpur, had started it. That's where I learnt to read and write a little. In the evenings, people would gather around telling stories, singing, dancing—at times it almost felt like I was back in the village. That's how I was able to find work. Dipu-da had seen me dancing one evening. He took me to Indrapuri Studios and was able to get me a job as an extra. Because of that I was able to rent a single room in Tollygunge basti. That's where I have been living for the last four years.'

'You live in a *basti*?'

'Yes, no mansion for me unfortunately. But you don't have to look so sorry for me Manu. I am doing all right. I have a job that gives me enough money for a roof over my head and two meals a day. And I have friends.'

'Your UCRC friends?' Manu asked.

'Yes. Dipu-da, Ranjan-jethu, Karuna-di and so many others. I owe them everything.' She smiled wanly. 'You remember how I used to make fun of you because you wanted to go to school?'

'Yes.'

'I was stupid. It's only after Ranjan-jethu taught me how to read and write, that I realised how important it is to be educated.'

'Really?' said Manu. Ever since he had become a manager in Regal Bearings, his reading had been restricted to invoices and purchase orders. 'What do you read?'

'Oh, mostly newspapers, and the party pamphlets that Dipu-da gives me. They have helped me understand a few things.'

'Like what?'

'Like why the police burnt down our village and why the government wants to close down the refugee camps and throw everyone out. And why the poor have to beg for a handful of rice while the rich feast on chicken and wine.'

Manu wasn't sure if her words had been meant for him, but they stung him like a slap on the face. Their paths had diverged so far from each other that it was difficult to believe that they had once started from the same place.

'Not everyone who is rich is bad, you know,' Manu said with a sheepish grin.

'I'm not saying that. I know you are a good person.'

'So is Raja-saab. You must meet him soon.'

'Maybe he is. The point is not about individuals. It is about the system. It's rotten to the core.'

'*Yeh azaadi jhootha hai*?' Manu said, almost to himself.

'Yes. And the sooner we understand that truth, the better it will be for everyone. You know Manu, if it wasn't for us extras, not a single film would get made in Indrapuri Studios. But you should see the way they treat us. It's disgraceful—twelve, fourteen-hour shifts. We can't even go to the bathroom sometimes because they say the costumes will get spoilt. And the wages are pathetic! We live like beggars while these stinking rich producers and star actors stay in their fancy air-conditioned bungalows in Alipore and party in Great Eastern Hotel.'

'You don't have to live like a beggar anymore, Mary. I am here and—'

'You don't understand me, do you?' Mary cut in. 'It's not about you and me. It's about changing the system.'

'You are going to change the system?'

'Yes, we are,' Mary's eyes lit up. 'Do you know we are trying to form a union of film technicians and junior artistes in Indrapuri Studios? And it's not just us. Everywhere, the poor, the farmers and the workers are uniting to fight against the rich. The day is not far when we will seize power and throw them all out!' she thumped her hand on the table so hard that her empty glass toppled over. She stuck her tongue out in embarrassment and said: 'I'm sorry, I got carried away. I didn't mean to give a lecture. It's the wine...I think I've had too much.'

'No, no, not at all. It's very interesting what you are saying,' Manu said.

'Please don't misunderstand me. We are not against the rich. It's just that we want everyone to be equal.'

'Thank god. I thought you were angry at me,' Manu smiled. After a pause he asked. 'Are you?'

'Why should I be?'

'Because I eat chicken. And I drink wine. And I left you all by yourself in Betla.'

'I was angry for a long time. But not anymore. I'm just glad that you still here, when everyone else is—'

'We have to try and forget the past Mary. Both of us. It's over and done with. We are together again. Isn't that more important?'

'Yes, it is,' Mary nodded. Her fingers brushed against his and they both smiled shyly. They looked just like the two children I had met on my first day here, ten years ago. And for a moment, the past that they both wanted to forget, leaked into the present, and they were again what they had once been.

***

Mary's return was the best thing that could have happened to Manu. He couldn't remember the last time when he had felt so alive, so full of hope and energy. His days fell into a familiar pattern and yet each one was touched with a magical quality, that made him want to stop the clocks and halt the march of time.

Every morning he would arrive early at the factory, complete his work as quickly as possible and drive down to Dhakuria Lake. There he would wait for Mary to arrive after she had finished her shift at Indrapuri Studios. I was happy too, listening to them chatting away for hours. Mary did most of the talking. She would tell him about the ridiculous films that were being made these days, of which actor was having a secret affair with which actress, of her life in the slum, of her work with the Communist party, of how much she missed the forest and how she dreamed of going back there someday.

On most days, they would head to a restaurant for an early dinner. Mary did not like going to the expensive restaurants on Park Street and soon Basanta Cabin in Bhowanipore became their favourite haunt. They watched the occasional play at Star Theatre and on another memorable occasion, they had even taken a boat ride on the Ganga from Princep Ghat.

But the most memorable incident happened one Saturday evening in December. The prince had gone to the club and the house was empty. Hormones bubbling under the influence of a few drinks at Basanta Cabin, Manu invited Mary home. She agreed. He then invited her to see his bedroom. She agreed again. If you want to know what happened after that, I'm afraid I cannot tell you. All I can say is that they weren't playing ludo in there.

One hour later, when Manu emerged from the bedroom, there was a silly grin plastered over his face. It was a historic moment—but not the sort that is usually recorded in textbooks.

Love and War

As an equally fine chronicler of his age had once written—it was the best of times, it was the worst of times. It was the winter of love and the spring of war. The hero of my tale had finally lost his virginity and he was leaving no bedsheet unturned to ensure that it stayed that way. Whenever the prince was away, Manu would smuggle Mary into the house and they would do the sort of things that twenty-year-olds do, when they get a room to themselves. But the lustful throbbings of their hearts were soon to be drowned out by the roll of war drums.

One morning in March, Manu arrived before the gates of Regal Bearings, to find his path blocked by a mob of angry factory workers. He brought the car to a halt and stepped out. 'What is the meaning of this?' he asked. 'Why are you not at work?'

A tall, lean man with a scraggly salt and pepper beard stepped forward from the crowd. He was attired in a wrinkled cotton kurta and dhoti that set him apart from the rest of the uniformed workers. He planted himself in front of Manu and said: 'Manager-babu, we are declaring a strike. No one will work until our demands are met,' he turned to the gathering and let out a loud cry. '*Amader dabi mante hobe!* (Our demands must be met!).'

'*Mante hobe, mante hobe* (Must be met, must be met),' the other men chorused in reply, pumping their fists in the air.

'*Taanashahi cholbe na,*' yelled the bearded man. (Dictatorship won't do! Won't do.)

'*Cholbe na, cholbe na*! (Won't do! Won't do!),' his companions roared back and the angry sloganeering continued unabated.

After a while, the bearded man called for silence and Manu was able to make himself heard. 'What is the meaning of this nonsense?' he asked.

'Nonsense?' spat the bearded man. 'Comrades, show it to him!'

One of the workers stepped forward from the throng and held out a steel bowl. It contained a small piece of fish submerged in a watery gravy. The bearded man picked up the fish and dangled it before Manu. 'You think this is nonsense?'

The pungent smell of rohu fish curry invaded Manu's nostrils. 'What is the problem? Has it gone bad?' he asked.

'No, but it's so small, that it might as well not be there,' said the bearded man as he released the fish. It fell into the bowl with a plop, sending the gravy splattering over Manu's laundered white shirt. 'Only fifty grams my brothers! Only fifty grams! How can anyone work on an empty stomach?'

'Shame, shame!' the gathering shouted. '*Inquilab zindabad*!' Long live the revolution!

It took several minutes before Manu could get a word in. 'If there is a problem with the food, then we can discuss it in a civil manner. What is the need for—'

The bearded man cut him off. 'Manager-babu, we don't need lessons in civility from any corrupt capitalist. Your workers are starving to death while you are fattening yourselves on their blood.'

'*Our* workers are starving? Rubbish!' exclaimed Manu. 'We take very good care of all our workers. In all these years, there hasn't been a single complaint about the food,' he gave the bearded man a once-over. 'And just who are you, if I may ask? I have never seen you here before. What business do you have in our factory, inciting our employees—'

'Your employees?' the bearded man cut him off. 'You think you own them? Listen carefully manager-babu, my name is Subodh Kumar Chatterjee. I am from the All India Trade Union Congress and under our leadership, all the workers of this country will now be united to fight against the capitalist dogs!'

Manu felt like giving the man a tight slap. But he controlled his anger and said: 'Mr Chatterjee, we take very good care of our workers. We don't need your union-baazi here. This is our factory and we will run it in the way we want to.'

'It's not *your* factory. It belongs to every worker who gives his sweat and blood to it. Their interests must be protected. And they will be protected! With force if need be!'

'Are you threatening me with violence?'

'Not right now. But if we have to, we will,' Mr Chatterjee said. 'Let me tell you something manager-babu—a new age is coming. The age of the people. The day is not far when we will snatch power from the hands of capitalists like you. With guns if need be. After all, as Chairman Mao says, power flows from the barrel of a gun.'

***

A few days after this incident, Manu and Mary met at Princep Ghat. They were sitting on a bench overlooking the Ganga, chatting about nothing in particular, when Manu said: 'Do you know a person called Subodh Chatterjee?'

'Subodh Chatterjee?' Mary frowned. 'That's the name of one of our party leaders. But why—'

'Is he a tall, thin man with a beard?' Manu cut her off.

'That sounds like him. But why do you ask?'

Manu ignored her question. 'So, he's...how do you say it...a comrade of yours?'

'Yes, and an important comrade too. Subodh-da is mobilizing factory workers to form registered unions.'

'Oh, it's Subodh-da now, is it? Sounds more than just a comrade to me.'

Mary stared at him. 'Why are you behaving so strangely, Manu? What's happened? Did Subodh-da come to your factory? Just spit it out instead of going around in circles.'

'All right,' replied Manu and went on to tell her of the demonstration at the factory. 'This is what your friends are really like,' he said. 'Goondas! Barging in and threatening me with guns.'

'Watch your language. Manu!' Mary snapped. 'Subodh-da is not a goonda. He's a friend and colleague. As for guns, Chairman Mao said—'

'Yes, yes, I know very well what your Chairman Mao says.'

'And you don't think he's right? Look what happened to us. We tried to fight the government's bullets with bows and arrows and—' she stopped and looked away from Manu.

'Look Mary, I am sorry for what happened to you,' Manu said gently. 'I really am. But two wrongs don't make a right. The factory is under lockout and its hurting everyone. The workers are not getting paid. Production is at a standstill. And there's a big order of bushings that we have to supply to Hindustan Motors. If we can't deliver it within the next two weeks, there will be huge losses.'

'Money, money, money!' Mary threw up her hands. 'Is that all that you can think of these days!'

'Why shouldn't I? Isn't money important? Who would know that better than me? I grew up with nothing—no father, no mother, no home. I had to work like a dog from the age of six. I used to live like a beggar. And I would have died like one, if Raja-saab hadn't picked me up from the streets. He gave me a home, an education. He made me his factory manager. He gave me a future. Because of him I can dare to dream today.'

'And what do you dream of, Manu?' asked Mary as she gazed curiously at him.

'Me? I want to make Regal Bearings the biggest, the best company in India. I want to take it to the top, the very top!' he exclaimed. 'And yes, I want to make money. I'm not ashamed to say it. Why should I? I want to make lots of money. Both for myself and for Raja-saab. So that he can use it as he wants—to make films, to get into politics.'

'That's what he wants. But what do *you* want, Manu?' Mary asked.

'What everyone else wants,' Manu said. 'A home and a family,' he sneaked a shy glance at Mary. 'A family that I can take care of and provide for.'

Mary burst into giggles. 'Such a diku you've become! A typical burjuaa!'

Her laughter cut through him like a red-hot knife, making him feel small and stupid. And it occurred to him that this wasn't the first time it was happening. Of late, he had begun to sense a subtle shift in their relationship. There was something in her manner that seemed to suggest that he wasn't good enough for her, that she was merely tolerating him. 'Sometimes I think I don't know you anymore,' he said.

She gave a small smile. 'Is that so surprising? We live in two different worlds, Manu. You eat at the best restaurants in town and stay in your fancy mansion. I eat rice and dal and live in a basti.'

'So you think I'm one of those rich, evil capitalists sucking the blood of the poor?'

'I never said that, Manu. I know you're not like those people.'

'I see,' Manu said. 'In that case, can I ask a small favour of you?'

'What?'

'Can you have a word with your Subodh-da and tell him what you just said to me.'

'I don't understand.'

'It's simple. Just tell this Subodh Chatterjee that Regal Bearings is not like other factories. Tell him that we take good care of our workers. And tell him to call off his bloody strike!'

Mary stared at him as if he had gone mad. 'What are you saying Manu? That's impossible. I could never do something like that. To go on strike or not is for the party to decide. How can I bring my personal relationships into party matters? How could you even suggest such a thing?'

Manu had only half-expected her to agree to his request. But the vehemence of her refusal felt like a punch to his gut. 'You can't do even this much for me? After I've told you how important it is. Didn't I say how badly we need this Hindustan Motors order? Mary, all I'm asking you is to talk to your party bosses and tell them that you know me!'

'It won't help, Manu. Even if I spoke, they wouldn't listen to me. I'm just an ordinary party worker, a small fry. My talking to them won't make any difference.'

'But it will make a difference to me!' Manu exclaimed as he got up from the bench and walked to the edge of the river. 'You may have forgotten, but I still remember. I remember the day when you and Lukabarsi talked to Rajinder Seth. I remember the difference that it made!'

A soft sigh escaped Mary. 'I remember too. Those were the good old days, weren't they? When we were on the same side?'

'And now we are not?'

'Can't you see, Manu? There is a war coming. And we will soon have to choose our sides.'

'Oh, so we are at war now, is it?'

'Not yet,' said Mary with a tenderness in her voice that stung at

Manu like a wasp bite. 'I don't know how to say this, Manu. You are my oldest friend. But we are not the same anymore. The times have changed and so have we,' her fingers grazed his face. 'The party means as much to me as your factory and Raja-saab mean to you. I don't see a meeting point between the two. Perhaps it's time for us to go our separate ways.'

Manu remained silent as he pushed her hand aside roughly.

'Don't do that, Manu,' she seized his hand again. 'I have treasured our times together and I always will. I would still like us to be friends, if that's—'

'Stop it, Mary,' Manu cut her off. 'I don't need your pity.'

All of a sudden, he found himself shrinking from this girl for whose touch he had thirsted until a day ago. He had loved her. He still did. He had dreamt of the life that they could build together. But she had only laughed at his dreams. Suddenly her new friends had become more important than her old ones. She had sniggered at him because he did not understand fancy words like burjuaa...but maybe she was right—maybe they were in two different worlds now, worlds separated by a vast chasm.

He lit up a cigarette and let out a cloud of smoke. And as he watched it drifting across the sun-speckled waters of the Ganga, the faint sound of a faraway commotion came to his ears—*'Amader daabi maante hobe! Inquilab Zindabad! Zindabad! Zindabad!'*

'Perhaps you are right,' he said in a low voice that Mary could barely hear. 'When the war comes, we will have to choose our sides.'

Book Three

Mary

Ten years had passed. Or rather I have decided to skip ten years. Mostly because they were rather tepid, compared to the ten that were to follow, as you will soon see. However, in the interests of historical continuity, here's a quick summary of what happened since the time we left Manu and Mary deciding that they would have to part ways.

Manu had chosen his side. And he had chosen well. By the summer of 1967, he had become Managing Director of Regal Bearings Ltd. The journey from manager to Managing Director hadn't been easy but it had been well deserved. Manu had given his heart and soul to Regal Bearings, working every day from eight in the morning till midnight. Lockouts, strikes, fires, floods, cunning competitors and complaining customers—he had weathered every crisis and come out stronger each time. His tireless efforts had made Regal Bearings a name to reckon with in the bushings business. Pleased by his performance, the prince had handed over the running of the factory entirely to Manu and had gone on to become a film producer and actor—which meant that he was willing to produce any film in which he was the lead actor.

In the eyes of the world, Manu had everything going for him—MD at only thirty, still handsome despite a small paunch and prematurely greying hair, still single and quite a catch in the marriage market. Of late, the prince had started hinting that it was about time that he got settled. But Manu showed little interest in women let alone marriage. In fact, he showed little interest in anything but work. His social life was non-existent and he was rarely to be seen anywhere outside factory and home. He avoided the usual haunts of the well-heeled—the Bengal Club, the golf course and the races. He turned down invitations to parties and rarely dined anywhere outside home. In short, Manu had built a wall around himself—a wall of work that kept out the past and left room for nothing but the future.

As for Mary, he hadn't seen her in ages. Or rather, she hadn't wanted to see him anymore. They had drifted apart, so swiftly and so far, that their days of togetherness seemed to be no more than a fairy tale. But the dull roots of memory and desire, long buried under piles of bushings, were about to be stirred once more into life, when on an April morning, a letter arrived from Mary.

***

It was more a hastily scribbled note than a letter. It said:

Dear Manu,

I am in a desperate situation and I need your help. There is no one else I can turn to at a time like this. I know that we have moved out of each other's lives. But if we can meet once, I would be very grateful to you. Will you please come to Dhakuria Lake, this Saturday evening at 5 o'clock? I will wait for you at our usual spot.

Yours,
Mary

Manu stared at the words in disbelief, reading and re-reading them, until finally his initial shock gave way to an excitement that he hadn't felt in years. *There is no one else I can turn to...*she had written. She still remembered him. He still mattered to her. A thousand incoherent thoughts tumbled over each other, leaving him skittish as a kitten.

He glanced at the calendar. It was Thursday. Only two more days to Saturday. He couldn't remember the last time he had felt so alive.

***

She arrived on the dot of five. Manu could barely recognise her. She looked much older than her years, her hair thin and grey, papery skin stretched tight across her cheekbones.

She gave him a small smile and said: 'I could barely recognise you. You look...healthy.'

Manu smiled back, glancing ruefully at his pot-belly. 'Healthy?

You mean I look like a fat, old uncle. But what to do? Ten years have taken their toll. You look just the same though,' he lied. 'But you do seem to have lost a lot of weight. Are you all right?'

'Getting along. But never mind me. Tell me about yourself. How has life treated you? What have you been doing?'

'Nothing much,' Manu shrugged. 'Life goes on. My work keeps me busy, that's about it. What about you? Still saving the world?'

'I don't know about that. But yes, I am a full-time party worker now.'

'Full-time? Don't you work in the studios any more?'

She shook her head. 'No, they threw me out two years ago. Only to be expected. With my looks, you think I'd get even a servant's role, let alone an apsara's?'

'How are you managing to make ends meet, then?'

She lowered her gaze and said: 'Somehow. The party gives me a small allowance. What about you? Are you married?'

The anger flared up inside Manu. There had been a time, a long time ago, when all that he wanted was a family and a home. He had just been an ordinary young man with ordinary dreams. But she had laughed at them.

'Can we get to the point?' he said brusquely. 'Why did you want to meet me?'

She sensed his anger. 'I'm sorry, Manu. It was stupid of me,' she said. 'I thought...you might have...gotten over it by now.'

'There's nothing to get over,' Manu said tersely. 'Now if you don't mind, I am in a hurry. So why don't you come straight to the point? What do you want from me?'

She avoided his gaze and said: 'You know, Manu, I stopped myself a thousand times before writing that letter to you. I know what I am doing is not right. But I didn't know what else to do. I feel so small...so mean...that I...' her voice trailed off and she became quiet.

She looked so desolate that his anger evaporated as quickly as it had erupted. 'Go on,' said Manu. 'It's all right. You can tell me.'

She looked up at him. 'I need some money, Manu. Ever since I stopped working at Indrapuri I have no income. The party allowance is enough for the food but not for the rent—it's only a little room in the basti, but enough for me. I have been paying it out of my savings, but they've run out now. If I don't get some money soon, I'll be out on the streets. I don't know what to do, Manu.'

'Aren't you married?'

'No, of course not,' she replied.

Manu's heart beat a little faster. 'Really? You haven't married yet?'

She smiled. 'Who would marry me?'

A flood of relief rushed through Manu. Now that he had got the answer to the question that had been gnawing inside him, everything seemed to change. Everything was all right now. Everything was possible.

There was so much that he suddenly wanted to do for her, to give her. Things that she had never had. Nice clothes, good food, maybe even a flat for herself...He could easily afford it. But wouldn't it be too much too soon? Besides, knowing her, she would probably be too proud to accept anything beyond the bare minimum. It was enough that she had remembered him. It was enough that she had returned.

'How much money do you need?' he asked trying to keep his voice steady.

'Anything will do,' she replied.

He took out two ten-rupee notes from his wallet and pressed it into her hands. 'This is all I have with me right now. There will be more if—'

She edged close to him and clasped his hand. 'I'm sorry, Manu.'

'What for?' Manu said.

'I wasn't nice to you,' she replied. 'I went away.'

'I went away too,' he said. 'It doesn't matter, now that you are back,' he gave her an awkward hug and the warmth of her body seeped through his skin like a comforting balm. Ten years of separation and resentment melted away in a moment.

Things were becoming a little mushy. I could almost hear the sound of violins playing in the background as Manu and Mary clung to each other. I thought they would welcome a little privacy and flew away. It was then that I noticed the stocky, middle-aged man who was sitting on the bench to their left. He was watching them. After a while, he pulled out a small Leica camera from his pocket and pointed it at them. He clicked a photograph and then another. A few clicks later, he seemed satisfied and replaced the camera in his pocket. He got up from the bench and walked out. I followed him into the street. The man kept walking until he came to a halt in front of a police jeep. He got into the jeep and left.

But I had the feeling that it wasn't the last we had seen of him.

***

The following day, they met at Dhakuria Lake again. Manu handed over another ten-rupee note to Mary, assuring her that there would be more whenever she needed it. Soon they were meeting at least once a week, revisiting their old haunts of Princep Ghat, Basanta Cabin and Star Theatre. Whenever Mary was with Manu, a little smile would appear on his face. After years, he was looking less like a depressed dung-beetle and more like a human.

I was happy to see him happy. But there were a few things that were niggling at me. Firstly, Manu was showering envelopes stuffed with ten-rupee notes on Mary and she was accepting them with alacrity, which the Mary we knew would never have done. By now he had probably given her enough money for two years of rent. He could afford it course and he didn't give it a second thought. But I couldn't help wondering what Mary was doing with all that money.

Then there was the mysterious photographer whom I had first noticed at Dhakuria Lake. Like a little lamb, wherever Mary and Manu went, the man was sure to go. I would see him lurking in the background, clicking away with his camera. What was he up to?

The final incident had happened two days ago. It was evening and Manu had accompanied Mary back to her home in Chitpur Lane as he sometimes did. He had been standing on her doorstep, gazing at her with his puppy eyes, when I heard the sound of a soft cough. It seemed to be coming from the kitchen. But Mary had said that she lived alone...so who did that cough belong to? My curiosity was piqued. I flew around to the back of the house and peeked through the window pane.

A tall, thin man in his forties, was standing in the kitchen pouring himself a cup of tea. He wore a shabby kurta pyjama and pair of thick glasses—an unremarkable looking man, except for the large, luminous eyes which gazed curiously at me. And as I stared back, it occurred to me that I had seen him before. But for the life of me, I could not remember where...

It was only when we were driving back home that it came to me—a blurred, black and white photograph that had appeared on the front page of the newspaper about two weeks ago. Although I wasn't absolutely sure, I think it was the same man. Apparently, he had been responsible for some sort of armed uprising in North Bengal in which a mob of peasants had attacked the police. A young officer had even died in the melee and the police had launched a manhunt for the mastermind behind the uprising.

As far as I could remember, he had a funny name, a woman's name...Champa...or something like that...

Alipore Jail

Dusk had fallen. The last rays of the setting sun slanted down the length of Chitpur Lane, its orange glow illuminating the shabby little tenement in which Mary lived. Manu was standing at the doorway with his usual will she ask me in today hang dog look on his face, when he felt something hard pressing against his spine. A hand slid across his mouth, clamping down roughly, and a low voice whispered into his ear: 'Keep quiet. This is the police. One squeak out of you and I'll blow your brains out.'

A stocky man with a large mole on his right cheek had Manu in his grip, twisting his arms behind his back. A second man had caught hold of Mary, his revolver rammed against her head. She squirmed to free herself, but he was too strong for her. A third man now appeared—a short, fat man, with even teeth that gleamed behind a crooked smile.

'Where is he?' the fat man hissed into Manu's ear.

Manu's bowels were turning into water. He threw a desperate glance at Mary. But she was avoiding his eye. 'What is all this? Who do you want?' Manu managed to croak.

'*Nyakaa*! Pretending to be so innocent, hah?' the fat man sneered. 'Who? Charu Majumdar. Who else? Where is he?'

Now I remembered! Charu Majumdar! Yes, that was the name of the man whose photograph I had seen in the newspaper, the same man who had been sipping tea in Mary's kitchen—Charu Majumdar, the most wanted Naxal in the history of India.

'You'll never catch him, you chutiyas, you bastards!' a strangled cry came from Mary.

Phattakk—a stinging blow from the fat policeman caught her square on the face. 'We'll see about that!' he said. He jerked his head towards the door. 'Get in there. Search the house,' he said to the man with the mole. 'I'll take care of these two.'

Terror and confusion chased across Manu's face. In contrast, Mary's coolness took my breath away. She had nerves of steel, that one. She looked as if she been carved out of a block of ice, as she calmly watched the policeman enter her house. If they found what they were looking for, it would be curtains for us.

***

But in spite of a thorough search of the couple of tiny rooms that the house consisted of, Charu Majumdar was not found. But what was found was almost as damning—a sheaf of papers containing eight monographs, written by the missing Mr Majumdar, with sabre-rattling titles such as:

What is the Source of the Spontaneous Revolutionary Outburst in India?
Build Armed Partisan Struggle by Fighting against Revisionism
Carry Forward the Peasant Struggle by Fighting Revisionism

I did not know it then, but the monographs were soon to stir the collective conscience of Bengal's brightest and best. The Historic Eight Documents, as they came to be later known, would inspire thousands of her children to choose Mao over *Ma, Baba, Bhai and Bon* (mother, father, brother sister). Hearkening to the Great Helmsman's call for a people's war, they would forsake their *maacher jhol* and monkey caps for machetes and revolvers. Thousands would walk down a blood-soaked path of encounter killings, torture and custodial deaths that would feed their battered bodies and broken spirits into the maws of history. The finest of Bengal's youth were to become but bloodied footnotes to the Historic Eight Documents, which the police now held in their hands.

Apart from the stash of incriminating documents, the search also uncovered three country-made revolvers, one hundred rounds of bullets and two brown manila envelopes stuffed with cash. From this point onwards, things moved forward with the swiftness of a kite swooping down on a field rat. Before I knew what was happening, Mary and Manu were handcuffed and bundled into a Black Maria van (which as an irrelevant but irresistible piece of trivia, I must tell you, is also called a 'Mother's Heart', apparently because it always has room for one more—one very scared golden sparrow, in this case, who had perched himself on its roof). Siren blaring, the van rumbled down the streets of Calcutta with its booty of two prisoners and one sparrow, until a short drive later, the towering red walls of Alipore Central Jail loomed into sight—grim and forbidding as a pisacha's parlour.

The prisoners were marched down the dark corridors of the prison as I flew above them fluttering near the high ceiling, taking care to stay out of sight. We went down rows upon rows of cells, the inmates jerking to life as we passed by them. They pressed themselves against the iron bars that separated us, howling at Mary and Manu. With ghoulish glee they called out after them—*notun maal esheche guru...Fresh meat, boss. We'll have a feast tonight...what did you do, murder, rape?*

But into my trained ear, there now floated other voices, faint yet clear, rising above the obscene cries of the prisoners—the whispers of the dead. Into my yaksha vision swam the grey ghosts of the long-dead men and women who had once been incarcerated within the same walls, who had once walked down the same blood-soaked path of encounter killings, torture and custodial deaths.

Here rises the spirit of Dudu Miyan, leader of the Indigo rebellion in Bengal. A little ahead, is the cell of Ramakrishna Biswas, the twenty-four-year-old soldier of Surya Sen's revolutionary army, who will swing from the gallows at the crack of dawn tomorrow. Speaking to him for one last time, disguised as his sister, is Pritilata Waddedar, who will kill herself a year later, when she chooses cyanide to capture. In the next cell sits Subhash Chandra Bose, his eyebrows hunched over his round eye-glasses, as he plans the Great Escape that will soon lead to his final journey aboard that ill-fated Mitsubishi bomber that is still flying inside the minds of a million never-say-die Bengalis. And then perhaps the most remarkable sight of all—Aurobindo Ghosh, incarcerated for the attempted murder of a British magistrate, silently transforming from revolutionary to saint, as he gazes in wonder at the image of Narayana that he can see in the sentry who stands guard over him.

The quest for freedom had led some prisoners to the gallows, others to their god. I wondered where it would lead Manu and Mary.

***

The atmosphere inside Alipore Central Jail was grim and forbidding as at a conclave of tantriks. A dark mood had gripped the police force. From the highest medallioned officer to the lowest hairy-kneed constable in his baggy, khaki shorts, everyone was talking about the Naxalbari uprising. I had read something of it in the papers of course, but it was only inside the jail that I came to know what had really happened.

The incident had occurred only a few days ago in the Naxalbari block of Siliguri, a small town nestling in the foothills of the Himalayas. Inspired by the revolutionary ideas contained in Charu Majumdar's Historic Eight documents, a group of peasants had seized land from the landlords of the area. Marking the boundaries of the captured land with red flags, they had begun harvesting their own crops on it. The movement was spreading like wildfire. Huge processions were being organised, and peasants armed with spears, bows and arrows were striking terror into the hearts of the landlords. The countryside was reverberating with the slogan *'March forward along the path of armed peasant revolution.'*

The situation was swiftly turning alarming. Armed police and paramilitary forces were brought in. The peasants retaliated and in the fracas that followed, one Inspector Sonam Wangdi was killed. This inflamed the police and they went on the warpath. Hundreds of peasants were beaten to a pulp and many of the movement's leaders either fell to police bullets or were arrested.

But their main leader Charu Majumdar was nowhere to be found. It was believed that he had gone underground and was hiding in Calcutta. No one knew where, but this much was clear by now—the police would stop at nothing in their search for the man who had killed one of their own—a search in which Manu and Mary had been caught like rats in a trap.

***

The prisoners were taken into a small, bare room enclosed by thick, scream-proof stone walls. In one corner of the room stood a wooden table illuminated by the ragged yellow light of an incandescent lamp hanging from the ceiling. At the centre of the table lay the incriminating evidence that had been found in Mary's house—two manila envelopes, one hundred rounds of bullets and three country-made revolvers.

The fat policeman walked in and leaned against the table. He turned his gaze to Mary and Manu and gave a crooked smile. 'Good evening friends, I am Inspector Rana Neogi.' He picked up one of the revolvers and ran a stubby forefinger down its barrel. 'From bows and arrows to guns, eh, madam Mary? Building your own little army to fight the police, is it? A people's army?' He locked eyes with her. 'But where is your general? Your great leader?'

Mary remained silent as the inspector went on: 'Is he hiding behind Mrs Mao's skirts? Or is he here? Right here in Calcutta? Hiding like a rat in the sewers, hanh? Your great leader has jumped from the sinking ship. Turned out to be just one more coward—like all great leaders.'

'He is no coward. As you will find out soon,' said Mary in a quiet voice.

'Oh? He is most definitely a coward, just as you are not. You are brave, very brave—all you innocent young people. Throwing away your lives to save Charu-babu's. What do you see in him I sometimes wonder? And where is he now, when you need him the most?'

'There is no revolution without sacrifice. I am prepared for it. We all are,' Mary returned.

'Indeed! What a noble sentiment,' the inspector sighed.

He pulled out a pack of cigarettes from his pocket. Slowly, deliberately, he drew a stick and sniffed delicately at it, as if he were savouring a glass of fine wine. The soft click of a lighter bursting into flame, the faint crackle of the stick being lit and then a hissing sound—like a piece of fish being thrown into a pan of sizzling oil, as the inspector plunged the glowing end of the cigarette into Mary's breast.

The smell of burning flesh curled into Manu's nostrils. A bitter stream of bile snaked into his mouth as the terror flooded through him, washing away every thought except one—survival. He had to somehow get out of this murderous stone-walled cage, get out before he was crushed alive in its fearsome jaws.

'See, it is like this madam—I am a chain smoker,' the inspector pursed his lips and blew out a cloud of smoke, 'and there is no ashtray here. So, I can keep smoking and stubbing out my cigarettes on you. Unless of course, you tell me where Charu-babu is. That way I can save my lungs and you can save—'

'Tell them, Mary! For god's sake, if you know where he is, then just tell them!' Manu screamed. The blood had left his face, his breath was short and ragged.

'Ah, the rich friend of the poor revolutionary. Or is it more than just friend, hanh?' the inspector smiled at Manu. 'I had almost forgotten about you.' He withdrew a ten-rupee note from the manila envelope and dangled it before Manu. 'This is your money isn't it? Your fingerprints are on these notes. Why have you been funding terrorists?'

'It's for her house rent,' Manu said.

'Two hundred rupees for rent! Does she live in the Victoria Memorial or what?' the inspector smirked.

'It's the truth. She said she had run out of money to pay her rent. I was just trying to help her,' Manu said.

'Leave him out of it. He's innocent,' Mary's voice was strangled. 'He has nothing to do with this. I am so sorry, so very sorry Manu,' she mumbled, almost to herself, an infinite sadness welling in her dark eyes.

'*Bah bah! Jail e boshe prem hocche!* Like two love birds in a cage, hanh? So touching,' said the inspector, with a smile that stopped short of his eyes.

'Please let him go,' Mary pleaded. 'I was...was...just using him. He doesn't know what the money was being spent on. He doesn't know anything.'

'Fine, I will let you friend go,' said the Inspector. 'But only if you tell us where Charu Majumdar is.'

'I don't know,' replied Mary.

'I see,' the Inspector said, gently rolling the cigarette between his thumb and forefinger, as if it was a string of prayer beads. 'I'm going to ask you one last time.'

'Please Mary!' Manu whimpered. 'Just tell him.'

Mary shook her head. 'I can't. I'm so sorry, Manu but I can't. I don't know.'

The inspector shrugged. 'Very well, then.' He jerked his head at the two constables who were standing guard by the door. 'You two can have her. Bring her to me when you are done.' He turned to Manu. 'But first let her watch her friend being taken care of,' he said.

Inspector Neogi brought the glowing end of his cigarette close to Manu's forehead. The strands of his hair crackled and curled and turned ochre from the heat. Moments later, the odour of burned flesh filled the air and the screams of the living joined the laments of the dead.

Inspector Neogi

Did Mary really not know where Charu Majumdar was or was she lying to the police? What was it that gave her the strength to bear the unspeakable atrocities of Inspector Neogi and his men? Was her love for the greater cause so great that she was willing to sacrifice herself as well as Manu for it? Or was her love for herself and Manu so little? Decades later, I still do not know the answers to these questions.

All I know is that no matter how many times the police questioned Mary about Charu-babu's whereabouts, her answer was always the same—*'I don't know.'* And after that, the inquisition would fall into a cruelly familiar pattern. There would a momentary hush and then the screams would begin. Screams that echoed inside the stone-walled jail, like the howls of a mad dog, as the police unleashed upon Mary all the weapons of their devilish arsenal—fire and water, iron rods and razor blades, pliers and chains, and a parade of cruel, hungry men who had been starved of women...

I have to stop. There are some things that one cannot speak of.

***

Three days had passed. Mary had been burnt, broken and torn from limb to limb. But she bore it all with the dead silence of a brick wall. I could not understand her. What stuff was she made of? What gave her such mad strength? The mere hint of torture had been enough to make even the great Galileo recant his proposition that the earth moved around the sun! Who did Mary think she was? Better than Galileo? Did she believe that her cause was greater than his? What madness had led her to believe that the changing of the world was more important than its turning?

And then there was Manu. Did she feel no remorse for having dragged her oldest friend into this inferno of her own making? For three days now, Manu had been in solitary confinement, trapped like a caged animal inside a tiny cell of stone and iron. Fortunately, he had been spared some of the worst excesses of the police who were focusing their energies on Mary. But he was in great pain and I could hear it every day in his increasingly mindless babblings and I could hear it in the long silences that followed.

By the evening of the fourth day, I was unable to bear their suffering anymore. It was then that I decided that I would do something about it. It wasn't an easy decision. Like a bee hovering over a garden of flowers, it is the historian's duty to dispassionately float above the great and small events of the times and deposit their essence into the honeycomb of history, without ruffling the petals of the past or the flowers of the future.

Unfortunately, I was turning out to be a bad historian (not to mention writing some of the worst mixed metaphors in history). But with every passing hour, I was becoming increasingly convinced of the necessity of action rather than observation—although mind you, even the mere act of observation can cause unpredictable changes to the observed, as good old Heisenberg taught us long ago. But to hell with Heisenberg, I said to myself. And to hell with history and hurricane-inducing Brazilian butterflies and gratuitous displays of gyaan! The only thing that mattered was Manu and Mary and I would do what it took to save them.

But do what and how? I thought about it long and hard until at last I settled upon a possible plan of action. As plans went, it was rather shaky and fraught with danger at every step. But it was the best that I could think of under the circumstances. Not one to let the grass grow beneath my feet, I immediately got down to work. I flew across to a deserted alley behind the east wing of the jail and concealed myself in a dark corner. After making sure that were no nosy parkers around, I closed my eyes and began to recite the Bahurupee Mantra.

Half an hour later, the golden sparrow had vanished. And in his place, stood Inspector Rana Neogi, in a spanking new uniform and full ceremonial regalia.

***

I waited until midnight so that I could be reasonably sure that the real Inspector Neogi was snoring in his bed. Tilting my police cap at a rakish angle, I gave my medals a quick spit and polish and strode towards the entrance of Alipore Jail. I was feeling tense as a tantrik without his chillum. I hoped I hadn't overdone the regalia, or the moustache for that matter. My heart lurched into my mouth but I marched forward bravely. There was no turning back now.

To my relief, my guise held up. As I approached the entrance, the guards snapped into a sharp salute and ushered me in. The rest of it was unexpectedly easy. The head jailor was awakened from his slumber and summoned before me. I informed him that I would be personally transferring Mary and Manu to the Lalbazar lockup. Immediately. For reasons that he did not need to know. Or check with anyone else for that matter. Or ask for any pettifogging paperwork. It was a top-secret operation. A matter of national security. Home Minister's orders etcetera etcetera.

So convincing was my acting, so impressive my appearance and so servile the head jailor, that he wilted under my orders like a lily in a thunderstorm. Manu and Mary were released from their cells and presented before me. I ordered for a police jeep, which in the interests of secrecy, I would drive myself (we yakshas are natural drivers, and quite frankly, compared to chariots, these modern cars are child's play). Before the befuddled jailor could start thinking, I marched the prisoners out and bundled them into a jeep that was parked outside.

Moments later, the jeep shot forward and the high walls of Alipore Jail fell away behind us. We were out of the frying pan. I could only hope that we weren't falling into the fire.

***

As I steered the jeep through the empty, midnight streets of Calcutta, I thought furiously of what to do next. Even to my bird brain, two things were clear. The first was to get Mary and Manu to a safe place. The second was for me to exit the stage and return to my rightful place in the wings. I had already caused too many ripples in the tides of time. If I didn't stop my meddling at once, they could swell into a giant wave that could wash away the future as we knew it.

But first things first—I needed a safe refuge to deposit my fugitive companions. I could only think of one. I stepped on the accelerator and a short drive later we were at Jodhpur Park, a few streets away from the prince's mansion. I brought the jeep to a stop and turned to face Manu and Mary. They were looking so dazed that I had to speak very slowly, as if to an idiot child.

'Listen carefully to what I am about to say. Your lives depend on it,' I said. 'First things first, I am not Inspector Neogi but only an impostor who looks like him. And it won't take long for the police to find that out. The moment they realise that they have been tricked, every constable in the city will be looking for you. You must hide. Go underground. And right now, there is only one place where you can go—the prince's house. So, go there as quickly as you can. You may be able to stay there for an hour or two. But not more. I'm sure the police already know where Manu lives and they will come searching for him there. So, you will have to find some other place to go hide. But now you must go home and then decide your next move. Go! Go now!'

Manu was goggling at me as if I had been speaking gibberish. 'Who are you?' he managed to say at last.

'It doesn't matter who I am. Stop asking stupid questions. Just go. Right now!' I threw open the doors of the jeep. 'Get out! Run!' I yelled.

Two ghost-like figures slowly emerged from the rear of the jeep, holding onto each other for support like an old couple. Run, fools, run, I muttered under my breath, they will be here soon! I had done my part. Now I could only pray that they would get away before the police arrived.

I waited until they had hobbled round the corner. As soon as they were out of sight, I started to recite the Bahurupee Mantra. Half an hour later I had returned to my sparrow form. With a flap of my wings, I took off into the sky and headed straight to Registan Manor. When I arrived there, I was relieved to see Manu and Mary sitting in the living room. The prince was there too, pacing furiously up and down the room. He seemed to be in a right royal tizzy.

***

'Do you hear me Manu? Can you even understand what I am saying?' the prince's voice sounded faintly inside Manu's head as if it were coming from a great distance.

Nothing was making sense to Manu. The arrest, the days and nights of torture, and now this theatre of the absurd, in which their tormentor, Inspector Neogi, had suddenly turned saviour. The whole world had gone mad! Or he had. Or was he trapped inside some sort of bizarre nightmare? He stared blankly at the vaguely familiar surroundings of this place that he had once called home.

'Not only are you in terrible danger, you have brought it right to my doorstep,' the prince threw up his hands in panic. 'If it was only you, I might even have managed to do something. Talked to the Commissioner for a pardon or something. But why the hell did you have to bring this Naxalite girl with you? Do you want to send us all to the gallows?'

Manu's gaze fell on the bloodied wreck seated beside him. Her body was a tapestry of angry burn marks and black bruises that stretched from her neck to her ankles. Her dark eyes were as dead as those of blind fishes that swam in the deepest oceans. Was she even Mary or one of the phantasms that had tormented him during those endless hours of solitary confinement?

'I am going to hand her over to the police. Right now,' the prince said.

'If you do that,' Manu heard himself speak, 'then you will have to hand me over as well. Mary and I are in this together—till the very end.'

He could not recognise his own voice. He could not understand what he was saying or why. He owed nothing but hate to this woman who had destroyed his life. In all the long hours of solitary confinement, he had lost count of the number of times he had cursed her for his plight. His anger had boiled over into a red-hot hate that had spread through his veins like molten metal.

And yet as he gazed at her now, this burnt, button-eyed, half-human, his hate evaporated like the morning dew and all that remained was pity. Yes, it was true that she had been responsible for his suffering. But she had paid the price for it, a far higher price than anyone should have to pay. Her pain had been too great and he would not let her endure even more.

He gently took her scarred hands into his and said: 'Raja-saab, we are in this together. I can't allow the police to get her again.'

'Are you mad Manu? Or just plain stupid?' the prince screamed. 'You want to risk your life for this woman? This Naxalite who has destroyed you? Who is she to you?'

'It doesn't matter. But I won't let anyone hurt her,' Manu replied.

'And what about me? What about my hurt? You disappear for days and then walk in like this at the dead of night with a wanted terrorist? Do you have any idea how worried I was for you all these days? I had nearly given you up for dead. I searched for you in every single hospital in Calcutta, even the morgues. I filed a missing person report with the police, met the Commissioner himself. The bastard didn't even tell me that you had been arrested.'

Manu remained silent as the prince went on: 'Do you know what is happening, you idiot? People are being taken to the Maidan at dawn and shot through their heads. Corpses are being thrown into the Hooghly. Young men and women are disappearing, just like that,' the prince snapped his fingers, 'and their families have no clue where they are. The police have become a law unto themselves. After Naxalbari, they won't stop at anything to get these Communist terrorists. According to the newspapers, this girl is with Charu Majumdar, the most wanted terrorist in India!'

'It's possible,' said Manu.

'Oh, it's possible is it? Then she won't be spared and neither will you,' he grabbed Manu by the shoulders and said: 'Look Manu, you are young, you have your whole life ahead of you. You have a business that you will inherit from me one day. You can marry, have children, make a life for yourself. Why are you throwing it all away for this mad woman and her mad revolution?'

'She's my friend and I have to help her. That's all,' Manu said. 'But I understand. It isn't right of us to put you into danger. We will leave.'

The prince stared blankly at Manu. His face turned grey and his shoulders slumped as if the weight of the world had fallen on it. 'You will leave?' he said in a low, hoarse voice. 'You will leave me, leave your home, throw away your future? All for the sake of this woman?'

'Yes. I am very sorry,' Manu's head sank to his chest. 'Raja-saab, you have been like a father to me. More than a father. But I can't leave her. Not in this state,' he rose from the sofa and held his hand out to Mary. 'Come, let's go.'

'No, I'm not going anywhere,' Mary said. Her voice was so feeble that it could barely be heard. 'Raja-saab is right. Please call the police, sir. I will give myself up.'

'Don't talk nonsense,' said Manu. 'You've caused enough trouble already. Just come with me. I'll figure out something.'

'No, Manu,' Mary freed herself from his grasp. 'I must give myself up. It's the only way. Please call the police, sir.'

The prince watched her curiously. After a while he said: 'I'm sorry, Manu. But Mary is right. I wish there was a better way out but unfortunately there isn't. I have no choice.'

He began to walk across to the telephone, when Manu blocked his path. 'I'm sorry, sir. But I have no choice either. We are going now. But I hope I will be able to come back one day to this place that I have always called home. Please forgive me if you can, Raja-saab.'

Taking hold of Mary's arm, he moved towards the front door. He was about to step out of the house when the prince called out from behind: 'Wait. Don't go.' Manu halted.

'There is a madness in you that I cannot understand,' said the prince, his voice sounding old and weary. 'But I suppose I will have to accept it. I don't want you to leave your home in this way. But you can't stay here either. It's far too dangerous—for all of us. You must go somewhere else.'

'That's what I was doing,' Manu said.

'But you have no place to go to, do you, you idiot!' the prince said.

'No, I don't,' Manu replied. 'But I'll think of—'

'It's best if you leave the thinking to me,' said the prince. He paced up and down the room, his eyebrows bunched in a frown. After a while he said: 'All right, here's what I suggest—I have a friend. He may be able to help you.'

But no sooner had he spoken, than I heard a familiar sound which made my feathers stand on end. It was too faint for a human to hear, but to my preternaturally sharp yaksha ears, it was clear as a bell—it was the growl of a police jeep, swiftly closing in on us like a hound that has caught the whiff of a hare.

Well, whoever was this friend that the prince was talking about, I hoped he was close at hand. Because in a matter of minutes, the police would be pounding on the door.

Jatayu Das

I was astonished and dismayed by the unseemly zeal of the Calcutta Police. It had hardly been an hour since we had made our great escape from Alipore Jail, and yet here they were—almost at our necks! It was a mystery how they had caught on to us so quickly, in spite of the fabulous job that I had done. (Although in hindsight, I probably should not have wished '*Hasta manana*' to the jailor as we were leaving...or cried '*Dilli ab door nahin,*' to the sentry standing guard at the entrance gate.)

Luckily the prince seemed to be doing a better job than me. You had to give it to the man's nerve. Even as we heard the police jeep screeching to a halt outside, he whisked Manu and Mary away through the back door, into the garden. His instructions were hurried but clear. Their only hope was to get out of Bengal as quickly as possible. Or they were sure to be captured in the manhunt that would inevitably follow. The first thing was to somehow reach the factory.

'If you can get to the factory,' said the prince, 'I will make arrangements for you to be taken to my friend's place. Once you reach there, you will be safe.'

'But who is this friend? Where does he stay?' asked Manu.

'Never mind all that!' the prince barked. 'There's no time for explanations! Besides, the less you know the better. That way you can't get my friend into trouble if the police catch you. Just trust me that if there is one person who can save your skins now, it is him. You just stay put with him until you hear back from me. But first you must reach the factory. You have to leave right now.'

'Go to the factory?' said Manu. 'At this time? But how can—'

'Walk! That's the only way. They are sure to check all cars. It's still dark. There's probably another three hours to go before day break. If you walk quickly, you may have just enough time to get to the factory. But you must be careful. Stay hidden in the shadows, avoid the main roads and watch out for the police vans. Once you reach the factory, someone will tell you what to do.'

'All right but—'

'No time for ifs and buts. Just go! If god is kind, perhaps we will meet again in better times. And one last thing, Manu—'

'Yes?'

'If you give up the woman, I may still be able to save you.'

'No,' Manu shook his head.

'I thought as much,' the prince sighed. 'All right then. What can I say? I only hope that you won't have to pay for your stupidity with your life. But enough talk. Go now. Leave!'

We left. And not a moment too soon. Even as we slipped out of the garden and into the street, I heard the heavy tread of police boots clattering over the marble porch of the mansion. The neighbourhood was swarming with policemen and the situation was looking grim. But just then, help came to us from unexpected quarters.

Like Kali, the fearsome yet loving goddess after whom she had been named, the great city of Calcutta now bestowed upon us the benediction of a moonless night. The darkness wrapped itself around us like a protective talisman, as our shadowy figures shuffled through the empty streets of the city. After a nerve-wracking journey, we finally arrived at the factory at the crack of dawn. We were received at the gate by the watchman, Jatayu Das, who immediately hustled us into the parking lot. A dilapidated goods lorry stood there, its carrier filled with boxes of bushings and bearings.

'Raja-saab telephoned me two hours ago,' Jatayu said. 'I have my orders. I am to drive you out of here,' he jerked his head at the lorry. 'Get in there, into the carrier. Quick, quick.'

Manu stared suspiciously at the bald, middle-aged watchman. With his thin, mouldering moustache and nervous manner, he certainly did not seem to be the type who would be able to carry out a rescue mission. 'You are driving us? Where?' Manu asked.

'Can't tell you anything, sir. Top secret,' Jatayu whispered conspiratorially. 'Just get into the carrier and hide behind the boxes. And stay there until I tell you that it is safe to come out. Come quickly! There is no time to lose.'

'But where are we going?' asked Manu, as he and Mary clambered into the carrier.

Jatayu Das pressed a finger to his lips. '*Kono proshno noy* (no questions),' he said and sat himself down in the driver's seat.

***

For two days and two nights, we had been travelling. But we seemed to be nowhere near our mysterious destination. Every so often, I would scan the horizon but all that greeted my eyes were the vast plains of Uttar Pradesh stretching out for miles in every direction—a flat, brown, monotone of baked earth.

Once again, we found ourselves on the same Grand Trunk Road that twenty years ago, had carried young Manhoos from the forests of Betla to the greatest city of the east. Except this time, we were travelling in the opposite direction, tossed inside a creaky goods lorry instead of an Oxford Morris. Manu and Mary were hidden inside the carrier, while I was trying to keep my perch on one of the boxes. The gut-wrenching tension that I felt every time we approached a police checkpost, was making me feel quite sick.

But on the bright side, we were far away from Calcutta—a thousand miles at least by my reckoning. I was finally beginning to feel a little more relaxed. So was Jatayu Das. He released Mary and Manu from the carrier and allowed them to sit beside him in the driver's cabin.

'In UP, there is no need to be scared of the police, babu,' Jatayu smiled. 'There are hardly any of them around. The problem in these parts is something quite different.'

'What is that?' asked Manu.

'Dacoits!' Jatayu whispered. 'But you don't have to worry about them, babu. I have taken precautions,' he furtively scanned the surroundings and then slid his hand below the seat, to pull out a flat, curved knife. 'Bhujali. Nepali weapon. For dacoits,' he said, brandishing the knife proudly.

'Are we going to Nepal then?' asked Manu. He did not expect an answer because until now Jatayu had flatly refused to divulge any information about their destination.

'Not Nepal, sir. Rishikesh,' replied Jatayu.

Rishikesh! My ears pricked up. It was my kind of place. Named after the tresses of Vishnu, Rishikesh was bristling with history. It was here that Lord Rama had performed his penance for the sin of killing Ravana. My spirits soared at the thought that we were not bound for some dusty, provincial hamlet of UP, but the hallowed land of Rishikesh, where the sunbeams reflected off the snowy peaks of the mighty Himalayas, shimmering like molten gold in the limpid waters of the holy Ganga.

My hopes were now rising as rapidly as my penchant for purple prose. Unlikely as it had seemed only two days ago, I began to wonder if our Bhujali-bearing driver might indeed be able to rescue us from the clutches of the khaki-clad Ravanas we were fleeing. Would history grant Jatayu the triumph that myth had denied him?

Even Manu seemed to have perked up a little at the news. He sat bolt upright and asked: 'Rishikesh? Really? That's where we are going?'

'Yes, sir,' replied the driver. 'Now that we are far away from Calcutta, I think I can tell you. Raja-saab has asked me to take you to his friend's house in Rishikesh.'

'Who is this friend? What's his name?' Manu asked.

'Mahesh Prasad Varma,' replied Jatayu.

'Mahesh Prasad Varma? Never heard Raja-saab talk of him before,' Manu said. 'Where does he stay?'

'At Chaurasi Kutiya Ashram,' Jatayu replied.

'What!' Manu exclaimed.

'That's what Raja-saab said. I am to take you to Chaurasi Kutiya Ashram. Once you are there, you are to ask for Varma-ji and he will take care of everything,' Jatayu Das' eyes narrowed. 'Yes, Manu sir, I know what you are thinking—highly suspicious.'

Blackbird

It had been an hour since we had crossed the holy town of Haridwar. Dense, green forests of pine, fir and juniper, rose high above the steep, winding road that led to Rishikesh. Jatayu Das dropped us off at the Lakshman Jhula and left. We crossed the bridge to the other bank of the Ganga and after a short walk, we arrived before the gates of Chaurasi Kutiya Ashram.

It was a picturesque place—standing upon a large hillock that overlooked the swift flowing waters of the Ganga. Even as we dithered in front of the gates wondering what to do next, a bearded young foreigner clad in flowing white robes approached us.

'Namaste,' said the man, joining his palms in greeting. 'Please come with me. Guru-ji has been expecting you.'

'Guru-ji?' Manu frowned. 'Well...actually we are supposed to meet Mr Mahesh Prasad Varma.'

'Guru-ji has many names,' the foreigner smiled. 'Who knows, Mahesh Prasad Varma may well be one of them? But everyone here calls him Maharishi—the great sage. Maharishi Mahesh Yogi. But what's in a name, my friend, innit? You've come to the right place. Come on now, follow me.'

With his blotchy white skin and tousled brown hair, he looked like any other firang who came to India to discover his soul. But there was something striking about him, something very special which I could not put my finger on. Maybe it was the dreamy eyes glinting behind the round, Gandhian eyeglasses, the delicately boned fingers that spoke of great artistry or the soft, musical quality of his voice. I found him rather impressive. But Manu's reaction was the opposite of mine. Where I saw gentle eyes and a musical voice, he only saw the unkempt hair and the scraggy beard. Where I saw a poet, he saw—

'A hippy,' Manu whispered into Mary's ear. 'This fellow looks like one of those foreigner hippies that the newspapers talk about,' he looked around suspiciously, 'God knows what sort of a place the prince has sent us to. We must be careful.'

We walked down a winding gravel path on either side of which stood rows of square stone huts with domed, egg-shaped roofs. 'Those are meditation chambers,' explained our escort when he noticed Manu staring curiously at them. 'There are eighty-four of them—hence the name Chaurasi Kutiya Ashram. Each chamber represents a different yoga asana. Together they represent the whole range of human life. Man! That's mind-blowing, innit, my friend? I mean—I've seen everything, I've done everything. I got everything that a man can want. But it's only after coming here that I've figured out the truth.'

'Which is?' asked Manu.

'That all you need is a cave,' said the man. 'Yeah, a cave and love—that is all you need,' he paused as if stunned by the brilliance of his own insight. After a moment he said: 'Although to be fair, Ringo needs digestive pills as well. The poor sap can't handle the food in this place. Too spicy he says. Yoko and I love it though. Yeah, we got all we need here. I think you will too. What's your name by the way? Where are you guys from?' he asked.

'I'm Manu. She's Mary. We've come from...Calcutta,' Manu replied hesitantly.

'Mary, eh?' the foreigner gave her a curious glance. 'Mary...eh... hmm...I see. She seems to have seen a lot of trouble, lately, eh?' he started to hum a tune to himself. 'Trouble...Mary...Mother Mary... hmm.... hmmm...when I'm in times of trouble...hmmm...hmmm.'

'And what's your good name?' asked Manu.

'I'm John. I'm from Britain,' replied the man. 'Yeah, I know. It's like across the universe, innit? And yet here we are my friend, together—on the same hill, under the same sun. Both of us searching for the same thing—peace. Yes, my friend. That's what everyone is searching for, innit? Peace and happiness.'

'Definitely a hippie,' Manu whispered to Mary. 'The next thing you know, he'll be offering us *charas*.'

But Mary was silent. She hadn't spoken a word since we had

fled from Calcutta. She seemed to be still trapped inside the dark dungeons of Alipore Jail. Her eyes were still dead as pebbles.

'Your friend looks as if she's suffered a lot,' said John. 'But that's the way of the world, innit, mate? Those who dream must pay the price for their dreams.'

I was beginning to like this fellow a lot but Manu still didn't seem too impressed. He rolled his eyes as we continued to walk through the ashram grounds. Soon we arrived before a high colonnaded building with a wide verandah.

'Guru-ji is inside,' said John. 'Go and meet him. He will help you,' his gentle gaze fell on Mary. 'I hope you find peace here, my friend. Remember—you may be a dreamer, but you're not the only one.'

***

Guru-ji turned out to be a short, plump man with a salt and pepper beard and a tendency to break into a high-pitched giggle for no ostensible reason. The moment we entered his room, he chuckled and said: 'Come, come, my son. I have been waiting for you.'

'Actually, we have come to meet Mahesh Prasad Varma,' Manu said.

A gale of laughter greeted his words. 'Mahesh Prasad Varma!' Guru-ji giggled. 'I had almost forgotten that I was once called that. Only my oldest friends know me by that name. Here they call me Maharishi,' he tried to look modest. 'Although I make no claims to any such greatness.'

'You and the prince are old friends?' asked Manu.

'Oh yes, very old,' said the Maharishi. He went on to tell Manu how he had met the prince twenty years ago in Registan, and how he had stood by his side when he had been forced by Patel and Menon to give up his kingdom.

'Surya beta, I said to him—you have lost a kingdom. So what?' the Maharishi chuckled. 'Build a new kingdom for yourself! Build an empire! As you know, I am a *trikaal darshi*—past, present, future, I can see everything. So, I looked into Surya beta's future and I told him to go east. Go east, young man! I said to him. That is where you will find your fortune. He took my advice and went to Calcutta. He has done well for himself, I believe. Isn't that so?'

'Yes, Guru-ji,' Manu replied.

'Yes, Surya may have risen high in life. But not so high that he has forgotten his old guru,' Maharishi waved his hands around, 'you see this ashram? It is the world headquarters of Transcendental Meditation—they call it TM—a practice which I have discovered. Ancient wisdom and modern energy—that is the gift that we are trying to give to the world. But without Surya's generosity I would not have been able to do it. I am happy that he has sent you here. Welcome, my friend, as you take your first steps with us on this great journey.'

'Thank you, Guru-ji,' Manu said. 'We are grateful that you have accepted us into your ashram. But how long can we stay here? I mean at some point of time we have to—'

The Maharishi lifted a hand and cut him off. 'Time? What is time? Nothing. Love. Love is all that matters. My old friend Surya has asked me to take care of you. I have given him my word that I shall. That is all. You shall stay here as my son and—' he stopped, as his gaze fell on Mary. 'Are the two of you married?' he asked.

Manu's cheeks turned brick-red. He shook his head. 'No matter, no matter,' giggled the Maharishi. 'As long as there is love, that is enough. Marriage is of no importance. We are not concerned with such worldly matters here. The two of you can stay together or in separate quarters—whatever you wish and for as long as you wish. Here we have enough room for everyone,' he stretched out his hands and placed them on Manu and Mary's foreheads. 'My poor children,' he sighed. 'I can see that you have suffered. You are broken. You must heal yourselves. Transcendental Meditation will help you. Come now, free your mind of all thought and chant with me. Om!'

Manu was a little taken aback by the request. But he felt it would be churlish of him to not do what his host wanted. He shut his eyes and began to chant. After a while, he felt an unexpected peace come over him. He sneaked a quick look at Mary. Her eyes were closed and she looked calmer than he had seen her in a long time.

Manu, Mary and the Maharishi continued to chant. And after a while, the primordial sound of the universe was joined by the strumming of guitars and a quartet of soft voices humming:

'Blackbird singing in the dead of night,
Take these broken wings and learn to fly...'

***

A word of unsolicited advice to urban Naxals, Tukde-Tukde, Khan Market and other gangs and assorted enemies of the Indian State. If ever you find yourselves in times of trouble, do not seek out Mother Mary, but get into a godman's ashram. Don white robes, wear a beatific smile and greet all and sundry with a Hare Krishna and it is unlikely that you will ever be suspected of being a seditious son of a bitch.

The strategy was working for Manu and Mary, at least. Like the Pandavas in agnatavaas (anonymous exile), they were finally safe from the prying eyes of the state. In any case, the Calcutta Police was too busy trying to put out the raging fires of Naxalism in Bengal, to be bothered about an ashram in remote Rishikesh.

But the ashram gave Manu and Mary much more than just a safe house. It healed them and mended their broken wings.

Ever since she had escaped from Alipore, I had my doubts whether Mary would ever be able to recover from the trauma of her imprisonment. She had fallen into an abyss of the blackest depression and we despaired if she would ever be able to climb out of it. Day after day she did nothing but lay on her bed and stare at the ceiling. She refused to bathe or eat or change her clothes and would often burst into uncontrollable fits of sobbing. On particularly bad days, she would lick the raw earth and stuff clods of mud into her mouth. On the rare occasions she could manage to fall asleep, she would wake up screaming, her body drenched in sweat. I wondered if the ghouls of the past would ever stop scrabbling at her with their bloodied claws.

But even as she wrestled her demons, Manu stood by her side like a rock. He bathed and fed her and persuaded her to go walking with him in the neighbouring forests and hills. He took her to the banks of the Ganga where they would watch the sunsets together. There were moments when it almost felt as if they were back together in Betla, wandering about in the forest by themselves. Except in those days, she used to chatter nineteen to the dozen, while now she would hardly utter a sound. But Manu did not give up. He made her attend meditation sessions and chant with the other residents of the ashram. He told her stories and jokes and even sang lullabies to put her to sleep. She had become almost like the child he had never had. And slowly, ever so slowly, like a sapling sprouting out of a long dormant seed, Mary began to heal.

One evening, when they were sitting on the banks of the Ganga, their feet dabbling in its clear waters, Mary took Manu's hands in hers and said: 'Thank you.'

'For what?' asked Manu. A flood of relief rushed through him in great, happy, waves.

'For everything,' Mary replied. 'If it hadn't been for you, I don't know...what...I don't...' It was the longest sentence she had spoken since coming to Rishikesh.

'Shush, it's all right,' said Manu. 'We are together. That's all that matters.' She looked up at him, her eyes glistening, as she pressed her lips against his.

Some of you would probably like to know where her lips pressed next. But I am afraid I cannot tell you that. I am a historian not Miss Malini. The reason I even mention this entirely private episode, is because it is a moment of historical significance—it is the first sign that broken-winged Mary is learning to fly again.

But as you are aware, the flapping of wings can sometimes be the harbinger of hurricanes.

The Symonds Company

Just as all politicians named Gandhi are not equally astute (or hirsute), all hurricanes do not hurry at the same speed. And the one that had been set into motion in the spring of 1968 by the fluttering of Mary's broken wings, was particularly tardy. It was to arrive only five years later, on 24 April 1973, when a gang of lumbermen from the Symonds Company trooped into the foothills of the Garhwali Himalayas.

As the lumbermen marched into an ancient forest of pine and ash trees, armed with axes and saws, they were greeted by an astonishing spectacle, that made them drop their jaws (and their saws as well). Blocking their path was a group of one hundred women who were—

But I am getting ahead of myself.

In my eagerness to ride into the storm, I have omitted to mention the five-year lull that preceded it. But well...would you rather listen to the Ride of the Valkyries, or know how their horses were saddled prior to aforesaid ride? However, keeping in mind my duties as a chronicler, let me pick up the threads from where I had last dropped them.

***

With Manu by her side, Mary was slowly climbing out of the dark abyss into which she had fallen. But more than him, I think it was the magic of the Himalayas that was healing her. The mountain forests brought to her a peace that she had not known for years. The swift flowing rivers and the little villages along the outskirts of the forests would transport her back to the Betla of her childhood. In the course of her wanderings, she discovered the village of Reni and it soon became her favourite rendezvous. It stood on a hill slope overlooking the Alakananda river and Mary could sit there for hours, watching its swirling white waters, and letting its currents gently wash away the trauma of Calcutta.

In the beginning, the villagers did not know what to make of this stranger who had appeared out of nowhere and would not talk to anyone. But over time, a quiet friendship began to grow between them and Mary. They would share the occasional cup of tea with her and chat about their humdrum lives. They would tell her stories of the mountains and the forests and the river. And Mary would remember the stories of her own childhood and the darkness would lift from her heart.

Manu on the other hand was becoming increasingly restless. Life had become like a cucumber—nice but bland. It was nice to do nothing except eat, sleep, and do TM. It was nice to have no worries. It was nice to snuggle up to Mary in the cold nights. But every day was yesterday once more. What Manu craved for was the rough and tumble of running the factory, the thrust and parry of business and the bright lights of Calcutta. Given a chance, he would have gone back there in a heartbeat. But the prince would hear nothing of it. Every week, he would write to Manu with strict instructions for him to stay put in Rishikesh. The Naxal situation was going from bad to worse and the Calcutta Police was on the warpath. The mere whiff of suspicion was enough for people to be whisked away to Lalbazar, where they would be brutally tortured or worse, have their brains blown out in pre-dawn encounters. Until the situation improved, there was absolutely no question of Manu's returning to Calcutta.

One evening, unable to bear the prospect of yet another session of Transcendental Meditation, Manu decided to go for a long walk. By the end of it, he arrived at a few conclusions. First—that long walks were an excellent way of clearing one's head. Second—that his lotus-eater life was driving him crazy. Third—that his parasitic existence off Raja-saab's money was hurting his self-respect and making him feel terribly insecure. Fourth—that he had seen many buses and trucks plying on the Rishikesh-Dehradun highway but hardly any garages. Fifth—that a good vehicle repair workshop in Dehradun was likely to do brisk business and help him earn his own living until it was safe to return to Calcutta.

Within a month, Manu and Mary bade farewell to Chaurasi Kutiya Ashram and moved into a small rented cottage off Rajpur Road in Dehradun. The landlord had been a little suspicious of their marital status but Manu had managed to convince him that they were as sanskari as the next couple. Within three months, he took a small loan from Raja-saab to set up a spanking new vehicle repair workshop in the Ghanta Ghar area of Dehradun. The signboard that was affixed to the entrance read:

Vishwakarma Motor Works

Your car is our karma

Within six months, Manu's garage was humming along quite nicely. Meanwhile, Mary had managed to find herself a teacher's job in the nearby primary school. By now she had become good friends with the villagers of Reni, and spent much of her spare time with them. In other words, by the winter of 1968, both Mary and Manu were gainfully occupied and quietly happy. In later years, they were to fondly remember their days in Dehradun as the most peaceful time of their lives.

Now, peace may be very good for the soul but it is very bad for history. As a colleague of mine, Graham Greene, had once remarked: *'In Italy, for thirty years under the Borgias, they had warfare, terror, murder and bloodshed, but they produced Michelangelo, Leonardo da Vinci and the Renaissance. In Switzerland they had brotherly love, and 500 years of democracy and peace—and what did that produce? The cuckoo clock.'*

Therefore, in keeping with the dismal demands of my profession, I must willy-nilly, relegate these, the happiest and most peaceful days of school teacher Mary and garage owner Manu to this short footnote. I must now advance the cuckoo clock of history by a full five years to the morning of 24 April 1973—when the lumbermen of the Symonds Company, a sports equipment manufacturing company, are trooping into the Garhwali Himalayas, to cut down three hundred trees for the purpose of making tennis racquets and cricket bats.

***

Armed with a license to chop, issued by the Forest Department of UP, the lumbermen of the Symonds Company had marched into an ancient grove of pine and fir in Chamoli taluk, when they were greeted by an astonishing spectacle that made them stop in their tracks. A hundred women were standing before the trees, their arms wrapped around them. Their frail bodies had turned into living shields of flesh and blood defying the sharp blades of the lumbermen's axes that glinted menacingly at their trunks (the women's and the trees', both).

As the lumbermen advanced upon the women, their voices erupted into a fierce battle cry—*'A chopped head is cheaper than a chopped tree.'*

Among the many women whose voices echoed through the foothills of the Himalayas on that glorious morning, were Gaura Devi, Bali Devi, Suraksha Devi, Sudesha Devi, Bachni Devi, Virushka Devi and last but not least—Mary Devi.

Confronted by these damnably difficult devis whose fierceness matched Durga Devi's, the lumbermen tried to get rid of them with the usual methods. They first tried to mansplain to them why it was essential to cut down ancient Himalayan forests to make bats and racquets for rich city dwellers. Could the women not understand that without a bracing culture of good, clean sports, no nation could ever become strong and healthy? And did they not want to see a strong and healthy India? How could they be so selfish, so unpatriotic? Freedom fighters had sacrificed their very lives for the nation. Couldn't they spare a few ash trees?

But the women led by Gaura Devi argued, that while they understood that tennis and cricket were important for building a strong nation, so were dal and chawal. *Jaan hain to jahaan hai*, they said, wagging their fingers sagely at the lumbermen, where there is life, there is the world. It is only after one ate, that one could play games. But if the forest was cut down, where would they get firewood to cook their food? Where would they find the herbs and berries that kept *them* strong and healthy enough to walk for miles every day, to collect a pot of drinking water?

Annoyed by the subversive logic of their arguments, the loggers now did what men usually do in such circumstances. They shouted at the women, abused them and threatened them with rape. And when that didn't scare them, they brandished their axes and guns and told them to get lost or else...

But the women refused to budge and their cries grew so loud that they could be heard in every nook and corner of the Terai. Village after village joined the resistance—Reni, Laata, Henwalghati. Homes emptied out as wave after wave of women joined their sisters in the forest. They tied rakhis around the trunks of their beloved arboreal brothers and kept guard over them in round-the-clock vigils. Eventually, after a four-day stand-off, the lumbermen had to beat a retreat and the women celebrated their victory.

But Mary did not join in their celebrations. She was not fooled. Twenty years after Betla, history was repeating itself in the Himalayas. Mary had learnt its lessons well. She knew that the war was far from over. The road ahead was long and hard and many more battles would have to be fought to save the forest. But save it she would, even if it cost her her life.

Mistress Mary Quite Contrary

That evening when Mary returned home, the Binaca Geetmala countdown was playing on the new Murphy radio that Manu had bought a few days ago. He was lounging on the sofa, a tumbler of whisky-soda in his hand and his head swaying to the latest song by Mukesh.

Manu looked up at Mary and said: 'Where were you the whole day? I was beginning to get worried.'

'In Chamoli,' replied Mary.

'Chamoli? Isn't that where the protests are going on?' Manu asked.

'Yes. That's where I was,' Mary replied. 'Those dogs from the Symonds Company are trying to cut down the forest and—'

Manu set aside his whisky and threw up his hands in exasperation. 'Mary! Mary! Mary! Why can't you just live peacefully like everyone else? Why do you have keep going off on your wild goose chases?'

'How can you say that, Manu?' Mary replied. 'How can I just sit and watch when a whole forest is being cut down in front of my eyes? That last time it happened I was too young to do anything about it. But this time—'

'Betla is history, Mary!' Manu cut her off. 'It's over and done with. How long can you remain stuck in the past? Can't you just forget about it?'

'How can you say that, Manu?' Mary said. 'I can never forget what happened in Betla. It's happening here again and I'm going to fight as hard as I can, to stop it.'

Manu gulped down his drink and poured himself another. 'Mary, just how many useless struggles will it take for you to learn your lesson? You wasted ten years of your life for your stupid Communism.

You were jailed. Tortured. We've spent five years here, hiding from the police! And what has come of your so-called struggle? Who has it helped? Where is your grand revolution now? Nowhere. It's over and done with. It's dead.'

'It is not!' Mary said, her eyes flashing in anger. 'The struggle—'

'—is finished,' Manu cut her off. 'The Naxals have all been killed or captured. Even your Charu Majumdar is dead!'

'What!' Mary gasped. Her face turned ashen as she slumped into a chair. 'Charu-babu is dead?' she said at last in a ragged voice. 'How do you know? How...when...when did this happen?'

'Last year, in July,' replied Manu. 'He died in police custody. Raja-saab wrote to me about it.'

'Last year? And you're telling me now!'

'I didn't want to hurt you,' Manu placed his hand on her shoulder. 'And I didn't want to tell you today either. But sooner or later, you have to face reality.'

Mary buried her face in her hands. Her shoulders were shaking as she sobbed and it took a while before she could recover herself. 'I suppose I always knew,' she mumbled. 'I think I always knew in my heart that he would go before any of us. He was too good for us, too good for this world. Such a wonderful man...so full of life, so full of dreams...'

They both remained silent until Mary spoke again: 'You know something, Manu, when we came here five years ago, I wanted to die. But I couldn't. I suppose I love life too much. So I tried my best to put the past behind me. I tried to love you. I tried to build a future with you. But you know what, Manu? The past never leaves you. It just keeps coming back, again and again. Twenty years ago, they destroyed Betla. Now they want to—'

'Mary, stop! Just stop!' Manu exclaimed. 'And listen to me for just once in your life. I know how much it hurts you to see these forests being cut down. But can you stop it? The government is too strong. There's too much money at stake. Why are you getting yourself dragged into this mess? Can't you see that it's a lost cause?'

'It's not,' Mary sat upright and squared her shoulders. The old fire blazed in her eyes as she said: 'Things are different this time. In Betla, we were weak, we were alone. But this time we are not. Every village in the Terai, thousands of people are willing to give up their lives to save the forest. Gaura Devi, Vimla-ji, Chandi Bhatt-ji, Sunderlal-ji—we are all together. The press is with us. The newspapers have already started writing about our protests. They are even calling it the Chipko Movement. People from all over India are supporting us. And I'm telling you that we will win. This time we are going to stop those butchers. This time our struggle will succeed.'

'When will you stop this madness!' Manu grabbed her by the shoulders and shook her hard. 'We have finally managed to make something of our lives. We live in a nice place, we have a nice home. The business is running well. The police aren't breathing down our necks anymore. Why can't we just be like any other normal couple? Why can't we enjoy life a little, grow old together? Why can't you leave the world to its problems and just be happy?'

'Happy? Yes, I would like to be happy,' replied Mary. 'Who wouldn't? But, do you know what makes you happy? Does anyone?'

'You are hopeless!' said Manu. 'Just hopeless!'

***

From that day onwards, something changed between Mary and Manu. There was a sudden shift in their relationship, as if an invisible switch had been flicked. They argued more than they talked and remained silent more than they argued. Manu's efforts to dissuade Mary from getting involved in the Chipko Movement only seemed to make her resolve grow stronger. It was as if she was back to her old Communist days. She was in the forefront of the protests, hugging trees and camping in the forests for days on end, leaving poor Manu with only his whisky and Binaca Geetmala for company.

Like leaves carried on a mountain river, Manu and Mary were drifting apart again. I do not think they had stopped caring for each other yet. But perhaps they had started caring a little less, perhaps they had become a little less important for each other. After all, they were on the wrong side of thirty—at that juncture of life, when middle-age lurks menacingly in the wings, causing one to stumble over the familiar lines that one is expected to recite from this point on. And soon to be middle-aged Mary and Manu were searching for the answers to that impossible but increasingly urgent question, 'What Is the Meaning of Life?'

If Mary had started to believe that her purpose in life was to save the forests, Manu was quite sure that his wasn't. His dreams of making Regal Bearings into a name to reckon with, had become more important and more urgent than ever before. Like the Pandavas, he was itching to end his enforced Himalayan agnatavaas and return to his Kurukshetra in Calcutta. But the prince would hear nothing of it and with every passing day, Manu's frustration became more intense.

But one January afternoon, in the winter of Manu's discontent, he received a letter that raised his hopes. As soon as Mary returned home, he sat her down at the dining table and said: 'I have wonderful news, Mary! We can go back home!'

Mary stared blankly at him. 'What do you mean?'

'What do you think I mean? We can go back to our home! To Calcutta!' Manu waved the prince's letter excitedly and said: 'Read this. Raja-saab writes that it may be safe to return to Calcutta in a few months' time. He says that ever since Siddhartha Shankar Ray took over as Chief Minister last year, the situation has been improving fast. Siddhartha Shankar has broken the back of the Naxal movement. Almost all the big fish have been either caught or killed. Things are finally getting back to normal.'

'So, it's all over is it?' Mary said softly, as if to herself.

'Let's hope so. You know, Raja-saab says he has inside information that the police may close the old case files—which means yours and mine. Isn't that wonderful?'

'Yes, it is.'

'We will still have to be careful, of course, until the situation is completely normal. But Raja-saab says that should happen soon—six months to a year perhaps. After that we can go back home! We can live freely once again. Do you hear me, Mary? We will be free again! Free!'

There was a strange look in Mary's eyes as she looked up at Manu. 'That is wonderful news Manu,' she ran her fingers down his chin. 'It's nice to see you so happy. You're looking just like a little boy.'

'I'm feeling like one too! I can't wait to get back home! We will have to start winding up things here soon. The garage shouldn't be a problem. Himatsingka Motor Works has been eyeing it for a while. I should be able to get a decent amount of money if I sell it to them.

Meanwhile, I think you should give notice to your school that you won't be around much longer.'

Mary did not speak. She was gazing out of the window at the mist-covered hills in the distance. After a while she said: 'I am sorry, Manu. But I cannot go back to Calcutta.'

Manu stared at her. 'What do you mean?' he asked.

'Please forgive me if you can Manu. But I can't go with you,' Mary replied. 'This is my home and I'm staying here.'

***

They were standing on Platform No. 1 of Dehradun Railway Station. In another two minutes the Doon Express would pull out of the station and begin its eastward journey towards Howrah Junction.

'So, time to say goodbye?' said Manu as he clasped Mary's hand.

'No goodbyes. I am sure we will meet again,' replied Mary, 'if you want to, that is. I know how badly I've behaved with you Manu... after all that you have done for me. I'm...sorry Manu. I really am.'

'It's all right. I'm getting used to it,' Manu smiled.

Now that the moment of parting had come, he didn't quite know what to feel. There was the joy of returning home after almost six years. But his happiness was soured by the sadness of returning alone. He had tried his best to convince Mary to join him but his pleas had fallen on deaf ears. It was the Himalayas that had given meaning to her life, Mary had told him. She had found friends here, she had found new purpose and new energy. And much as she loved Manu, she could not leave the mountains and the forests and go back to Calcutta. She was terribly sorry for what she was doing. She would never be able to repay the debt that she owed to Manu and she could only hope that he would forgive her.

In the beginning, Manu had been deeply hurt. But when he calmed down and thought about it, he did not have the heart to blame her. How could he? The mountains had given her peace and hope, and Calcutta only pain and suffering. What was there for her except the pieces of her broken dreams?

A shrill whistle sounded. The station master was waving a green flag. 'I have to go now,' Manu said. 'But I will write to you. And I'll come and see you whenever I can.'

'I hope you will,' Mary said. She ran her fingers gently across his cheeks. 'And Manu...I just wanted to say something before you go.'

'Yes?' asked Manu

'You are the nicest, kindest person I have ever known. Please don't change,' said Mary.

'I'll try. But I can't promise,' Manu smiled as he climbed into the train. 'Goodbye, Mary.' With a grunt and a whistle and a cloud of steam, the Doon Express heaved out of the station. Manu leaned out of the door, waving at Mary's receding figure, until she was out of sight.

A few moments later, he settled down in his seat, feeling a little empty. He was gazing through the window pane, when he noticed his reflection staring back at him. How old he looked...flecks of grey salted his once dark hair. The lines on his forehead were now clearly visible. The heaviness of time had spread across his face like slowly congealing blood. He wasn't young anymore—already thirty-seven, mid-way upon the journey of his life and slouching steadily towards inevitable middle-age.

But he wasn't there yet, he told himself. He was still young. Young enough to dream, young enough to take another stab at life—the life that had been put on hold for six long years. But at long last, his Himalayan exile was finally over. He was returning to his lost kingdom. An inexplicable feeling came over him—one that made him feel happy and guilty at the same time.

And as the Doon Express shot forward towards the city of Kali, he heard a voice whispering inside his head—a single word repeating itself like a drumbeat to the rhythmic clatter of the train's wheels: Free! Free! Free!

Book Four

The Prodigal Returns

In Registan Manor in Jodhpur Park, Prince Surya Pratap Singh was awaiting Manu's return with much anxiety. As soon as Manu walked in, the prince enfolded him in a bear hug. 'Oh, how happy I am to see you again, Manu! Thank god you're here at last! You don't know how much I have missed you.'

Manu bent down and touched the prince's feet. 'How are you Raja-saab?' he asked. 'Is everything okay?'

'No, Manu beta,' the prince replied. 'Nothing is okay.'

'Why? What has happened?' asked Manu.

'I'll tell you everything,' said the prince. 'But first you freshen up and let's have lunch. It's been so many years since we have had a meal together.'

That afternoon, after lunch, the prince told Manu what had happened. 'To put it briefly, I'm in trouble, Manu. The business has gone to the dogs and apart from that—' the prince paused.

'Yes?' asked Manu.

'How do I say this, beta,' the prince sighed. 'But I've lost a lot of money in this miserable film business.'

'I see,' said Manu. He wasn't surprised. He only hoped the losses weren't too bad. 'How much money?'

'Too much, too much,' the prince groaned. 'I have managed to produce three flops in a row. The last film especially—*Beder Chhele Jochhon (Jochhon, Son of the Snake Charmers).* It's been a box-office disaster. I have no idea why—it had such a great storyline. Jochhon, the son of a poor snake charmer falls in love with the rich zamindar's daughter. But naturally, the zamindar cannot tolerate such nonsense. He sends his goondas to thrash the boy and then...anyway, you get the idea...romance, fights, nagin dance—it had everything. First time in Bengali cinema, the hero and villain do Kung-fu fighting in the climax scene. I spent a fortune making the film. I was sure it would run for at least three hundred days. But instead of a super hit that bloody *Beder Chhele* turned out to be a super flop. This public, I tell you! God knows what they want!'

'How much money did you lose?' asked Manu.

'Nearly one lakh,' the prince said, staring shamefacedly at his feet.

'One lakh! But where did so much money come from?'

'From the business, of course. Where else?'

'And you say the business is doing badly?'

'Terrible,' the prince sighed. 'After you left, everything just collapsed. Sales are half of what they used to be. So is production. Lockouts, machine failures, power cuts—one problem after another. It's been a nightmare. And I have been so busy with my films that I've hardly had any time for the factory,' the prince looked up at Manu. 'But now that you are back, Manu beta, I am sure that things will be much better.'

'I'll try my best. You know I used to feel so guilty sitting uselessly in Dehradun, unable to help you in any way,' Manu said.

'That's all right. Now you will have enough and more to do. Manu, I want you to take charge of the factory. Run it like you used to in the old days.'

'You want to leave everything to me, Raja-saab? And what about you? Are you planning to do more films?'

The prince almost jumped up in alarm. 'Are you mad? No more films for me, baba! Not in this lifetime. I have learnt my lesson. No, Manu, I will be doing something far more important.'

'What, Raja-saab?'

'Politics, Manu, politics!' said the prince. He stood up and began to pace up and down the room. 'This is the right time for me to get into politics. The tide is turning and I must grab it with both hands.'

From my perch on the window sill, I listened carefully to the prince as he outlined his plans to Manu.

'You see, Manu,' said the prince. 'While you were hiding in Rishikesh, Calcutta has changed completely. You know how many Bangladeshis have come to West Bengal during the last four years? Ten million!'

'Ten million!' Manu exclaimed.

'Yes. It all began when that Pakistani thug Yahya Khan sent in his army to Dhaka to show the Bangladeshis who was boss. '*Kill three million of them, and the rest will eat out of our hands*'—that's what the bloody fellow said. And that's just what the Pakistani army did. They went on the rampage, raping, killing and plundering.'

'I read something about it in the newspapers,' Manu said.

'No newspaper report can tell you how bad things were. Lakhs of Bangladeshis fled to West Bengal to escape the Pakistani army. It was just like Partition. Once again, the refugee camps mushrooming everywhere, once again the women and children begging for a bowl of gruel, crying *'Ektu fyaan dao maa* (give us some rice gruel).' But Mrs Gandhi saved the day. Much as I dislike her, I have to give it to that woman. She has more guts than the whole Nehru khaandaan put together. It's because she sent in the Indian Army to Dhaka and threw out the Pakistanis, that the Bangladeshis have their own country today.'

'I know all that,' said Manu. 'But what does it have to do with you, Raja-saab?'

'Everything,' the prince slapped his thigh. 'You mark my words Manu—Mrs Gandhi's greatest triumph is going to become the cause of her downfall. And the day she falls, so will the Congress party. And that is where I come in.'

Mrs Gandhi's victory in the Bangladesh war had made her obnoxious, said the prince. Success had gone to her head, swelling it to such an extent that her carefully arranged coiffeur had become three inches higher. People had started calling her Maa Durga and the slayer of Yahyasura had wasted no time in grabbing power with all her ten hands. The woman, who had until recently been derided as a Goongi Gudiya, a dumb doll, had reduced her detractors to her boy-toys. Then one by one, she had appointed her loyalists to the ranks of power. The civil services, the police, the banks, the courts were now all headed by her favourite sycophants. But the real power lay with her son, Sanjay. These days, his word was writ. Little happened without Sanjay's knowledge and nothing without his nod.

'These bloody Congressis!' exclaimed the prince. 'First it was Motilal-ji and Nehru-ji. Then it was Nehru-ji and Indira-ji, and now

Indira-ji and Sanju-baba. You tell me Manu, it's nearly thirty years since we won independence. But still this father-daughter-mother-son team is playing kabaddi-kabaddi with the country! How many more years must we put up with these Gandhis? Do they think India is their father's property, their baap ka jagir or what? *Arre baba*, if this country was to be run by only one dynasty, then what was wrong with mine? Never mind the country, they could have at least left Registan for me, no?' the prince gazed at the portraits of his ancestors hung on the wall and said: 'But Nehru-ji took that away from me in 1947. And twenty-four years later, his daughter even took away my privy purse! Not just that she has raised my income tax to 93.5 per cent. It's daylight robbery! But her days are over. I'm telling you Manu, she and her Congressi chamchas will be kicked out very soon.'

'Why do you say so, Raja-saab? The Congress party looks as strong as ever to me.'

'That's because you have no idea of what is happening! Don't you see that people are sick of the Congress? They have ruled this country for twenty-seven years. And what have they given in return? Nothing! No roti, no kapda, no makaan. Only empty slogans and corruption and taxes! People are looking for a change. And that is why this is the perfect time for me to make my entry into politics.'

'What do you have in mind, Raja-saab?'

'The general elections are two years away and this time I am going to contest.'

'But on whose ticket? I hope you are not thinking of standing as an independent candidate. That would be a disaster.'

'I'm not that stupid, Manu. I have thought about everything very carefully. I plan to contest on the Jana Sangh ticket. In fact, I have already met some of their top leaders to discuss the idea. They are open to it.'

'The Jana Sangh?' Manu's eyebrows shot up. 'But why? I don't know much about them but I don't think they are very popular. How many people have even heard of them here in West Bengal?'

'Ah, but West Bengal is where the Jana Sangh was born. Shyama Prasad Mookerjee founded it here in Calcutta in 1951. He was elected to Parliament from the Calcutta South East constituency, right where we are sitting. Anyway, that was a long time ago. Why talk of the past? It is the future that is important. Business and politics—that is the double engine that will lead us to power. That's why I need you so badly, Manu. You will have to take care of the business, so that I can take care of the politics.'

'Of course, Raja-saab,' Manu replied. 'I will do my very best. But I'm still not sure that the Jana Sangh is the right choice.'

'It is Manu, it is. Politics is all about winning elections. And winning elections is about two things—money and vote banks. The money will come from you and—'

'From me?' Manu interrupted.

'I mean from the business, of course, which you will run for me.'

'Yes, of course. And the vote bank?'

'There are one million in Calcutta alone, one million Hindus who no one cares about. Except me. And the Jana Sangh.'

'And this is your vote bank? Who are these people?'

'The refugees of course, Manu. There are one million Hindu refugees from Bangladesh in Calcutta today. Who is thinking of them? No one. Not the Congress, not the Communists. There is only one party today that is fighting for the Hindus and that is the Jana Sangh. If we can consolidate the local Hindu vote plus the votes of the Bangladeshi Hindu refugees, then we can throw out the Congress and the Communists. But you leave all that to me. It is your job to make the money and my job to get the votes. And together, we will become powerful. Together we will do something for the Hindus of this country. That's something worth working for, isn't it, Manu?'

'Yes, it is Raja-saab,' Manu replied. 'I will try my very best.' He didn't care too much for the country but the prince was a different matter. He would do what it took to make his dreams come true.

***

During the next six months, Manu gave his heart and soul to Regal Bearings. Like the prince had said, the business was in bad shape and it was taking a great deal of hard work to bring it back to its feet again. But Manu revelled in it. He felt like he was back home. The familiar clang of machines churning out one bushing after the other, the chatter of workers, the clattering of typewriters as they spat out payment receipts and the soft rustle of currency notes—they were all music to his ears. Especially the money. It was the balm that not only soothed his old insecurities but also made him feel that he was repaying his many debts to Raja-saab.

Meanwhile, the prince was busy currying favour with the Jana Sangh for an election ticket. He had recently installed a giant portrait of Shyama Prasad Mookerjee in the drawing room of Registan Manor, in the hope that it would impress the assortment of Jana Sangh leaders and RSS karyakartas, who would often drop by. The prince would ply them with turmeric-milk (for the sanskari traditionalists) and single malt (for the modern), and as they sipped their drinks, he would deliver fiery speeches of how he would kick the Congressis and the Commies right into the Bay of Bengal. One evening, after a particularly impassioned speech, I even thought I saw Mr Mookerjee stroke his painted moustache in approval.

But while milk and whisky were helpful in lubricating the prince's passage into the inner circles of the Jana Sangh, its leaders were still not convinced that a non-Bengali outsider could win an election from Calcutta. Both the Congress and the Communists were formidable opponents and in a three-way contest, he would be squashed underfoot like an ant caught between two duelling elephants. Even so, they were willing to give him a chance. But he would have to first convince them that he had both the money and the manpower required to win an election.

The prince wasn't too worried. Ever since Manu had taken over the running of Regal Bearings, business had been improving fast and a decent amount of money was coming into the bank. The important thing was to get an equally decent number of people into the vote bank. But the prince did not see that as a major problem. After all, he had money and even if money couldn't buy love, it could certainly buy loyalty—the loyalty of lakhs of people, who had been stranded on the shores of Calcutta by the tides of history.

The stateless, homeless Hindu refugees of Bangladesh were looking for a saviour. And he, Surya Pratap Singh, was ready to become one.

***

One morning in December, a goods lorry lumbered into Barasat, a shanty town north of Calcutta. The carrier of the lorry was packed with rations—rice, potatoes, lentils and onions. A banner had been strung across the front of the lorry. It bore a giant photograph of the prince, his palms joined in greeting, his lips parted in a wide smile. Across the top of the banner, written in Bengali, were the words: '*Baastuharar Bondhu*, Surya Pratap Singh'—friend of the homeless, Surya Pratap Singh.

As the lorry approached Barasat Refugee Camp, a flood of people crawled out of the tarpaulin-covered tents that stood on either side of the narrow pathway—snot-nosed children with bloated bellies, fat flies buzzing across their faces, men and women, hobbling on their stick-thin legs. Like rats to the call of the Pied Piper, they followed the lorry, until after a while, it came to a halt in the middle of an open field. An announcement was made over the loudspeaker that Shri Surya Pratap Singh, Jana Sangh leader, would now give a speech.

At the mention of a speech, the spark went out of the hollow eyes that had been hungrily eyeing the rations being unloaded from the lorry. But they waited patiently as Surya Pratap Singh, friend of the homeless, seized a mic and launched into his speech. He told them how he too had once been driven out of his birthplace. How he too, had been forced to flee to Calcutta, leaving behind his ancestral lands and properties forever. Their wounds were his wounds, said the prince and they were like his own brothers and sisters, bonded by the pain of a lost homeland. But now that he was at their side, they had nothing more to fear. After much maudlin meandering, the prince finally came to the part that everyone had been waiting for.

Each family, the prince announced, would be given 5 kilos of rice, 3 kilos of lentils, 1 kilo of potatoes, etcetera. etcetera. No one would have to pay a paisa for this. It was all free! A roar of applause greeted the prince's announcement. And this was only the beginning, the prince went on. More rations would be provided in the next month (lusty cheers) and the month after that (lustier cheers) for as long as it took. After the applause had subsided, Manu announced that the rations would now be distributed. The head of each family was asked to come forward and provide the details of his family members. These would be noted in the register, after which the rations would be given.

Much to Manu's relief, the distribution proceeded in an orderly fashion. The men queued in front of the lorry and one after one they stepped forward to receive a sack of rations from a beaming prince. By the end of two hours, almost seven hundred families had collected their sacks. Manu quickly scanned the register in which he had noted down the details of each family. The names of almost two thousand adults had been entered in the register.

Not bad, he said to himself, two thousand adults in two hours of work. A decent start to the vote bank. And Barasat was just the beginning. There were several more refugee colonies to go. He threw a quick look at the prince. He was surrounded by a throng of people—the men thanking him with folded hands, the women thrusting their babies at him while he patted their heads with the ease of a seasoned politician.

'I suppose you are doing this to get our votes?' a voice sounded at his side. Manu turned to see a woman looking curiously at him. And for a moment, his heart stopped.

'Mary!' he whispered in disbelief.

Citizen Khan

Even I was baffled by Mary's sudden reappearance, so what to say of Manu? Although he hardly ever spoke of her I knew that a part of him had always stayed back with her in Dehradun. The woman who had approached us had an uncanny resemblance to her—the same sharp cheekbones, the same thin hair pulled back in a severe bun, the same fire flashing in the same dark eyes. So, it wasn't unnatural for Manu to have mistaken her for his forever but ever lost love. Except that she wasn't—a realisation that was now slowly dawning upon Manu.

'Who are you?' Manu asked, still gaping at the stranger.

'A refugee,' the woman replied, 'just like everyone else here. Queuing up for your alms. But never mind me—why have you come here? Why this sudden generosity?' she jerked her head at the baby-hugging prince. 'Is that your leader? Is he going to stand for elections?'

'He might,' replied Manu. 'But that's not the only reason why we are here. It's so that we can help—'

'If your help means free rice and potatoes, then we don't need it,' the woman cut in. 'We don't need your charity. What we need is jobs. We need work. We need the right to live in peace, without being chased out of the refugee camps by the police. Can your leader help us with those? Or will he only give nice speeches and hug babies like all other politicians?'

Manu was stumped for words. She was so much like Mary, this woman—the same intensity, the same anger. And yet so different too. There was the hardness of steel and concrete in her words, and the pungency of petrol fumes that spoke of the city and not the forest. As I listened to her, it almost felt like a wine tasting—I could detect the fruity notes of a convent school education, the smooth confidence of a university degree and the harshness of halogen street lights. And the way she was firing away her questions, I was beginning to suspect that she was a lawyer.

'May I know your name please?' asked Manu.

'I'm Sayoni,' the woman replied. 'Sayoni Khan. I am a lawyer.' Bingo! I said to myself, as the woman went on: 'Or rather I used to be, back home in Dhaka. Now I run a temporary school for the children of this camp.'

'Khan?' Manu frowned. 'But I thought all the Muslim refugees had gone back to Bangladesh.'

'I'm Hindu. That's why I had to stay back in India. Bangladesh isn't a very safe place for people like us these days.'

'A Hindu Khan?'

'Yes, a Hindu Khan,' she said, rolling her eyes. 'I suppose there are some people who know that there are some Hindus with the surname of Khan. But it looks like you are not one of them. Anyway, to come back to the point. Why are you giving us these rations? If it is for our votes, then I hope you know that we can't give them to you. We are still citizens of Bangladesh. We can't vote in your Indian elections.'

'But that is precisely one of the reasons why we are here,' Manu replied. 'You see our party, meaning the Jana Sangh party, is demanding that the Hindu refugees from Bangladesh should be given Indian citizenship. So you see, we are not giving you only rice and potatoes. We are trying to give you a home, a place where you can live as free citizens of a free country.'

'Really? Then why didn't your leader talk about all this in his speech?' asked Sayoni.

'We have to go one step at a time, isn't it?' Manu said. 'After all, this is only the first day. But I can assure you that the Jana Sangh is fighting for your rights and it will continue to do so.'

'What about giving us ration cards and identity papers to begin with?'

'The party is taking up these issues as well. You can ask Raja-saab about it. He knows more about it. But I can see that you are a lawyer. And a good one too, by the looks of it.'

Sayoni smiled. 'I used to practice in Dhaka High Court. And yes, it was quite a decent practice. You know how much we East Bengalis love litigation.'

'And your family?'

Sayoni's face turned pale. After a while she said: 'I have no family. My mother died long ago. And my father and brother...' she paused, '...they were tortured to death by the Pakistanis. Only I escaped. Walked for days to come here to Calcutta.' There was a distant look in her eyes as she said:

'A million are dead, the million who can
Walk toward Calcutta from East Pakistan.'

No one spoke for some time. 'You write poetry?' Manu broke the silence.

'Not me,' she said. 'Some American poet wrote that. Ginsberg or something like that, I think his name was,' she gave her head a shake. 'I'm so sorry, I don't know what's come over me. Talking to you like this. It's just that each day here is such a struggle. Sometimes it just gets to me and...'

'I can understand,' Manu replied. 'You don't have to apologize. By the way I'm Manu. Manu Pratap Singh.'

'Nice to meet you, Mr Singh,' Sayoni said. 'And thank you so much for the rations. I am sorry if I was rude. I didn't mean it. Anyway, I should be going now. But it was nice talking to you. Goodbye.'

'Goodbye,' Manu said. He wished she wasn't leaving so quickly. He couldn't remember the last time he had enjoyed a conversation so much. She was already walking away when an idea struck him. He called out to her. 'Excuse me, Sayoni-ji, but can I have a quick word with you?'

She turned around: 'Yes, Mr Singh?'

'Please call me Manu,' he replied. 'I was just thinking—'

'Yes?'

'I have a factory. We manufacture bushings and bearings. Maybe you've heard of it? Regal Bearings?

'I'm sorry. But I don't know much outside this refugee camp. But why do you ask?'

'So the thing is that I am always busy managing the day-to-day operations, production, sales. But I need some legal help from time to time—taxes, business contracts, union negotiations, things like that. So, I was wondering if you would be interested in helping me out? You will be paid, of course.'

Sayoni Khan's eyes lit up. 'Mr Singh, are you offering me work?'

'I might. At least, I would like to discuss the possibilities with you.'

'Really?' she stared at him in disbelief. 'But why?'

'It's just that...I don't think this is the right place for you. You deserve much better. And if I can help you in some way, then why not?'

'That's very kind of you, Mr Singh, really very—'

'Manu, please. Not Mr Singh.'

'Yes, sorry...Manu. I don't know what to say. If I can get some proper work, it would mean the world to me. But there is a problem,' she said.

'What?'

Her face fell. 'I can't practice law here in India. I'm not an Indian citizen.'

'Oh, don't worry about that right now. It's only office work that I am talking about. You won't have to appear in court. Not immediately at least,' replied Manu. 'But why don't we go one step at time? If you come to my office, at say ten o'clock on Monday morning, we can have a more detailed discussion,' he fished out a visiting card from his pocket. 'This is the factory address. So, will you come?'

She took the card from him as if it was a knighthood. 'Of course, I will.'

***

At the stroke of ten, on the following Monday morning, Sayoni Khan arrived at Manu's office. She looked tense and nervously patted down the pleats of her saree as Manu asked her about her qualifications and experience. But she needn't have worried. A short conversation later, Manu offered to employ her as his assistant. She would be paid a salary of two hundred rupees a month along with provident fund and other allowances. I think it was a fair bit more than Sayoni had been expecting, and she jumped at the offer. She was ready to start working from the next day itself.

What had prompted Manu's generosity towards a stranger that he hardly knew anything about? Was it because she reminded him of Mary? Or was it because she reminded him of himself, as he had been twenty-eight years ago, alone in the world without home, family, or future? Or had he been somehow touched by the spirit of Calcutta, that terrible yet beautiful city, which had always made room for the millions of people who had streamed into it in search of life and livelihood—Chinese, Jews, Armenians, Parsis, Rajasthanis, Biharis, Tamilians, Bangladeshis and what-not.

Whatever be the reason, Manu felt good when he was with Sayoni. For their relationship was based on that all-important four-letter word which is the foundation of all good relationships—talk. In the days that followed, Manu told her all about Betla and Calcutta and Dehradun. He spoke about the prince and Mary and what they meant to him. She in turn told him of her life in Bangladesh. She spoke of her father and her brother and of the happy days they had spent in Dhaka, until the time when the Pakistani fighter jets had swooped down on them like a swarm of locusts and destroyed their lives.

When Sayoni was around, Manu could not take his eyes off her. And when she was away, he would pass the time in the company of romantic Rafi instead of melancholic Mukesh. As the days went by, it was becoming quite clear that Mr Singh was falling hook, line and sinker for Ms Khan. It was only a matter of time before he would turn into a tepid version of the lover boy Mr Khanna.

Luurve was in the air and it did not take my extraordinary olfactory abilities to smell it.

***

While I was fairly certain that Manu had developed lovey-dovey feelings for Sayoni, I didn't quite know what she felt towards him. There was no doubt that she was grateful for the job that he had given her. Because of it she had been able to leave Barasat Refugee Camp and rent a small two-room flat in Belghoria. She was even able to afford a little bit of fish and the occasional mutton on Sundays. There were moments when she could not believe that her four nightmarish years in the refugee camp had ended at last. And she would utter a silent prayer of gratitude for the small, clean flat that she could call home and for the man who had made it possible. There was nothing more that Sayoni wanted from life. At least, not at the moment.

But if a one-bedroom flat was enough to make Sayoni happy, nothing less than the throne of India would do for Indira. It was another matter that as the serving Prime Minister, she was already seated upon it. But she feared that it would be snatched away by her formidable enemies, who were attacking her from all sides.

In Bombay, the socialist leader George Fernandes, starter of strikes and stopper of trains, was making fiery speeches against her. In Patna that old Gandhian Jayaprakash Narayan, had emerged from his long hibernation and was out on the streets calling for total revolution. And the unkindest cut of all, in Gujarat, her own finance minister, Morarji Desai *urrf* Brutus was openly defying her. Seized by the need to save India from Indira, Morarji-bhai had gone on a fast unto death, shunning food, water, and even his own urine.

It was enough to piss anyone off and a pissed off PM can be dangerous. Especially if she happened to be Mrs Gandhi. We were sitting on a keg of gunpowder. The fuse had been lit and it was burning a swift path to the inevitable explosion.

Actually, make that two explosions—one small and one huge, both of which erupted on the same day, 25 June 1975.

The Explosions

25 June 1975. An unforgettable day. Especially for me. It was the day on which I nearly went permanently cock-eyed, trying to keep track of the momentous events that were unfolding simultaneously in Delhi and in Calcutta. It was like watching a tennis match on a thousand-mile-long court.

The first volley was fired in Delhi by Mrs Gandhi when she arrived at the 340-roomed Rashtrapati Bhavan to meet the President. At about the same time, Manu was knocking on the door of Sayoni's one-bedroom flat in Belghoria. Indira was accompanied by the Bengal Chief Minister, Siddhartha Shankar Ray, and Manu by Chief Historian, Prem Chandra Guha.

As Manu waited nervously at Sayoni's doorstep, hoping perhaps for some action, my sixth sense told me that the real action was about to begin in New Delhi. Guided by my supernaturally sharp instincts, my head swivelled northwards. All-seeing for an instant, I watched a tense President Fakhruddin Ali Ahmed ushering the visitors into his palace. My head now turned back east where Sayoni Khan was welcoming Manu into hers. Back to the north, where Indira was telling the President how her gareeb subjects, instead of being grateful for her Garibi Hatao program, were hell-bent on hataoing her instead. Eastward ho, and Sayoni was telling Manu for the umpteenth time how grateful she was to him.

In Delhi, mustachioed bearers, balancing silver trays on white-gloved fingers, padded silently across thick Kashmiri carpets to offer tea and biscuits to Indira. In Calcutta, Manu picked up a biscuit from the dented hindalium plate that Sayoni held before him and nibbled shyly upon it. In Delhi, they spoke of big things—of internal disturbances and constitutional amendments and matters of national security. In Calcutta, they spoke of small things—of the price of onions and how Sayoni had bought a new sari for herself after four years. In Delhi, Indira and Siddhartha discussed some Very Important People—Communists and Jana Sanghis, political opponents and newspaper editors, and made plans to get rid of them before the night was over. In Calcutta, Manu and Sayoni discussed very unimportant people, like Mary and the prince. In Delhi, Indira and Siddhartha talked of the perfect future that they would build together. In Calcutta, Manu and Sayoni dared not talk of the future, for fear of ruining a perfect present.

The hours flew by. In the north, thunderclouds darkened the skies. In the east, the city gleamed in the silvery light of a million moonbeams. And then, when the hands of the clock were about to close upon the midnight hour, there came two sounds. From the north, the faint rustle of pen on paper and from the east (and I blush as I say this) a soft gasp of pleasure.

The lighted fuses have burned to their ends. The explosions have been set off.

In Delhi, President Fakhruddin Ali Ahmed has just signed a piece of paper declaring that India is in a state of internal emergency. In Calcutta, Manu and Sayoni are also in a state of emergency (albeit without the paperwork...and the clothes...and a great deal more pleasurable).

And now, having secured the presidential signature that she needs so desperately, Indira is heading back to her residence on 7 Race Course Road, where she and Siddhartha will spend the rest of the night plotting and planning their next moves. Manu and Sayoni, on the other hand, are heading for the bed. Their moves need no planning, for they seem to be coming quite naturally.

And in the early hours of 26 June 1975, as thirty-eight-year-old Manu and twenty-eight-year-old India are both being screwed, let us draw a modest curtain over these most private of proceedings and pause for a brief interlude. We shall resume our tale on the morning after.

The Morning After

All happy memories are alike, an unchanging melody played on loop. Every unhappy memory is unhappy in its own way—a protean raga with its shifting textures and meanings. My recollections of the morning of 26 June 1975 includes both.

First, the happy memory, always in the present, always the same.

I see Manu and Sayoni, wrapped around each other, a sunbeam slanting across the crumpled sheets that half-cover their naked bodies. I see his hand on her bare hip and hers on his tousled hair, both lost to the world. Born of long years of habit and hardship, she awakens first and smiles at the man lying on her bed. As if in reply, he opens his eyes and smiles back. They make love again. There is only half an hour or so before Manu must leave for the factory, but it is enough. Time enough for both to realise that perhaps they are like the couple in the Wills Navy Cut advertisements—Made for Each Other.

Then the unhappy memory, which always leaves me wondering how I should begin and what I should say. For lack of a better alternative, let me begin with the mystery of the missing newspaper.

Like the dog that did not bark in the night, the first indication that something had gone wrong, was the missing newspaper. It irked Sayoni no end for reading the newspaper over a cup of tea was as much a part of her morning ritual as brushing her teeth.

'This is so irritating!' she said with a scowl.

'Were you expecting us to make the headlines?' asked Manu. He was still stretched out on the bed, following her with his eyes. 'Not that I would be surprised. Last night was...quite something, no?'

She gave a shy smile. 'Yes, it was...it was nice,' she sat down by his side, running her fingers through his hair. 'Now get up and get ready. We have to go to the factory.'

'No, we don't. I'm taking the day off,' replied Manu. 'And so are you. That's an order.'

'Okay, boss. And what will we do the whole day?'

'This?' said Manu, pulling her down to his side.

'Stop it,' she said playfully. 'We hardly know each other.'

'Then we should spend more time together, don't you think? How about taking a boat ride with me on the Ganga, Miss Khan?'

'Don't you think you are rowing your boat too fast, Mr Singh,' she replied, pinching him on the cheek.

'Can you blame me? It's been stuck on the shore for too long,' he replied.

She turned away from him, suddenly serious as she gazed through the open window: 'I need some time, Manu. This has all been too sudden, too quick.'

Manu raised himself on his elbows. 'But it feels right to me. Doesn't it to you?'

'Yes. What I mean to say is that...I like you Manu. I really do. But what happened last night may just be an accident. The past is still too close, too fresh for me. I don't want to get hurt.'

'I won't hurt you ever. I promise.'

'What about Mary?'

Manu sat up. 'Mary! What has Mary got to do with anything? What is it that are you trying to say?'

'You left her.'

Manu threw up his hands. 'I didn't leave her! She left me.'

'But she still means a great deal to you, isn't that so?'

'There was a time when she meant everything to me. But not anymore. She's a friend, but nothing more than that.'

'Are you sure?'

'Of course, I'm sure. Look Sayoni, three years have gone by and we haven't met even once. In the early days, we used to write to each other once in two–three weeks. But that's gone down to a letter once every six months, maybe. Just a line or two, that's all. Mary is in her own world, Sayoni. Busy with her forests and hills. She's different from the rest of us. She's not interested in the usual things that other people want—money, home, family and all that.'

'Then what does she want?' asked Sayoni.

'To save the world, I suppose,' Manu gave a small smile. 'Anyway, that's enough about Mary. What do you want?'

Sayoni looked out of the window and said:

'There is no time, no time, so, don't be fussy,
Take whatever is close at hand
And quickly make a little bundle of things,
Then get out, get out, while you still can.'

'We are udbastus, refugees,' she continued. 'What can we want? Just a small bundle of things that we won't have to pack up at midnight and run. A safe place that we can call home, a job—that's all we want.'

'I think that's all I want as well,' said Manu. 'You see? You and I, we are the same.'

'Manu, last night was...beautiful,' said Sayoni. 'But can we go a little slowly, please? Sometimes I feel so scared. Things can change so suddenly, so quickly. Anyway, enough of all this serious talk. It's time for a good cup of tea.'

'That would be nice,' said Manu as Sayoni headed into the kitchen.

'And can you please turn on the radio?' she called out. 'Let me listen to the news at least since I can't read it.'

Manu switched on the radio and the signature tune of All India Radio floated out on the airwaves. Plaintive notes of violin, cello and tanpura blended harmoniously with the soft bubbling of the water simmering on the kitchen stove. After all these years, I often remember that moment—Manu pottering around in his banian, Sayoni humming softly as she pours out two cups of tea...it was the very picture of domestic bliss and middle-aged love. Suddenly the momentous events that had occurred in Delhi only a few hours ago, seemed inconsequential. But then the music stopped abruptly and over the airwaves, loud and clear as an akaashvaani, came the voice of Mrs Gandhi.

'The President has proclaimed an Emergency. There is nothing to panic about.'

Most of India, of course, did just the opposite.

***

After many decades of living in India, one thing has become clear to me—whenever a Prime Minister assures the nation that there is no need to panic, there usually is. And the events that were to follow Mrs Gandhi's announcement were to prove me right.

To begin with, it wasn't only the newspapers that had mysteriously disappeared on the morning of 26 June, but thousands of people as well. The previous night, when Manu and Sayoni were busy doing their hanky-panky under the bedsheets, Indira and Siddhartha were doing theirs (on bond paper sheets, though). And as they say in Bengal—the sheet was soon about to heet the fan.

Pre-dawn raids were taking place across the country. Like circling vultures, the police were swooping down on any person who had ever dared to utter a squeak against Mrs Gandhi and bundling them off to jail. The list of names was long and impressive—old Jayaprakash Narayan, his I-don't-give-a-damn attitude wrapped around him like armour, a rather pissed-off Morarji Desai, an unshakeable Atal Bihari Vajpayee, a livid Lal Krishna Advani and many others.

The arrests had been made in secret and Manu knew nothing about them. But as he listened to Mrs Gandhi's speech, an uneasy feeling began to come over him. She was speaking of conspiracy, of national security and enemies of the state...there was a familiar ring to these words. He had heard them before, eight years ago...when the government had declared Mary and him as its enemies. What if eight years later, the government decided that Raja-saab was an enemy of the state as well?

Perhaps he was exaggerating the situation, Manu tried to reason with himself. After all, Raja-saab was no Naxal, shooting arrows and bullets at policemen. He was only a struggling politician, like thousands of others. But then it occurred to him that, of late, the prince had been making rather incendiary speeches against the government.

In a recent rally at Barasat Refugee Camp, Raja-saab had openly accused Mrs Gandhi of abandoning the Hindu refugees who had come from Bangladesh. It was now an Islamic country, Raja-saab had thundered, and Hindus were being butchered there by the barbaric Mussalmans. It was the government's dharma to save our Hindu brothers and sisters from Islamic persecution and provide them sanctuary. After all, he said, India was to the Hindus what Israel was to the Jews. Every Hindu had the right to call India his home, no matter where he came from. But four years had passed since the Bangladesh war, and Mrs Gandhi had done nothing for the refugees. Well then, if she hadn't, he would. He, Surya Pratap Singh, vowed to fight for the rights of the Hindu refugees, so that they could live legally in this country as equal citizens. He would fight for their ration cards, identity papers, jobs and most importantly for their right to vote.

Apart from being hugely popular with the refugees, Raja-saab's position appealed to many of the native residents of Calcutta as well. Many of them believed that the refugee problem could not just be swept under the carpet. Since the government was unable to send them back to Bangladesh, they would have to rehabilitate them. Otherwise, they would turn out to be an even bigger problem. Already the refugee colonies had defaced their beloved Calcutta beyond recognition. More importantly, many of the refugees were now living with their relatives in Calcutta. But how long could they go on feeding them? After all, there were limits to their hospitality. The sooner the government accepted Bangladeshi Hindus as bona-fide citizens, the sooner they would be able to stand on their own two feet and give their hosts a respite.

Two weeks ago, the prince had addressed another rally in which over five thousand people had turned up. It was large enough for the Jana Sangh leaders to sit up and take notice. Even the press had covered the event and Prince Surya Pratap Singh's photograph had appeared in the newspapers. He was excited as a rabbit in springtime. His strategy of trying to consolidate the Hindu vote seemed to be working.

Manu had been equally happy at the time. But now, a feeling of foreboding swept through him. Wasn't Raja-saab going overboard in creating divisions between Hindus and Muslims just to gain popular support? Wasn't that how the Partition had happened? Wasn't that why all those wretched people had lived and died like sewer rats in Bijoygarh refugee camp? Yes, his loyalty to Raja-saab was unshakeable but he just didn't feel good about what he was doing these days. Besides it could prove dangerous to Raja-saab himself. What if his activities had attracted the government's attention? What if he had already been marked out as an enemy of the state? If so, Raja-saab was in danger.

Fear and guilt chased through Manu as he berated himself for having spent the night away from home. As soon as Mrs Gandhi's speech ended, he rushed back to Registan Manor, praying that everything was normal. But as soon as he stepped inside the house, he knew that something was wrong.

Old Prahlad was sitting forlornly in a corner, his head slumped over his chest. He looked up in relief at Manu's arrival and told him what had happened. At about five in the morning, he had heard the doorbell ring. Raja-saab, who was already awake by then, opened the door and Prahlad went back to sleep. When he awoke two hours later, he discovered that the front door was flung open and Raja-saab was nowhere to be seen. He looked all around the house but couldn't find him. Four hours had passed since then, and he was still missing.

In short, Prince Surya Pratap Singh seemed to have vanished into thin air.

The Missing Prince

Two days had passed since Mrs Gandhi had announced the Emergency. Chaos and confusion reigned supreme in the land. No one seemed to know what was happening. The newspapers seemed equally confused and news articles had been replaced by blank pages and inspirational poems. That morning, my eye fell on a small insertion in the obituary column of the *Times of India*. I chuckled aloud as I read it.

'D.E.M. O'Cracy—beloved husband of T. Ruth, loving father of L. I. Bertie, brother of Faith, Hope and Justicia, expired on June 26.'

I read it out to Manu, hoping that he would be amused as well. But he skewered me with a frosty glare. 'Can you please be quiet?' he barked. 'I have enough to worry about without having to listen to your bakwaas!'

I beat a hasty retreat. I should have realised Manu was worried sick. There was still no news of the prince. It was as if he had been swallowed by a black hole. Fighting off his fear of the police, Manu had gone to the local thana to enquire after the prince's disappearance. But it took three days before he was finally granted an audience with the officer in charge, one Inspector Ghosh.

The inspector was a corpulent, swarthy man, who liked tracing circles around his navel with his forefinger. 'Sorry, sorry Mr Singh,' said Inspector Ghosh with an insincere smile. 'This Emergency has been keeping us very busy. Hardly a moment to even breathe these days. So, tell me sir, what is the problem?'

When Manu had finished telling him about the missing prince, the Inspector stared at him with a strange expression and said: 'Surya Pratap Singh, is it? I know him. Going around saying all sorts of big-big things these days, isn't he? RSS man, right?'

'Jana Sangh. Not RSS,' Manu replied.

'Same thing. All the same, these people. Always trying to make trouble between Muslims and Hindus and increasing our work.' Inspector Ghosh caressed his navel. 'Look here, Mr Singh, I am a good Hindu myself. I have no problem if we throw every single Muslim out of this country. But that is a job for the army, isn't it? Get the army, put them all on a train and send them back to wherever they came from—Bangladesh, Pakistan, Afghanistan. How can the police manage such huge numbers? But no! Instead of doing the real work, all these RSS people do, is start one fire here and another fire there. And we police people have to keep running to put them out. Do you know, after the Hindu-Muslim riots in 1964, it took me over six months to just do the paperwork. You only tell me, how can a country run like this?'

'I understand, sir,' said Manu. 'But let us come back from 1964 to today. Raja-saab has been missing for three days and I am really worried. Please tell me frankly—has the police arrested him? I hear many people have been arrested after Mrs Gandhi declared the Emergency, and that's why I am asking.'

The Inspector shrugged. 'How can I say, sir? It is true, that thousands of people have been arrested during the last few days. See,' he pointed at a stack of files. 'Lists and lists of arrests. Just the paperwork is killing me, it will take at least one month to finish. You please come back after that and I may be able to help you then.'

'Come back after one month! But he is missing *now*! He is nowhere to be found. He is an old man. He had diabetes; his heart is weak. What if something happens to him?'

'That only a doctor can say. But if you ask me, your Raja-saab should have thought of his health before doing his RSS-giri, isn't it?' he leaned forward and whispered. 'Between you and me, Mr Singh, I think the CBI is behind this. So I am sorry but I can't help you. I have enough on my hands as it is...' he looked sadly at the stack of files and heaved a deep sigh.

'But can't you understand what I am saying, sir,' Manu said. 'He is missing.'

'Then please file a missing person report and we will look into it,' barked the Inspector. 'That is the standard procedure.'

'But sir—'

'No more ifs and buts,' the Inspector slammed his hand on the desk. 'One more word and I will throw you straight into the lockup. This is Emergency. Police can do whatever we want to do, no questions asked. Please don't try my patience any more, or it will go very badly for you. Please get out now,' he looked at the constable standing guard and barked: '*Ei khotta khankir chhele ta ke ekhan theke baar kor toh!* (Kick out this North Indian son of a whore, right now)!'

***

Three weeks later, the situation was as bleak as before. There was no trace of the prince. I shuddered to think what was happening to him if he was indeed in jail. The memories of Alipore were still fresh in my mind. Manu hadn't forgotten either and he was frantic with worry. He had checked with all the hospitals and the morgues but there was no report of a likely looking death. He practically laid siege at the local thana, and when that failed, he squatted at the police headquarters in Lalbazar to meet the Police Commissioner. But all his efforts were in vain.

Unable to make any headway with the police, Manu now sought to meet the Chief Minister himself. It was extremely unlikely that Siddhartha Shankar Ray, chief architect of the Emergency, would give a flying fig about an arrest that he himself had probably sanctioned. But this did not deter Manu. He spent days waiting in the reception of Writer's Building begging for an appointment to meet the CM. But his pleas fell on deaf ears and after several fruitless attempts, he was forced to give up.

He then approached journalists and editors of every newspaper worth its name. But most of them were too scared of writing anything for fear that they would be jailed as well. The Emergency had given the government absolute freedom to do whatever it pleased. Even the courts were powerless before it, so what to speak of mere journalists.

After much bowing and scraping, Manu was finally able to get an appointment with the editor of a prominent newspaper. But the man showed little interest in his woes and just as we were leaving his office, I overheard him mutter to his colleague: 'Mrs Gandhi has screwed over the country with this Emergency. But if there's one good thing that she's done—it is banning the RSS and throwing all those Jana Sanghis into jail. Can't stand the lot. Communal bastards, all of them.'

By now, my usually buoyant self-confidence had yielded to a gnawing fear. My antennae, ever attuned to the tenor of the times, told me that we were in the midst of an extraordinary age. This wasn't the India that we knew—the old laws, the old verities were breaking down. Overnight, the lumbering, bumbling, indolent Indian state had turned into a sleek, well-oiled monster, swallowing anyone who dared to stand in its way.

We could only hope that the prince hadn't become one of its many victims.

***

A dark desolation had taken hold of Manu. If it wasn't for Sayoni he would probably have broken down. But she was by his side all the time, doing everything possible to keep his spirits up. She moved in to Registan Manor, so that she could keep a watch over his food and sleep. She cooked his favourite dishes, read out her favourite poems and forced him to go to the factory to take his mind off things. She even started to draft a habeas corpus petition for him, in the belief that it might force the police to produce Raja-saab before the court.

But Manu had little faith in the courts and was beginning to lose all hope. The air was thick with rumours that political prisoners especially those with RSS or Communist connections, were being brutally tortured in jail. Manu could not imagine how Raja-saab would be able to withstand even a minute of torture after the luxuries that he had enjoyed all through his life. There were times when he could not help but think that Raja-saab had already died in custody. That was probably why the police were so tight-lipped about him.

Days turned into months and we had almost given up the prince for dead, when one night we received a telephone call that was to both revive our hopes and ignite our fears. It was on the stroke of eight p.m. that the telephone rang.

***

'Shri Manu Pratap Singh?' a man's voice said at the other end of the line.

'Yes,' replied Manu. 'Who is this?'

'That doesn't matter,' replied the man. 'Let me come straight to the point. I have news of Surya Pratap Singh.'

'What! Where is he? How is—'

'He is in Bangalore. You must come here as soon as you can. Tomorrow, if possible. Take the first flight out.'

'Bangalore? But where?'

'Victoria Hospital. I will meet you there.'

'Hospital! Is Raja-saab all right?'

There was a pause before the voice said. 'Yes. But please come here as soon as you can. I will meet you at the hospital.'

'But who are you? What is your—'

'Manu-babu,' the voice cut him off peremptorily. 'I am a friend. I am trying to help you and you have to trust me. I don't have much time. So, listen carefully—all our leaders are in Bangalore Central Jail. Advani-ji, Vajpayee-ji, all of them. Your father was also taken there soon after his arrest in Calcutta.'

'But you said he was in Victoria Hospital?'

'Yes, they moved him from the jail to the hospital two days ago because he wasn't feeling well. But don't worry. He is being treated now and we hope that he will get better.'

'But what has happened—'

'There's no time for so much talk, Manu-bhai. The phone lines may be tapped. If you want to see your father, then come to Bangalore as soon as possible. That's all I can tell you for now. *Baaki aapki marzi*—the choice is yours—take it or leave it.'

'But why should I believe you?'

'That is up to you.'

'All right, let's say I come to Bangalore, to Victoria Hospital, yes?'

'Yes.'

'And then what? How will we meet? How will I recognise you?'

'I will come to you. I have seen your photograph.'

'When? How?'

'Your father carries a picture of you in his wallet. He showed it to me.'

Manu felt a lump swelling in his throat. He took a moment to recover himself and said: 'If you know my father that well, I probably know you too. What is your name?'

'You don't know me. My name is—' there was a pause. 'Prakash... Prakash Singh.'

'Prakash Singh? Really?' Manu asked. Although he was quite sure that it was a false name, he tried to remember if Raja-saab had ever mentioned a Prakash Singh. But nothing came to mind. Was this some sort of hoax? Was he walking into a trap? But in spite of everything the man sounded sincere. In any case, he was the only lead to Raja-saab and there was no choice but to see it through.

'All right, Prakash-ji,' said Manu. 'I will do as you say. I'll take a flight to Bangalore tomorrow itself if I can.'

'Good. After you land go straight to Victoria Hospital and wait for me there. What time will you land?'

'I don't know. I'll have to check with Indian Airlines. I don't even know if there are any tickets.'

'Please try your best and take the first available flight. Come quickly. Time is short.'

There was a click and the line went dead.

Prakash Singh

It was late afternoon when the Indian Airlines flight from Calcutta landed in Bangalore. Manu took a taxi from the airport and headed straight to Victoria Hospital, an elegant stone building that looked more like an English castle than a hospital. Manu stood outside the main gate waiting for the mysterious Prakash Singh to make his appearance. But after an hour, there was still no sign of the man and he began to have a sinking feeling that he had been made a fool of.

After some time, he grew tired of hanging around uselessly and decided to take matters into his own hands. He walked into the reception. It was teeming with people clutching thick files of medical reports. There was a long queue at the reception counter and it took Manu the better part of an hour to reach the bored-looking man with a drooping moustache who was sitting behind it, leafing through a Kannada film magazine.

'*Idhar Surya Pratap Singh bolke koi patient admitted hai kya?* (Is any patient named Surya Pratap Singh admitted here?),' Manu asked.

'*Yaaru*? (Who?)' said the man without lifting his eyes from the magazine.

'Surya Pratap Singh?' Manu repeated. 'Any one by that name here?'

The man looked up in annoyance and said: '*Kannada, saar, Kannada dalli mathadi* (Speak in Kannada, sir).'

'*Mataji nahi*,' Manu tried to explain. 'Pitaji. I am looking for my father. *Main apne pitaji ko dhoond raha hoon.*'

The man slammed the magazine angrily on his desk and said: '*Aaii, yaaru neevu? Kannada dalli mathadi athva illi inda hogi*. You please talk in Kannada or get out from here.'

'Excuse me, but I have come all the way from Calcutta to—'

Manu began, but the man standing behind him pushed him aside roughly and took his place at the head of the queue.

Three hours later, we were still waiting for the mysterious Prakash Singh to turn up. And at five p.m. sharp, we were kicked out into the street by the security guards. By then, Manu was kicking himself for his own gullibility. The whole trip had been such a waste of time and money, not to mention the agony of having his hopes dashed to the ground.

He was on the verge of calling it a night and checking into a hotel, when an autorickshaw skidded to a halt just behind us. A short Sikh man, with an exceptionally broad chest, emerged from the auto. He was attired in a tight blue safari suit and matching blue turban. Most of his face was covered by a beard and a pair of large, oval-shaped sunglasses that he did not remove, although the sun had called it a day a while ago.

The Sikh man threw a quick glance at Manu and then furtively slipped behind the trunk of a massive gulmohar tree that stood nearby. Pursing his lips into a circle, he made a sort of smooching sound that was clearly intended for Manu. Either he was a Bombay taxi driver or he was making a pass at Manu, I said to myself, as Manu stared suspiciously at the stranger.

'Pssst, Manu-bhai,' the Sikh hissed, waving his hands frantically from behind the tree. 'Manu-bhai, come here.'

Manu advanced tentatively towards the gulmohar tree. When he was almost there, the stranger grabbed him by the collar and pulled him into the shadows. 'Hide, hide. The police may be here and we should not be seen with each other.'

'Who are you?' Manu asked angrily, wrenching his shirt out of the man's grip.

'Prakash Singh, who else?' replied the Sikh. 'I am sorry I got so late. I got on to a wrong bus and it took me half the way to Mysoor. I just couldn't get the conductor to understand where I wanted to go. No one speaks in Hindi in this place. It's such a pain. One day, I am going to do something about it.'

'Please stop your bakwaas,' Manu said. 'You said you have news of my father. Where is he?'

There was a short pause before Prakash Singh said: 'I am sorry,

Manu-bhai. But I don't have good news. Your father is no more. He passed away last night. He had a heart attack.'

The blood drained from Manu's face. For several moments, there was no sound except the rasping of his breath and the chirping of cicadas somewhere in the distance. And then, like the report of a fired pistol, came the sound of a sharp, short crack.

'You are lying!' said Manu as he landed a stinging slap on Prakash Singh's cheek.

***

We were at Sukh Sagar, an ill-named restaurant that stood a stone's throw away from Victoria Hospital. Prakash Singh placed a cup of watery coffee in front of Manu and tipped two teaspoons of sugar into it. 'Drink that. It will do you good,' he said. 'You are in shock.'

Manu took a sip as Prakash Singh said: 'I am so sorry that you could not be beside your father in his last moments. We tried our best. But we were too late. We ourselves did not know exactly when they shifted him out of the jail and brought him to the hospital. He had been kept in a different block from the rest of our leaders. Otherwise, we could have told you much earlier.'

'I couldn't even see him,' Manu's voice was hoarse. 'I couldn't perform his last rites. He did so much for me but I couldn't do anything for him. He had so many dreams, so many—' he broke off and his body started shaking as the sobs racked through him.

Prakash Singh waited until Manu was calmer. 'Don't blame yourself Manu-bhai. You did everything that you could. It's not your fault. It is the Congress that killed him.'

'Those bastards!' Manu snarled. 'I will get those bastards, if it is the last thing I do. I will drag them to the courts—all of them. I will have them thrown in jail. The police, the Chief Minister, the Prime Minister. Every single one of them. Let them rot and die there, like my father.'

'*Shanti*, Manu-bhai, peace,' Prakash Singh said. 'You must not become emotional. You must remain strong and calm.'

'My father has been murdered and you are asking me to be calm! No Mr Singh! I will not be calm. I will haul this government and the police to court and—'

'And the courts will simply throw out your petition,' Prakash

Singh cut him off. 'The judges have become lapdogs of Mrs Gandhi.'

'Then what do you want me to do? Sit at home wearing bangles?'

'Manu-bhai, in politics revenge is a dish best served by the ballot. The way to defeat the Congress is not in the courts but in the streets, in the rallies, in the polling booths. If we all work hard together then the people will throw out Mrs Gandhi and her chamchas in the next elections.'

'That is what Raja-saab also dreamed of,' said Manu. 'And I will fulfill his last wishes. I will stand for elections myself. Believe me Prakash-ji I will do whatever it takes for the Jana Sangh to win from Calcutta. If I don't rub the noses of these bloody Congressis in the mud, then my name is not Manu Pratap Singh.'

'I salute your enthusiasm, Manu-bhai,' said Prakash Singh. 'But mere *josh* will not be enough to win the battle. We need *hosh,* as well. We must work smartly. Now, first of all, we have no idea when the elections will be held. Secondly, Calcutta is not the best place for us to contest elections. Apart from the fact that you are not a Bengali, the Communists and Congress are much stronger than the Jana Sangh in Bengal. No Manu, before we go East, we will have to go West. Not Bengal but Gujarat. That is where it will all begin. With the blessings of Shri Ram, Gujarat will become the laboratory in which our movement will be born. And from there, one by one, we will capture the whole of India.'

'Why Gujarat?' Manu asked.

'To understand that you will have to come to Gujarat and see the kind of work we have started doing there,' Prakash Singh said. 'After all this is over you must come down to Ahmedabad and meet me.'

'I will try. But do you mind telling me who you really are? And what is your role in the party?'

Prakash Singh smiled. 'There will come a day when all your questions will be answered. But not today. In any case, I should go now. The longer we are together, the greater is the risk to both of us. But before I leave, let me tell you something, Manu-bhai—your father's sacrifice will not be in vain. One day we will have a Congress-mukt Bharat, and on that day, your father's soul will finally find peace.'

'But I can't just sit around until that happens,' said Manu. 'I want to help you. I want to do something!'

'But Manu-bhai, you are already doing something very important,' said Prakash Singh. 'The most important thing of all, much more important than contesting elections.'

'What am I doing?' asked Manu.

'You are running a business, Manu-bhai. You are making money. See, I know you are from Calcutta and your thinking may have become contaminated by the air and water of that place. But if there is one thing, we Gujaratis know, it is that money makes the world go round. And the road to money is dhando, business. Dhando is destiny and money is power. The party needs funds which only businessmen like you can give us. The Congress has Tata-Birla in their pocket. Who do we have? Only bechara Dhiru-bhai and he is scared of supporting us openly.'

'What do you want from me, Prakash-bhai? Just say it, and it is yours,' said Manu.

'Go back to Calcutta, Manu-bhai. Grow your business, become big, become rich! That is the best way you can support us.'

In spite of the turmoil raging inside him, Manu was struck by the sense of power and raw confidence that seemed to radiate from the man. He would go far, this Prakash Singh, whoever he was. He would do many things, thought Manu, great things even...but whether they would be for good or not, only time would tell...

Manu nodded. 'Yes, perhaps you are right. That's what Raja-saab used to say as well,' he grasped Prakash Singh's hand and said: 'Thank you for everything. Without you...'

'It's all right, Manu-bhai,' said Prakash Singh. 'That's what friends are for.'

Manu lowered his gaze and said: 'Also, I am sorry...I am very sorry that I...I...slapped you last night.'

'*Arre*, it's nothing,' Prakash Singh slapped himself on the chest and said: '*Yeh chhappan inch ki chhati hai,* Manu-bhai. This 56-inch chest can take all the blows of the world. You did not slap me. You only extended your hand in friendship. Today I have made a new friend and I never forget my friends,' he joined his palms in a namaste and stood up to leave. 'Goodbye, Manu-bhai, until we meet again,' he said and walked away.

Manu stared at the receding figure of Prakash Singh. And as he did so an eerie feeling came over him that he just could not make sense of—it was as if someone was walking over his grave.

A Proposal

The prince's death plunged Manu into an abyss of grief. The old memories haunted him—their chance encounter in Betla which had changed his life forever, his first ice cream at Buckingham Place hotel, the day when the prince had shown him into his own room, the night when he had saved Mary and him from the clutches of the police...there were so many memories. Now that the prince was gone, the emptiness of Registan Manor gnawed at him like a rat. He tried to relieve the pain by immersing himself in work. But every inch of the factory reminded him of the early days when they had built it up together, brick by brick from nothing.

But along with his grief, there was also a burning anger at the sufferings that the prince had endured and his helplessness festered inside him like a raw wound. Prakash Singh's advice to concentrate on the business seemed too timid, too cowardly a response and his mind kept going back to the possibility of approaching the courts for justice. Soon after his return to Calcutta, he asked Sayoni about it. But she wasn't encouraging.

'Unfortunately, I don't think the legal route will work, Manu,' Sayoni said. 'In this situation, the courts will do nothing.'

'Do nothing?' Manu exclaimed. 'Raja-saab was murdered by the police. He died in custody, without basic medical treatment. I wasn't even allowed to see his dead body, let alone perform his last rites. In which civilized country do such things happen? How can these criminals, these murderers go scot free?'

'This is no longer a civilized country, Manu,' Sayoni replied. 'There was one last hope. But with the latest Supreme Court judgement, even that has gone.'

'Meaning?'

'The Supreme Court has ruled that even a habeas corpus writ petition will not be admitted in court from now on.'

'I'm not a lawyer,' said Manu. 'What does that mean?'

'Habeas corpus. Meaning—show me the body,' Sayoni replied. 'Under habeas corpus, any person arrested by the police had the right to be produced before a court of law. And it was the court's prerogative to determine if the detention was lawful or not. But last week, your Supreme Court passed a judgement that suspends habeas corpus indefinitely. In the ADM Jabalpur *vs.* Shivkant Shukla case, the court has ruled that the right to habeas corpus does not hold good in a state of Emergency. Far worse, they have even ruled that Article 21, which guarantees the right to life and liberty, stands suspended during the Emergency—a majority ruling passed by four out of five judges of a Constitutional Bench—no less.'

'This sounds totally mad. Do you mean to say we don't even have the right to life anymore?'

'Yes. But I am not saying it. Your Supreme Court is.'

'Are you sure of all this? You practiced law in Bangladesh. What do you know—'

'I know, Manu. Bangladesh, Pakistan, India—there's hardly any difference in our laws. And I am a good lawyer.'

Manu's shoulders slumped. 'So, there's nothing we can do?'

'Not through the legal route at least. You just have to accept it and move on.'

'Is it so easy to just move on?'

'No, it's not,' replied Sayoni. She wrapped her arms around him and hugged him tight. 'And who knows that better than me? You lost your father. So did I. When I ran away from Bangladesh, I lost everything that was dear to me. But I have learnt to move on. I have learnt to let go. If I can do it, so can you.'

'It's hard, so hard,' mumbled Manu.

She gently stroked his hair and said: 'Time is the best healer. Don't waste your time fretting over things that you can't change. Do what you can do. Do what Prakash Singh told you to—build the business, get rich, get powerful and get back at the Congress. That is the best way to avenge your father's death.'

***

Manu was praying hard for the destruction of the Congress. But he wasn't the only one. Mrs Gandhi's son, Sanju-baba, had recently turned his attention to the population problem and had launched a nation-wide family planning drive. And across the fair and fertile land of India, millions of grown men were quaking in their langots, in dread of their private bits being snipped off. Every time Manu went out, I would utter a small prayer for the safe return of his crown jewels.

But it wasn't only Sanjay Gandhi's sterilization programme that was sapping the country of its vital juices. On one hand, the Red Queen and her son were ordering off the heads of anyone they didn't like. On the other, they were exhorting the citizenry to rise to the occasion by issuing alarmingly earnest edicts such as—

'Talk less, work more.'
'There is no substitute for hard work' and
'Twenty-point program is a blueprint for progress.'

Every day, we were being bombarded by such inspiring messages. It was enough to get any normal person down, what to say of poor Manu. I did my best to lift his spirits but my efforts proved fruitless. I whistled merry tunes to cheer him up, first thing in the morning, but he would shoo me away. I would read out the inspirational poems that appeared in the newspapers, in place of the actual news. Even the radio failed to improve his mood. The peppy Kishore Kumar songs, that he liked so much, had been banned ever since Kishore-da had refused to sing at a Congress convention, in praise of the Emergency. Instead, we were subjected to endless renditions of Mahendra Kapoor's *Mere desh ki dharti sona ugle*, until the bile uglo-ed in our mouths. I even tried light literature. But this backfired spectacularly, after I read out a passage from a recently published book entitled *World's Wisest Wizard: Psychography of a Cosmic Mind*, realizing only too late, that it was a biography of Sanjay Gandhi.

Luckily, apart from me, Sayoni was also there by Manu's side. She had become his Woman Friday—advisor, assistant, troubleshooter and girlfriend all rolled into one. When Manu found himself unable to bear the demands of running the factory, she stepped in and took the load off him, shielding him from the day-to-day problems of the business. Whether it was a delayed order, a breakdown in the equipment, an angry customer or an even angrier union leader, Sayoni managed it all with an energy and astuteness that surprised everyone.

The workers of Regal Bearings, all men, were not very happy that a mere female was calling the shots these days. A woman's place was in the kitchen, they said, not on the shop floor. What was the boss thinking of, they asked? The answer, of course, was quite obvious. She was a single woman and he was a single man—so what else could he be thinking of?

But Manu was only too relieved to have Sayoni by his side. She had excellent business sense and was quite capable of handling all her responsibilities. He realised how dependent he had become on her ever since Raja saab had died, and how close...

Naturally, tongues had started wagging and the rumours were flying thick and fast—last week, Manu and Sayoni had been sighted taking a boat ride at Princep Ghat. Three days ago, they had been seen huddling close to each other at Mocambo and so on. A reliable gossip at the factory even confirmed that Sayoni had started spending the nights at the boss's house.

But the thing with rumours is that they are often true. By the winter of 1976, Manu and Sayoni had become almost inseparable. She often spent the nights at Registan Manor, chatting about this and that, cooking a meal for him or listening to the radio together. It almost felt like they were a married couple. With Sayoni beside him, the darkness that had taken hold of Manu began to slowly recede.

***

It was only a matter of time before the inevitable happened. And one evening in the January of 1977, Manu popped the question that been on his mind for a while.

'Do you know that people are talking about us in the factory?' Manu asked. 'I heard some things recently that I didn't like at all.'

'Of course, I know,' Sayoni replied. 'I'm not deaf or blind. It's been going on for a while.'

'Really? I only came to know a few days ago.'

'They are too scared to talk in front of you. With me they aren't so polite.'

'And you never told me? It doesn't bother you?'

'It used to. But not anymore. I've gotten used to it.'

'You should have told me before. I would have—'

'You already had a lot on your mind, Manu. I thought you could do with one less thing to worry about.'

'I don't like the way they talk about you.'

'Why does it bother you so much? It's just idle gossip.'

'And how come it doesn't bother you? Any other woman—'

'Listen, Manu. I walked all the way from Dhaka to Calcutta. I saw horrors that no one should have to see. I lost everything and I thought my life was over. And then I met you. You gave me a job, you trusted me...it's you that I care about Manu, not the cheap talk of a few people.'

'You do?'

'Isn't that obvious?'

'I care for you too. A lot.'

'Thank you.'

'I was just wondering...'

'Yes?'

'So...I mean...should we get married?'

'Are you proposing to me?'

'Yes, I am.'

'Then propose properly.'

Manu took Sayoni's hand in his and asked: 'Will you marry me?'

'Finally! I was wondering if you would ever ask,' she replied.

'And?'

'Of course, I will, you silly man.' She bent down and sealed her answer with a kiss.

Marriage Parties

Ah, spring! Season of sweet love and sweaty marriages.

The sweet love you have just read about. Of the sweaty marriages, there were two. The first took place in Delhi on the Ides of March. But the romance that had preceded the marriage had been sparked off two months earlier. One cold January night, Mrs Gandhi surprised everyone by abruptly declaring that the Emergency was over and elections would be held soon. Electrified by this shocking but welcome announcement, the four principal opponents of the Congress party decided to meet for a quick group date.

The date went off so well that it ended in a proposal of marriage, or more accurately, a *ménage à quatre*. Spurred by their hate for the Congress and their love of power, the four different parties came together to form a polyamorous union named the Janata Party. And when the Lok Sabha elections were held later that year, the hastily cobbled alliance was swept to power. Much to Manu's delight, India had its first ever Congress-mukt government. The alliance included the Jana Sangh and it comforted Manu to think that the substantial contributions he had made towards the party funds might have contributed to the victory. Raja-saab's sacrifice hadn't gone in vain.

Mrs Gandhi's drubbing at the hustings sparked off celebrations all across the country. All India Radio played appropriate music like *Waqt Ne Kiya, Kya Haseen Sitam (What Sweet Torture has Time Wrought)* and Manu declared an early Durga Puja bonus for his employees to celebrate the goddess' long overdue exit from her father's jagir.

More celebrations were to follow three months later, when the second sweaty marriage of 1977 took place in Calcutta. In June that year, Manu and Sayoni finally tied the knot in a small private ceremony that was attended by a handful of profusely perspiring friends and colleagues. It wasn't the ideal time to marry, but Manu and Sayoni did not want to wait anymore and provide more grist to the gossip mill. A few guests grumbled about how they hadn't even been able wear their best clothes because of the horrible weather. Others made snide remarks about the unseemly ardour of middle-aged lovers who insisted on a mid-summer wedding. But Manu didn't care. After a long time, he was too happy to be bothered about the small stuff.

He had good reason to be happy. He was married to a woman he loved, in reasonably good health, owner of a decent business that provided a reasonable income and in possession of a mansion in Jodhpur Park. When he thought about how far he had come from his Betla days, he felt grateful. And like thirty-year-old India, forty-year-old Manu had much to be grateful for. Impoverished, illiterate and in the servitude of a cruel master for many years, both had shaken off the chains of the past and had made their own trysts with destiny. Manu had arrived at that stage of his life when he was beginning to feel that his *azaadi* wasn't *jhootha* anymore.

For years now, his life had been centred around the lives of other people—Rajinder Seth, Raja-saab, Mary. He had done whatever he could for them. But now he was beginning to feel that he was finally free from his debts, free of the shackles of the past, free to shape the future as he wanted to. If the first half of his life had been about surviving, the second half would be about thriving.

He would become rich. And powerful. He would become untouchable. Never again would he or his family be at the mercy of the government. Never again would any of his loved ones be thrown out of their homes, tortured and killed in jail by the government. Because it would be *his* government, and the government would be his. Now that the Jana Sangh was part of the ruling alliance, it wasn't merely a pipe dream, but the beginning of a new age...

Middle-aged Manu had come to that point, which comes but rarely in one's history, when he was striving to step out from the old to the new, when an age had ended, and when his soul, for long suppressed, yearned to find utterance. (Sometimes I am surprised by own eloquence, not to mention my tendency to pass off other people's writings as mine. But I suppose that is par for the course for any historian.)

***

We were about to voyage into new seas. Uncharted waters lay ahead and everyone was struggling to navigate through them. Mrs Gandhi and son were thinking of retiring from politics and living in a chateau in the Himalayas for the rest of their lives. Comrade Jyoti Basu, who had become the first Communist Chief Minister of West Bengal, had gotten his spotless white dhoti in a twist at the prospect of launching a rebellion against his own bourgeois government. The new Prime Minister, Morarji Desai, was agonizing over the appointment of the whisky-swigging Atal Bihari Vajpayee as his foreign minister.

Manu and Sayoni were struggling to adjust to their new lives as well. Fortunately, the questions that confronted them were far less weighty—limited to whether they should go to Gangtok or Shimla for their honeymoon (they chose Gangtok) or whether blue curtains would look better in the living room or pink (pink). But all said and done, married life was agreeing with Manu. After many years of being occupied by two bachelors, there was finally a woman living inside Registan Manor. And her deft touch had turned it into a home—there were flower vases and framed photographs, the aroma of freshly cooked meals. It felt wonderful to share a life with someone—cups of tea, radio programs, LP records, dinner at Mocambo and a warm bed. Sayoni's presence lifted Manu's spirits. He applied himself to the business with a renewed vigour and with Sayoni by his side, he hoped that he would finally be able to fulfil his ambitions of becoming a respected industrialist instead of a small-time businessman.

The country's spirits were high as well. After decades of mean-minded foreigners predicting that India was on its way to becoming a basket case, the world was now praising the wisdom of the Indian people for being flagbearers of democracy. Effusive reports were published in the *New York Times, London Times* and such-like. And although only about 9.37 per cent of the country could read English, it did not stop everyone from congratulating each other.

Everywhere I looked, change was in the air.

***

But three years later, it was clear that I had been mistaken. The Eighties were almost upon us but it seemed that we were still stuck in the Sixties.

In Delhi, the Janata Party was disintegrating faster than a limp biscuit dunked in a cup of tea. The awesome foursome in whom the country had placed its trust, was looking less like a *ménage à quatre* and more like a menagerie of squabbling sparrows. Sensing a turn in the tide, Mrs Gandhi and son postponed their Himalayan retirement plan and plunged straight back into battle. And when the Lok Sabha elections were held in 1980, Mrs Gandhi stormed back to power. Maa Durga was back in her father's home and the Jana Sangh was back in the wilderness.

Meanwhile in Calcutta, the Left Front government was back to its revolutionary ways. But evolution had been guillotined out of the revolution and even as the rest of the world moved forward, in Calcutta, the chorus of '*cholbe na, cholbe na* (won't do, won't do*)*', had even stopped the hands of the clocks. Three years of Communist rule had gifted the city its own unique version of the Pax Romana. I called it the pyak-pyak Bangaliana.

Pyak-pyak clacked the tongues of penurious Bengali poets, addicted to addas and cigarettes at the Coffee House on College Street, pyak-pyak clucked the tongues of parents rebuking their children for doing rock-baaji instead of studying bajaar notes on 'How to Succeed in Joint' (the engineering exam variety, and not the marijuana), pyak-pyak went the Leftist comrades, complaining of New Delhi's stepmotherly treatment towards Bengal, pyak-pyak went the ceiling fans croaking to a halt as load-shedding plunged the city into darkness and despair, pyak-pyak went the pages of *Anandabazar Patrika* flapping open in the hands of a million babus as they settled down to the morning chit-chat and pyak-pyak creaked the shutters of factories shut down by unending strikes, gheraos and lockouts.

The situation in Regal Bearings was particularly grim. The workers had gone on strike for over four months now and production had ground to a standstill. But Jyoti Babu's government did nothing about it. Capitalists had already been marked out as class enemies but Manu began to have a strong feeling that he was being singled out for special treatment. After all, by now, many people knew that his father had been a staunch supporter of the Jana Sangh and while Manu had kept his own political leanings a secret, there were whispers along the lines of 'like father, like son'. Both the Congress and the Communists detested the Jana Sangh and with the former at the Centre and the latter in the state, Manu felt as if he was caught between the hammer and the anvil.

One day, he returned home late and collapsed upon the sofa in exhaustion. He looked so grey and weary that Sayoni was worried that he had fallen ill.

'What's happened? You look terrible,' she said, as she placed a glass of water before him.

Manu gulped down the water and said: 'Thanks. I needed that badly. Haven't had a sip of water the whole day.'

'What happened?'

'There was a gherao in the factory!'

'Again!'

'Yes, and every time it's getting worse. They wouldn't even let me go to the bathroom. I had to sit in my office the whole day and listen to their slogans. I have such a splitting headache,' he lay down on the sofa and closed his eyes.

Sayoni sat down by his side and gently pressed her fingers against his temples. 'What do they want now? I thought you had increased the wages only two months ago.'

'Different issue this time. I fired three men last week. Not that I wanted to but I had to. They were just sitting around and smoking beedis all day long. The union is demanding that I have to take them back. And give a written undertaking that no one will ever be fired in the future.'

'Ridiculous!' said Sayoni.

'I don't know how long we can go on like this,' Manu said. 'If push comes to shove, we may have to shut down the factory or go somewhere else.'

'But where?' asked Sayoni.

'Maharashtra or Gujarat. That's where everyone is going these days.'

'But you know nothing of these places. You will have to start from scratch.'

'Yes, but it may be easier starting afresh rather than continuing here. Things are becoming just impossible. You know, they even threatened to set fire to the factory if I didn't take back those three men.'

'What?' Sayoni gasped. 'We should call the police.'

'They won't lift a finger against the unions. You know that, Sayoni. They have their orders.'

'But they are threatening you openly now. What if they do something to you?'

'Ah, don't worry so much. They say such things all the time. But their bark is worse than their bite.'

Sayoni looked up at him. 'I am scared, Manu,' she said. 'How can we go on like this?'

Manu stayed silent. He had asked himself the same question but he had no answer. Once again, the future seemed uncertain, the path ahead obscured by mist. Mid-way upon the journey of life, Manu could feel his dreams slipping through his fingers. The business that meant so much to him was being steadily destroyed by powerful forces over which he had no control. Like a phoenix, the Congress was rising from the ashes of his father's dream, and all he could do was to look on helplessly.

But what rankled the most was that even after three years of marriage, they were still childless. By now, Manu was already in his forties and it wasn't long before Sayoni got there. Aware that the biological clock was ticking away furiously, he and Sayoni were going at it hammer and tongs. The romance of the early days had almost faded away and these days, their lovemaking had turned into a Grim Project to Make a Baby. But it wasn't working. The doctors had assured Sayoni that there was nothing wrong with her. They recommended that Manu get himself checked up. But she could not bring herself to say it to him, for fear of hurting his ego. Even so, there were times when she wondered, only half in jest, whether he had been a victim of Sanjay Gandhi's nasbandi programme and had kept it a secret from her.

As the days went by, I could see that Manu was rapidly slipping into a mid-life crisis. He had only a few years to go before he turned fifty and all he had to show for himself was a string of failures. He had failed Mary, he had failed as a businessman, he had failed as a husband, and as a son.

Loser, loser, loser, an insidious voice kept whispering into his ear with the insistence of a drumbeat. With each passing day, the voice grew louder, and by the summer of 1984, the winter of Manu Singh's discontent had reached its peak.

But Manu wasn't the only discontented Singh. There were thousands, lakhs of others—from the yellow mustard fields of the Punjab to the snow-covered streets of Canada, who also believed that they had lost out. And they held the Indian state responsible for their woes. I only had to tilt my head westwards to hear the war drums beating loudly inside their hearts.

And with the sound of beating drums, there now came a vision to me...unclear, fuzzy as if I was peering through a thick fog, I saw the hazy outlines of a huge dome arching gracefully onto the skies... it appeared to be a temple...a glittering temple made of gold. Shining, yellow gold.

Another temple now swam into my vision—a temple of white gold somewhere in the forests of Betla. I saw bullets flying...men, women and children screaming. I saw their blood spill out and darken the earth...

The wheel of time was turning; the past was once again leaking into the future. But there was nothing I could do except watch, as the alchemy of time turned the temple of white gold into a gurudwara of yellow, glittering gold, and then into a masjid, and then a temple again, and then a church, and a temple.

Round and round the wheel was going...mandir, masjid, church, gurudwara shapeshifting from one to the other like the patterns of a kaleidoscope gone crazy, each one as different from the other as the gods that dwelt within them. Except for one thing—the cold, red blood that stained them was the same.

Book Five

1984

By the autumn of 1984, the jury was still out on whether George Orwell's terrifying vision of the future would come true or not. But of my vision, there was no such doubt.

Wherever I looked I saw blood. In the west, it was the blood staining the ramparts of the Golden Temple of Amritsar—the dried, still-warm blood of the Khalistani militants and the Indian Army soldiers who had fought a pitched battle inside the temple turned fortress. And in the north, in New Delhi, it was the blood of Mrs Gandhi, felled by a hail of bullets unleashed by her own bodyguards in retaliation against her assault on their beloved Golden Temple.

Mrs Gandhi's assassination plunged the country into shock. Numbed and lost, a billion people were praying for a saviour—a safe pair of hands to steady the rocking boat and steer it through the storm. And who could be better suited for such a job than a sailor... or a pilot. As luck would have it, there happened to be just such a man—a professional pilot by the name of Rajiv Gandhi. Hours after his mother's assassination, Rajiv was sworn in as interim Prime Minister. And for the first time in history, the golden sparrow of India was being flown by an expert pilot.

Our hopes rose but only to fall. For instead of guiding our beloved *sone ki chidiya* into safe havens, within hours of taking off, Mr Pilot-turned-PM managed to crash her into a tree—a fallen tree, at that.

***

'*When a mighty tree falls, the earth shakes*,' Manu read out from the newspaper. 'Can you believe it? Thousands of Sikhs are being butchered all over the country and this is all that Rajiv Gandhi has to say. Under his very nose, the Congress leaders are rioting on the streets of Delhi, armed mobs are shouting: *'Khoon ka badla khoon se lenge* (Blood will be revenged by blood).' These fucking Congressis!' he spat. 'How much more blood do they need?'

Sayoni shuddered. 'Don't! Please don't! I don't want to listen anymore.'

'But it's happening Sayoni, whether you want to listen or—'

'Stop!' Sayoni cut him off. 'Just stop! I can't hear of any more blood. It's bringing back the nightmares...the terrible, unspeakable things that I saw happening years ago in Dhaka. I'm scared Manu... I'm so scared.'

Manu grasped her hand and gave a gentle squeeze. 'I'm sorry. I should have realised...I'm scared too Sayoni. Let's just hope that the madness stops. What else can we do?'

It took a while for Sayoni to recover herself. 'Yes, what else can we do but hope?' she said with a deep sigh. After a while she asked: 'Do you have any Sikh friends in Delhi?'

'Not really, no,' Manu replied. 'Nowhere else either,' his eyebrows knotted into a frown, 'Unless you count Prakash Singh.'

'Prakash Singh? The man you met in Bangalore during the Emergency?' asked Sayoni.

'The same. Not really a friend I suppose, although he did help me when I was in trouble. But after that he just disappeared. I don't even know if he is actually a Sikh. He was probably in disguise. And given the situation now, I certainly hope he was. I hope he's safe... wherever he is...he said he was from Gujarat. Who knows, maybe things aren't too bad over there.'

'Let's hope so. Although I have to say one thing,' Sayoni replied, 'of all the places we could have been in, I'm glad that we are here in Calcutta. I think Jyoti Babu has handled the situation really well so far. The policing, the imposition of curfew, it's all helped. I don't think any Sikhs have been attacked here.'

'Can't disagree with you there,' said Manu, 'It's true they have kept the peace so far. But don't let that fool you. These Communists can be just as bloodthirsty as the Congressis. Look at how they killed those Ananda Margis on Bijon Setu. Seventeen monks burnt alive in broad daylight while the police just looked on. This is a lawless country, Sayoni.'

Sayoni gazed pensively at Manu and said: 'Sometimes, I am glad we don't have a child.'

Manu's face darkened. 'I know how much you wanted a baby. I am...I'm sorry that I failed you.'

'Don't be stupid,' Sayoni said. 'These things are not in anyone's hands. When I see what's happening around us, I think god didn't want us to bring a baby into this world. The riots, the killings, the blood—when will they ever stop!'

'I feel like that too. Sometimes I feel like just giving it all up and going off to the hills like Mary.'

'Mary?' Sayoni looked up. 'How come you've suddenly remembered Mary? It's been years since you mentioned her.'

'I don't know. But somehow, I've been thinking of her.'

'Have you heard from her recently?

'I got a letter from her last month.'

'Oh, why didn't you tell me?'

'Just like that.'

'I see. What did she write about? Is she still in Dehradun? Has she married yet?'

'Mary and marry?' Manu smiled. 'She was never the type. Don't think she ever will marry. She's too busy with her work. And yes, she's still in Dehradun.'

'What's she doing these days?'

'The same old nonsense. She and her jholawallah friends are trying stop some dam from being built. The Tehri dam, I think, she had written.'

'Nonsense? How can you say that? So typical of a man to dismiss anything a woman does.'

'It has nothing to do with her being a woman, Sayoni,' Manu replied. 'I've known Mary from childhood and she always had a screw loose. Why would anyone want to stop a dam from being built? I mean, for a change, the government is trying to do something useful. But then, all these activist types have to go and stop it. Dams stop floods from happening, dams generate electricity. And god knows how badly we need electricity in this country. My machines sit idle for hours every day, because of load shedding. And when the power comes back, the workers go on strike. And if by chance everything is okay, then riots break out. How the hell am I supposed to run my factory like this? How can I make a living? How can I provide for you?'

'You worry too much. If things go really bad, I can try and practice law again.'

'I hope it won't come to that. Speaking of which, there is something I have been meaning to talk to you about.'

'What?'

'I've been thinking about it for a while. Maybe it's time to shut down the factory.'

'Shut down the factory? But it's our only source of income. What will—'

'There is hardly any income these days. We've been running on losses for the last six months.'

'You never told me—'

'I am telling you now, right? Listen, I've tried everything. But it's no longer possible to keep Regal Bearings going.'

'What do you have in mind?'

'I'm thinking of getting into real estate.'

'I don't understand.'

'Real estate. It's the best business these days.'

'Yes, but—'

'It's simple, Sayoni. I'm going to make flats and sell them.'

'But where? How?'

'I'll demolish the factory and use the land to build flats. There's a good market for low-cost flats in Calcutta these days.'

'But you don't know anything about real estate.'

'There's nothing to know. It's much simpler to make flats than motor parts. All you need is land and I have almost one acre.'

'But that land was given out on an industrial usage lease. How will you get it converted to residential usage? Is it even possible?'

'It is. I've found out.'

'But it'll be a nightmare. You will need to get permissions from dozens of government departments.'

'Let's see. I've been talking to some people. They say they can get it done. It'll require some hefty bribes, of course.'

'How much?'

'A few lakh rupees perhaps. But even after all the bribes I should be able to make a decent profit. I've done all the calculations.'

'May I see them please?'

'Of course, I would have asked you anyway.'

'Tell me something—who's going to buy these flats? Uttarpara is miles away from Calcutta. Not exactly a prime location is it?'

'No, but the trick will be to make them affordable. There's a big market for budget flats these days. People are flooding into Calcutta. Garia, Patuli, Naktala—they are full of Bengalis who are running away from the Northeast to settle here. From Assam and Meghalaya especially because of the anti-foreigner agitations going on there these days.'

'Foreigners? You mean Bangladeshis? Like me?'

'You could say so. But they have been living in India for many years now.'

'And you are going to build homes for them?'

'It's clear the business is going nowhere and this is the only thing I can think of right now. Let me give it a try at least. What do you say?'

'It won't be easy. But if that's what you want to do, then who am I to stop you? After all, who knows better than me what a home means?'

***

If Manu's business was on the brink of collapse, so was the Jana Sangh's. Recently renamed as the Bharatiya Janata Party, it seemed to have attracted very few Bharatiyas. In the elections following Mrs Gandhi's assassination, the BJP had been able to win only two Lok Sabha seats against the four hundred and twenty-six won by the Congress. In spite of having dashed the golden sparrow against a mighty tree, the dashing young pilot was now flying high on the sympathy wave caused by the fall of the aforementioned tree.

Like Manu, the BJP was struggling for survival. And like Manu, the BJP too had realised that the path to salvation began with construction. But where Manu had chosen to build flats for the newly prosperous, the BJP decided to build temples for destitute gods.

I only wish they had checked with me once before going down that path. Me, being a divine being and all that, with first-hand experience of dealing with the gods—both major and minor. And believe you me, in all my long and distinguished career, not a single god have I known has ever needed to be saved by a mere mortal, let alone a politician. But then if politicians didn't fight over gods and votes, what would they do for time-pass? Build schools and hospitals hna? Ewww...so boring....

But the BJP had zero interest in the gratuitous advice dished out by the Ramchandra and Prem Chandra Guhas of the world. Their attention was consumed by a far more important person—the Mughal emperor Babur. The BJP claimed that Babur had torn down a temple that stood at the very spot where Lord Rama was born in Ayodhya, and had built a mosque on the ruins. This was an impossible, intolerable situation, a civilizational wound, an insult to Hindus. Something needed to be done about it and something was. Soon enough, the BJP and its extended family launched a nationwide campaign for the construction of a grand temple for the homeless Lord Rama at the site of the Babri Masjid.

Manu's ambitions were far more modest. All he wanted was to shut down his ailing factory and construct low-cost flats for the middle-class on his one-acre plot of land in Uttarpara. But whether it was modest 2-BHK flats for mortals in Uttarpara or grand temples for the gods in Ayodhya, construction in India is a difficult affair. And if it requires land usage conversion, from industrial to residential or from masjid to mandir, then things can become really messy.

But the futures of both the Singh and the Sangh parivars were at stake and they were determined to do what it took to survive. They hunkered down, donned the war paint, girded their loins and prepared themselves for the long, hard struggle ahead.

It wasn't a pretty sight...I can tell you that much.

Computers

But two years later, neither Manu nor the BJP were anywhere in sight of the promised land. For between them and their dreams stood the Lakshman Rekha of the law. Occupation was nine parts of the law and if a piece of land was occupied by a masjid, then it could not simply be torn down overnight to build a mandir. The same rule applied to factories and flats.

But Manu was undeterred. Leaving the day-to-day operations of Regal Bearings to Sayoni, he made the rounds of the law courts, and the Inspector of Factories, and the Labour Department, and the Registrar of Stamps and Duties and the Hooghly Municipal Corporation and every other pettifogging official whose signature he needed on some pettifogging piece of paper or the other. Of the lot, the Municipal Corporation was the worst—packed to the rafters with some of the most corrupt specimens of humanity that it had ever been his misfortune to meet.

And so it was, that Manu had become a regular visitor to the offices of the Hooghly Municipal Corporation. Like a rat in maze, he scurried up and down its dingy corridors every day, a wad of notes in his pocket, a briefcase bulging with files in his hand and a prayer on his lips.

It was on one such day that he met the man who was to nudge him into the next lap of his journey.

***

He was a tall, lean man, with a morose moustache that hung limply in the damp heat of Calcutta. Like everyone else, he too had a briefcase of files in his hand and a resigned expression on his face as he waited patiently for the babus to have their morning cups of tea, read their newspapers, solve their crossword puzzles, finish their addas and play a few hands of rummy before finally settling down to an honest half hour of work.

Manu had seen the man a few times at the Municipal office. On each occasion, he had been struck by his appearance. Unlike most of the other supplicants who thronged the offices of the Corporation, he was attired in a tailored grey suit, expensive leather shoes and a blue striped tie. There was a suppressed energy in him, like that of a coiled spring that was at odds with the general air of apathy that pervaded the place. Today, he was pacing up and down the reception, his face grim as a thundercloud. After a while, he walked up to the reception desk and slammed his files under the nose of the bored clerk who was manning it.

'*Aur kitna time lagega*!' he barked at the clerk in a clipped English-afflicted Hindi. 'How much more time? I've been waiting for two hours. *Mere ko plane pakadna hai aaj, 4 baje ka flight hai.* I have a plane to catch—my flight is at four o'clock.'

The clerk lifted his gaze from his newspaper. '*Plane dhorna ha to jaao dhoro. Ham kya air hostess lagta?* (Go catch your plane then. Do I look like an air-hostess)?' he replied as he scanned the intruder from top to bottom. '*Suit tie porta hai to nijeke laat shaheb samajhta hai kya* (Do you think you are a big saheb just because you are wearing a suit and tie)? Bloody nonsense character,' the clerk said and returned to his newspaper.

The man threw him a furious look and returned to the seating area. Swearing under his breath, he sat down heavily on the chair next to Manu.

'These people should be hanged,' Manu said. 'Just see the way they treat us. Is this why we pay our taxes?'

'I know!' the man exclaimed angrily. 'Five days in a row I have been coming here but my file hasn't moved forward by one inch. And I have to get back to Bangalore today.'

'Oh, you are from Bangalore, is it?' asked Manu.

'Yes. Have you been there?' the stranger asked.

'Only once,' said Manu. A lump formed in his throat, as he remembered himself sitting at Sukh Sagar, listening to Prakash Singh's account of Raja-saab's death. 'It was a very short stay.'

'I have nothing against Calcutta,' the man went on. 'It's not as if things are all hunky dory in Bangalore. But it's nothing compared to this. It's so difficult to get any work done here. And it's going from bad to worse, I can tell you.'

'You don't have to tell me. I know it only too well. So, what brings you to Calcutta?'

'I have a warehouse here in Howrah. I wanted to convert it into an office space for my new business. But I need their blessings for that,' he jerked his head at the ranks of clerks huddled over their tables in the adjoining hall.

'You have your own business?' asked Manu.

'Yes, manufacturing. I'm into vegetable oils—sunflower, vanaspati, that sort of thing. It's been around for a while. My father started it in 1945 and I inherited it from him when he died.'

'Is it? What a coincidence. I am into manufacturing as well—bushings and bearings. Inherited it from my father, just like you. Vegetable oils sounds like a good business to be in. People will always need oil, right? How are the margins? Good?'

'Not too bad. But to tell you the truth, I am totally bored of vegetable oils. I'm trying to get into computers now. That's why I need to set up an office here quickly—for my programmers. There are a lot of bright young engineers in these parts—from Shibpur, Jadavpur, Kharagpur. I thought, why do they have to come all the way to Bangalore, if they can work from Calcutta. They will be happier here and I can also reduce salary costs.'

'But what about union problems?'

'That is not likely. Computer programmers are highly educated, middle-class people. They are not cut out for all this union nonsense. That's another reason I want to get into the computer business.'

'I am afraid I know nothing about computers. I've never seen one in my life.'

'Next time you are in Bangalore, come and visit us. I'll show you. Computers! It is the future, sir—you mark my words.'

There was a gleam in the man's eyes as he spoke. He seemed to have magically perked up at the mention of computers. Manu took a closer look at him. He was probably in his early forties, younger than him but not much. Another middle-aged man with youthful dreams. At least he wasn't the only dreamer...

'Certainly,' said Manu, 'if I come to Bangalore, I would definitely like to see your computer factory.'

The man threw a curious look at Manu. 'That's right. That's exactly right. Funny, how I never saw it that way...a computer factory,' he muttered, as if he was speaking to himself. 'Yes...that's exactly how it should be run—like a factory. Men, machines, raw materials, finished products...' he looked up with a start, 'I'm sorry. It's just that your words set me thinking.'

'No problem, sir. I know how it is when you are trying to do something new. You think about it all the time. I'm trying to start a new business myself.'

'I see. What line?'

'Real estate. Flats.'

'Ah, real estate! A tough, tough business. But very profitable if you can make it work.'

'You think so? I'm quite new to it so I don't really know how it will go. But I'm trying.'

'Aren't we all? But let me tell you, sir. You have chosen a good line. Real estate is going to boom in India. It's already started to happen in Bangalore.'

'Really?'

'Oh yes. Bangalore is the new Calcutta. Everyone is coming there. Why don't you think of starting something there as well? The land is still cheap, especially compared to other cities. But it won't stay that way for long.'

'Let's see. Let me start with Calcutta at least. Like they say, you have to crawl before you can walk.'

'True, true. Well, it has been nice chatting with you,' the man said. 'But I should go now and find out what's happening to that file of mine. But here's my card,' he extracted a visiting card from his pocket and offered it to Manu. 'Next time you come to Bangalore, do come and visit us.' Manu took the card and offered him one of his own.

'Mr Manu Pratap Singh,' the man said as he glanced at the card. 'I see. Very nice to meet you Mr Singh. Good luck with your new venture and until we meet again, goodbye,' he shook Manu's hand and rose to leave.

Manu looked at the card in his hand. It read:

Ameer Premjee
Managing Director
WEEPRO
(Worldwide Electrical and Electronic Products Ltd)
Doddakannelli, Sarjapura Road,
Bangalore—560 035

Manu gazed at Mr Premjee's receding figure. He had a feeling that their paths would cross again.

Uttarpara Housing Society

While the BJP was giving its heart and soul for the construction of Ram Lalla's new home in Ayodhya, Manu was giving his to the Uttarpara housing project. But the mills of god and government grind exceedingly slow and neither Lord Rama's bhakts nor Manu had made much progress so far. But after many torrid months of *chakkar-katoing* and palm-greasing Manu was finally able to secure all the three hundred and thirty-seven permissions required to shut down the factory and construct a housing complex on its premises. And in the winter of 1986, the moment that he had both been dreading and hoping for finally arrived.

Cranes rumbled through the gates of Regal Bearings and wrecking balls swung into action. Under their onslaught, the walls of the factory began to crack and crumble. The foundations shuddered, the high roofs shivered and before you could say *'Budget flats wahi banayenge'*, the building collapsed like a house of cards.

The shockwaves from the crash travelled all the way from Uttarpara straight into the BJP headquarters at Jhandewalan, jerking its dejected leaders out of their stupor. It was as if they had heard the sound of Shiva's bow being broken by Lord Rama. An electrifying idea now entered their heads. And as it began to sink in, they winked and nodded at each other, their lips moving silently as if to say: *'Manu beta, tera number toh aa gaya, ab hamara bhi aayega* (Manu, your luck is turning, and soon, so will ours).'

But to Manu, the demolition of the old factory felt like the loss of his own child. Something died inside him and as he gazed at the mound of concrete and rubble to which it had been reduced, the memories flooded through him and he had to blink back his tears. Things would never be the same again. The old order had ended and the new had begun. But whether it would be for better or for worse, only time would tell.

***

In the spring of 1987, Regal Bearings Ltd was given a quiet burial and replaced by the newly incorporated Regal Estates Ltd. With new hopes and new energy, newly minted property developer Manu Pratap Singh stepped into the muddy, murky world of real estate. But it did not take him long to realise that Mr Premjee had been right.

The construction business was tough. Extraordinarily tough. It is true that the labour problems were less severe because of the steady supply of poverty-stricken construction workers from Bihar and UP who were too disorganised to go on strike every other day. But almost everything else was maddeningly difficult, enough to drive anyone up the half-constructed walls.

From ensuring adequate supplies of cement and sand, to getting building plans approved by the municipality, to filing applications for water, electricity and sewage connections—everything took enormous time and huge bribes. And even then, one couldn't be sure that the work would finally get done. And the worst problem of all—the problem of happiness.

The success or failure of a construction project depended on the builder's ability to spread the happiness. The long list of people who had to be made happy included the MLA, the councillor, the sewage inspector, the health officer, the block development officer, their brothers, nephews and other assorted friends and relatives. Cement had to bought from the MLA's first cousin twice removed, sand from the councillor's second cousin once removed and so on. And then there were the clubs—the Howrah Sarbojonin Club, the Evergreen Boys Club, the Uttarpara Forever Friends Club and a host of other happiness seeking clubs.

A host of unidentified young men who claimed to be office-bearers of these clubs, swarmed around Manu like a cloud of locusts, their left hands clutching thick receipt books, and right hands stretched out for donations. The ostensible purposes of these donations were as eclectic as they were noble—Durga Puja, Kali Puja, a new carrom board for the club, a statue of Diego Maradona, a Kumar Sanu evening and on one occasion, a sponsorship for the Miss Uttarpara Universe competition. Manu had no option but to pay up, for as the boys would gently remind him, people who wanted to swim in the river, were advised to keep the crocodiles happy.

***

Three years of blood, bribes, sweat and cement went into the Uttarpara project. But it was done at last and one spring morning in 1990, Manu was able to stand on his one-acre plot of land and gaze proudly at the two hundred 2-BHK flats that had been constructed upon it. Under the circumstances, he had done well, far better than the BJP certainly, who hadn't been able to lay even a single brick for Ram Lalla's home in all these years. Where they had failed, Manu had succeeded. But the success had come at a heavy price. The project had barely broken even, and his financial situation was the worst that it had been in years.

These days, when he looked at himself in the mirror, a tired, haggard face stared back. He was fifty-three and he felt every year of it. He felt it in the stiffness of his joints, the odd spasm of pain in his heart and the increasingly frequent failures in bed. How had he become so old so quickly? Where had all the years vanished? It seemed only yesterday that he had been a ten-year-old boy roaming the forests of Betla with Mary. Waves of regret washed over him. He had so little to show for his fifty-three years—no wealth, no child, no name and fame...only broken promises and unfulfilled dreams.

He stared out of the window. The city lay before him like a vast grey canvas. Oh Calcutta! The city that had taken away as much as it had given, this terrible, beautiful city that was so difficult to like, and yet so easy to love...for in spite of everything, he had grown to love Calcutta. But there were times when he felt her grey sameness, her inertia, her great weariness seeping into him. Was he becoming like her, exhausted by struggle and spiralling into irrelevance? Had he been made so weak by time and fate that he had lost the will to strive and to seek? Or did he still have it in him to make one last charge at life before it slipped away like grains of sand through the neck of an hourglass? Did he dare to throw the dice for one last time?

***

'Are you all right?' Sayoni asked, a concerned expression on her face. 'You don't look well. Maybe you should you see a doctor.'

'I'm okay. Just a little tired. This Uttarpara project has taken its toll on me,' Manu replied.

'I can see that. And what has it given in return?' Sayoni said. 'I was looking at the final numbers yesterday. They don't look very good.'

'I know.'

'I don't want to add to your worries, but you should know that things are already getting a little tight money-wise.'

'How tight?'

'If all the flats get sold, then we should be okay for the next eighteen months or so. But after that we will run out of cash. The bank loans have to be paid off as you know.'

'I know.'

'I'm beginning to get a little worried, Manu.'

'We'll manage somehow,' Manu lit up a cigarette. 'We always have, haven't we?'

'Yes but—'

'I'll think of something. Anyway, listen—I'm planning to go out of town for a few days.'

'Where?'

'Bangalore,' replied Manu, taking a drag on his cigarette.

'Bangalore!' Sayoni raised her eyebrows. 'What for?'

'I want to see the place for myself once. Everyone's talking about Bangalore these days. I thought it might be worth a visit. Who knows, I might be able to find some good business there.'

Manu was right. These days, all the newspapers were nattering on about how Bangalore was becoming the fastest growing city of India, if not Asia. If the reports were to be believed, hot, new computer companies were mushrooming in every street corner. Manu found himself thinking of his brief visit there in 1976. In spite of the circumstances, he remembered how impressed he had been by the clean, orderly city with its smooth, tree-lined roads, its uninterrupted power supply and its brilliant weather. Especially the weather. Although he had gone there in May, he hadn't had to switch on a fan even once. Cool, casual Bangalore had been as different from hot, humid, chaotic Calcutta as chalk from cheese. If Calcutta was like an arthritic old tabby, content to watch the world go by, Bangalore was like a frisky puppy straining at the leash to explore it.

But Sayoni didn't seem to share Manu's enthusiasm. 'You know nothing about Bangalore. What do you hope to achieve by going there?'

'When Raja-saab came here to start his business he didn't know anything about Calcutta either,' Manu replied. 'He had to start from scratch and he succeeded. Because he wasn't scared. I remember him telling me how much he admired the Marwari businessmen, who were bold enough to go wherever there was business.'

'Are you seriously telling me that you are planning to start a business in Bangalore now?' asked Sayoni.

'I'm not saying that. But there's no harm in thinking about it, is there? Look Sayoni, it's obvious that Calcutta is a dying city. It has no future. Certainly not for a businessman like me.'

'Maybe it doesn't, but what makes you think that Bangalore will be any better? This is India after all.'

'Oh, come on! Bangalore and Calcutta are worlds apart. For every company that is shutting down here, five new ones are opening there. There's a whole new industry coming up in Bangalore—computers.'

'You are going to start a computer business in Bangalore? Manu, you have gone mad!'

'I am not that stupid, Sayoni. I know what I can do and what I can't. Listen, it's simple. From what I know, computers have to be run by people. Lots of people. And people need houses to stay in. And if that is so, then why shouldn't I make those houses? I know I can do that. All I need is land and I hear that it's still cheap in Bangalore. I can smell an opportunity, Sayoni, and I want to find out more about it.'

'I think you are just daydreaming, Manu. Who's been telling you all this? What do you know about these computer companies anyway?'

'I've been reading about them. Besides there's someone I met who had told me about how Bangalore was going to become the computer capital of India. And I think he's right. In fact, his photo appeared in *Business Today* just the other day. Looks like he's doing very well for himself in the computers line.'

'Who's this person? How do you know him?'

'A man called Ameer Premjee. Quite an impressive fellow. We met a few years ago by accident and started talking. That's when he invited me to visit his computer factory in Bangalore. I am curious about it. I've never seen a computer in my life, you know. I hope he agrees to meet me though. It's been a long time. But even if he doesn't, it's not a problem. I'll take a look around the place and come back in couple of days.'

Sayoni wasn't convinced that either Ameer Premjee's factory or Bangalore were worth visiting. But she let Manu have his way. One week later, he took a flight to Bangalore and checked into Hotel Minerva on J.C. Road. The following morning, he called the WEEPRO office to seek an appointment with Mr Premjee. He was pleasantly surprised when Mr Premjee's secretary called him back to confirm the meeting. When he arrived at the WEEPRO office at Sarjapura Road, he was even more surprised to discover that Mr Premjee remembered him quite well.

They spoke for about an hour, after which Mr Premjee gave him a tour of his computer factory. It was an eye opener for Manu. He gazed admiringly at the rows of young men and women hunched before grey TV-like boxes, their fingers diligently tapping away on flattish typewriters. The atmosphere of quiet, concentrated work was so different from the ruckus of the shop floor in Regal Bearings.

Mr Premjee informed Manu that the TVs were actually computers and that the men were programmers.

'But what exactly are they doing?' Manu asked. 'I don't see them making anything.'

'Oh, but they are. They are making software,' Mr Premjee replied.

'Software? What is that?' Manu asked.

'How do I explain this?' Mr Premjee frowned. 'Basically, software is what tells a computer what it should do.'

It was clear as mud to Manu but he nodded understandingly. 'I see. And how much do you pay them?' he nodded at the programmers.

'Oh, about two or three thousand a month for freshers,' Mr Premjee replied. 'Double that in three years' if they stay on. Unfortunately, good programmers don't come cheap.'

The answer took Manu's breath away. These people were barely twenty-one and they were making so much money! Such a thing was unheard of in Calcutta.

Mr Premjee seemed to have read his thoughts. 'Yes, they make good money,' he said. 'And they spend it well too. The new generation is not bothered about savings, Mr Singh. They want to enjoy life—they spend all their money on clothes, beer, holidays. Which, by the way, brings me to the reason that I thought I should meet you.'

'I don't understand.'

'Let me explain. You see Mr Singh, WEEPRO is growing fast. We are hiring hundreds of people every year, thousands even. They are coming from all over the country to Bangalore. They need good houses to stay in and they can afford to pay for it. Which is where builders like you come in. There is a high demand for decent quality flats in Bangalore and not enough supply. So why don't you fill the gap? It will be good for you, good for my employees and good for me. What do you say, Mr Singh?'

'It all sounds very exciting,' Manu replied. 'But why are you telling me all this, sir? I mean...you hardly know me.'

Mr Premjee smiled. 'No, but I know this much, Mr Singh—if you could manage to run a business in Calcutta for so many years, then you have plenty of brains and balls. And that's what the real estate business takes.'

'I don't know about all that. But thank you, sir. I must admit it hasn't been easy doing business there.'

'I can imagine. Besides there is something else too.'

'Yes, sir?'

'I hope you won't mind me saying this, Mr Singh. But I see a little bit of myself in you. After all, neither of us is exactly young, are we? But we are both trying to do something new. We are trying to build something where nothing existed. That's not easy and I admire people who try to do the difficult things.'

Manu tried to look modest. 'I don't know what to say, sir. That's very kind of you.'

'I am just a businessman. But I think you are a fighter and I like fighters. Think about it, Mr Singh—if my computer business goes well, I will need a reliable property developer by my side. Housing, offices, IT parks—there are tons of things that will have to be built.

You mark my words. Bangalore is going to become the Silicon Valley of India. A gold rush is about to happen, Mr Singh, a gold rush.'

Mr Premjee spoke with such confidence and passion that it was difficult not to be swayed by his words. By the end of the meeting, Manu was convinced that Bangalore's business prospects were booming. He decided to stay on for a few more days to get a better sense of the place. And the more he saw of it, the more he felt that Mr Premjee hadn't been exaggerating. Bangalore was a city on the move, and it was only a matter of time before it would leave the likes of Calcutta far behind.

By the time Manu returned home, he had made up his mind. He might be an old, greying prospector but his hunger for gold was still green. And he wasn't going to miss the last gold rush of his life.

The Great Reboot

According to the Chinese calendar, 1991 was the Year of the Goat. In India however, it turned out to be the Year of the Great Reboot.

It was the year in which the country's foreign exchange reserves had plummeted to such perilous levels that only a total reboot of the economy could save the situation. It was also the year in which the assassination of Rajiv Gandhi had forced the Congress party to reboot itself, thereby precipitating an unprecedented transfer of power from the Nehru family to an outsider, P.V. Narasimha Rao. It was the year in which his wise old vizier, Manmohan Singh, would have to press the reset button to rescue India from the financial crisis into which it had been plunged. And it was the year in which Manu Singh would have to do to himself what Manmohan Singh was doing to the country—reboot.

In short, 1991 was that magical year in which fifty-four-year-old Manu and the forty-four-year-old republic would both have to turn their backs on the failures of the past and give themselves another chance to make good their futures. (And as it turned out, 1991 was the year of the GOAT not only for China, but for India and for Manu as well—of all years it was quite simply, the Greatest of All Time.)

***

If Manmohan Singh was placing his bets on India, Manu Singh was placing his on Bangalore. It had been six months since he opened a small branch office of Regal Estates in that salubrious city. He had taken a bank loan to make two investments which he fervently prayed would pay off. The first was a plot of land in a locality called Indiranagar. It had cost him a pretty penny but he still had a little money left over. With it he bought a one-acre plot of land in Koramangala, a thick jungle on the outskirts of Bangalore. Both deals had been based on Mr Premjee's advice.

'If you want to get into the real estate business in Bangalore, then start with Indiranagar,' Mr Premjee advised him. 'It's an old residential locality and the land is a little expensive. But I expect its value to shoot up in the next two years. This is the right time to buy. Build good-quality flats, hold them for a year or two and sell them. You're sure to get a good return.'

'And Koramangala?'

'Ah, now that is a little more risky. It will take a while to come up but when it does, it will be big. I believe Koramangala is going to become the next Indiranagar. If you have any money to spare, put it there. You could hit the jackpot.'

'Why do you say that, sir?' Manu asked. 'I've seen this Koramangala place. It's so far from the city. There's nothing but a jungle there. Jackals howling after dark. Who will be crazy enough to even think of buying a house there? Not in the next ten years. Not even thirty, I would think.'

'Thirty!' Mr Premjee laughed. 'Three to five years is all it will take. I'm telling you again, Mr Singh, Bangalore is going to become the Silicon Valley of Asia. And when that happens Koramangala will become its heart, and Electronic City its head. Have you seen Electronic City, by the way?'

'Yes, I went there yesterday. Quite a few offices, although it looks as if there are plenty of open sites still.'

'There won't be for much longer. Every day five new companies are opening their offices there. Three years from now, Electronic City is where people will go to work. And Koramangala is where they will live. You see, it's the perfect location—mid-way between Bangalore and Electronic City. Demand will just shoot up. If I were you, I'd buy some land in Koramangala before it becomes too expensive.'

Manu nodded. 'All right, if you say so. After all you know Bangalore much better than me. I'm just an outsider here.'

Mr Premjee smiled. 'So, what's the problem? Outsiders are good. Outsiders work hard. They are self-made people. We are all outsiders.

I came here from Bombay. Eighty per cent of my employees are from outside Karnataka. They are young, smart and hungry. Bangalore is the future, Mr Singh, not Delhi or Calcutta or even Bombay. Bangalore is all about creating wealth, not inheriting it. If anyone has an idea, this is the place to be. This is where ideas can be converted into money. Bangalore is the closest thing we have to the American Dream.'

Manu didn't know if Bangalore was India's version of the American Dream. But after Calcutta, it certainly felt like a breath of fresh air. These days he was shuttling back and forth between the two cities and the difference was palpable. If Calcutta reeked of mothballs nestled in old clothes, Bangalore was redolent with the heady perfume of youth and energy.

'I hope you are right, sir,' Manu said. 'It's a huge change for us to leave everything and settle here. My wife is quite scared, to tell you the truth. She doesn't want to move from Calcutta. And then there are the language issues, the food and—'

Mr Premjee raised his hand and cut him off. 'Tell her not to worry about such small things. Thousands of my own employees are from West Bengal. So many of them in fact, have already started calling it Bengal-uru,' Manu smiled as Mr Premjee went on. 'Set aside your doubts, Mr Singh. This is the right place and this is the right time. The reforms announced by Dr Manmohan Singh have the potential to totally change the way business is done in India. The economy will go into a new orbit and if we play our cards right, we will all make a lot of money. I'm telling you, Mr Singh, the gold rush has just started. But if you want to cross the river of gold, then you can't have your feet in two boats.'

After a great deal of dithering and deliberation, Manu and Sayoni finally jumped boats from Calcutta to Bangalore. It wasn't easy to say goodbye to the city which had been their home for so many years and on the day they boarded the flight to Bangalore, their eyes were moist. But for better or for worse, the decision had been made and they would have to live by it.

***

Manu had rented an apartment in Indiranagar, a cozy two-bedroom flat on the fourth floor that overlooked a leafy street. It was comfortable enough but a far cry from Registan Manor. It took Manu and Sayoni some time to adjust to their new surroundings, but all said and done, the reboot turned out to be easier than either of them had expected.

One evening, when a gentle June evening shower was pattering outside, Manu said to Sayoni: 'How does it feel to be here? I sometimes wonder if I did the right thing by asking you to move to Bangalore.'

'I can't say I don't miss Calcutta once in a while,' Sayoni sighed. 'The place has its charm. But then I must admit, so does Bangalore. Especially the weather! It's just amazing! I'm wearing a sweater in June. Can you believe it?'

'I think the weather is the main reason why the people here are so nice and polite.'

'I know. Even the milkman says hallo to me every morning, when he hands over the milk.'

Manu smiled. 'Not hallo. He says *halu*, which means milk in Kannada.' In the last few months, Manu had picked up a smattering of Kannada from the local contractors with whom he had started working.

'Oh, I see,' Sayoni laughed. 'How's it going with the business?'

'Pretty decent. I'm glad I took Mr Premjee's advice. Do you know all the Indiranagar flats have already been booked? And we've just about laid the foundation.'

'That's excellent! And what about Koramangala?'

'Going on. The electric lines, access roads are all in place. We should be able to start construction in a few months. There's only one small problem though.'

'What?'

'There are no drainage and sewage connections yet. The municipality hasn't laid the lines in that area.'

'What? But how will you build flats without sewage connections?'

'They'll come in five or six years. It's part of the city master plan.'

'But what will you do until then? Five years isn't a short time.'

Manu shrugged. 'There's a sort of drain nearby. Challaghatta Valley, it's called. I think it used to be a river a long time ago but now it's just a drain. The other builders are pumping in their sewage there. So I suppose that's what I'll have to do as well.'

Sayoni frowned. 'But that's illegal, isn't it? More importantly, it isn't right.'

'Yes, but everyone is doing it—Raheja, Shobha, Purvankara, all the big builders. Who can afford to wait for five years? Infosys and WEEPRO have already set up their offices in Koramangala. There's a demand for five hundred new flats at least. I have to move fast or I'll miss the boat.'

'Five hundred flats! Who's buying them?'

'All these young software people. They can afford it with their fat salaries. Twenty-five-year-old kids are making thirty thousand rupees a month!'

'That's a lot of money.'

'I know. A house costing 15-20 lakhs is nothing for these people. The banks are queuing up to give them loans. Who could have thought of it ten years ago? People had to wait until they had retired to be able to buy a house with their Provident Fund. But not anymore. It's amazing, just amazing, what's happening in India these days. I've never seen anything like it before.'

***

It was true that we had never seen anything like it before. Good old India was changing right before our eyes at a blistering speed. The strong medicine administered by the good doctor Manmohan Singh had not only taken the economy out of the ICU but had catapulted it straight into the gym. Businesses were getting fitter and their owners fatter. Shopping malls were going up, single malts were going down, and Mercedes cars were going any which way they pleased. The golden sparrow had finally been released from its cage and it was flying high.

As Mr Premjee had foreseen, the software business was booming in Bangalore. The demand for techies was so high that the giant technology campuses in Electronic City had put up signboards which read: 'Trespassers Will Be Recruited.' Tidal waves of techies were washing up to the shores of Bangalore. They worked hard and partied hard. It was COBOL and C++ by day, beer and curd rice by night and a sweet salary cheque at the end of the month.

But if it was boom time in Bangalore, in Ayodhya it was

demolition time. Thousands of kar sevaks, primed by the grim leaders of Hindutva, brought the domes of the Babri Masjid crashing to the ground in just hours, using iron rods, shovels and pick-axes. The very name of God was turned into a weapon and cries of '*Jai Shri Ram*' shook the land.

More was to come. Riots broke out across the country, the worst of them in Bombay, where Muslims paid the heaviest price. Retaliation came barely four months later, and that great big city of ten million souls was ripped apart by a series of explosions. Blood spilled on the streets and in the local trains again. Trishuls and AK-47s stabbed the air, and the acrid smoke of RDX mingled with the exhaust fumes of Audi cars.

In all my years of exile, I had never seen anything like it. India had been rebooted. The old operating system had become obsolete, and it was impossible to say what the new one would have in store for the country.

The Golden Bird Flies

In three short years, the country had changed beyond recognition. But the new India was working out rather well for Manu. His Koramangala flats were selling like hot Gobi Manchurians on a rainy Bangalore evening. A river of gold was flowing into Manu's pockets. But along with it was flowing a river of raw sewage, pouring out of the flats that he had sold to his techie customers. Every morning when they squatted on their gleaming white commodes, their shit flowed straight into the Challaghatta Valley and the many lakes that lay scattered across the city like a broken string of emeralds, turning their clear, green waters into frothing, stinking cauldrons of black filth.

The wings of the golden sparrow were dripping with shit and blood. But frankly, my dear reader, no one gave a damn. For she was flying high and we were all flying with her, flying higher than we had ever flown before.

Both Manmohan and Manu couldn't have been more pleased. Their gambles had paid off. Business had never been as good as it was now. There were times when Manu had to pinch himself to make sure that he wasn't dreaming. It had been only three years since he had arrived in Bangalore to set up his real estate business. But how it had grown! Both the Indiranagar and Koramangala projects had been grand successes. Regal Estates was flush with funds and an emboldened Manu was buying land like there was no tomorrow.

Apart from the business, Manu had made rapid progress on the personal front as well. He had recently bought himself a plush bungalow in posh Lavelle Road, and before long, a couple of BMWs were adorning the driveway. He had donated his Old Monks to his newly appointed gardener and had restocked his bar with

Glenmorangies. By any standards, Manu was quickly climbing up the mountain of gold. But the speed at which he was doing so, was beginning to worry me. And it was worrying Sayoni too.

'Aren't you doing too much, too soon, Manu?' she asked him one day. 'Shouldn't you slow down a little?'

'Slow down? Now?' Manu exclaimed. 'Sayoni, all my life I've struggled to make something of myself. And just when I finally seem to be getting somewhere, you are telling me to slow down?'

'All I meant was that you should be a little more careful with your money,' Sayoni said. 'Take the BMWs for instance. One I can understand. But what was the need to buy two? It's a lot of money.'

'Why shouldn't I? Haven't I worked like a dog all these years? I'm almost fifty-six now, Sayoni. When will I enjoy myself a little? When I'm eighty?'

'All right, fine! But what about all these sites that you have been buying left, right and centre? Didn't I tell you that many of them don't have clear titles? I checked the sale deeds myself. I warned you. But you just ignored me and went ahead!'

'Just leave these things to me. You are making a fuss over nothing. It's easy to regularise property over here. The government here is quite cooperative, if you know what I mean.'

'I hope you understand the risk you are taking Manu. All your funds are tied up in these properties now and if you can't sell them, then you'll be in a deep mess.'

'I don't think you understand this business, Sayoni,' Manu replied. 'In the real estate business, land is everything and if I don't move fast, there will be nothing left to buy. Koramangala is already running out of good land parcels. People have already started moving to other areas. Just the other day, the Prestige people bought ten acres of land in HSR Layout because it's closer to Electronic City. Infosys has already started building its new campus there. It's huge. Do you know how many people they expect to have there?'

'How many?'

'Between thirty and fifty thousand over the next three years is what I hear. And that's just Infosys. WEEPRO is the same, TCS will probably add another twenty thousand employees. Lakhs of people are coming to work here in Bangalore. That means there are lakhs of flats to be made and sold. But I can do that only if I have enough land. After that no one will be able to stop me.'

'But where is it that you want to go? What do you want, Manu?' Sayoni looked pensive. 'You're so busy that you hardly have time to breathe. Do you remember the last time you spent some time at home...or with me?'

'But Sayoni, I just—'

'It hasn't been easy for me, you know. Leaving Calcutta, coming to a new place,' she looked away from him. 'I miss you, Manu.'

He took her hand and said: 'But I'm doing it for you. I want you to have the best.'

'Forget about me. What do you want for yourself?'

'Nothing. I only want you to be happy.'

Manu was lying of course. I knew that he longed to see himself on the covers of magazines, of winning Businessman of the Year awards, of rubbing shoulders with the Tata-Birlas of the world, like Raja-saab had once dreamt of. He had already made something of a name for himself in Bangalore's real estate circles. But it wasn't enough. He hungered to take his business to the next level and that was a different game altogether. For that, the politicians would have to be in his pocket and they didn't come cheap.

Yes, Manu was flying high. But he wanted to fly higher, as high as Icarus. His eyes were set on the sun and although I could see that his waxen wings were becoming just a little sticky, a little soft, Manu didn't notice a thing.

***

Bangalore was turning out to be a fairy-tale for Manu. Like Rumpelstiltskin, he was spinning land into gold and the gold into more land and so on, in a virtuous cycle that showered him with more riches than he had ever thought possible.

There were times when he would sit in the garden of his five-thousand-square-feet bungalow silently gazing at the BMWs and Audis parked in his driveway. How far he had come! It seemed only yesterday that he had been a homeless urchin, crouching under the belly of a broken-down jalopy, engine oil dripping on his grease-blackened face. And today he employed two uniformed chauffeurs who were too snooty to even wash his BMWs. Not to mention the three maids and two gardeners who made sure that his home looked like Buckingham Place Hotel on steroids.

Oh yes, he had come a long, long way from his Netarhat days, when Raja-saab had picked him off the streets. Otherwise, he would probably still have been rotting there, a homeless old man, scrounging for scraps. He heaved a sigh of regret. The prince had done so much for him, but there was nothing that he had been able to do in return. If only he hadn't died in prison...

This was like an ache that pierced his heart as he grew older. What did all the wealth and success matter when the only parent he had known was no longer with him? And I, the constant companion who could read his mind, saw this sorrow turn slowly to rage and hate. It changed him. It poisoned his heart.

The bloody Congressis, he would swear to himself. How he hated them! Although he grudgingly accepted that it was a Congress government to whom he owed his business success, nothing would have made him happier than to see them consigned to the dustbin of history. Not that he wasn't doing his bit to try and help that along. Only two months ago, he had made a substantial donation to the BJP, so substantial that he had even received a personally signed letter from Atal Bihari Vajpayee, the tallest leader of the BJP, thanking him for his contribution. Manu was flattered but he wondered if his contribution would make any difference. Would Raja-saab's dream of seeing a Congress-mukt Bharat ever come true?

He often thought back to the day in the Barasat camp when the prince had stood shoulder to shoulder with the thousands of Bangladeshi refugees who had fled all the way to Calcutta to escape the tyranny of the Pakistani army. 'They are all Hindus,' Raja-saab used to say. 'Our fellow Hindus, almost all of them. But apart from leaders of the Jana Sangh, there is not a single politician who has spoken up for them.' Manu felt that he hadn't understood how brave Raja-saab was—until it was too late. Raja-saab had paid with his life for his beliefs. The Congressis had murdered him—they did not want a true Hindu to rise, so they had killed him. Who knew how many others like him had been locked up in prison and tortured to death? It was now twenty-five years since they had silenced his brave and generous Raja-saab, but the Hindus of Bangladesh and Pakistan were still at the mercy of their Islamic oppressors.

'Forget the Hindus of Bangladesh and Pakistan,' Manu would tell himself, 'who speaks for the Hindus of India? The belligerent Muslims have always held this country to ransom. Raja-saab understood this long before I did. I wish I hadn't been so blind, I should have supported him. I should have worked to make him a great leader.'

Manu had convinced himself that India's fifteen crore Muslims were all fanatics, every last man, woman and child. Their azaans blared from loudspeakers five times a day, arrogantly claiming ownership of the country...He held them responsible for keeping the country on the boil. He held them responsible for India's backwardness—they voted en masse for the Congress election after election and let that party of murderers ruin the country.

And their numbers were only growing by the day. 'We're paying the price for our prosperity, for our booming economy,' he would fume sometimes. 'Shouldn't someone stop them? Those Bangladeshis, streaming into India like greedy flies to a honey pot.' No, he said, no one would ever stop them. Except the BJP. It was the only party which spoke about the danger of our people being swamped by these foreigners. Manu had seen it happening under his very nose in Calcutta—hordes of strange, bearded men in skull caps who had taken over entire localities of the city and strutted about with their burkha-clad begums in tow, as if India was their *baap ka jagir*.

At least Bangalore wasn't that badly off so far, but for how long? Already he could overhear several of the labourers at his construction sites speaking in a strange Bengali tongue, which he was sure was a Bangladeshi dialect. When he asked them where they had come from, they said Calcutta. Except of course, that they didn't know a thing about the city. They were, however, cheap and hardworking and it made business sense to hire them. But nothing more. He was under no illusion that if left unchecked they would soon pose a real threat to the fabric of Indian society.

Fifteen-twenty crore Muslims, with their one God and one Book, united as a clenched fist and multiplying like a colony of termites... The only way to check them was to unite the Hindus. But who could ever unite eighty crore squabbling Hindus with their thirty-three crore squabbling gods...it was a task worthy of a Bhagirath!

But Manu's despair had soon given way to hope. Against all odds, in the winter of 1992, such a Bhagirath had at last emerged—in the form of the balding, bespectacled Lal Krishna Advani. As leader of the Ram Janmabhoomi movement, this unlikely Iron Man—whom Manu had instinctively started referring to as 'Advani-ji'—had proudly ridden his chariot across the breadth of India, all the way from Somnath to Ayodhya. And when the Babri Masjid was razed to the ground, it felt as if a cooling balm had at last been applied upon the centuries-old wound that had been festering inside every Hindu heart. For once, Manu felt, the Hindus were united and speaking in a single voice.

The unceasing wails of '*Allah-hu-Akbar*' from the mosques were finally being answered by cries of '*Jai Shri Ram*'. If the same spirit somehow prevailed until the next general elections, Manu thought, then the BJP had a real chance of coming to power. The tide was turning and this time he would take it at the flood...he could afford to.

He picked up the phone and called his secretary. 'Manjunatha, you remember that cash I told you to keep in the safe? How much is there?'

There was a brief pause before Manjunatha replied: 'One crore, sir.'

'Keep it ready in my briefcase. I will need it soon.'

'Sure, sir.'

One crore was a lot of money. But it was a small price to pay for Raja-saab's dreams.

***

To Manu's delight, Raja-saab's dream was soon to come true. In the Lok Sabha elections of 1996, the BJP and its allies won an unprecedented number of seats and Atal Bihari Vajpayee became the first BJP Prime Minister of India. On that day, Manu hung a garland of lotuses on the portrait of Shyama Prasad Mookerjee and threw a grand party at his bungalow for several top leaders of the BJP.

It was late at night when the guests had finally left and Manu was relaxing on the sofa with a single malt. 'What an amazing day, hanh? Historic!' he said to Sayoni. 'If Raja-saab was here, he would have been so happy.'

'Yes, I suppose so,' Sayoni said. 'It's nice to see you happy too.'

Manu looked up curiously. 'What's the matter? You look a little dull.'

'It's nothing...it's just that I wasn't feeling very comfortable with the sort of talk that was going on in the party tonight.'

'What sort of talk? It was just normal politics.'

'Normal?' Sayoni snapped. 'Was that awful young man saying anything remotely normal?'

'Which man?'

'That fellow who was sitting opposite you at the dining table... the young, bearded guy in a pink kurta—remember him?'

'Yes. I don't know him though. Some young party worker who was sent down here from Delhi as an observer. His name's Anurag, Abhilash...something starting with A...can't remember.'

'Never mind,' Sayoni said. 'So this fellow says—"*Babur ki aulaadon ko, goli maaron saalon ko*" (all these sons of Babur's, shoot the buggers). And everyone starts laughing as if it's some big joke. How sick can one get?'

'I didn't laugh,' Manu avoided her gaze.

'No, but you didn't say anything either. You just stood there as if you were deaf and dumb. How can you mix with these people?'

'Because I need to, okay? Stop blowing things out of proportion. They are just politicians. You shouldn't expect any better from them.'

'Please don't invite them home next time, these new friends of yours.'

'*Arre baba*, they are not my friends. A couple of them are my business partners, that's all. The rest are just hangers-on. I'm not all that fond of them myself. But what to do? You can't be in the real estate business without the right political connections. Anyway, now that our party is in power, things should become a lot smoother,' he pulled her over to his side and offered his glass. 'Drink?'

'No thanks,' she replied pushing away the glass.

'What's wrong with you?' said Manu. 'Come on! Join me for a drink. It's a day to celebrate!'

She looked down at her feet and said: 'I don't know, Manu. But all this talk of what Babur did and what Aurangzeb did and how it's high time that the Muslims were put in their place just made me very, very...scared.'

'What for? You of all people shouldn't be saying that,' Manu replied. 'You had to run away from Bangladesh because you were a Hindu.'

'You don't understand Manu. I had to run away because I spoke Bengali not because I was Hindu. The Pakistani army was going after every Bengali speaking person that they could get their hands on—both Hindu *and* Muslim. You didn't have to be a Hindu to get raped by them—only a Bengali-speaking woman. And that's exactly why I hate what your new friends were saying. Two wrongs don't make a right. This whole business of creating an enemy because he's a Muslim or a Bengali or whatever else just leads to more bloodshed. Only the politicians gain from it.'

Manu sat up. 'I don't think our party is trying to make an enemy out of the Muslims. All we are saying is that we won't stand for any more Muslim appeasement. No more vote bank politics. No more Shah Banos. No more different laws for Hindus and Muslims. You are a lawyer. You tell me, how can the law allow one community to have four wives while everyone else can have only one. One country, one law—'

'And one wife!' Sayoni cut him off. 'Okay! I get it. But if you keep ranting this way for much longer, you may not have even that one wife anymore. I hope you understand.'

'I think it's you who doesn't understand. All we are saying is—'

'We?'

'Yes, we!' Manu slammed his whisky glass down on the table. 'I may not be a politician but I believe in the BJP. And I believe that Vajpayee-ji will change this country. He will right the wrongs of the past, all the wrongs that the Congress have turned a blind eye to for the last fifty years!'

'How? By tearing down more mosques and building temples over them?'

Manu shrugged. 'I don't support the way things happened in Ayodhya but it happened for the right reasons. You can't make an omelette without breaking eggs.'

'Manu, we are not talking of eggs. We are talking of human lives.'

'And you think lives weren't lost when the Muslims invaded us? Do you think the Khiljis and Ghaznis came to India on some sort of cultural exchange program? To teach us how to sing khayal and thumri? No, they came here to crush us and convert us. They came here to do jihad!'

'Come on Manu! Your newly made friends seem to have really brainwashed you. Next you'll be telling me that every Muslim who is ever born wants to become a jihadi so that he can go to jannat after dying! Are you jealous of them by any chance? Because they can have four wives on earth and seventy-two virgins in heaven?' Sayoni burst into laughter.

It was a mistake. Hell hath no fury like a man scorned, especially by a woman. Just as Draupadi's amusement at Duryodhana's clumsiness in the palace of illusions, had sown the seeds of the Mahabharata war, Sayoni's laughter had set off a domestic Kurukshetra.

'You can joke all you like, Sayoni,' Manu spat. 'Do you even know how many Hindu temples they destroyed to build their mosques? Sixty thousand!'

'Really? Sure it wasn't sixty thousand, two hundred and seven? Just check your spreadsheet once and see.'

'What spreadsheet?' Manu looked startled.

'The one in which you were keeping a count of how many temples were being destroyed by Ghazni and Khilji and Aurangzeb and the rest of them? Because you were there when it happened, right? You were right there watching them doing all those terrible things, yes? Or else how can you be so damn sure that there were only sixty thousand temples and not sixty thousand, two hundred and seven?'

'This is not a joking matter, Sayoni!'

'I'm deadly serious. I really want to see that spreadsheet. And also the other one.'

'Stop your nonsense, Sayoni! What other one?'

'The other spreadsheet in which you kept count of the number of Buddhist stupas that were destroyed by Hindu rulers. Because I kept count too. My number is 27,318. What's yours?'

'You're ridiculous,' Manu snapped. 'It's a waste of time talking to you. Let's just stop.'

'Yes, let's stop,' Sayoni's shoulders fell and a sigh escaped her. 'At least we agree on one thing—it's ridiculous, so ridiculous that...it's almost funny. Except that it isn't. It's no longer funny when people... real people with real lives, with families and children, have to die today because of something that did or did not happen hundreds and thousands of years ago.'

'Like it or not, we all carry our histories with us. It's the burden we all have to bear.'

Sayoni stared at him for a while and said: 'I sometimes wonder which part of your history you've carried with you. You've changed so much since the time I first met you that I sometimes can't recognise you...you've become so much harder, hungrier...' she said in a soft voice that could barely be heard.

Manu averted her gaze as he sipped on his drink. 'Everyone changes, Sayoni. And everything. But change can be good as well. Isn't it good that these Congress thieves have been kicked out at last? For fifty years they have been looting this country—Bofors, Jain hawala, this scam, that scam. But now that they are finally gone, people like me can think of making an honest living. This country will finally make progress.'

'Country? Which country are you talking about, Manu? India? Because the India that I once knew and loved has gone! Your friends in the Ram Janmabhoomi movement took a dagger and plunged it straight through her heart. Who knows how many years it will take for the wound to heal, if ever?'

'Oh come on! Stop being so dramatic. The Ram Janmabhoomi movement wasn't a knife through India. It was an operation needed to unite the Hindus and win power. But now that we've won, it's over and done with.'

'That I doubt. Since it worked once, they will try such things again and again.'

'*Arre nahin*. Vajpayee-ji is not like that. He's a sensible, moderate person. And he will change this country. You just watch. Five years from now, India will be shining.'

'I hope you're right, Manu,' she said softly. 'I sincerely hope you're right.'

'I know I am,' Manu replied. His face was shining as well. But whether it was because of the dreams in his head or the drink in his hand, I could not say.

Gujarat Shining

The end of the millennium was fast approaching. Petrified by the havoc that could be wreaked by the Y2K bug, the world was making a beeline for Bangalore. Every global company worth its name was queuing up at the gates of Electronic City to avail of the pest control services being offered by the likes of Infosys, WEEPRO and TCS. Millions of lines of computer code that were suspected to be infested by the Y2K bug would have to be cleaned out before the midnight of 31 December 1999. Otherwise, from Australia to America, the whole world would be royally bug-gered. The predictions were dire—the electricity grid would crash, fire would break out, planes would plummet, ships would sink and everybody's bank balances would be reset to zero.

But on the last day of the last millennium, at the stroke of the midnight hour, when the soul of every nation was quaking in fear—nothing happened.

Far from the world ending with a bang, it sailed on with barely a whimper. And instead of everyone's bank balances being wiped out, there were many whose shot up to stratospheric levels. In the process of killing the Y2K bug, the techies of Bangalore had also made a killing for themselves. The new India was shining and more millionaires had been created in the two years preceding the new millennium, than in the two thousand before that.

One such millionaire was Manu Pratap Singh. He had no idea what a computer bug was, but his business had flourished because of it. Bangalore's IT boom had catapulted the construction industry into a new orbit altogether. Everywhere I looked, something or the other was being built—flats, flyovers, offices, malls. And Manu had a finger in almost every pie. By now, his portfolio had gone far beyond flats. It included giant IT parks, gated communities, five-star hotels and high-end resorts. The hotels and resorts business, in particular, was doing extremely well—partly because of the shortage of good hotels in Bangalore and partly because of the abundant support of the tourism ministry in Delhi. These days it was headed by a senior BJP leader from Karnataka who was rather fond of Manu. And naturally so, for Manu was now donating upwards of two crores to the party funds every year.

With the tourism ministry behind him, Manu had already built two luxury resorts in Karnataka. The first was on the banks of the Cauvery river in Kabini, and the second on the outskirts of the Bandipur forest. Of all the projects he had undertaken, the Bandipur resort had given him the greatest satisfaction. But it had also caused him the greatest trouble. Mid-way through the construction, a bunch of environmental activists had created such a ruckus over it, that the project was on the verge of being cancelled. It was only with the help of his New Delhi connections that Manu was able to salvage the situation and complete the construction.

But his efforts had been worth it. The Bandipur resort turned out to be most impressive. Its aesthetics and luxurious facilities were outstanding, so much so, that people were even comparing it with the best wildlife resorts in Kenya. To Manu's delight, it had recently even been featured on the cover of a national travel magazine.

If Manu was doing well, the BJP was doing even better. Since their conquest of New Delhi in 1996, the states of Uttar Pradesh, Himachal Pradesh and Gujarat had fallen into their bag in quick succession. Raja-saab's dream of a Congress-mukt Bharat, which had once appeared to be a mere fantasy, was now beginning to look like a possibility.

And in the month of October in the year 2001, there emerged from the shadows, the man who believed that he would fulfil that old, old dream of Hindutva. He had a salt and pepper beard and an exceptionally broad chest. His name was—

***

'Prakash Singh!' exclaimed Manu. 'He looks just like Prakash Singh.' He was staring at the television screen where a bearded man in his fifties was speaking into a microphone. He was speaking in Gujarati but Manu could make out what he was saying:

'...swear in the name of God that I will bear true faith and allegiance to the Constitution of India as by law established...'

Sayoni was reading a magazine. 'Can you change the channel please?' she said. 'I don't know how you can watch this boring political news all the time.'

'Can you be quiet please? The new Chief Minister of Gujarat is being sworn in. I want to watch.'

'So what? Chief Ministers come and go all the time.'

'Yes, but I think that man is Prakash Singh. I missed hearing his name in the beginning.'

Sayoni set aside her magazine and looked up. 'Prakash Singh? Really?'

Manu frowned as he leaned forward and stared at the TV screen. 'Well...he looks just like Prakash Singh. I can't be sure it's him, of course. It was almost thirty years ago. He was wearing a turban and dark glasses then. But he seems so familiar. Especially the voice...' said Manu as the metallic voice boomed through the TV speakers.

'...that I will do right to all manner of people in accordance with the Constitution and the law without fear or favour, affection or ill-will.'

'Well, it may be good for you if he's actually Prakash Singh. He might remember you and it may not be a bad thing to know the Chief Minister of Gujarat.'

'I hope he doesn't remember that I had slapped him on the day we met.'

'You slapped the Chief Minister of Gujarat!'

'No, no, I only slapped a man who called himself Prakash Singh! And it wasn't a slap, really. More like an...outburst. I couldn't control myself when he told me that Raja-saab had died.'

'Oh, that's nothing. Perhaps you should try and meet him sometime. Ask him if he is the same man. It might be interesting to find out.'

'Yes, it might certainly be interesting,' said Manu. 'Although it's not very likely that he will meet me. He's a big man now.'

***

But within months of Prakash Singh's look-alike assuming office, Manu received an official letter from the Chief Secretary of Gujarat inviting him for a meeting in Gandhinagar. The purpose of the meeting was to discuss potential investment opportunities in the state. Manu was a little surprised to receive the invitation. It was true, that by now, Regal Estates was a well-respected name in the south, but he had no idea that its reputation had travelled as far as Gujarat. But why look a gift horse in the mouth, he said to himself. There could be a potential business opportunity and with a bit of luck, he might even be able to meet the Chief Minister and ask him the question that had been niggling in his head.

A week later, Manu took a flight to Ahmedabad. When he arrived at the Secretariat in Gandhinagar, he was greeted by a smart young woman in a sharp suit who escorted him to the Chief Secretary's office. He was a podgy, smiling man in his fifties, with a bald patch that gleamed like the polished mahogany desk behind which he was sitting. Framed portraits of Gandhi, Vajpayee and the new Chief Minister hanging on the wall behind beamed down at Manu, as the Chief Secretary said: 'Welcome to Gujarat, Mr Singh. I hope you had a comfortable flight. Would you like some tea, coffee?'

'Thank you, sir. Just a glass of water will do,' Manu said. 'Very hot here.'

'What to do, Mr Singh, we are not as lucky as you Bangalore people,' the Chief Secretary smiled.

'Now, let me come straight to point, Mr Singh. As you may know, our honourable CM-ji is on a mission to attract huge investments in Gujarat. And we want people like you to come here and do business with us.'

Manu cleared his throat and said: 'First of all, let me say that I am thoroughly impressed by everything I have seen here so far. Naturally, as a businessman, I would be very interested in your proposal. But what do you have in mind?'

'Yes, yes, let us get down to brass tacks right away. As you may know, our CM-ji is a man in a hurry. So, Mr Singh, tourism is a big focus area for our government and we have been hearing about the luxury resorts you have built in Karnataka. In Bandini or some such place, isn't it?'

'Bandipur and Kabini, actually.'

'Yes, yes, same thing,' the Chief Secretary waved his pudgy hands. 'As I said, we know about the work you have done there and we like it. We want you to build similar resorts here in Gujarat. Our beautiful state has many beautiful places to see—Somnath, Dwarka, Rann of Kutch, Gir National Park. But the tourist facilities are bad, very bad. However, with our new CM-ji's leadership, all that will change. Big investments are going to be made. In fact, we are even planning to get Amit-bhai to do an advertising campaign for Gujarat Tourism.'

'Amit-bhai? You mean Amit Shah?' As preparation for his meeting, Manu had been doing some background research about the Chief Minister's inner circle. Amit Shah was reputed to be the CM's closest confidant and the second most powerful man in the state.

The Chief Secretary bared his teeth in a smile. '*Arre* no, sir, not that Amit-bhai. I am talking about the other Amit-bhai, the one and only Amitabh Bachchan.'

'Amitabh Bachchan!' Manu was impressed. He was quite sure that Mr Bachchan wouldn't come cheap.

'Yes sir, we are thinking of making Bachchan saab the face of Gujarat Tourism. What do you think of it?'

'I think it's like tossing the Sholay coin sir. You can't lose!'

'Let us hope you are right. Anyway, let's not digress. I'll come straight to the point. Are you interested in working with us, Mr Singh?'

'Of course, I am. But—'

'Excellent! When can you start?'

'Start what?'

'Building the resorts of course. Didn't I tell you that our CM saab is a man in a hurry?'

'But how can I say anything now? I have no details. What resorts, where, how etcetera etcetera.'

'Of course, we will tell you everything. But in principle, are you committed to our plans?'

'Definitely. But first, I have to see the proposed location, understand what budgets you have, how large you want it to be, what facilities. There are a thousand things to be discussed. Then there is the question of getting all the permissions, the land acquisition, the—'

'*Arre* Mr Singh, why are you worried about all these small, small things?' the Chief Secretary cut him off. 'You just leave all that to us and we will take care of everything. This is Gujarat, sir. Things happen here like this,' he snapped his fingers. 'You just give us your commitment that you will work with us and we will manage everything else—land, labour, loans, approvals...'

'That sounds incredible,' Manu leaned back in his chair. 'I have never experienced such cooperation from any other government.'

'Didn't I tell you, sir? This is Gujarat. We are different. *Dhando*, business, that is our true religion here. So, what do you say, Mr Singh? Shall we shake hands?'

'I am feeling a little overwhelmed to tell you the truth,' Manu said. 'I don't even know where you want me to start.'

'Oh, I should have mentioned that. We have already decided. Our first project will be in the Gir Forest. Naturally, you have heard of Gir?'

'Yes, I have,' Manu lied.

'Gir forest—pride of Gujarat, home of the Asiatic lion. It will be our flagship project and we will count on you, Mr Singh, to do a fantastic job there.'

'I will have to think about it, sir. I have never worked in these parts before and it is a big responsibility.'

'It is a big opportunity and we are very keen that you should do it. Which is why we haven't talked to any other company so far. But I am sure the biggest builders in India will give an arm and a leg for winning this deal.'

'I understand.'

'So, you have to make up your mind quickly. More importantly you have to get the work started quickly. You see, the bye-elections are coming up next year and we want to showcase this work to the people. So, let me ask you, Mr Singh—do I have your in-principle agreement that you will undertake this project?

Manu thought about it for a moment. He couldn't understand why such an attractive deal was being handed over to him on a platter. It sounded too good to be true. But he could find no good reason for turning down the offer and many good ones for accepting it. If he could pull it off, he would be able to expand his footprint beyond Karnataka. It would take him one step closer to becoming a national player, and perhaps even international...he took a deep breath and said: 'All right, sir. I will do it.'

'Excellent, Mr Singh, excellent!' the Chief Secretary gave a wide grin. 'Very good.'

'But I will need your cooperation and support at every stage, otherwise the project will fail.'

'Don't worry about that. The Gujarat government will be with you one hundred and ten percent. The paperwork and contracts will be completed in the next ten days. We will do everything possible to help you. However—' he paused.

'Yes?' Manu asked.

'There is one condition that we have.'

'What sir?'

'The project must be completed in time. No delays, no excuses. In exactly nine months' time, you will have to hand over a world-class tourist facility for us—better than the one you made in Bandipur. Is this clear?'

'Look sir, technically it is quite possible to finish the work in ninc months. But if there are delays on account of land acquisition then I cannot guarantee anything. Environmental activists are stopping everything these days. They nearly managed to get my Bandipur project cancelled. I'm sure they will cause trouble here as well.'

'You are right there, Mr Singh. Bloody nuisance these jholawallahs!' the Chief Secretary slammed his palm on the desk. 'Saving trees, saving tigers, saving pangolins and whatnot. *Arre*, who will save the people, I want to ask them? Who will give them jobs, electricity, roads, cars? Who will feed the hunger of millions of our people? All these bleeding-heart liberals! All they can do is protest.'

'I agree. But—'

'*Arre* Manu-bhai, you don't have to worry about those loafers. This is Gujarat. We know how to manage them here. Look at that mad woman Medha Patkar. For ten years she has been doing her dharna on the Narmada. But let me tell you—she won't be able to do a damn thing. The Sardar Sarovar Dam will be completed no matter what she tries to do. The farmers of Saurashtra will finally get water and electricity. This is Gujarat, sir. Things that have never before happened in India will happen here with our new CM-ji. The question is—will you make them happen with us?'

'That goes without saying, sir. Of course, I would. It would be my privilege to work with you. But I have to ask you something, sir.'

'What is it?'

'Why am I being given this red-carpet welcome, sir? I have never seen anything like it before.'

The Chief Secretary's eyes twinkled. 'It seems you have a good friend in this government. A very powerful friend. And he has given me strict instructions to cater to your every need. I believe you go back a long way. *Purana rishta hai hamara*, we go back a long way, he told me, when he asked me to invite you here.'

'*He* asked you to invite me?'

'Yes, in fact he wanted to meet you personally. But at the last moment, he was called away by some urgent work.'

'Who is this person, this powerful friend of mine?' Manu asked.

'*Arre*, Mr Singh, why pretend to be so innocent? I am sure you can guess,' he winked at Manu as he extended a handshake. 'Anyway, now that we are going to work together, I am sure you will meet him soon enough. Welcome to the team, Manu-bhai. Let us make Gujarat great again.'

The Blackbuck

It had been three days since Manu had arrived in Gir to kick-start the resort project. Most of the time had been spent in making a thorough survey of the land that had been allocated for the purpose. On the morning of the fourth day, he was scanning the dense forests that lay on the western boundary of the land, when his attention was drawn by a silvery light glinting in the distance. Manu made his way through the foliage and soon arrived before a small stream, its clear waters twinkling like diamonds.

Manu ambled along the banks of the stream. 'This seems like a good spot to build the cottages,' he said. 'What do you say Mansukh-bhai?'

'Two hundred per cent, Manu-bhai. I am also thinking the same,' replied Mansukh-bhai. 'It's an A-one location.'

Mansukh-bhai was a short, podgy man in his forties, attired in a white safari suit and in white leather shoes that were quite unsuitable for a walk in the woods. But he had come highly recommended by the District Collector. Mansukh-bhai, the Collector had informed Manu, was the best government contractor for miles around. He was the master of jugaad. Sand, cement, labourers, legal hassles—whatever help Manu needed, he just had to tell Mansukh-bhai and it would be done.

So far, Mansukh-bhai had lived up to his reputation. It had been only four months since the Gujarat government had awarded Regal Estates a handsome contract for building a luxury resort in Gir. But thanks to Mansukh-bhai, a great deal of progress had already been made. The five-acre parcel of land that had been allocated by the government, had been levelled and cleared of all foliage. A ten-kilometre-long road connecting the resort to the Junagadh-Somnath highway was almost ready, and in a few weeks' time, the electricity and water lines would also be laid.

With the basic civil works in place, Manu was now in a position to start designing the resort itself and his plans were ambitious. His resort would have to be among the top ten in the world.

'Mansukh-bhai, I was thinking,' Manu said, 'can we supply the jacuzzis in our super-deluxe cottages with water from the stream?'

'No problem Manu-bhai. We just have to lay the pipes and pump in the water.'

'Very good. Then we can advertise that our resort has natural spring water jacuzzis.'

'You mean stream water sir?'

'No, no—spring water. That will sound much better. But are you sure it can be done?'

'One hundred and ten percent, Manu-bhai. If you want, I can even make kiddies pool for you. You ask anyone in Gujarat about me and they will say—*Mansukh hai to mumkin hai*. You just leave it to me sir. So, how many super-deluxe cottages you want?'

Manu didn't reply. His attention had been caught by a young blackbuck that had emerged from the forest and was trotting towards the stream. Oblivious to the men watching her, the blackbuck lowered her mouth to the stream and lapped at the water.

'Blackbuck sir,' Mansukh whispered to Manu. 'Wildlife animal.'

'Such a beautiful creature,' Manu said softly. 'It's been ages since I saw one.' Ages indeed...the last time he had seen a blackbuck had been nearly fifty-five years ago...on a hot summers' day when he and Mary had bumped into a family of blackbucks on the bank of the Koyal river. The long-forgotten memories now came rushing back... he remembered the mother buck scolding her calves for not eating enough grass, he remembered the father complaining bitterly about Lajwati the leopard, who had become even greedier in her old age.

'Yes sir, please see the blackbuck, sir. Good for looking and good for hunting also,' Mansukh was saying. 'Recently only some film stars also came here to do hunting. But they were too drunk to even shoot straight. Only managed to hit one rabbit. Better they stick to shooting item numbers instead of blackbucks, heh, heh—what do you say, sir?'

'Shhh,' Manu raised a finger to his lips and tip-toed his way towards the blackbuck. But she saw him approach and her large, dark eyes widened in fear. She backed away and was about to bolt into the forest when Manu made a curious barking sound. The blackbuck paused and looked curiously at Manu, her head inclined sideways, as if to ask: 'Sorry, what did you say?'

Manu made the barking sound again. The blackbuck stared at him as if he was an idiot. I could almost see her rolling her eyes. Manu moved closer. The blackbuck stamped her hooves nervously on the ground. Slowly, he walked towards her until he was by her side. She edged away but did not flee. He stretched out his hand and brought it close to the blackbuck's face but she shrank from him.

The two stood still for a while, when all of a sudden, the blackbuck stepped forward and rubbed her head against Manu's legs. He smiled in delight and made another barking sound. But once again she gave him a blank stare. She nuzzled her head against his hand and gave his fingers a quick lick. Then with a sudden leap, she was off and away. Within moments, she had disappeared behind the trees.

With a small regretful sigh, he watched her go. Her gentle touch was still warm against his skin. He could still see her large, dark eyes staring at him in incomprehension. The thought that he hadn't been able to speak to her, twisted inside him like a knife. He had tried his best but it was clear that she hadn't understood a word of what he had said.

And yet, there was a time when he had been able to speak to all manner of animals—horses, hares, birds, blackbucks...he could converse with them as easily as if they were human. It was a gift that had been given to him by god...and by Mary...an immeasurably precious gift that had enabled him to make his tryst with destiny. It had rewarded him with riches beyond his wildest dreams. But now the gift was gone...just like Mary was gone too. He had lost them both. No...not lost...discarded...deliberately thrown away like old-fashioned clothes that were too embarrassing to be worn anymore, clothes that reeked of the mud and mahua of the jungle that he had wanted to get away so badly from, that he had followed a stranger all the way to Calcutta.

But coming to Calcutta was only the beginning. He had soon

realised that if he had to remain there, he would have to leave the jungle behind for good. He would have to blend in with the city, become like the babus who lived in it. And no babu ever talked to animals...

And so he had wilfully thrown away the gift that had brought him so far, so that he could go even further. And to his credit, he had come a very long way, beyond all his dreams...but even so, he could not help but wonder just how much he had lost, how much he had thrown away, in that fifty-five-year long journey from Betla to Gir.

***

It had been six days since Manu's encounter with the blackbuck. He had put up at the government circuit house, about ten kilometres away from Gir national park. It was a small bungalow, nothing fancy, but quite adequate for his needs. Its proximity to the project site made it the most convenient place to stay in. A government jeep would pick up him up every morning and take him to the site, where Manu would spend the rest of the day working with Mansukh-bhai and his team of architects.

But this morning, Manu's mind was not on work. Every now and then, his gaze would wander to the stream and each time the bushes rustled, his pulse would race faster in the hope that the blackbuck had returned. But each time his hopes were dashed. His head told him that it was unlikely she would come to a place which was bustling with men and machines. But his heart thirsted to catch a glimpse of the blackbuck, if only to ask her forgiveness for what he was doing to her home.

With an eye on the forthcoming bye-elections, the government had fast-tracked the Gir project. Men, materials, money—whatever Manu asked for, he got. As a result, construction was galloping ahead at a furious pace. Already the land had been cleared and now, the boundary wall was being raised. As Manu gazed at the line of concrete slabs slicing through the forest floor and leaving a thick, gray wound, he was suddenly overcome by an intense feeling of guilt and regret, such as he had never felt in all his long years in the construction business.

Strange thoughts were running through his head today...what if he tore down the wall, stopped the construction? What if he pulled out of the project? These were crazy thoughts, he knew, but he couldn't help thinking them. If only he could stop...but how could he? He was bound, hand and foot, by contracts, clauses, penalties and legal obligations...he had no choice but to go on.

In the evening he returned to the circuit house and poured himself a drink of the Old Pirate whisky that Mansukh-bhai had bootlegged for him. It smelt like horse-piss and tasted worse but it would have to do. He grimaced as he took a sip. He was praying that the alcohol would drown the incessant chatter inside his head, when there was a knock on the door.

He opened it to see an old woman standing before him. The whisky glass slipped from his fingers and smashed against the floor.

***

It took a while before either of them could speak.

'Can't hold your drink these days?' said the old woman at last, eyeing the broken glass at his feet. 'Have you really become as old as you look?'

'Yes...I suppose so. But...you...you look just the same,' he stammered and immediately regretted his clumsy compliment as she rolled her eyes at him.

The gray-haired lady standing before him bore no resemblance to the little girl with whom he had danced in the moonlit forests of Betla or the young woman for whom he had risked his very life in the streets of Calcutta. The lines had cut deep into her face and she was tanned brown as a peanut. She was much thinner too and looked positively frail in the faded, cotton sari draped around her slight frame. But there was no doubt that she was still the same old Mary.

Mary gave him a small smile. 'Aren't you going to ask me in, Manu?'

'Of course, please, please,' Manu gestured her into the room. 'So stupid of me. Please come in. Have a seat.'

Mary's eyes narrowed as she sat down on a chair and watched him. 'Are you all right? You are not looking well.'

'Just a headache,' Manu replied. 'But never mind me. What on earth are *you* doing here? How did you know I was here? After...after what...almost thirty years?'

'Yes, it's been a long time. Very long.'

'1973. Dehradun railway station—the last time we saw each other. You remember?'

'Yes, I remember.'

'A lifetime ago. Things have changed so much since then.'

'Yes, they have. Just like we have changed. Although you seem to have done very well for yourself, Mr Manu Pratap Singh—Chairman and Managing Director of Regal Estates, uncrowned king of the construction business, honoured guest of the Gujarat government.'

Manu didn't hide his surprise. 'You seem to know a lot about me. Yes, I may have come a long way, but I'm just the same poor boy you knew in Betla,' he smiled. Mary did not return the smile. There was a coldness in her gaze that made him nervous. 'Anyway, enough about me. What about you? What have you been up to? Saving the world as usual?' he gave an uneasy laugh.

'Yes, and failing as usual,' Mary replied. 'Listen Manu, I don't have much time, so let me get straight to the point.'

'Just hold on. We are meeting after so long. Let me offer you a cup of tea at least. Or if you prefer, some Old Pirate whisky. It's horrible but—'

'No thanks. I really have no time. I have to get back to—'

'Oh please! We are meeting after thirty years. Surely, we can spend thirty minutes together. You haven't told me yet—how did you manage to track me down here?'

'Big people are easy to find, Mr Manu Pratap Singh, Managing Director of Regal Estates. It's the small people like us who just... disappear...as if we'd never existed. Anyway, to answer your question—we have been following you and your company with interest for a while now. Our sources informed us that you were here in Gir.'

'We? Sources? You're sounding like some sort of spy, Mary.'

'Whatever you want to say, Manu. We are not spies. But we have our networks, our friends. They may not be as rich and powerful as yours, but they are good people. They care for this country. Some of them are even in the government. After all, not everyone is in love with our great leaders. These friends tell us what's goes on in the corridors of power. Who is doing what, who is getting which contract for which project—things like that.'

'I see. So, this is what it's all about. Cards are on the table, eh?

Very good! So what is it that you and your friends want me to do? Put a stop to the Gir project?'

Mary rose from her chair, a wild look in her eyes. 'Yes, Manu. Please stop it! You can do it if you want to. That's why they asked me to meet you. To see if I could convince you.'

'Who are these people who are filling your head with this nonsense, Mary? Is it the Medha Patkar gang? Or the Sunderlal Bahuguna gang? Or is it—'

'Manu, just stop it. You are talking nonsense now.'

'No, you are the one who's talking nonsense. Do-gooders like you who want to stop anything and everything good that happens in this country! Can't you see how much this project will benefit the people of this region? Don't you want them to get jobs? Don't you want their children to go to good schools? Don't you see how badly they need this project!' But even as he spoke, he felt the hollowness of his own words.

'That's what these people need?' Mary exclaimed. 'Jacuzzi-fitted luxury villas in the middle of a forest? Just stop and think for a moment Manu. This project will destroy the forest and everything that lives in it. Are a few temporary jobs worth that much? And the jobs are unlikely to go to the local people anyway. Most of them will be forced to give up the homes they have been staying in for generations and live in slums somewhere.'

'Please don't exaggerate. It's a huge forest. My resort will only occupy a couple of acres.'

'Who are you fooling, Manu? The access road itself will destroy another fifty acres. Roads are linear projects, cutting through our forests like a sharp knife through the heart. Don't you see what's happening? They are dying, Manu—our forests, rivers, lakes, and everything that lives in them. They are all dying. And these people, whom you claim to care so much about—even they are dying!'

'Rubbish!'

'Really? Do you know that only last year, there was a mysterious virus attack in Siliguri? In a matter of days, forty-nine people dropped dead from an uncontrollable fever.'

'So? What on earth does this have to do with my Gir project?'

'Everything! People suspect that the Siliguri deaths were caused by a zoonotic virus.'

'A what?'

'A zoonotic virus, Manu. A virus that passes from animals to humans, when the boundaries between them get erased. It happens when forests are destroyed, when wild animals don't have any more space left for themselves. There are no vaccines to protect us from zoonotic viruses, Manu, no cures. They can spread fast and become pandemics in which thousands, lakhs of people can die.'

'Nonsense. Do you think I'm a kid to believe your science fiction stories?'

Mary sighed. 'If only you were still a kid. You were so much better then.'

There was a long silence before Manu spoke. 'I'm sorry, Mary, but I can't stop now,' his breath was laboured as if at the end of a long, hard run. 'I have to go on. And even if I stopped what use would it be? There are ten more to take my place. What will you do then?'

'We will fight them too, we will fight all of them.'

'How long will you keep on fighting Mary?'

'As long as there is something left to fight for. Which may not be long, the way things are going. Manu, I'm begging you once again. Please stop this project.'

Manu looked away from her. His voice was barely a whisper when he said: 'I'm sorry, Mary. But I can't. I've gone too far and I can't stop now.'

'Then when will you stop, Manu? When the last dolphin has died? When the last forest has been turned into a desert? When your photo appears on the cover of *Business Today*? When Manu?'

His head sank to his chest. 'I don't know,' he said. 'I don't know.' He cupped his face in his hands. He felt too tired to speak, to think even.

They sat in silence, exhausted by the argument. After a while Mary got up and said: 'You remember something, Manu?'

'What?'

'When you left Dehradun, I had told you that you were the nicest man I ever knew. But now you've changed so much that I can barely recognise you. And changed for what? Money? Power? Fame? Such a disappointment you have been, Manu. Such a sore disappointment. For thirty pieces of silver, you've sold yourself.'

Her words seared through him like a red-hot knife. Yes, he had always wanted money. It had been the chimera that he had chased all his life. He had been seduced by its shape-shifting promises—survival, security, luxury, power, justice. Were those such terrible things? Was he wrong in desiring them? Was he wrong in working hard to get them? But lacerated by her disappointment, he remained silent.

'I am sorry. I can see that I have wasted your time,' Mary said. 'I will leave now. But if you should ever change your mind, call me at this number,' she jotted down a telephone number on a chit of paper and placed it on his bedside table.

Manu tried to swallow his hurt and act normal. 'Shall we talk of something more pleasant? What is your program like? Staying here for a few days more?'

'That's none of your business,' she replied curtly.

'Fine, fine...as for me, I am leaving tomorrow for Ahmedabad. In fact, Sayoni is coming down from Bangalore as well. We are planning to take a small break, see a little bit of Gujarat.'

'Sayoni? Your wife?'

'Yes. We often talk about you.'

'Really? She must hate me then.'

'Don't be stupid. She admires you. A lot.'

'What for?'

'For your work, your commitment. I know that she would like to meet you.'

'I would probably like to meet her as well.'

'So why don't we? Come to Ahmedabad with me. Meet Sayoni. Maybe we could have dinner together? What do you say?' Mary did not reply. 'Come on,' pleaded Manu. 'Let's put aside our differences for once. Just one dinner? For old times' sake?'

Mary stood up. 'No, Manu, the old times have gone. I don't think we will ever meet for dinner. The courts are much more likely. Or the streets. But do give my regards to Sayoni,' she was about to walk out of the room when she stopped: 'I'm sorry if I hurt you, Manu. I didn't mean to. Don't take what I said to heart. Just an old woman's foolishness,' she smiled sadly. 'I wish you all the best and I hope you and Sayoni have a long and happy life together.'

She turned and walked out without a second glance.

Police Hamarey Saath Hai

On the morning of 27 February 2002, Manu finished his work in Gir and headed back to Ahmedabad. Upon arriving, he checked into a suite at the Taj Hotel. It was a blessed relief from the rundown circuit house in Gir and after days of roughing it out he was looking forward to a nice, hot bubble bath. He filled up the bathtub and sank into it with grunt of pleasure. Submerged in a fragrant pool of lather, he watched the wisps of steam rise lazily and swirl before his eyes like the morning mist.

And as he watched, the mist seemed to take on a human shape—the silhouette of a thin, frail woman in dusty chappals and a thin, frayed sari...*such a disappointment you have been*...the mist sighed... *such a sore disappointment...for thirty pieces of silver, you've sold yourself...*

Quick as flame, the mist changed shape again. The woman vanished and in her place appeared a blackbuck, bolting in terror as a giant earth mover hurtled towards it, smoke streaming out of its steel underbelly, its wheels crushing rocks into dust...

And then came the sound of a hiss...*sssuch a dissssapointment...* the mist had turned into a snake...*sssuch a sssore dissssapointment...* said the snake as it slithered up Manu's spine and coiled itself around his neck.

Get off me, gasped Manu, flailing helplessly at the snake. *Get off me!*

Remember me? said the snake.

No. Who are you? asked Manu.

It's me. Lukabarsi. Remember now?

Manu had to think for several moments and then it all came back to him...*Lukabarsi, Mary, Seth-ji's garage....*

Lukabarsi! Yes, I remember! I remember now!

Yesss, you remember now, the snake hissed. *But too late! It's too late!* the coils tightened around his neck.

Let go of me, Luka. I can't breathe...I can't breathe...

Neither can we, Manu. Neither can we, said the snake as it pressed down hard.

The room grew dark and Manu let out a strangled scream.

***

Manu was still screaming when the telephone rang and woke him up. He sat up in the bathtub, gasping for air. After a while he recovered himself and padded across the suite to reach the telephone.

Sayoni was on the line. 'Hello, have you reached Ahmedabad?' she asked.

'Yes, just got in this morning,' Manu replied hoarsely, as he gingerly ran his fingers across his neck.

'You don't sound okay,' Sayoni said. 'Anything the matter?'

'I'm tired. Very tired. That's all. The government is behind me to finish everything before the bye-elections. There's so much work to be done and I...I...just don't feel like...anyway, never mind. I'm fine. I think I just need a break.'

'That you do. I don't remember the last time that you took even a day off. Manu, you really need a proper holiday. Sabarmati, Mount Abu, Palitana—we are going to see everything. No mobile, no calls, no email. Just rest and relaxation, all right?'

'Whatever you say. You are reaching here in the evening, right?'

'Yes, the flight lands at 7 p.m. I'll come straight to the hotel.'

'It will be good to see you, Sayoni. I've missed you so much.'

There was a pause on the line. 'Missed me? Are you sure you're okay, Manu?' asked Sayoni.

'Yes, yes I'm fine. You know...you won't believe who I—' Manu stopped.

'What?' asked Sayoni. 'What did you say?'

'Nothing. I'll tell you later. It's just that some...well...some strange things have happened during these last few days. And I am feeling...a little...how do I put it...confused. I think I really need a break. Just to think things through. You just come over as soon as you can.'

'I'm on my way, Manu. Just hold on till I come.'

'Great. I'll see you in the evening then. Just take a pre-paid taxi from the airport. The service is quite decent. Come to the hotel directly. I'm in Room Number 119.'

'Okay. See you soon.'

'Oh, and one more thing. Just be a little careful, will you? There are rumours of some trouble in the city.'

'What sort of trouble?'

'I'm not really sure. But the cab driver was talking of a train that caught fire this morning. The Sabarmati Express, I think he said. Caught fire at Godhra railway station. Around sixty or so people may have died, mostly women and children.'

'Sixty! That sounds like a bad accident.'

'Some people are saying that it wasn't an accident. There are rumours that the train was deliberately set on fire. Not the whole train actually, but one particular coach.'

'That's strange. Why would anyone set fire to a single coach?'

'Apparently that coach was full of pilgrims coming back from Ayodhya. People are saying that it was done to take revenge for Babri Masjid.'

'Oh my god! If that's true, then it's a terrible thing to have happened. What's the situation like in Ahmedabad now?'

'Seems okay so far. But you know how these things can flare up. Doesn't take any time for rumours to turn into riots. Come to think of it, I'm wondering if it's even safe for you to come here. Maybe you should cancel your trip. Why take an unnecessary risk?'

'No, I'm coming! We've been planning this holiday for such a long time, Manu. I'm not going to cancel it at the last moment.'

'Even if I tell you to?'

'When have I ever listened to you, Manu Singh?'

'All right, fine. Come then. It will be good to see you. I have so many things to talk to you about.'

'Like what?'

'The business, for example. I have been thinking about it. I don't know if—' Manu stopped himself.

'Go on,' Sayoni said.

'I'll tell you when we meet,' Manu paused. After a while he said: 'Can I ask you something, Sayoni?'

'Yes, of course, anything.'

'It's a really stupid question. Promise that you won't laugh at me.'

'Of course not, Manu. What is it?'

He took a deep breath and said: 'Have I been a good person? Have I done the right things?'

There was a long silence before Sayoni replied. 'Of course, you have been a good person, Manu. You've cared for me, for Raja-saab, for Mary, for all the people who work for you. Why are you asking such weird questions?'

'I don't know,' Manu said with an embarrassed laugh. How could he explain to her why he was suddenly feeling so lost, so confused? Why the solid ground upon which he had been standing for all these years was slipping beneath his feet? He tried to get a grip of himself. 'Anyway, we will talk when we meet,' he said.

'Yes, I think we need to. You just take care of yourself until then, okay? I need to run to the airport. I'll see you very soon. Bye for now.'

'Goodbye,' said Manu and replaced the phone receiver on the cradle. He towelled himself dry and collapsed into bed. After tossing and turning for a while he fell into an uneasy sleep.

But even as Manu rested on the snow-white, lavender-scented pillows of the Taj Hotel, waiting for Sayoni to come, a foul wind was racing towards the city of Ahmedabad. It smelt of burning flesh and death.

***

It was 7.30 in the evening when Sayoni boarded a taxi from Ahmedabad airport. She had tried to call Manu at the hotel, but the receptionist informed her that he wasn't picking up the phone. It worried her. He had sounded so strange when they had spoken earlier in the day.

'Can you drive fast, please?' she said to the taxi driver. 'I'm in a hurry.'

The driver was a lean, bearded man in his thirties with a snub nose and small eyes. He squinted at her through the rear-view mirror and said: 'I'll try my best, madam. I also want to finish up quickly and go home. Things are not good in the city.'

'Why what's happened?' Sayoni asked.

'Some trouble has broken out in Kalupur. Because of what happened in Godhra.'

'The train bogey which was set on fire?' Sayoni said. 'But wasn't it an accident?'

'Most likely, madam,' the driver replied. 'But some people are spreading rumours that it was a planned operation. Tell me madam, who will make plans to burn women and children alive? What do they think we are? Butchers?' his gaze shifted to the rearview mirror. A metal carving was dangling from it.

A sudden fear rippled through Sayoni as she noticed the carving. It said 786. 'Please take only the main roads, bhaiyya. No shortcuts please.'

'Don't worry madam, I'll get you safely to your hotel. Only fifteen minutes more and we will be there,' He touched the carving to his forehead and pressed down on the accelerator.

As the taxi shot forward, Sayoni gazed through the window, trying to push down the little tendrils of fear that were crawling inside her stomach. She glanced at her wristwatch. She would soon be safe and sound in the Taj with Manu. Five minutes later, the car came to a halt at a traffic signal. Sayoni peered out of the window. Things seemed to be quiet...a little too quiet perhaps. Why were the streets so empty...and why was the signal stuck at red when there were no cars on the road? She was about to tell the driver to get moving when she heard the shuffle of feet behind her. Before she knew what was happening, two men appeared out of nowhere and planted themselves in front of the taxi.

One of the men lowered his head to the driver's side window and smiled: '*Kem chhe? Majama*? (How are you? Good?).'

'I'm okay, bhai-saab,' the driver replied uncertainly.

The smile vanished from the man's face. '*Kya naam hai tera? Kidhar jaa raha* (What's your name? Where are you going)?' he barked.

'Just dropping madam to Taj Hotel,' the driver stammered.

'I asked for your name,' the man barked. '*Naam bata jaldi* (What's your name)?'

'Name? I...my name is Jignesh. Jignesh Patel, saab,' the driver said. 'I'm Hindu, saab.' His forehead was dripping with sweat. He was wiping his brow with the back of his hand, when the other man let out a jubilant cry.

'*Bhai-log idhar aa jao sab* (come here everyone)!' he shouted as he pointed at the metal carving hanging from the rearview mirror. '*Abbe 786 ka aulaad, tera number toh aa gaya* (Oy, you son of 786, your number's up)!'

'No, I'm Hindu. This is my friend's car,' the driver whimpered. The blood had drained from his face and he was shivering uncontrollably. 'Please let me go, saab, please let me go,' he sobbed.

But ten more men had emerged from the shadows, their knives glinting red in the light of the traffic signal. One of the men yanked open the front door, while another caught the driver by the collar and dragged him out. He screamed and kicked in terror, but the men slammed their fists into his face and put an end to the screaming. Another pair of men grasped his hands and dragged him across the street. They hurled him to the pavement and as he lay squirming, a third man walked up, a plastic jerrycan in his hand. He held the can above the driver, tilting it at an angle. The petrol sparkled as it streamed out of the can and spilled all over him, until he was drenched from head to toe.

The stench of petrol filled the air. Sayoni could feel the bile rising in her throat. She was on the verge of throwing up, when one of the men popped his head through the open window and said: 'Your name aunty-ji?' He had a scar on his left cheek and his breath stank of tobacco.

'I...my...name,' Sayoni mumbled. She was finding it difficult to breathe. 'My name is Sayoni Kh—' she stopped herself in the nick of time.

A crooked smile appeared on Scarface's lips. 'Sayyonee, hanh? Sayyonee what?'

'Sayoni, not Sayyonee. Sayoni...Singh,' she replied.

'Is it? You have any ID proof, madam?' Without waiting for a reply, Scarface thrust his hand through the window and grabbed her handbag. A moment later, he drew out a PAN card and waved it around like a prize, as he called out to his companions: '*Yeh dekh re, bhai-log* (Brothers, come and see). Sayyonee Khan has come to meet us.'

Hoots of laughter greeted his words as Sayoni stammered: 'No, I'm Hindu. I'm Bengali Hindu. I'm—' The door opened. Scarface grabbed her by the hand and dragged her out.

'Which of you bastards wants to take her?' he shouted.

'*Arre*, aunty is too old for me,' someone replied. 'You only take her, uncle.'

They broke into raucous laughter. After it had subsided, Scarface grinned and said: '*Phir toh bahut sara Vaseline chahiye hoga. Lagta hai bahut din se kisi ne aunty ka servicing nahin kiya* (I'll need some Vaseline on her though. Looks like aunty hasn't been serviced in a long time).'

'*Petrol hai na, uncle. Wohi laga lo. Waise bhi baad mein petrol hi daaloge na mooh mein? Neeche bhi thoda daal lo* (No Vaseline here, uncle. Use petrol instead. Anyway you will put it all over her. Put some down there also, no)?' one of the men replied.

'Please believe me. I'm Hindu!' Sayoni screamed. But someone gave her a hard shove from behind and she crashed face down upon the stone pavement. From the corner of her eye, she saw Scarface taking off his khaki trousers.

It was the last thing that she saw before the man hurled himself upon her. She cried out in agony as he rutted her like a machine gone mad, but her screams were drowned by the whistles and cheers of his companions.

***

The embers of Godhra had sparked off a raging inferno in Ahmedabad. Thousands of attackers fitted out in saffron scarves poured into the streets, swearing to avenge the victims of Godhra. They brandished kitchen knives and cleavers, swords and trishuls. But their most powerful weapon was entirely innocuous—computer printouts of the Ahmedabad Municipal Corporation, containing names and addresses of all the Muslim householders of the city. Armed with their deadly checklists, the mobs quickly got down to business. With clinical precision, they went from house to house, hunting down one family after another, as their chilling cries rent the air:

> *Yeh andar ki baat hai*
> *Police hamarey saath hai*
>
> (This is the news from inside
> The police is on our side.)

But while the marauding mobs were sweeping through the city murdering, raping and burning with impunity, the police were nowhere to be seen. Flaming torches were flung into the bedrooms of Muslim families; petrol was forced down the throats of children and they were set ablaze in front of their mothers; pregnant women were dragged out into the street and their foetuses ripped apart with swords. Rivulets of blood flowed into the waters of the Sabarmati, burnt corpses drifted past the Gandhi Ashram on her banks. But still, the police were nowhere to be seen.

And what of Manu and Sayoni? How I wish that I did not have to write anymore. I am tired. Tired of blood and fire and riots. How I wish I could fly away and not have to write on and on. But I am cursed and it is my dark fate to record the happenings of that accursed evening and the accursed nights and days that followed.

So I will write. But no more than the bare facts—it is all I can manage.

When Sayoni did not arrive at the Taj Hotel, Manu moved heaven and earth to find out where she was. After increasingly frantic calls to her mobile phone went unanswered, he somehow managed to find a cab that would take him to the airport (no easy task in the middle of a riot). The Indian Airlines staff confirmed that she had boarded the Bangalore-Ahmedabad flight. But they had no clue where she had gone after landing.

By now it was nearly midnight, and Sayoni was still missing. There was no choice but to approach the police. The groggy eyed police inspector at the Airport Police Station had no interest in Manu's case. He shook his head sleepily, saying that he wouldn't be able to do a thing tonight. Riots had broken out in the city and all his men were busy managing the situation, he said with a sly smile. This was no time to look for a woman who was stupid enough to travel alone in a taxi at night.

An infuriated Manu demanded that the inspector file a Missing Person Report right away and get cracking. He was here at the invitation of the Gujarat government. He knew top ranking IAS officers, the Chief Secretary, the Chief Minister even.

The inspector looked at Manu in amusement: '*Chaliye, achha hai. Phir toh aap directly CM saab se hi mil lijiye. Woh chahenge to aapko aapki bibi bhi mil jaayegi* (That's good. Then you go meet the CM saab directly. If he wants it, your wife will be found),' he winked.

A desperate Manu tried calling the Chief Secretary, the Home Secretary and every major and minor government officer he knew. He even tried Mansukh-hai-to-mumkin-hai-Bhai. But all his calls either went unanswered or were met with a sympathetic apology. The situation was bad, people said, it was every man for himself.

And when the bloody night of 27th February turned into a bloodier dawn, Sayoni was still missing.

After the riots, when the city was being cleaned up, the charred corpse of a woman was found lying on a street in Gomtipur. She was burnt beyond recognition. Her only identification was a PAN card which bore the name: Sayoni Khan. An abandoned taxi stood near the corpse. The metal carving that dangled from its rearview mirror, read 786—the numbers representing the holy words in praise of God: *Bismillahi Rahmani Raheem.*

In the name of God, the Most Gracious, the Most Merciful.

When Manu made his umpteenth visit to the police station, the inspector didn't try to conceal the irritation he felt. 'Here,' he said, shoving the card across the table. 'This is your wife's, isn't it? We found it...next to her body. Burnt.' He could give no further details.

Manu never did find out how Sayoni met her end. And thank god he didn't.

Book Six

The Crane

Whichever gods Manu believed in (if he believed in them at all anymore) were turning out to be anything but merciful. They had snatched from him every living soul he had ever loved. The prince had died in prison, Sayoni had died a horrible death in the riots. The cruel gods had denied him even the closure of performing their last rites, let alone being by their side in their final moments. Yes, Mary was still alive, but he was as good as dead to her. And so in the spring of 2002, sixty-five year old Manu found himself to be utterly alone, abandoned even by the beasts of the forest.

But it was Sayoni's death that he was finding impossible to come to terms with. Night and day, a red-hot guilt burned inside him, for he held himself as responsible for her murder as her unknown assailants. Wasn't it his thirst for money, his hunger for political power that had brought him to Gujarat? Wasn't it his obsession with the Gir project and the long separations that had made Sayoni want to join him in Ahmedabad? Hadn't she warned him that the saffron-clad senas of India were no different from the skull-cap wearing jihadis of Bangladesh? She had managed to escape from one, only to fall into the murdering hands of the other...and he had been responsible for it.

Like a cancer, the pain cut deep into the very marrow of his bones. He felt as if he had been hollowed out and a terrible emptiness ached inside him. He had nothing to live for, nothing that he wanted anymore—neither love nor vengeance, neither power nor fame. He had even lost his hunger for money—the one desire that had been the lodestar of his life ever since he had tasted his first ice cream in Buckingham Place Hotel. From that moment onwards, his insides had forever whined for more—more ice cream, more money, more stocks and shares, more bungalows and BMWs. But now, their very thought nauseated him.

Within a few weeks of Sayoni's death, Manu got rid of all his possessions. He sold off his cars, properties, shares—everything. He closed his bank accounts and shut down his construction business. Then he looked up Mary's NGO on Google and sent across a cheque for the entire proceeds of the sales (a most handsome amount, if I may say so), keeping only a few lakh rupees in cash for himself. He moved into a small rented house in Kumbalgodu, a remote village on the banks of the Vrishabhavati river, miles away from Bangalore city. And there he spent his days, cut off from the rest of the world, smoking endless cigarettes and staring blankly at the Vrishabhavati river.

You did not have to be a soothsayer to predict that Manu's days were numbered. He was dying of heartbreak.

***

I may be a bad historian, but it is as a soothsayer that I really suck. As it turns out, Manu did not die of heartbreak or from the sheer boredom of staying in Kumbalgodu village. A wounded bird returned him to life.

It was I who first noticed the bird. One day, during my usual morning jaunt over the Vrishabhavati I saw a large white bird on the left bank of the river. Swifter than Salim Ali, I identified the bird as a sarus crane (or *antigone antigone* for the ornithologically obsessed). The moment I saw it, I did a quick double take. For instead of standing upright, as cranes invariably do, it was lying flat on its back. I craned my neck and took a closer look. There was no mistake. It was definitely a sarus crane, red-crowned, long-necked, white-winged—the works. But it was lying on its back—a most unnatural sight, almost as unnatural as a road without potholes in Bangalore; for apart from Indians, cranes are the most aatma-nirbhar species I have known—they learn to stand on their own two feet from a very early age and must remain that way until they die.

I glided down to the bird and greeted her: 'Hello there. How are you doing today?'

The crane snapped its beak angrily and said: 'Can't you see I'm in pain?'

She pointed her wing tip at her right leg and showed me what was troubling her. The poor thing was in a mess. Instead of being straight, the portion of her leg above the knee (if that's what they call it for cranes) was bent at an angle of almost ninety degrees. Clearly, it was broken.

'What happened? Did you 'brake' too hard while landing?' I asked, wiggling my wings to mime the quotation marks.

The crane groaned and said: 'No, you idiot. A bloody dog did that to me. A filthy mongrel that was scrounging for food in the garbage that people throw into the river. Must have thought I would make a tasty meal and attacked me. Snapped my right leg when I wasn't looking and bit it right through the bone. I pecked and pulled and tugged and somehow managed to escape. But the damage was already done. That bloody dog has finished my leg,' she wailed.

'Oh dear,' I said. 'How horrible.'

The crane's eyes darkened with pain. 'You have no idea what I have suffered. I will never stand up on my two feet again, I will never soar in the skies again and feel the sun on my wings,' she sobbed. 'I will just lie here in the dirt until I die. And what a mercy that will be! Oh dear god, what a mercy that will be.'

I was deeply moved by her plight. It was awful to see this beautiful creature writhing in pain, waiting for death...and it was then that I was struck by a brilliant idea. I did not know whether it would work. But it was a ray of hope. If fire could fight fire, I thought, then perhaps darkness could fight darkness? Worth a try... definitely worth a try.

'Listen my friend,' I said. 'I'm going to leave you for a bit now. But I'll be back soon with help.'

'Please don't,' the crane groaned. 'The last thing I want is *your* help. I just want to die in peace.'

'No one is going to die. Not yet,' I said as I took off into the skies and headed straight for home.

***

'What do you think?' I asked. 'Will she live?'

Manu frowned as his gaze swept over the crane's leg. He gently stroked her head and made little clucking sounds to soothe her. But his actions only seemed to agitate her even more.

'Why have you brought a man here? He'll slit my throat and roast me for dinner!' the crane shrieked angrily at me. 'I knew you were an idiot the moment I saw you.'

'Oi—watch it,' I said. 'A little less beak and a lot more gratitude, if you please. I'm trying to help, you know.'

'By bringing a man to my deathbed? Give me a pack of wild dogs any day!'

'Hush! This one isn't like other men,' I said, nodding at Manu. 'He's kind. He'll try and help you if he can,' I said. 'You will save her, won't you Manu.'

'Me? What can I do?' Manu replied. 'I am not capable of doing anything anymore. Come, let's go back home.'

I smacked him hard on the head with my wing and said: 'Manu Singh! I have had enough of your self-pitying! It's high time you stopped going around as if the weight of the world was on your shoulders and made yourself useful for a change.'

'Just what is it that you want me to do?' Manu snapped back.

'Take that poor bird to the vet and get her leg fixed. You can do that much at least, can't you?'

Manu glared at me. He didn't feel like doing a thing except lying on his bed and staring at the ceiling. What was the use of doing anything when everything he did went wrong. A harsh croak sounded at his feet and he started.

'What now?' I asked.

He was staring at the crane as if she were a ghost. 'I think she is trying to say something to me,' Manu replied slowly. 'I can't make out exactly what it is but I thought she said...*die*. I'm quite sure she said it...*die*...twice at least. Am I right...or just imagining things?'

'No you are not,' I replied. 'She said—*let me die. For god's sake, please let me die.*'

'Really? You mean...she's talking to me?' Manu's eyes lit up in wonder. 'She actually spoke to me?' He knelt down, cradling the crane gently in his hands and squawked a few times. In response the crane let out a terrified shriek and kicked at him with her good leg.

'Why is she getting angry? Manu asked me. 'I just said that I'll try and take her to a vet.'

'Sure, that's what you *meant* to say. What you ended up saying was—*I'll keep you as a pet.* But good try,' I patted him on the back. 'Once the vet fixes her leg, you should brush up your Cranish with her.'

'Yes, I would like that, I would like that very much indeed,' said Manu. His gaze met the crane's and each saw their pain reflected in the other's eyes. He ran his fingers ever so gently across the crane's feathers. This time she did not shrink from him and instead let out a volley of long plaintive squawks.

'What is she saying?' asked Manu. 'Something about a forest, if I heard her right?'

'Yes. She's saying that before she dies, she would like to see a forest. A real forest, in which there are no wild dogs and rats scrounging in garbage. A forest with bird-song and berries and tall trees upon which she can perch in peace. And a small river into which no sewage flows, with fishes and frogs and juicy snail on which she can dine, and then dance in her moonlit waters.'

Manu gazed silently at the crane. After a long time he said in a barely audible whisper. 'I know a place like that. I used to live there once upon a time...so long, so very long ago...more than half a century ago. I had almost forgotten about it. But the memories are coming back now, like fireflies in the dark they are coming back to me at last,' his eyes glistened as he turned to the crane. 'Listen my friend. Don't worry about a thing from now on. I'll take care of everything. First of all, we'll go to the vet and get your leg fixed. Then I'll take you to my home and look after you until you are up and about. After that we will—'

'Hold it. Just hold it for a second,' I cut in. 'Just what have you been smoking? How on earth are you going to keep this great big crane in that tiny little house of yours? We will be knee-deep in bird droppings in a day.'

'Not that home, bird-brain!' Manu replied. 'I am talking about Betla.'

I stared blankly at Manu. 'What? We are going to take her all the way to Betla?'

'Yes, as soon as she is better,' said Manu. 'We will all go to Betla. We will all go back home.'

I was about to say something sarcastic about this harebrained scheme of his. But I held my tongue—for a faint smile had lit up Manu's face. For the first time in many months, Manu was smiling—the dreamy smile of a little boy returning home, after a long, long time.

Home Again

Like Odysseus, no traveller ever returns to the home that he has left, for by the end of the journey, both have changed. In the winter of 2002, when Manu returned to Netarhat, there was as much resemblance to the place that he had left fifty-two years ago, as there is between Salman Khan and Salman Rushdie.

The once comatose strip of mud leading into Netarhat town had now become a two-lane metalled road, choked with bumper to bumper traffic. We realised, too late, that we had made the mistake of arriving in town on New Year's Eve. Pretty much everyone in North India (and their uncle), seemed to have descended on Netarhat, all determined to watch the last sunset of the year from the newly minted Magnolia Sunset Point before heading to the New Year's Gala Party 2003 at the Pavitra Paradise Hotel. I shuddered at the prospect of having to spend the evening rubbing shoulders with sweaty hordes of the aforesaid uncles, sedately swinging their booties to the beats of *'Say Shava Shava'*.

I heaved a heartfelt sigh and a cloud of petrol fumes swept into my lungs. 'Ahh, the heady smell of vikaas,' I rasped hoarsely as I turned to Manu and asked: 'What next? Where are we going now?'

'The Dak Bungalow. It's a good thing I had made an advance booking,' he replied. 'We'll stay there for the night and first thing tomorrow morning, we will release Kangana (the name we'd given her) into the forest,' he clucked at the crane who let out a sad chirp in reply.

Poor Kangana was miserable. And who could blame her? For three nights and three days, she had been cooped up inside a wooden crate in the back seat of the jeep which Manu had driven from Bangalore to Netarhat.

'Don't worry little one. We are almost there,' Manu said. 'By this time tomorrow, you will be feasting on the juiciest snails to be found in the Koyal river.'

He gazed into the distance. Beyond the long line of cars, the green-gold outline of the Betla forest was glimmering in the horizon. Bamboo, sal and mahua trees swayed in the mild winter breeze, and the long-buried memories came flooding back to Manu. He could almost hear the Koyal calling out to him, inviting him to watch blue-throated kingfishers dive into her waters, like they had many years ago, when Mary was by his side.

***

Even the best laid plans of mice and Manu can go oft' awry.

Although he did not know it yet, the Betla of Manu's childhood was gone. It still existed of course, but not as the free-for-all forest in which anyone could romp around as they pleased. It was now a National Park—a protected wildlife reserve under Project Tiger, Mrs Gandhi's splendid scheme to save her favourite animal from extinction.

Nearly twelve hundred square kilometres of forest land had been cordoned off by the government and a tall, concrete Mughal style archway stood at the entrance of the park. Sentries stood guard at the gate and forest officers patrolled the jungle to chase away poachers, cattle grazers and women from the nearby Betla village, foraging for firewood. Entry to the park was strictly regulated and visitors had to stick to the officially permitted routes. In other words, it was not the sort of place where one could simply walk in with a crane (and that too one as cranky as Kangana) and release it into the wilderness.

That much became clear to us on the following morning when we arrived before the gates of Betla National Park. Manu's jaw dropped as he watched the throng of tourists buzzing like flies at the ticket counter, jostling for first dibs on the jeep safari.

'Oh my god!' he exclaimed. 'Is this Betla? Or Brigade Road on Friday night? How on earth am I going to get Kangana in there?'

'Quite frankly, I don't think it's possible,' I replied. 'Besides, even if you somehow managed to sneak her in, I don't think you should. It's not safe for her.'

'What do you mean?' asked Manu.

What I meant was that in saving Kangana's life, Manu had unwittingly taken away her ability to live on her own. During the last few months he had spared no effort to get her up and about. He had got her leg fixed at the Bangalore Veterinary Hospital. To protect her from stray dog attacks, he had built a small fenced enclosure on the banks of the Vrishabhavati. He would visit her every day and feed her berries and nuts and water. He would tell her stories in his broken Cranish to lift her spirits. And as he nursed her back to health, he had come to love her like the child he never had.

But like many who become parents in their old age, Manu was blind to his child's shortcomings. He could not see that although Kangana's leg had healed, it wasn't what it used to be. She had developed a limp and she could not fly as swiftly as before, for her muscles had grown weak during her long convalescence. But as birds of the same feather (only a little smaller and browner), I could see what Manu couldn't—that Kangana wouldn't survive in the wild for more than a week. For an outsider like Kangana, the jungles of Betla could be as dangerous as the mean streets of Bangalore. She was easy meat, and would soon end up in the clutches of some hungry predator. Until now, I hadn't had the heart to reveal my fears to Manu. But the time had come for me to speak my mind. And I spoke.

The wrinkles on Manu's forehead grew deeper as he listened to me. 'I hate to admit it, but you may be right,' he said at last in a low, sad voice. 'Now that you say it, Kangana may not be strong enough to live in the wild. Besides, she may have become semi-domesticated. Damn it! Why didn't I see this coming? What am I going to do with her now?'

'Well...I believe there is a zoo in Ranchi,' I said. 'Perhaps you could ask them if...' I petered to a halt because Manu was glaring so furiously at me that I thought he would wring my neck.

'A zoo!' he snapped. 'You think I'm going to hand over my little baby to a zoo! Not over my dead body!'

'All right fine!' I said. 'But think calmly for a moment. You can't keep her here. And you can't take her back to Bangalore. So what will you do?'

Manu's scowl darkened. 'I don't know. Just stop asking me stupid questions and let me think.'

He paced up and down, his fists clenching and unclenching in frustration. A few moments later, he stopped abruptly and turned to me: 'I promised Kangana that I would find her a home in the forest. And I will keep my promise,' he stabbed a finger at the gates of the Betla National Park. 'If she can't stay in that forest, then she will stay in a different one.'

'A different one? Which one?' I asked.

'The one that I will make for her,' replied Manu, a fierce gleam in his eyes.

'What?' I exclaimed.

'Yes, my friend,' Manu smiled. 'I am going to make a forest for her. I have no idea how, but I will do it.'

'You've lost your mind, Manu,' I squawked. 'Either that or a sunstroke. I think you are talking non—'

'I don't care what you think,' Manu cut in harshly. 'I don't care if it sounds crazy. I don't care if it's impossible. All I know is that I have to do it. Don't you understand? For the first time in my life I can see clearly what I must do. And if I can raise a forest, a small one, or even a little grove, it will be the best thing I will have done in my life. If I can't...well...at least I will have had the satisfaction of trying. And that will be enough for me. I don't want anything more from this life.'

For once, even I was at a loss for words.

***

For all his faults, Manu had one admirable quality. When his mind was set on something, he just did it. Had he been younger and fitter, I might have taken him seriously, but not now. I was sceptical of his big talk of growing a forest out of thin air. It was just an emotional outburst, I said to myself, the delusions of a sixty-five year old man who had lost the battle of life, and probably his marbles as well. But I was wrong. Manu hadn't lost his mind. He had found a reason to live.

In the days that followed, Manu took up his forest project with an energy that I had never seen before. The first thing he did was to enlist the services of one Bhupati Munda who was reputed to be the real estate king of Netarhat. Bhupati turned out to be a sharp operator. Within two days, he managed to find us a place to live—a ramshackle bungalow with a large garden, in which the good-hearted landlord was willing to let Kangana stay, provided he was paid double the rent. With the living arrangements out of the way, Manu now turned his attention to the far more thorny problem of finding a piece of land on which he could raise his forest.

There was plenty of land in and around Netarhat. But the large land blocks were mostly farm land or belonged to the government. The government properties were untouchable of course. And soon, so was Manu. He had begun his search by approaching a few farmers from Betla village. It was a mistake. The moment they found out that Manu wanted to buy land, the alarm bells went off in their heads and they turned hostile.

Within days, every farmer in Betla village had heard of the greedy diku from Bengaluru who was out to grab the land that they had tilled for generations. The rumours flew thick and fast. Some said the diku wanted to build a mall, others said it was an amusement park, yet others said it was an IT park, for that was the only thing that Bengalureans built. And no matter how hard Manu tried to convince them, that all he wanted to do was plant trees and raise a forest, not one person believed him. Who would be stupid enough to spend good money to grow a forest, they scoffed, and chased him away, calling him a liar.

Manu's pipe-dream seemed to be going up in smoke. He was in despair. On one hand, that spoiled brat of a crane kept shrieking for her forest, on the other he was nowhere close to finding a half-decent piece of land. He was wondering whether his grand project had stalled even before taking off, when good old Bhupati Munda came to the rescue.

'Manu babu,' said Bhupati. 'There is a piece of land that I know of. No occupants, no construction, no cultivation. Only acres and acres of empty land with not a soul in sight. Are you interested in seeing it?'

Manu sat up with a jolt. 'Where is this land?' he asked. 'It sounds too good to be true.'

'Oh, it is true Manu babu. Cent percent true. Bhupati Munda never lies,' replied Bhupati. 'And in a very good location too. Just a few kilometres off the highway.'

'What is this gold mine that you are talking about?' Manu asked eagerly.

'Good joke, Manu babu. It may not be a gold mine but it is a bauxite mine.'

'Bauxite? You mean aluminium ore?'

'Cent percent correct, sir-ji,' Bhupati gave an oily smile. 'You see, sir-ji, once upon a time, there used to be an aluminium plant in these parts. The ore was supplied by the mine that I'm talking about.'

'And where is this plant now?' asked Manu. 'Aluminium plants don't just vanish into thin air.'

'As good as vanish only, sir-ji. Aluminium plant, bauxite mine—everything is gone. You see, about ten years ago, the government decided to shut it down.'

'But why?'

'Because there was no more bauxite left to mine, sir-ji. In fact, the ore had run out even earlier, sometime in the 1980s only—at least that's what my father says. But the government kept the plant running until 1992.'

'But if there was no ore, then why keep running the plant? What were they hoping to get from it?'

'*Arre* sir-ji, a government factory is like a treadmill. Both keep running without getting anywhere. At least employees were still getting salaries, no? But finally in 1992, the government decided that enough was enough. They gave VRS to everyone and shut down the plant, the mine, everything. And they have stayed shut these last ten years. No one goes there anymore. Just an empty factory building and empty land gathering dust.'

'But it is government land. We can't just walk in there and start planting trees.'

'Why not sir-ji, why not? Let me tell you something—no one is bothered about that place, least of all the government. They haven't even kept a security guard at the plant. And the mine is fully open. Anyone can walk in there and do whatever they want. Besides, why should the government object if someone wants to spend his own money to plant trees on a barren piece of land? In fact, the government will be happy that someone is doing their job for them.'

'Okay, assuming for a moment that you are right, I will still need official permission before I even think of touching government land, right? An authorisation letter, lease agreement, an MOU, some paperwork, right? How will I manage that?'

'*Arre* Manu babu,' Bhupati swatted aside Manu's concerns, 'why you have to manage anything when I am there? Just pay me a small service fee and give a little extra for chai-pani for the government babus and I'll get you your papers.'

'What papers?' Manu asked. 'Is it a lease agreement or a sale deed or—'

'*Arre* whatever you want, sir-ji. All you city people are always so worried about papers. Over here papers don't matter. Only connections. And I have all the connections—from chaprasi to Chief Minister, Bhupati Munda knows everyone and everyone knows Bhupati Munda,' he said, thumping his chest.

'Really,' Manu cocked an eyebrow. 'So exactly what sort of connections do you have?'

'It's simple, sir-ji—I am Bhupati Munda, the local Zilla Parishad President is Prajapati Munda and the Chief Minister is Arjun Munda. Now Prajapati-ji is my cousin's uncle and Arjun-ji is Prajapati-ji's co-brother-in-law's niece's husband—which makes Arjun-ji and me brothers. Yes or no?'

'I have no clue,' replied Manu. 'But we are jumping the gun here. Your brothers and uncles can wait. The first thing is to see this land of yours.'

'No problem, sir. We could have gone today itself but it's a little late. I'll take you there, first thing tomorrow morning.' Bhupati said as he rose to leave, when he seemed to be struck by a thought. He turned to Manu and said: 'I hope you don't mind me asking one question, sir-ji. Are you superstitious person, Manu babu? Do you believe in the supernatural?'

Manu looked at him in surprise. 'I haven't really thought about it. But I don't think I'm particularly superstitious. Why do you ask?'

'Good, that's good,' Bhupati let out a sigh of relief. 'I was thinking and thinking whether I should tell you or not. You may have got scared. But now I can tell you.'

'Go on!' Manu said impatiently.

'You see there is a reason why no one goes to the mine anymore. Some say that it is the same reason why even the government babus don't want anything to do with it.'

'What reason?'

Bhupati lowered his voice to a dramatic whisper. 'Manu babu, they say the land is cursed. They say that ghosts live there.'

'Ghosts?' Manu laughed.

'Yes sir, ghosts. The unhappy spirits of dead men and women who once used to live there. But—' Bhupati paused as a sharp breath escaped Manu's lips.

'But what?' Manu said urgently. 'Why did you stop? Go on.'

Bhupati sighed. 'It is not a happy tale, babu. It goes back many years, around the time when my father was born. The old-timers say that in those days, there used to be a Santhal village where the aluminium plant stands now. It was a small village—with a hundred, two hundred people maybe. They mostly kept to themselves, deep inside the jungle. Few saw them but those who did used to say that they were a happy, hardworking lot, who never did anyone any harm.'

Manu's face had turned white as a sheet. 'What happened to them?' he asked hoarsely.

'No one knows for sure. But one fine day they simply disappeared. As if they had never been there. Some say they left to go to another part of the jungle, further away from the highway. But others say that they were killed.'

'By whom?' Manu managed to ask.

Bhupati shrugged. 'Who can say? No one saw what actually happened. On the day that the Santhals disappeared, the police came and sealed off the entire area. For months after, the only people who were allowed entry were the aluminium factory people. But my father told me that the shells of fired bullets were found lodged inside the trees surrounding the village. Someone may have attacked the Santhals—maybe poachers, maybe illegal timber loggers, maybe even the—' Bhupati stopped abruptly and shook his head as if to dismiss the thought that had occurred to him. After a while he said. 'The only people who could have said what really happened on that day were the Santhals themselves. But there was no one left to tell. Since that day, not one person from the village was ever seen again. Everyone had vanished.'

'Not everyone. One remained, only one,' Manu whispered in a voice that seemed to come from the depths of a bottomless abyss. 'And she is still there. I think she is still there, on that cursed land.'

The Ghosts of the Past

The land was truly cursed. She had been strip-mined, her skin and flesh torn apart, the marrow crushed out of her bones until she was ripe for the taking. She had lain helplessly as metal-jawed excavators dug out her precious bauxite and ladled every last crumb of it into the belly of the smoke-belching factory, where it was digested in vats of burning chemicals and transformed into alumina—that magical snow-white powder that looked like cocaine and was equally addictive. And when the deed was done, all that was left of her was a toxic red mud which seeped into the soil and poisoned the clear waters of the aquifers that lay beneath her.

'This is the land, sir,' Bhupati said, spreading his arms in an expansive gesture, like a tour guide showing us the Taj Mahal. 'I know it looks terrible now, but they say it was once a forest.'

'Yes it was,' Manu murmured. 'I knew that forest. And I knew those who lived here.'

'What's that, sir-ji?' asked Bhupati.

Manu did not reply. His eyes glistened as he gazed at the desolate landscape before him. The forest that had once bloomed upon her breast was long gone. Now there was not a single stick of bamboo, not one shrub, not even a blade of grass. No birds chirped there, no frogs croaked, no wolves bayed in the moonlight for her—only acre upon silent acre of blood-red dust, spread out like a gaping wound and in the distance, an abandoned bulldozer, its blade arm raised high like a giant praying mantis stalking its prey.

The tears were rolling down Manu's cheeks now. He turned away to hide them from Bhupati, as he fought to stop them from coming.

'Did we really have to do this?' he asked hoarsely.

Bhupati did not seem to have noticed the anguish in Manu's

voice. He merely gave a hearty shrug and said: 'What to do, sir-ji? We are like this only, yes or no? Complan boy and Complan girl put together, isn't it?'

'What?' Manu exclaimed.

'What I meant sir-ji, is that we are growing so fast—just like Complan boy and girl. We need more. And more. And more. So many people, so many needs. Take yourself for example. You came from Bangalore to Ranchi on plane, yes or no?'

'Yes, but—'

Bhupati cut him off. 'Plane is made from aluminium, isn't it, sir-ji? And everyone wants to fly on planes these days. Even my useless brother-in-law wants to fly. And why only brother-in-law? Take my own wife only. These days she is wasting good money to buy aluminium foils. To keep rotis warm, she says. But I think it's just to make our dining table look more hi-fi—like in four-star hotels. What to do sir-ji, we are like that only.'

I thought Manu would give him a tight slap. But he listened quietly and after a while he said: 'Maybe you are right, Bhupati. We all have our needs. But so do they. Did we really have to take everything away from them? What right did we have to do such a thing?'

A strange look came over Bhupati's face. He put his hand gently on Manu's shoulder. 'You are right, sir-ji. I am a Munda and I know what you mean. Today we all need aluminium foil and fancy phones and planes and trains and whatnot. But hardly fifty-sixty years ago, my forefathers lived in the jungle. They hunted wild boars, brewed mahua, ate, drank and made merry. That's all it took for them to be happy. But can I go back to the jungle and live like them? We can't change the past or change what we have become, sir-ji. We can only do something with the time that is given to us. Where one man has cut down a forest, another man can grow it, no?'

'That's what I wanted to do. But sometimes I feel so stupid,' said Manu. 'I don't know if it is possible or even worth trying. Some things can never come back once they are—'

He stopped abruptly, startled by a low wail that sounded almost human. And out of nowhere, there came a gust of wind, whistling past our ears and kicking up clouds of red earth at our feet.

Bhupati nearly jumped out of his skin. 'Ghosts!' he whispered, his voice trembling in fear and awe. 'The ghosts have come. Can you hear them, Manu-babu? Can you hear them?'

As if in a dream Manu nodded his head. Yes, he could hear the ghosts. There were thousands, millions of them—the lost souls of the lost forest. Yes, he could hear them—the laments of a million dead birds, beasts and men, all wailing as one.

But of the many voices that came to his ear, there was one that sounded above all the others. Borne on the wind, it was faint as a moonbeam but clear as a bell—the voice of a little girl, rising above the chorus of unhappy wails, crying: *Give us back our home, give us back our home.*

And in reply, Manu whispered back to the wind: *I will try, I will try.*

***

And Manu tried as perhaps no man before him had ever tried. It was as if he had been possessed by the ghosts of the forest and in his quest to give them back their lost home, he was prepared to sacrifice all he had—his time, his money and his sanity.

His quest began, like all quests of the modern age—with the paperwork. Let alone a forest, not a blade of grass could be grown on government land without clearances from every pettifogging Competent Authority in the system, from panchayat chief to Chief Minister. It was a daunting but not impossible task and Manu wasn't fazed by it. After all, as a former real estate magnate, he had had plenty of experience of dealing with government authorities on matters of land. Besides, what objection could they have if some crazy private citizen wanted to take a blighted, bauxite mine off their hands and turn it into an afforestation project. And that too when he was ready to spend his own money and asked for nothing in return?

It was a no-brainer—I mean if I were the Competent Authority I would have jumped at this opportunity to become an environmental hero with zero public expenditure or movement of my butt. I would have simply leased the damned land to Manu and taken selfies with admiring Amazonian activists after winning the Magsaysay Prize for Public Service. But, alas, I was no authority, not even incompetent, and the ones that were, had neither my imagination nor my intelligence.

What they did have was red tape and reams of it. And in no time, poor Manu was tied up in all sorts of knots, caught in a chakravyuh, a maze, of government files, filings, papers and procedures. But like the young warrior Abhimanyu, old Manu too fought back with all his might. Doggedly limping from one department to the other, from one corrupt officer to the next and from one file stopper to his boss, he kept going. He stumbled and fell at every step but he never gave up.

Slowly but surely, Manu's efforts bore fruit. It took 79 petitions to the government (mostly addressed to one or the other of Bhupati's relatives), 537 different meetings involving 2 sympathetic ministers, 5 supportive bureaucrats and 313 corrupt lower division clerks but by the spring of 2007, Manu had finally obtained all the clearances required to start planting his forest. Like a good Nike model, Manu had just done it.

The arrow of time had cut deep lines into his brow, his skin had been burned by the scorching northern summers and his hair whitened by regret and sorrow. Yet on the day that seventy-year-old Manu received the final piece of paper sanctioning his forest, the years seemed to roll off his back. His eyes shone like a young boy's and his heart was green with hope.

Well begun is half done, and I was sure that Manu would see it through to the bitter end, even if it was the last thing he did. Even if he had to do it all by himself.

'*Ekla chalo re*—we will walk alone if we have to, but we won't stop,' I murmured to myself.

But as it so often happens, my poetical musings were both mispronounced and misplaced. For Manu would not have to walk alone much longer. Fate was about to join him with a companion—a young boy who would be at his side, until the very end.

Tat Tvam Asi

How well I remember the day when the boy came into our lives. It was a balmy morning in March. The festival of Holi was round the corner, but the forests of Betla were already coloured a dusty pink by thick clouds of mahua flowers in full bloom. Earlier in the day, Manu and I had set off on a horticultural expedition to a secluded part of the jungle. Soon after arriving there, Manu got down to work under my watchful eye.

Manu was kneeling on the ground, carefully loosening the soil around a mahua sapling, when I realised that someone else was watching him too. A young boy, of about ten or so, was standing behind a clump of bushes, staring curiously at Manu. He wasn't much to look at—just your usual poverty stricken, Rural-Indian kid. There are lakhs of them and they all look the same to me—thin, dark-skinned, dusty-haired, hungry-eyed.

The boy was nibbling on a blade of grass as he watched Manu. After a while, he walked up to him and asked: 'What are you doing?'

Manu looked up at the intruder. A glimmer of recognition seemed to appear in his eyes as he peered at the boy. Then, as if to clear the thought, he shook his head and said: 'I'm trying to take out this mahua sapling without damaging the roots. Not an easy task.'

'Why do you want to take it out?' asked the boy. 'It will get hurt. Plants feel pain just like we do. Trees, bushes, even grass—they all feel pain.'

Manu smiled. 'You seem to be a very clever boy. Did you learn that in school?'

The boy shook his head. 'No, I never went to school. But my father taught me all about plants and animals and...and buffaloes and many other things...but then he...' his voice shook and he became quiet. 'He died...two years ago,' he said after a while.

'I'm very sorry to hear that. And your mother?' Manu asked gently.

'She's dead too. Ammi, abba...they both died on the same day... in a bus accident...' he looked away. Manu let him be until the boy had collected himself. Pointing at the mahua sapling, the boy asked again: 'Why do you want to pull it out? It will die if you do that.'

'It won't. I'm going to put it into a pot full of soft soil, water it and take it to its new home. There I'm going to make a nice, deep hole in the earth for it, plant it and take good care of it.'

'Where is this new home?' the boy asked suspiciously.

'In a forest, where the old bauxite mine used to be,' Manu replied.

'You're lying. There's no forest there. Only ghosts. My father told me about them. You shouldn't go there. If you do, the ghosts will twist your neck and you'll die.'

'*Arre*, nothing will happen to me. The ghosts are my friends. They won't harm me.'

The boy shrank from Manu. 'Are you a ghost yourself?'

'No, I am not a ghost,' Manu smiled.

'Who are you then? Do you live in this forest? How come I haven't seen you here before.'

'I am...well...you could say I'm a gardener. I've come here to take a mahua sapling for my garden. But enough about me. What about you? You look too young to be roaming around alone in the forest.'

'I'm not alone,' the boy replied. 'My friends are with me.'

'Which friends?' asked Manu, as he looked around the empty forest.

'My best friends,' the boy replied and counted them off on his fingertips. 'Madhuri, Malaika, Karishma, Kareena.'

'Where? Where? Where are they?' I squealed in excitement. My heart had started to pump harder than Salman Khan pumps iron. After sixty long years of my decidedly unsexy exile, I was finally about to see not one, not two, but four-four Bollywood hotties in the flesh (and a fair bit of flesh too, if they were filming a rain dance in the forest)! But only moments later, my hopes were dashed to the ground.

'There they are,' the boy said, pointing towards a small clearing in the forest, some fifty yards ahead. Four buffaloes stood there, placidly chewing on the fresh, green grass.

I groaned in disappointment as the boy informed us that the buffaloes belonged to a local businessman who had named them after his favourite actresses. By now I had lost all interest in the boy and his bloody buffaloes. But for some strange reason, Manu wanted to know more. So I listened glumly as the boy told us about his depressingly unglamorous life.

He came from a long line of cattle herders, said the boy. His father, grandfather and all their fathers before them, had grazed buffaloes in the forest. And ever since he had come of age, so had he—for it was the only thing he knew how to do. But he didn't mind. In fact, he rather enjoyed roaming freely in the forest with his buffaloes. He considered them to be his friends, unlike their owner Mukesh bhaiyya, for whom they were only machines to be milked for profit.

As it turned out, this Mukesh bhaiyya was equally adept at milking both buffaloes and human beings. He had a money lending business that operated on a simple but effective principle—to lend money to poor people at such exorbitant interest rates that they could rarely repay their debts. And when that happened, Mukesh bhaiyya would make sure that they paid their dues, in other equally profitable ways.

It was a sad but familiar tale. There are lakhs of Mukesh bhaiyyas in India and lakhs more victims. One such victim was the boy's father. Apparently, some seven years ago, the poor man had taken a loan of twenty thousand rupees from Mukesh bhaiyya to get medical treatment for a broken leg. The leg got fixed but the loan was to break the backs of the next two generations.

'Abba was able to return only five thousand rupees out of the twenty thousand. To repay the rest, he had to work for Mukesh bhaiyya until the day he died,' the boy said. 'But he got paid only fifty rupees a day and the loan never got cleared. After abba died, Mukesh bhaiyya said that I would have to now work for him. So that's what I am doing, although I get paid only twenty-five rupees a day.'

'What!' Manu exclaimed. 'Only twenty-five rupees for grazing buffaloes all day long? What nonsense! We are not in 1947 anymore. How can such things happen in this day and age!'

'Maybe it doesn't happen in the cities, babu-ji. But this is jungle area. *Yahaan sab kuch chalta hai,* here anything can happen. But it's okay, babu-ji. Mukesh bhaiyya gives me two meals a day and a charpoy to sleep on in the verandah of his haveli. It's enough for me. I am able to save most of my money. If I can keep saving it, then maybe one day, I will be able to clear my father's debt. Except I don't know when,' he looked up at Manu. 'Babu-ji, if I save twenty-five rupees per day, how long will it take me to save two lakh rupees?' he asked hopefully.

'Two lakhs!' Manu's eyebrows shot up. 'What will you do with two lakhs?'

'That's what we owe Mukesh bhaiyya.'

'What? Who says so?'

'Yes, that's what abba told me. Before he died, he said that we owe two lakhs to Mukesh bhaiyya. And Mukesh bhaiyya also said the same thing to me.'

'But that's impossible! How can a loan of twenty thousand become two lakhs?!'

'I know. I also couldn't understand it. So I asked abba again. He said that Mukesh bhaiyya had made him put his thumb print on some piece of paper which said that the loan would have to be returned with *vyaj* (interest). If not, abba and his family would have to work for Mukesh bhaiyya—on his terms and conditions. I don't know what this *vyaj* is babu-ji. But it must be some jadugar only, a magician, if it can turn twenty thousand into two lakhs.'

Although he didn't know it, the boy was right. As my good friend Einstein had once said: *'Compound interest is the eighth wonder of the world. He who understands it, earns it; he who doesn't, pays it.'* Two generations of cattle herders hadn't understood the black magic of compounding and had paid heavily for it.

'Sometimes I think I'll also have to graze buffaloes all my life, just like my father and grandfather,' the boy muttered as he gazed wistfully into the distance.

Manu gently placed his hand on the boy's shoulder. I could see that he felt for the poor boy. After all, their childhoods were so alike that they might have been the same. Both had been orphaned at an early age and deprived of a home and parents. Unschooled and illiterate, both had been at the mercy of tyrants for a roof over their heads and two meals a day. Their childhood had been lost forever and their future portended only poverty and hardship.

'Tat vam asi'—out of the blue, the long-forgotten words of an ancient mantra rang inside Manu's head, with the clarity of temple bells at dawn. He had heard them before, these strange words...but when, where...and what did they mean? He strained his memory, trying to remember, and slowly it came back to him.

Tat tvam asi—thou art that...it was a Mahakavya, one of the four great sayings of the Upanishads. He had learnt it long years ago, in an ashram in the foothills of the Himalayas. He remembered Maharishi Mahesh Yogi teaching him to repeat the mantra endlessly so that he could find peace. And he remembered how he would chant it mechanically just to get it over with, for it meant nothing to him and it gave him no peace.

That was then. But now as he gazed at the forest around him and the reddening sky above and the light of the setting sun leaping from the horizon and falling gently upon his wrinkled face and upon the young face of the cattle herder's son beside him, he understood at last what the Maharishi had tried to teach him—that he was one with the world and all that lived and died in it—Raja-saab, Mary, Sayoni...forests, fireflies, fishes...birds, blackbucks and boys who grazed buffaloes. And once again the mantra whispered inside his head—*thou art that, you are the world and the world is you, you are he and he is you, all are one, all are same...*

Except they were not the same. They were different. Their debts were different—if the boy's debt was to a money lender, Manu's was to the world itself.

For all that it had taken away from his childhood, this world, this life had also given him much—the gift of speaking to birds and beasts, Polson's butter, chocolate ice cream, the bright lights of Park Street, Chicken a la Kiev and red wine at Mocambo, boat rides on the Ganga, money in the bank and BMWs in bungalows. He had been orphaned and alone, but soon the world had given him a friend, a father, a wife...what more could any man ask for?

He gazed again at the cattle herder's son...how much he had received from the world and how little had the other. Yes, they both had debts to pay. But his, by far, was the heavier.

He was seventy now, his days were numbered. He had been born and raised in servitude. But he would die free. Freed of all his debts. The time had come to repay his debts to the world, give back to life what he received from it. Not that he could ever give it all back. But whatever he could, he would.

His mind was made up. Squaring his shoulders, he turned to the boy and asked: 'So, what do you want to become when you grow up?'

The boy looked bewildered. 'Become? I...I have never thought about it. I mean...what can I—'

'Suppose you could become anything you wanted to,' Manu said, 'then what would you become? Teacher, farmer, policeman?'

The boy frowned as he contemplated these pleasurable but impossible scenarios. After a moment his face lit up in a big smile and he exclaimed: 'I know. I know. A doctor! A bone doctor! When I grow up I want to become a bone doctor. And I want to open a free hospital so that people won't have to borrow money from Mukesh bhaiyya for getting their broken legs fixed. How does that sound?'

'It sounds fantastic,' Manu smiled. 'A bone doctor, eh? Very good, very good. So how big will your hospital be, Dr...oh...I just realised, we don't even know each other's names. Time to introduce ourselves properly, I think. I'll start. My name is Manu. Manu Singh. What should I call you?'

'Ismail,' the boy replied. 'That's my name, saab.'

'Pleased to meet you, Dr Ismail,' I chirped merrily.

Ismail couldn't understand what I was saying of course. Or maybe he could. For his smile had grown even wider. Maybe bone doctor Ismail was already dreaming of his big hospital.

The Deal

And so it was that guilt and debt-ridden Manu embarked upon his final mission—to free himself of his self-imposed burdens so that he could die a free man. The day after his chance encounter with Ismail, he paid a visit to Mukesh bhaiyya's house. Mukesh bhaiyya was in his forties, a bald, beady-eyed man with a shiny, pointed moustache and stubby fingers which kept stroking the thick, gold chain peeking through the folds of his soft fleshy neck.

Manu came straight to the point. He was prepared to make an immediate cash payment of twenty thousand rupees to Mukesh bhaiyya, provided Ismail's loan was written off in full and he was immediately released from his duties.

'Twenty thousand?' Mukesh bhaiyya chuckled. 'Have you gone you mad, Singh-ji?' he leafed through a dog-eared file placed on the table at his side and said: 'Ah, here it is. So, the total amount due to me from Ismail's father is two lakh, thirty-four thousand, nine hundred and ninety-six rupees!'

'That is ridiculous,' Manu said. 'The loan amount was only twenty thousand. The rate of interest you are charging is exorbitant. It's illegal.'

'Illegal, hanh? See Singh-ji, if you want to go to court, you can go. But I have papers on which the boy's father has put his thumb print. *Chailye*, I will round it off to two lakh. Give me the cash and take the boy. Although what you want him for, I can't imagine. He is only good for grazing buffaloes.'

'And if you don't help, that is all he will ever do. Just look at the poor boy, Mukesh-ji,' Manu pleaded. 'You know very well that he will never be able to return such a huge amount to you.'

Mukesh bhaiyya shrugged. 'That's why I am giving him a chance to work for me and pay back in labour what he cannot pay in cash,' he ran his fingers across his gold chain, 'Singh-saab, I hear that you have come here, all the way from Bangalore to grow a forest. Is that true?'

'Yes,' said Manu. 'But I am not here to discuss my forest.'

'Yes, yes...although why you want do such a mad thing I can't imagine,' Mukesh bhaiyya shrugged. 'But people have all sorts of funny hobbies these days...especially you city people. However, one thing I know, you definitely must have lots of money to do such a crazy thing. So let's make a deal. You give me 50 percent of the outstanding—one lakh, and take the boy. What do you say?'

Manu's shoulders slumped. I knew that he didn't have anywhere close to that amount to spare. And whatever little he had, he had kept aside for his forest. His face darkened as he said: 'I'm sorry Mukesh-ji, at best I can manage seventy five thousand. That's all.'

'Then no deal, Singh saab, I'm sorry,' said Mukesh bhaiyya. 'But I still can't understand why you want to do this?' he looked at Ismail. '*Kya lagta hai aapka*? Who is he to you?'

'Never mind that. What matters is that the boy wants to make something of his life. He wants to become a doctor. And I want to help him. That's all. I want to send him to school to study so that—'

Mukesh bhaiyya broke into a guffaw. 'Become a doctor? *Arre*, Singh saab, even if you feed him and clothe him and send him to school, at the first chance he gets, he will run away to some madrasa, grow a beard and get married by fifteen. That's what all of them do, these Mohammedan good-for-nothings.'

'Keep your mouth shut!' Manu roared. 'You are a vile, pathetic man,' he turned to Ismail, who had been standing behind him all this while, listening silently. 'Come, let's get out of here. We will go straight to the police. This is a case of child labour and I'm going to file an FIR. Let's see what you do then. I should have done that in the first place. My mistake that I came here today. But now I am going to show you—'

'*Arre* go, go!' Mukesh bhaiyya cut in. 'The police is in my pocket. You won't be able to bend a single hair on my head!'

'We'll see about that,' Manu returned. 'Come Ismail, let's go,' he grasped Ismail's hand and began to walk out of the house

'Babu-ji, wait, please wait!' Ismail stopped him. He freed himself of Manu's grip and said: 'Is it really true babu-ji?' There were tears in his eyes as he spoke, 'is it true that you will send me to school... make me a doctor? You really mean it?'

'Of course I mean it. I mean every word. I said so yesterday itself, didn't I?' Manu replied. 'Don't you believe me?'

'Yes, but I thought you were...I mean I wasn't sure...' Ismail said in a broken voice. 'I'm so sorry that I...doubted you. It's just that no one has ever done anything for me.'

Manu enfolded Ismail in a hug. 'Even I don't know what I can do for you, but I'll try my best.'

Ismail took a deep breath and said: 'Then I'll try too, saab. If you can do so much for me, I can also do something for myself. I'll tell you what, saab—you don't have to give any money, you don't have to go to the police. There is a night school for adults in Netarhat. I can study there. I can graze buffaloes by day and go to school by night. If you can help me with my studies sometimes, I will manage. I'll study hard, I promise. You will help me, won't you?'

Manu had never been a father but in that moment, he thought he knew what it felt like to be one. His eyes were glistening as he hugged Ismail tightly and said: 'Don't worry, Ismail. I'll help you with your studies. And I'll make sure you go to a good school.'

'Then, let's go,' Ismail said with a grin. 'We will do without you, Mukesh bhaiyya. But since Kareena and Karishma and the others won't be able to do without me, I'll come back and take them out as usual.'

We marched out of the house when we heard Mukesh bhaiyya calling out from behind: 'Wait! Wait, Singh saab. You seem to have taken my words to heart. *Arre*, I was only joking,' he waddled up to us and said: 'See, I know this boy for many years now. Even I want him to do well in life.'

'Yes, that much I can see,' Manu replied. 'But what is it that you really want? Be quick.'

'Heh, heh, I just want to help both of you,' Mukesh bhaiyya gave an oily smile. 'Singh saab, why don't we do a deal? You give me that seventy-five thousand rupees and I will let the boy go to school four days a week. The other three days he must work for me. What do you say?'

'I say that I won't give you a paisa!' Manu exclaimed. 'I will go straight to the police and file a complaint against you.'

Mukesh bhaiyya shrugged. 'Listen, Singh saab. The thanedaar at the police station owes me seven lakh rupees. He won't lift a finger against me. If you want to waste your time with the police you can do that. But it won't get you anywhere. See, I am a businessman. Live and let live, that's my policy. Just give me the seventy-five thousand and I will consider Ismail's father's loan closed. Of course, he still has to work three days a week for me. Deal?' he said, his eyes gleaming greedily.

'You don't have to give him any money,' Ismail said. 'I will go to night school and I will continue to graze his buffaloes. We will manage.'

'Just a second, Ismail. Wait,' said Manu. He thought for a few moments and turned to Mukesh bhaiyya: 'How many years must he work for you? All his life? Like his father?'

'*Arre* no, Singh saab, no,' Mukesh bhaiyya simpered. 'Let's say for ten years. By that time he will have finished school. I will even continue to pay him his twenty-five rupees per day for his work. He can use it for his school books. Or if he saves it, he will have a nice little pot of money by the time he is ready to go to the big medical college in Ranchi, isn't it, Ismail beta? So Singh saab, what do you say?'

Manu was silent. After a while he said: 'All right, here's my final offer. Firstly, Ismail will stay with me and you won't have to take care of his food and accommodation anymore.'

'Okay, okay, very good,' Mukesh bhaiyya rubbed his hands gleefully.

'Next, he will go to school, five days a week and work for you for two days, during the weekends. This he will do for the next ten years and you will pay him fifty rupees a day for his work.'

'What? But I said three days and twenty five—'

'So this is the deal,' Manu said, ignoring the interruption. 'First thing, tomorrow morning, I will give you seventy-five thousand rupees. In cash. In return, you will permanently close Ismail father's loan and hand me over any papers that he may have put his thumb print on.'

'But...'

Manu raised a hand and cut him off. 'If you agree to all my conditions we have a deal. Otherwise I am going straight to the police. And you can tell your thanedar that if he doesn't take action, I will go to the Chief Minister. You may not know it, but I have been dealing with ministers and thanedars for years, and I know how to go to the top if I have to. I have my connections.'

'But...but...' stammered Mukesh bhaiyya.

'Deal or no deal?' Manu said.

Mukesh bhaiyya cursed, cajoled, blustered and bargained but Manu was implacable. In the end, unable to resist the lure of easy money, Mukesh bhaiyya caved in and with a sorrowful shake of his head, he muttered: 'Deal.'

Ismail

Nine years had passed since that deal-making spring of 2007. It was a period marked by hectic deal-making far beyond the boondocks of Betla. All over the world, very big people had been busy cutting very big deals. Crooked bankers in Wall Street had cut underhand deals worth trillions of dollars and had plunged the world into its worst financial crisis since the Great Depression. Closer home, the good Dr. Manmohan Singh had been plunged into his own great depression, after the ordeal of trying to get a nuclear deal signed with the USA. And in the summer of 2014, the BJP made a deal with the Indian electorate to run the country for the next five years and the CM of Gujarat became the PM of India.

For the old Manu, the BJP's sweeping victory would have been a very big deal. But when the new Manu heard the news on the radio, his face turned to stone. He switched off the radio and walked out of the house, spending the rest of the day working like a madman in the forest. When I asked what had come over him, he replied: 'Just leave me alone. I don't want to talk to anyone.' And indeed, whatever be the reason, Manu didn't speak a word for the next three days.

But speaking for myself, those nine years from 2007 to 2016 were among the most peaceful, most wonderful times of my long exile in India.

Soon after he moved in with us, Manu had admitted Ismail to a good school in Netarhat. But the education of Ismail was no easy task. He was way behind the rest of his class and quickly became the butt of their cruel jokes. They called him buffalo boy and junglee and whatnot and even the teachers smirked when he was unable to write even his own name at the age of ten. There were times when Ismail just wanted to run away and graze buffaloes in the jungle. And if Manu wasn't around, he probably would have.

But Manu wasn't having any of it. 'I promised to make you a doctor and so I shall,' he told Ismail. 'But you have to work hard and do as I say.'

And so every evening after dinner, Manu would sit Ismail down and teach him for four straight hours—reading, writing, arithmetic, science...the works. He would help him with his homework and his classwork and prepare him for his exams. Manu's efforts bore fruit and slowly but surely, the gap between Ismail and his classmates began to close and his confidence began to grow.

And there came a day, when it struck Ismail that no one had made fun of him for a whole week. Not just that, teacher ma'am had praised him for solving a particularly tricky arithmetic problem that required him to measure exactly 5 litres of milk out of two jars containing 3 and 7 litres of milk each. From that day, there was no stopping Ismail.

He slept half as much as everyone else and worked twice as hard. He never missed a day's class, nor did he ever default on his commitment to graze Mukesh bhaiyya's buffaloes twice a week. By the time he reached high school, he was topping every exam and winning every prize. He had become the darling of his teachers and great things were expected of him. His dream of becoming a doctor was no longer a fantasy but a distinct possibility.

Manu was as proud of Ismail as any father could be of his son. He saw in Ismail a reflection of his younger self—the will to rise above the circumstances of his birth, the hunger to make something of himself and to succeed against all odds. Meanwhile Manu himself was succeeding against the odds. Within days of securing all the necessary permissions, he had plunged into his afforestation project with the boundless energy of a teenager. From the largest corporate to the smallest shopkeeper, from the snootiest NGO to the humblest jholawalla, Manu knocked on every door. He hustled, harangued, badgered and begged them for donations until he had raised enough money to fund his forest.

Money apart, Manu's prodigious efforts would have had Bhagirath himself stroking his beard in approval. It included the digging of 7,297 rainwater harvesting pits, the construction of 213 open wells, furious Googling of the Miyawaki forest growing technique, the planting of thousands of saplings, eye-watering quantities of gobar and gaumutra, innumerable setbacks and unimaginable labour. But nine years after he and Ismail had together planted the first mahua sapling on the site of the abandoned bauxite mine, Manu's dream had come true. Two hundred acres of bloodied earth and poisoned water had turned into a lush, green oasis in which a young forest had taken root.

Black-breasted quails nested on the branches of her chir pine trees. Ochre flowers of palash burst into bloom in the spring time, setting the forest on fire. And on the full moon, the wolves went mad with joy, baying until silvery night had turned into crimson dawn. And Kangana, now mellow in middle-age, celebrated her twentieth birthday, a good age for a sarus crane, knee-deep in the pond by the bamboo grove, tossing juicy snails into her mouth and crooning in delight whenever Ismail or Manu passed her by.

The villagers called it Manuvan, the forest of Manu Baba, the bent old man who looked like a sadhu, with his flowing white beard and gentle eyes. It was their way of honouring the crazy, old man who had created a forest out of dry earth and thin air, with nothing but his two gnarled hands and all his love. It was probably the finest thing that Manu had done in his life. And the last.

***

I must come now to the final notes of the final bars of my sparrow song, for the music has died and I can sing no more. In the blinking of an eye, nine good years have come and gone and it is the 18th of March, 2016—the day the music died.

How well I remember the day and how I wish I could forget it. But I am cursed. No matter how hard I try, I cannot forget. My memories have become my own worst enemy. They have robbed me of the last droplets of the peace that I crave for, but will never know again. I have battled the demons that torment me. With all my might, I have hewed and stabbed at them. I have tried to cut them out of my mind. But like the spilled blood of the asura Raktabeej, each time I have erased one evil memory, ten more have sprung up in its place.

I do not know what to do anymore. But I must keep trying or else I am sure to go mad. So let me make one more attempt. One last attempt to find peace. I will not fight my memories anymore but give them expression. I will take a piece of paper and write down what happened on that fateful day. Then I will burn it and throw the ashes into the Koyal river. And I will fly away, fly far away from this place. And only then, perhaps, will I be freed of my demons...

So let me put pen to paper and earn my freedom.

***

It was the 18th of March, 2016, the day before Manu's seventy-ninth birthday. Not that one knew the exact date on which Manu (then Manhoos) had been born, not even his long dead parents. And so it had fallen upon Raja-saab to settle the matter once and for all. Raja-saab in his wisdom, had decided that Manu had been born on the 19th of March, the day on which he had first arrived in Calcutta to begin his new life. Since then, for all legal and practical purposes, the 19th of March had become Manu's official date of birth.

Until a few years ago, Manu's birth date had been of little significance—nothing more than a fictional set of numbers printed on ration cards and Aadhaar cards and the like. But Ismail's arrival was to change that. All his classmates celebrated their birthdays, Ismail told Manu, and many celebrated their parents' birthdays as well. He wanted to do the same. He wanted both him and Manu to have proper birthday parties with cake cutting and candle blowing and gifts and the rest of it. Brushing aside Manu's protests that he was too old for such things, Ismail had taken on the responsibility of organising the celebrations. And thanks to him, since the last eight years, Manu's birthday party had become a much-awaited annual fixture in our little home.

But this year was special. Manu was about to leave behind his seventh decade and step into his eighth and Ismail wanted to give his old man a special gift. He had set his heart on a new pair of Duckback gumboots to replace the old, leaky ones in which Manu tramped about in his forest. Unfortunately he didn't have the money to buy them. Much of his cattle grazing income had already gone towards school books and uniforms and he was running short. But as luck would have it, an opportunity to make a quick buck had recently presented itself. A few days ago, Mukesh bhaiyya had offered Ismail the princely sum of three hundred rupees, if he herded six buffaloes to the cattle market in Chatra district, where they were to be sold.

Although it was a school day, Ismail jumped at the offer. He said nothing to Manu, for he knew that he wouldn't be permitted to miss school and instead, quietly hatched his plans. And on that fateful day of Wednesday, the 18th of March, 2016, Ismail crept out of the house at the crack of dawn, to embark upon his secret mission.

Manu was still sleeping but I was up and about. Having nothing better to do, I decided to tag along with Ismail. A short while later, he had taken charge of Mukesh bhaiyya's buffaloes and we were on our way to the cattle market of Chatra. We had been joined by a second cattle herder whom Mukesh bhaiyya had hired for the day—a lean, grim-faced, man in his mid-thirties by the name of Musharraf Shaikh. Ismail tried to make some small talk with him, but he wasn't the chatty kind and so the procession of six buffaloes, two cattle herders and one sparrow proceeded silently towards our destination. Before long, we were passing through Balumath forest in the vicinity of Jhabbar village, when the quiet dawn was shattered by a loud cry: 'Stop!'

A group of men had emerged from the surrounding forest. Within seconds, they spread out and corralled us in a tight circle. Unnerved by their sudden appearance, the buffaloes snorted nervously and staggered to an abrupt halt. Tails swishing, they stared at the strangers with their great, black eyes. There were eight men. At first sight, they seemed unfamiliar but when I looked closely I knew that I had seen these men before.

Since the dawn of history, in every age and in every place, these men have been there. Sometimes they wear skull caps, sometimes their foreheads are smeared with vermillion or sandalwood paste, sometimes crucifixes dangle from their necks. Like the colours of a chameleon, their outer appearance keeps changing, but they are the same men—their eyes reddened by anger and fear, hearts blackened by hate, hands grasping shovels, swords and chains that gleam with bloodlust.

One of the men stepped forward and grabbed Ismail by the throat. 'Name?' he barked.

Ismail had gone pale. His teeth were chattering so badly that he was unable to speak. The man asked him again but Ismail could only mumble incoherently. The man now turned impatiently to Musharraf and asked his name. He somehow stammered out a reply which seemed to please his interrogator.

'Musharraf!' he announced proudly to his companions. '*Bhaiyon, mil gaya*! Brothers, we have found who we were looking for!' he jerked his head in the direction of a chir tree and said: 'That tree will do. Two of you get it ready for Musharraf mian.'

'R...ready...f...for what?' Musharraf stammered.

'For what?' the man roared in laughter. 'Your nikaah, your marriage, mian Musharraf! What else! Today we will put a garland around your neck and unite you with your god!'

'Senapati-ji, what about the boy?' someone asked. 'He looks young. What should we do with him?'

The man called Senapati-ji threw an impatient look at his questioner and snorted: 'Young or old, these people are all the same. Catch them young, I say. Bhaiyon, this is not the time to be weak. Our rules are clear—if the boy is a *katwa* we will put a garland on him. If not, we will let him take his cows and go.'

The blood had drained from Ismail's face. He was shivering uncontrollably, but summoning every last bit of his courage, he said: 'Saab, they are not cows. They are buffaloes.'

Senapati-ji gave a crooked smile and said: 'And what if I say they are cows?'

'B...but...they are not...they are buf...buff....' Ismail tried to explain, when the man raised his hand and brought it down on his face like a scythe. Ismail staggered and fell crashing to the ground. A gash opened up in the corner of his mouth and blood streamed down his chin.

'Buffaloes, hanh?' Senapati-ji scoffed. 'Buffaloes, cows, they are all the same to you people. You dare to touch our mother, hanh? You dare to slaughter our mother to make your kebabs and biryani? Today, we will make kebabs out of you,' he turned to the other men and raising a clenched fist, he shouted: '*Gau mata ki raksha karenge, Bharat mata ko bachayenge* (We will protect our cow mother, we will save our Mother India).'

In one voice, the other men took up their leader's cry. '*Gau mata ki raksha karenge, Bharat mata ko bachayenge,'* they bellowed, stabbing the air with their shovels and swords.

'All right, that's enough!' Senapati-ji commanded and the cries subsided. 'We have work to do. Tie them up and take them to the tree.'

'But senapati-ji, what about the boy?' one of the men asked. 'We don't know his name, yet. Shouldn't we—'

'Ah! Bunty, you talk too much,' Senapati-ji cut him off in an irritated voice. 'Why don't you just take off his pants and check if he is a *katwa,* instead of wasting time with your stupid questions?'

'Sorry Senapati-ji,' Bunty mumbled, 'I'll do it right away.' He grasped Ismail's hands and twisted them behind his back. 'Hey, what are the rest of you doing? Take off his pants and see.'

Two men stepped forward and grabbed hold of Ismail's trousers. They were pulling them off his waist, to see if he was circumsised, when Ismail started screaming—the howl of a terrified beast, echoing endlessly through the silent forest. until I could not bear to hear it anymore. I closed my ears but the screaming did not stop. And then, above the screams came Senapati-ji's voice: 'Just shut up that damned boy! Where are the bloody rags? Ram them inside his mouth before he wakes up the village!'

There was the sound of a brief scuffle and then...silence. All was quiet. So quiet that even the fluttering of a butterfly's wings sounded loud as a war drum. And then through the deathly silence came a calm, almost casual voice: 'Take them to the tree and hang them by their necks.'

I couldn't take it anymore. I couldn't bear to see what was happening. How could I? I am nothing but a useless, spineless storyteller. I can talk big and tell tall tales. But that's it. I don't have the courage to face reality. I choose to ignore what goes on under my very nose.

And so like the coward that I am, I close my eyes, ears and mouth and I silently wait for the inevitable to happen. The noose tightens around Ismail's throat, squeezing the life-breath out of him. He gasps, struggles and kicks. But it is useless. Minutes later he is dead.

And suspended from a tree branch, his young, half naked body, swings gently in the morning breeze, like a giant pendulum.

The End

It did not take long for the villagers of Jhabbar village to discover the cold, dead bodies of Ismail and Musharraf. The police arrived shortly after and an investigation was ordered into the lynching. Around mid-day, a police inspector escorted Manu to the scene of the crime.

A huge crowd had gathered at the site. A pair of constables had to clear a path through the assembly, for Manu to pass through. The inspector hadn't divulged too many details yet and Manu couldn't quite understand what was going on. The chaos and crowds confused him further and as he hobbled slowly towards the tree from which Ismail had been hanged, he kept asking the inspector why he had been brought here.

A few moments later, they were at the foot of the tree. The inspector requested Manu to look up and said: 'I am sorry that you have to see this Manu baba, but it's necessary,' he placed his hand gently on Manu's shoulder. 'Look carefully and tell me. Do you know the boy? The boy on the right.'

As if in a trance Manu craned his neck and gazed at Ismail's corpse dangling above him. He stared at it for a few moments, blank with incomprehension. And then the light left his eyes. One moment, it was there, and the next it had vanished, like the snuffed out flame of a candle.

'Do you know this boy?' the inspector asked again.

'No,' mumbled Manu. He turned and began to hobble away. He was bent double and his knees were giving way. He was about to fall down when the inspector grasped his arms and held him up. He lowered him onto the ground and waited until Manu had recovered his breath.

'I know how painful this must be to you, Manu babu,' the inspector said. 'But this is a case of homicide, double-murder. Unless we can identify the bodies, we won't be able to start our investigations. So please help us, Manu baba.'

Manu remained silent. 'Mukesh bhaiyya informed me that this boy stays with you. His name is Ismail. Is this true?' the inspector asked.

Still, no answer. Manu's head fell, he hugged his knees close to his chest, curling up like an unborn child inside its mother's womb.

'Is this your boy Ismail?' the inspector asked once again.

And this time Manu replied. 'No, he is not Ismail. My Ismail has gone to school. He's gone to school.'

All of a sudden Manu staggered to his feet and got up. Clutching at the inspector he said: 'What am I doing here?' There was a wild look in his eyes and his voice was shaking uncontrollably. 'Ismail will be back home soon. I have to get his food ready. I have to teach him. His exams are starting next week.'

'Manu baba, please! I know how difficult—' the inspector said.

'You don't know anything, you idiot!' Manu hissed like a snake. 'I'm telling you that the boy hanging from that tree there is not Ismail. My Ismail is in school. He is the best student in his class and he's going to become a doctor! Do you hear that, you stupid idiot! My Ismail is going to become a doctor,'

He shoved the inspector aside and hobbled away, pushing his way through the crowds as he muttered: 'Let me go! Let me go! I have to get back home before Ismail returns from school. My Ismail is coming home.'

***

All day long Manu sat on the doorstep of our house waiting for Ismail to come home. Day turned into night, but Ismail did not come. The arms of the clock turned in their relentless circles, the earth spun slowly on its axis, the sun fell and the constellations rose. But Ismail did not come and Manu did not budge. Still and silent as a mountain, he sat on the doorstep and kept sleepless vigil for his missing son.

Through that long, dark night, I too sat by the side of the

shrivelled, old man and watched over him. For what else could I do? But shortly before day break, my weary eyes closed and I fell into an uneasy sleep. I could not have dozed off long but when I awoke Manu was missing. I looked for him everywhere—the house, the garden, the street...but he was nowhere to be seen. And then I noticed that his gumboots were missing and I immediately knew where he had gone.

Without losing a moment, I took off into the skies and headed straight to Manuvan. My guess was right. There he was, in the forest of his dreams, lying on the soft green grass below the mahua tree that he and Ismail had together planted all those years ago. I called out to him but he did not reply. I tapped his cheeks with my wing tips and gently pecked his nose. Nothing...a great fear turned my stomach into a block of ice. I placed my ear on his chest. But there was nothing...I could hear nothing. And I knew why.

Manu had given his heart to the world, down to the very last bit. And when there was nothing left to give, it had simply stopped beating.

***

I have become a block of ice. I feel nothing. I can do nothing. Except sit by Manu's side and stare at him. An eternity passes before I finally notice the piece of paper clutched in his cold, stiff fingers. I peer at it. It is a water colour painting, still unfinished. But there is little doubt as to its subject. It is the portrait of an old man, with a flowing white beard, twinkling eyes and a peaceful smile. At the bottom of the picture, written by hand are the words—*'Happy Birthday, Abba—Love, Ismail.'*

Suddenly I start to cry. And I cannot stop.

Epilogue

Six years and more have passed since Manu died. The grief that has fallen upon me like a heavy, grey fog refuses to lift. And all I can do is brood. But it isn't just Manu's or Ismail's or Sayoni's deaths that have left me hollow as a husk. A strange new virus has been dancing its ghoulish dance across the length and breadth of the country, swatting aside lakhs upon lakhs of lives as if they were flies.

I am tired. I am sick and tired of all that I have heard and seen these last two years—the unceasing wail of ambulance sirens in the dead of night, the long queues of dead bodies waiting to be burned in makeshift pyres, of men, women and children walking back home on bleeding feet, of desperate people waiting for an oxygen cylinder or food rations.

I am sick and tired of this land of fire and blood and death. I have been here for nearly seventy-five years and I want no more of it. Wherever I go, I am followed by the stench of bloodied, burning bodies—from the refugee camps of 1948, to the killiings of 1984, and from the burning train and blood-soaked streets of Gujarat to the flaming pyres of the pandemic.

These days I find it difficult to even fly. How can I? My body is full of wounds. They run long and deep...old wounds give rise to new and the blood spurts out again and again, every drop multiplying endlessly, until I am drenched in blood—the blood of the brilliant young students of Presidency College shot through their heads in pre-dawn encounters in the Maidan, the blood of the Dalits gunned down on the island of Marichjhapi, the blood of the peasants butchered in the killing fields of Nellie, the blood of kings and cattle herders, and the blood of an entire Santhal village wiped out in the jungles of Betla. The blood of sweet, innocent Ismail...

All I want is to go home, crawl back with my tail tucked between my legs and never again set my eyes on this benighted country. Night and day I pray to be released from my never-ending exile so that I can go home. But no one listens to my pleas.

***

A new day has dawned. Nothing has changed and nothing ever will.

But all of a sudden, a streak of lightning crackles in the cloudless skies, jolting me out of my grey gloom. A roar of thunder shakes the tree upon which I am perched, and a cavernous voice booms out:

'Prem Chandra Guha, this is an aakaashvani from Mount Kailash. Listen carefully, for it will not be repeated. It is Sharad Purnima, the birthday of his His Majesty, the most merciful Lord Kubera, and this year He has decided to grant a general amnesty to all convicts who have served fifty or more years of their sentence. As you have completed 75 years of your exile, your punishment is now deemed to be over. You may return to Kailash where you will be required to submit the written records of your stay in Bharatvarsha, in triplicate, to the competent authority.'

I am too stunned to comprehend what I have just heard. It takes a while before the words sink in. And then I let out a great whoop of joy, do cartwheels in the air, kiss Kangana on the cheeks and generally make a damn fool of myself in front of the puzzled residents of Manuvan. They think I've gone mad. But who cares! I am free! Free at last!

I bid a quick farewell to everyone and without further ado I leap into the air. At last I am going home!

***

Before long I am flying over the mighty Ganga. The vast plains below me are crisscrossed with mysterious strands of silvery thread, that I have never seen before. It takes me a while to realise that they are the spanking new highways built during the time I had been mourning the deaths of Manu and Ismail. Dotted along their length are petrol bunks, restaurants and garages. In fact, I can see at least three garages by the name of Vishwakarma Motor Works. But they are manned by smart-looking mechanics in crisp overalls and not skinny ten-year-olds in greasy banians. In fact, almost every ten-year-old that I can see is inside a school. And it gladdens my heart to know that they are reciting their multiplication tables and not hawking wild berries on the highway or cleaning out the carburettors of broken down vehicles.

I continue my journey along the left bank of the Ganga and soon I am at Benares, oldest living city in human civilisation, older than history, older even than legend and myth. Be that as it may, it is the thousand peppy ring-tones of a thousand shiny smartphones that greet me as I fly over its serpentine alleys. At the Assi Ghat, the chants of Sanskrit shlokas rise and fall with the sonorous strains of Raag Bhairavi on Bismillah Khan's shehnai, playing on a distant radio. I am enchanted by the eternal magic of this ancient city. I listen quietly and watch the flames of the burning brass lamps leap skywards, and I cannot help but wonder how different they are from all the other fires I have seen—how tender with warmth, how glowing with life...

But I must move on and soon I am flying over the Triveni Sangam, that sacred point where the Ganga, Yamuna and Saraswati converge like the three strands of a sparkling emerald necklace. Their green waters look cool and refreshing. In all the years that I have spent here, they have never looked clearer and cleaner than today. They lift my spirits and I offer silent thanks to those who have helped cleanse the holy rivers. But even as I look upon the clear, green waters below, I am suddenly conscious of the filth that clings to me. My body reeks of the uncountable sins that I have known for seven decades, and all the waters of all the holy rivers of this land will not be enough to rid me of their stench.

I am just a tiny sparrow, wounded and weak. I need rest. I need peace. I hear the waters calling out to me. They cannot grant me absolution but as I listen closely, I think they are offering me a chance of redemption. I swoop down and dive in.

The Yamuna is redolent with the scent of lotus flowers inlaid in the white marble walls of the Taj Mahal. Her fragrance sweetens the melted snows of the Himalayas that her sister, Ganga, has borne from distant Tapovan. Below them, quiet flows the Saraswati, river of knowledge and wisdom, invisible, except those who treasure her above all else. Their waters flow over me like a soothing balm, healing the wounds that have festered inside me for decades, cleansing my blood-caked wings. I begin to feel a little better. The darkness inside my heart lightens and I feel stronger.

I fly onwards until I reach the foothills of the Garhwali Himalayas and it suddenly occurs to me that I have flown a very long way indeed. I have been stabbed, slashed, burned and lynched and yet...I am still flying. I wonder if I can also sing...

I open my beak and let out a soft trill. In spite of long years of disuse, my voice still sounds melodious and I am struck by the wonder of it. Bloodied rags have been rammed down my throat, iron hands have strangled my neck, nooses have throttled me. But in spite of everything that has been done to silence me, I still have my voice, I can still sing.

Yes, in spite of the gods, and against all the odds, here I am—still flying, still singing.

With renewed hope and energy I press forward. As if by a miracle (or is it my intent), I am flying over Chamoli village. On the slopes of a pine-covered hillock I see a frail, old woman, brown and wrinkled as a shrivelled raisin. Even after all these years I recognise her at once. For the one constant in an ever-changing world is Mary.

Her eyes still sparkle like stars, as she stands ramrod straight before a group of children. They have assembled in a neat circle around a flag pole. Mary's gnarled hands tug on the rope and a neatly folded flag climbs up the pole. When it reaches the top, the tri-colour spreads out like the wings of a majestic eagle and saffron, green and white ripple as one in the mountain breeze. And a thought comes to me—that as long as there are people like Mary and Manu, and Sayoni and Ismail, in this world, there is still hope for this land of the *sone ki chidiya*...

The children cheer and clap and then they begin to sing the national anthem. My gaze falls on a little boy whose voice is sweeter than the others. A skinny boy of nine or so, with unkempt hair, like a crow's nest. I cannot help but wonder how much he looks like Ismail, on the day I first met him. Or is it Manu? Or is it the million other Manus across the length and breadth of this country, whom I have never met. It doesn't matter, I say to myself. He is who he is. He is singing sweetly and that is enough. Our gazes meet briefly and I find myself singing along with him.

And then from the high hills and the deep valleys, from the teeming cities and the tiny hamlets, from the forests and rivers and seas of this great land, I hear a billion and more voices joining my small, feeble voice. And we are all singing the freedom song of India and I feel as one with them.

And I suddenly realise that I cannot go back home. For I am already there.

The alchemy of time and love has turned the land of my exile into my homeland. I do not think I can leave now. And I do not think I want to. My return to Kailash must wait. For I can sense that a new journey is about to begin. A journey on which I must walk side by side with a billion and more of my people, along that long and uphill road that may one day, lead us to the mythical amrit that we all seek.

And until that day comes, the golden sparrow will sing her song.

Acknowledgements

My sincere thanks to:

Renuka Chatterjee—editor extraordinaire, without whom this book would have remained a flight of fancy.

Ravi Singh—Publisher, Speaking Tiger for his many insights and ideas to make this a better book.

Rupa, my sister—who read this manuscript when it was only half-baked but believed that it could someday become a half-decent cake.

Sumedha, my daughter—for her persistent efforts to make me a better writer and human being in spite of her repeated failures to do so.

P. Rajesh, friend and colleague—for being my first reader and for his invaluable feedback and thoughtful suggestions.

Jug Suraiya and Hansda Sowvendra Sekhar—for their generous cover quotes and for the pleasure that I have derived from their writings.

Anurag Basnet, friend and former editor—for introducing the book to the good folks at Speaking Tiger.

Maithili Doshi—for designing such a fabulous cover and lending a patient ear to my many unsolicited suggestions.

Pampa, my wife—for everything, always.